D0266155

WITHDRAWN
FROM
MERTON PUBLIC
LIBRARIES

LANDSCAPE OF LIES

Also by the same author
The Caravaggio Conspiracy
The Nazi's Wife
Crusade

MERIDEN PUBLIC LIBRARY
CW

MADISON PUBLIC LIBRARIES
CW

LANDSCAPE OF LIES

Peter Watson

Hutchinson
London Sydney Auckland Johannesburg

© Peter Watson 1989

All rights reserved
This edition first published in Great Britain by
Hutchinson, an imprint of Century Hutchinson Ltd,
Brookmount House, 62–65 Chandos Place, London WC2N 4NW

Century Hutchinson Australia Pty Ltd, 89–91 Albion
Street, Surry Hills, Australia NSW 2010

Century Hutchinson New Zealand Ltd, PO Box 40–086,
Glenfield, Auckland 10, New Zealand

Century Hutchinson South Africa (Pty) Ltd,
PO Box 337, Bergvlei, 2012 South Africa

British Library Cataloguing in Publication Data

Watson, Peter, *1943-*
  Landscape of lies.
  I. Title
  823'.914 [F]

  ISBN 0–09–173884–9

Phototypeset by Input Typesetting Ltd, London

Printed in Great Britain by
Butler and Tanner, Frome, Somerset

MERTON PUBLIC LIBRARIES

E|F 355 560 03A

6|89 MAC

NATIONAL PORTRAIT 1996 GALLERY

17857

Author's Note

This is a work of fiction.
All of the characters and some of the
locations are inventions

For Katie

Prologue

The moment Isobel awoke she knew there was someone else in the house. She didn't know why she was so certain of it – only that she instinctively held her breath. She couldn't see her watch but from the way the May moon sliced its shadows across the bedroom carpet she guessed it must be after three. As she started to get out of bed she heard the study door, downstairs, click in its lock. Isobel had been brought up in this house, lived in it for most of her twenty-nine years, and that noise told her how the intruder had got in: a window was open in the dining-room. The study door always rattled when the dining-room windows were opened. She had known, ever since she began to live alone in the big house, that the low bay windows of the dining-room were a security risk, but she had never really believed a burglar would take advantage of them. Now it was too late.

She slipped out of bed and silently put on her dressing-gown. At first she had no fear – rather, she was intrigued to know what the burglar had come for. There was nothing of any real value in the house, not even a decent set of silver. Since her father had died and left the farm to Isobel, she had been fighting a losing battle. Gradually she had sold off the Chinese porcelain, the Japanese lacquer, the jade carvings that her father, a diplomat in the Far East before he retired, had collected. There was nothing left to steal.

It was only then that Isobel began to be afraid. Perhaps the intruder had come not to steal but to assault *her*? There were so many stories these days about rape. Maybe she would know him. Maybe he would kill her afterwards. Afterwards . . . she shivered.

She shivered but didn't hesitate. She knew the house and its character inside out. As a very young girl, before her father was sent abroad, she had often crept on to the landing in the evenings to watch when he was entertaining downstairs and no one had ever guessed she was there. So she knew that if she pushed the bedroom door before she turned the handle it would open without complaint. In the corridor she knew just where *not* to tread to avoid making any sound.

As she moved down the corridor no one came towards her and she breathed more easily. It was a burglar she had to deal with, it seemed, not a rapist.

She turned a corner and stopped. Here the corridor became a gallery overlooking the hall. There was an oak balustrade. She inched towards it and peered down. *There he was.* A tall, shadowy figure stood in front of a painting in the hall. He was reaching up to lift it off the hook.

Isobel was suddenly filled with an immense anger. It was as if the fear she had felt a moment ago had redirected itself to another part of her: she was awash in fury. It was widely known in the area that she lived alone. Now it seemed she was fair game, that anyone could come into this great house and help himself to whatever he wanted.

Immediately she had a plan. She wanted to stop the theft, but she also wanted the man to know that she wasn't afraid – that although she lived alone she wasn't helpless.

She half turned to where she knew there was a large pewter vase on a table. It had been in the family for ever, so she had been told, and had an ivory collar, a carving of some sort, around its base. Once it might have been valuable but the pewter was knocked about a lot and the ivory was chipped: it was ideal for what she had in mind. Noiselessly she lifted it off the table: it was cumbersome but not too heavy.

Raising it with her right hand, she reached across with her left and held the light switch. She paused, telling herself that she would have the advantage of surprise but that, for a moment after the light went on, both she and the intruder would be blinded. She tried to memorise where he was standing.

She took a breath – and threw the switch.

As the hall was flooded with light, the figure grunted, a sound of muffled surprise. The man – he was much too tall to be a woman – was wearing a motor-cycle helmet. It turned her way. Behind the darkened glass of the visor she thought she could see two startled eyes. The helmet with its shiny, anonymous skin was menacing; it unbalanced the proportions of the figure and transformed it into a kind of distended growth, bulbous and threatening. Isobel didn't wait any longer.

She pitched the vase as hard as she could into the hall. She didn't aim at the man's head. That struck her as too dangerous even in the circumstances and she knew that the law had some weird ideas about the rights of criminals. In any case he was wearing the helmet. She aimed at his feet.

The vase was top-heavy and slid out of her hand with less control than she would have wished. Still, she had the advantage of height, and the helmeted figure was not far away. Before he could move, the vase had skidded on to the stone slabs of the hall floor about a foot in front of his feet. Dropping the picture, he instinctively jerked to one side – but that was his undoing. As the vase hit the floor, the ivory collar snapped off and shattered into several pieces. The vase itself, however, being metal, bounced up again and struck the intruder below the knee on his left leg.

Isobel winced as she heard the crack of bone, and the man's scream drowned the rattle of the vase as it clattered back on to the stone slabs. Despite the pain he must have been in, however, the figure immediately stooped again to pick up the painting. Seeing this, Isobel nearly exploded in fury and turned to look for other weapons that were within reach. All she could see was a dish of alabaster eggs in the middle of the table near where the vase had stood. Her fingers closed over one of the eggs – but then she checked herself. This little nest would do far more damage as a job lot. A ladylike form of shrapnel, she thought grimly.

She gripped the dish with both hands and carried it to the balustrade. The figure downstairs was now clutching the painting and straightening up. One leg was curled under him in a way that showed he was still in great pain, but even so he wasn't giving up.

Neither was Isobel. Without faltering she leaned over the balcony and tipped the eggs on to the intruder. There must have been fifteen of them in the dish and three scored direct hits. One cannoned on to the man's shoulder. Another – surely the most painful – caught him on an elbow. The voice within the helmet screamed again and he dropped the picture a second time. The third egg cracked against the helmet. The figure would have felt little pain from this but the helmet visor was fractured and a splinter fell to the floor. Now Isobel stood a chance of seeing who the burglar was.

She quickly ran round the gallery to where there was another of the mementoes her father had picked up in the Far East, a Japanese scimitar. Still swamped in anger, she grabbed the blade, tearing it from its mount on the wall, and launched herself down the stairs.

But now the figure in the helmet had turned away and, half running, half hopping, was making for the dining-room and the open window by which he had entered.

Reaching the cold stone slabs of the hall floor, Isobel turned to give chase, but her bare right foot stepped on to one of the ivory fragments that had broken off the vase. This cut painfully into the ball of her foot but, worse, caused her to skid on the stones. As she put out her hand to break her fall she fell against the edge of the scimitar. Luckily the blade missed her eye but it bit deep into her cheek and immediately drew blood. The force of her fall caused the scimitar to slip from her fingers and when she got to her feet and ran to the dining-room the figure had gone. The net curtain hung limp in the open window. In the silver moonlight outside the house there were no moving shadows. Isobel waited a moment, listening, then closed the window. In her bare feet she could not give chase.

She returned to the hall, warm blood still oozing from her cheek. When she inspected the painting the helmeted figure had tried to steal, Isobel saw that the frame had broken at the corner and a small area of paint was scratched. As she examined the scratch mark, one hand still dabbing her sticky cheek, she heard in the distance the sound of a motor bike retreating into the night.

1

'You may be richer than you think, Michael. Come over here and I'll show you why.'

Julius Samuels smiled and lifted a glass to his lips. The liver spots danced on his old throat as he swallowed his whisky. It was not quite 10 am. He was seated in a worn mahogany swivel chair and wearing a white coat smudged with paint. His left hand held a large oval-shaped palette with squibs of pigment laid out in a curved spectrum near the edge. A cigar thicker than a thumb burned in a tray on a shelf near his right shoulder.

Michael Whiting picked his way past stacks of gilded frames, tins of oil, bottles of varnish brown as beer, rows of canvases, their faces turned confidentially to the wall. He edged around a large easel, careful not to snag his corduroy suit on the wood, and stood next to the massive bulk of London's most venerable picture restorer. Behind and below them the traffic in Dover Street rumbled forward in the sunshine.

In front of the two men, on the easel, stood a painting. It showed a woman: her skin was pale but she had the faint blossom of pink in her cheeks. She was wearing a blue hood – except that half the hood was missing. It had been removed by the restorer. Under it was revealed a thick mane of chestnut hair.

Samuels reached for his cigar and drew on it. The end glowed like the curly filament in a small lamp. 'I took off the varnish, then applied some diluted acetone and white spirit.' He cleared his throat. 'The blue came off straight away, as easy as wiping your nose. I

13

found all this lovely hair underneath. Then I found the earring . . . that's when I called you.' He wedged the cigar back into his mouth.

Michael was examining the chestnut hair. It was beautifully painted; he could almost count the strands. 'Perbloodyfection. But why would anyone cover up such lovely hair with that hideous hood?'

'Rum bunch, those Victorians. But I've come across this before. People were more religious then than they are now. Italian religious art was fashionable in those days – and that made it expensive. But it wasn't hard to "doctor" one of the family portraits, which were much more common and therefore cheaper. Get a nice-looking woman, safely dead so she couldn't complain. Cover up the jewels, the cleavage, the fashionable hairdo. In no time you have a saint or the Blessed Virgin.' He chuckled, though it sounded as if he was gargling. 'They were rogues in those days.'

Michael smiled, carefully keeping his eyes on the picture. 'You should know.'

Samuels replied without removing the cigar from his mouth. 'Have a whisky, Michael. You're not thinking straight this morning. I sometimes "improve" paintings, I know. All restorers do. That's what customers want – old masters that look as though they were painted at the weekend. But I never invent.' He reached across for the Bell's and a glass.

He continued as Michael helped himself. 'The reason I phoned you was this: if you give me the go-ahead and I clean all this Victorian mush away, you might be able to identify the lady from her jewels. There might even be a coat of arms in the background. If you *can* identify her you know better than I do how much that will improve the value of the picture. That's why you may be richer than you think.'

Michael's eyes were watering slightly from the strength of the whisky so early in the day but he tried not to let it show. He felt a quickening of the pulse that wasn't due to the alcohol and stared again at the canvas. This was one of the main reasons he had become an art dealer: for the thrill of discovery. True, he loved just looking at paintings. English ones especially. Michael thought English painting was very underrated across the world. The Americans appreciated it, but the Italians, the French and the Germans had never regarded English art as equal to their own. The few occasions when Michael had sold paintings to foreign museums had been the proudest moments of his career. But the discoveries he had made – those were the most *exciting* times.

He leaned forward to inspect the picture again. The hair and the jewel were certainly a cut above the blue hood. As old Jules said, underneath this dreary Victorian saint, which he had acquired at a house sale along with something else he valued more highly, there might just lurk a much better painting.

Julius had taken down from a shelf a large book. Like all good restorers he kept a meticulous record of what he did to paintings. He made notes and little drawings, partly to cover himself should there ever be any dispute about the authenticity of something he had restored, partly as an *aide-mémoire* in case, as regularly happened, a work came back to him on a later occasion. He opened the book and showed Michael a tiny drawing on one of the pages. 'This is how much I've taken off so far. The rest shouldn't take me too long. What do you think?'

In reply, Michael placed his hand on the old man's shoulder. 'If this woman turns out to be Lady Luck, Jules, it's not going to do your liver much good.' They had a deal that Michael always paid in whisky, to avoid the tax man.

Samuels gave a throaty chuckle. 'Michael, by my age your liver becomes your favourite and most useful organ.' Samuels chuckled again and the liver spots did another jig on his throat. He pointed at Michael's glass. 'Knock that back and let me get on. You must have a shop to go to.'

This time Michael laughed and finished his drink. Samuels delighted in calling dealers' galleries their 'shops': he knew how it hurt their sensibilities.

Out in the sunshine, Michael turned south, towards Piccadilly. He had broken his cardinal rule of never drinking anything other than single malt whisky – as he always did when he visited Julius. But he was smiling; an encounter with the old man always put him in a good mood.

He dodged the traffic in Piccadilly and walked down St James's Street. He passed White's, turned into Jermyn Street, then right opposite Fortnum and Mason into Duke Street. His own gallery was in Mason's Yard, halfway down the street on the left, through an archway. It wasn't Duke Street itself, of course, or Old Bond Street, come to that, but it wasn't bad. He and his partner could afford more space there, and anyone who knew anything about British painting knew where to find them.

He passed a couple of other galleries. In the window of one was a portrait and he stopped to admire it. It was a small Degas pastel, smudges of powdery pink, pale blue and apricot splashing out from the dark charcoal lines. It showed a middle-aged man, bearded and balding, but elegant in a close-fitting jacket and a high collar, with a flowered handkerchief cascading from his breast pocket. A comfortably off figure from the comfortable world of the nineteenth century, the world of servants, bicycles, picnics. A world that lots of people wanted to return to, in art if they couldn't do it in real life.

Michael looked past the portrait to his own reflection in the window. Corduroy suits, he had been told a thousand times, were a thing of the past. They reeked of jazz and coffee bars, the archaeology of the twentieth century, in the words of his ungovernable younger sister, Robyn. But, at thirty-three, he couldn't quite bring himself to abandon what he had got used to. Nor was the art dealer's uniform – dark, double-breasted suit, sea island cotton shirt, black shoes, shiny as olives – all that enticing either. The brown velvet of the corduroy suited Michael's colouring too. He'd been even blonder as a baby but he was still very fair. Robyn was jealous of his hair and its waviness, even though he couldn't seem to keep it in place. His gaze shifted to the cigar in his hand. The tobacco was a weakness, of course. Cigars were expensive, made him look older than he was, and lots of people, women especially, hated the smoke. But Michael was hooked. He loved the smell, the crackle of the leaves, the *colour* of the leaves. He relished the deliberate ritual of cutting and lighting a cigar, of rolling it in the flame of the match. He rolled the cigar between his fingers now, then jabbed it into his mouth and straightened his tie, using the reflection in the window.

Michael sighed. He always seemed to have an unravelled look, no matter how hard he tried. He took another glance at the apricot splashes in the Degas and moved on through the archway which led into Mason's Yard. His gallery was at the far end where its sign

16

could be seen by passers-by in Duke Street. The green and gold lettering read: 'Whiting & Wood Fine Art'. Michael had a partner, Gregory Wood, an accountant who had many contacts in the City. All galleries had to borrow from the banks so that they could maintain sufficient stock to give customers a decent choice. If Greg could borrow money at a better rate than other galleries were getting they were ahead of the game.

Michael and Greg got on well – they had to, given the fact that they were a small firm and in each other's pockets for most of the time. While Greg raised loans and chased customers who hadn't paid it was Michael's job to find the paintings and the customers. The only slight shadow on their relationship was coming towards Michael now as he opened the door to the gallery and stepped inside. The pleasure Michael took in their current 'star' – a small Gainsborough oil sketch, a landscape with a low, pepper-coloured horizon and a firebrick sky – was soon wiped out as Patrick Wood greeted him.

Had Patrick not been Greg's son Michael would never have allowed the boy – for he was barely twenty – anywhere near the gallery. Snobbish, pompous, someone who imagined that dealing in paintings made him better than other people, he was a not unfamiliar type in the art world. Worse, a thin gold chain dangled from the buttonhole in his left lapel and he affected brightly speckled bow ties. Today's was pink with dark red spots.

'Good morning, Paddy.' Michael knew how Patrick hated being addressed as if he were an Irish bricklayer. 'What were you doing in the inner sanctum?'

The 'inner sanctum' was the viewing room at the back of the gallery, where favoured customers were shown paintings they might like to buy. It had easy chairs, a hidden bar and two velvet-covered easels. Access to the sanctum was supposed to convey a sense of privilege, or achievement, denied to ordinary mortals. Patrick had just stepped out of it, leaving the door half open.

'You have a visitor. I was hoping to keep her all to myself – though it seems she's here to see you.'

'A woman?'

'Not just any woman, Michael. This is Rita Hayworth, Princess

17

Diana and Zelda Fitzgerald all rolled into one. As the Michelin Guide might say: "Well worth a detour".'

Michael grinned at Patrick. The boy was improving, almost human. 'Keep that up and we'll have you writing catalogue entries soon. Think you can make some coffee without spraying speckles on that lovely bow tie?'

Patrick nodded. These sparring matches were normal and they both knew Greg approved. He said he wanted the spots knocked off his son.

Michael cast a brief glance over the walls of the gallery. It was late May and the art world was preparing for its big season, June through to mid-July. Soon Michael and Greg would be putting their best wares on the walls in readiness for the foreign collectors who would descend on London for the big auctions and the fancy antique fairs. For now, however, the gallery was showing some of its less intimidating pictures: a small Hoppner portrait, a Cozens landscape and a wonderful, almost abstract, cloud study by John Thistle in peach, cream and crimson. Michael adjusted the picture, which was not quite straight on the wall, and went through to the inner sanctum.

The room stuck out at the back of the gallery with nothing built above it, and Greg and he had been able to equip it with a glass roof or skylight so that pictures could be viewed for much of the time in natural light. The sun streamed in through the glass panels and on to the woman who was waiting. Patrick had not been entirely wrong. She wasn't young enough to be Princess Diana but she had the Hayworth hair, long and sweeping down the side of her face so that it almost covered one cheek. Deep eyes, dark as damsons. A warm, wheat-coloured skin. But the face was dominated by the sharp arch of her eyebrows, which were somehow curved and angled at the same time. It gave this woman's face an amused, quizzical, sardonic cast. Michael noticed that she had a thin plaster across one cheek. She hadn't taken off her raincoat, hadn't even unbelted it; that, he supposed, was what gave her a Fitzgerald air. It was as if she had an open car waiting for her nearby.

'Hello,' he said, holding out his hand. 'You're here to see me? You're not the taxman, I hope?'

She stood up, smiled, and shook hands. In high heels she was an inch or so shorter than he was – taller even than Princess Diana. Her hands were surprisingly rough. 'Isobel Sadler.'

'Please sit down,' he said. 'I've just been to see a man who insisted on offering me a large Scotch – at this hour! – so I for one need some coffee. Would you like to take off your coat?'

The coat masked the woman's figure so he was disappointed when she refused. Instead, she unbelted it and let it hang loose. Underneath she was wearing a white cotton shirt and a kilt. She sat back in her chair and crossed her legs.

Before she could speak the phone rang. Michael picked up the receiver and took a fresh cigar from his top pocket. As he listened he lovingly rolled the thick tube between his fingers. 'I don't believe it,' he said into the receiver. 'Again? Imbloodypressive. How many divorces is that – four? Five! Yes, I'm in, of course. Good idea. Three weeks, I'd say. If Miss Masson is divorcing, it can only mean she's ready to get married again. Okay? 'Bye, Nick.' He replaced the receiver, licked the end of the cigar and began to fiddle with his matches. 'Sorry about that. Where were we?'

Isobel Sadler said, 'It's good of you to see me. I gather it's normal to have an appointment. As if you were a doctor.' An eyebrow lifted a fraction. A mocking movement?

Michael shrugged and breathed blue smoke into the room. 'You're lucky I'm here,' he said. 'I travel a lot. You might have wasted your time.'

'I hope I'm not wasting yours. Edward Ryan suggested I come to you.'

'Oh yes? I wonder why.' Ryan was a dealer in oriental things. Michael tapped the first of the cigar ash into a lacquered tray.

Isobel Sadler smiled. 'He said you weren't too old or too young, that you weren't too rich or too hungry, that you weren't too straight or too bent, and that you liked a gamble.'

'Hmm. Who are Ryan's solicitors? I'll sue.'

'Save your money. He also said you thought like a detective – that's why you've made so many discoveries. Well, I have a mystery for you.'

As she said this, Isobel Sadler reached down to a packet at the side of her chair. From the shape it looked like a painting. She unwrapped the paper. Michael admired her movements but noticed once more the rough skin on her hands. In profile, her nose was too long to be perfect, and in an ideal world her lower lip would not have been so fleshy. But those eyebrows, which seemed to move independently of the rest of her face, gave her expression a jolt of electricity, radiation as much as warmth. It was one of those faces where none of the individual parts was in itself remarkable but where the whole added up to considerably more than the sum. Michael liked it.

She got up and placed the picture on one of the velvet easels, then sat down again in her chair.

Michael looked at the painting. He could usually tell straight away how good or bad something was but it was hard on people to respond too quickly. They were more flattered, and more convinced, if he took his time over it, and less devastated if the verdict was unfavourable.

He noticed immediately that the frame of the picture was broken at one corner and that some paint had chipped off nearby.

The picture showed a landscape of sorts. There was a valley in the background, and some buildings behind a copse of trees. In the foreground was a ring of figures – he counted nine – and, it appeared, all were male. Each figure was dressed differently: one was in a tunic, another in what looked like a monk's habit, and yet another appeared to be a skeleton wearing a mitre. One of the figures lay in front of a ruined window that made a kind of arch, through which the countryside could be seen. The ruin contained a number of columns, one with a carved capital, and to one side there was what looked like a small chapel area screened by a red cloth.

Conscious of Isobel Sadler's eyes on him, Michael stared at the landscape for a while, pulling on his cigar. So Edward Ryan thought he liked a gamble, did he? Gambling was just one of Michael's sins. Most of the other things he enjoyed – whisky, cigars, red meat – were rapidly becoming crimes these days. He let the smoke fill his mouth, then breathed out slowly, feeling his chest and shoulders relax: the taboo comfort of tobacco. He got up and examined the picture more closely. It was not in good condition. The panel was cracked in at least three places, and one of the cracks looked quite new. Besides the paint loss he had already noticed, there were patches of dirt and discoloured varnish. He turned the panel over.

Sometimes the back of a picture told you more than the front: who had owned it, when it had been sold and where, whether its supports had been changed. Not this time: apart from the fact that two of the cracks went all the way through to the reverse side of the panel and there were several worm holes visible, the back of the painting told him nothing new. He replaced it on the easel, sat down again and tapped more ash into the lacquered tray.

'No problems here for the taxman. Your picture has decorative value only, I'm afraid.' He wondered if Miss – Mrs? – Sadler knew that this was the time-honoured way of saying something was virtually worthless. 'It is probably English, northern European certainly, but not by anyone I recognise . . . Not that I am the best judge,' he added quickly. 'Although it says "English paintings" on our window outside and on our business cards, our speciality is really the late eighteenth and early nineteenth centuries. Your picture, I would say, is much earlier – sixteenth century by the looks of it, and to judge from the panel . . . However, apart from the poor condition it's in' – Michael pointed with his cigar to the cracks and the abrasions – 'it is a very odd composition. To put it bluntly, it's not at all well painted.' He tapped one of the faces, on the right of the picture. 'This head, curiously, is well done, but the rest' – he waved his hand over the other figures – 'are very weak, clumsy even. The proportions are wrong; the heads are awkward on the bodies and the features on some of the faces are coarse.' He said all this as gently as he could, not wanting to crush his visitor's hopes too harshly but at the same time not wanting to mislead her. 'I must say I have never seen such a composition before.' He pointed to the figure in the tunic, which had curly designs on it. 'This man, who appears to be holding a clock, looks like some sort of mythological figure.' He pointed to another man. 'There's a skeleton holding a crosier.' Then to a third. 'This one seems to have some sort of plant growing out of his middle – I haven't a clue what that is. Very odd.'

He stared at the picture for a while without speaking, then turned to look at Isobel Sadler. Her hair had fallen forward over one eye. It made her seem as though she was hiding from the bad news he was bringing.

He spoke softly. 'In short, it's an old picture but not a very good

21

one. I can't put an exact figure on it but it's worth hundreds at the most, not thousands. Sorry.'

He placed his cigar back in his mouth. People, he had found, responded to the bad news in one of three ways. There were those who let their disappointment show. There were those who laughed it off – nervously; they were disappointed too. And there were those who had never really believed in the first place that they could be lucky enough to have stumbled across something truly valuable. They sometimes let their resentment turn into anger and would storm out of the gallery.

Isobel Sadler did none of these things. One eyebrow rose a fraction. She tapped her teeth with a fingernail, pushed her hair back from her eye and said, 'Yes, you've confirmed what I thought.'

Though Michael was genuinely passionate about cigars, and smoked them in the bath or when he was fishing, there were occasions in the art business when they were useful to hide behind, to buy time. He could puff regularly, without speaking. It was almost as if cigar smoke contained some sort of soporific. People accepted delay more willingly. He played for time.

Isobel Sadler was an odd lady, he reflected. As odd as her picture. Before he could say anything, however, Patrick appeared with the coffee. The young man set the tray on a side-table and handed the cups across. Michael waited for him to leave before saying, 'If you knew the picture was nothing special, why bother to come? It was a waste of time after all – '

'I didn't say that!' Isobel Sadler didn't exactly shout but there was something – an edge – in her tone and Michael was brought up short. His coffee-cup rattled in its saucer.

She went on, the edge still there in her voice. 'I agree that on the face of it this picture has little or no value, Mr Whiting. I have a soft spot for it – mainly because it's been in my family for ever. But that doesn't blind me to the fact that it is not – well, a fine work. I come from an old West Country family and there is a tradition that Holbein was a friend of our ancestors. But I never really believed this was by him. As you say, a lot of it is clumsy and the composition is – well, you called it odd and I wouldn't disagree. If I didn't have a soft spot for it I would probably think it horrible.' She looked at Michael fiercely, as if to say that he didn't

22

need to be gentle in his professional opinions with *her*. 'But – and this is the odd thing – I *do* think it may be special. Now I can get to the mystery. It's not how valuable this picture is, or who painted it, but why, two nights ago, someone tried to steal it.'

Michael set down his coffee-cup. The sharp way in which Isobel Sadler had addressed him had caused him to flush slightly. He did not reply for a moment but sat, coaxing the smoke out of his cigar. His sister had a sharp tongue: Robyn would like the woman opposite. Then he said, 'That proves nothing. Thieves don't always know about art. They could have tried to take it by mistake or, because it was "art", imagined that it must be valuable.'

'No,' she said quickly. 'The thief made straight for the painting. I know because he woke me up breaking in and I disturbed him. I don't have any Ming in the house, or silver. But there's the usual hi-fi equipment. Thieves always go for electronic stuff first, or so I've been told. What's more, after I interrupted him – I managed to hit him in the shin with a vase that I threw at him – he escaped on a motor cycle. He could never have carried bulky hi-fi equipment on that. No, he definitely came for the painting.'

Michael pretended to examine the leaves of his cigar. The idea of this woman lobbing a vase at a burglar fascinated him. She was clearly a brave lady – but then the tone in her voice had told him she was red-blooded. Another thought struck him. If she was tackling burglars single-handed, did that mean she lived alone? He could feel her gaze fixed on him, the calculating eyebrows. 'You may be right, you may be wrong,' he said. 'I don't know. What I do know is that no amount of interest in this picture by thieves can make it valuable. It's not.'

Isobel Sadler's hair had fallen over her eye again and she brushed it away impatiently. 'I'm telling you my story backwards, Mr Whiting, and that is probably confusing. I apologize. I haven't told you about the coincidence yet. I wanted to be sure that it meant something. The fact that you confirm the picture is worthless only makes the coincidence more marked.'

Michael said nothing. A layer of lazy smoke drifted between them. As it approached Isobel Sadler she pointedly waved it away.

'I said I had a mystery for you, but the picture is only part of it. I suppose I should tell you something about myself – it will help.

My family, the Sadlers, can trace our ancestors back to Tudor times. We are no longer rich' – she held up her hands – 'I have had to work my parents' farm since they are both dead, but yes, we go back many generations.' Her eyes probed his. 'We have one famous ancestor – or perhaps "notorious" is a better word. Sir William Sadler: 1480 to 1537.' She smiled. 'I can never forget his dates. Anyway, he had a rather controversial role in the dissolution of the monasteries – he was called a "Visitor" and his job was to help Henry VIII dispose of all their assets, so it didn't exactly make him popular. The point is that because of Sir William – "Bad Bill" we called him in the family – I've always been interested in history, especially local history, anything to do with the family or the area we come from, near Painswick in Gloucestershire. For instance, I get all the catalogues of the manuscript sales at the auction houses and a few weeks ago I noticed that some papers relating to Bad Bill were due to come up for auction at Sotheby's.' She rubbed an eyebrow with her knuckle. 'For most people I would imagine they are thoroughly boring. They consisted of inventories mainly, relating to monasteries which Sir William had had a hand in dissolving, and there were a few letters he'd written, including one to another member of the family. That's what I was mainly interested in. They weren't expensive – a hundred and fifty to three hundred and fifty pounds for the lot. I thought I would have no bother getting them.' She smiled.

'But you did?' Michael had no idea why he was listening to this story, which had nothing to do with art.

Isobel Sadler nodded. 'I started bidding at the low end of the estimate: one hundred and fifty pounds. But there was someone else just as interested as me. I got carried away and so did this other person. The price went over five hundred pounds. Then to six hundred. I was astonished. At seven hundred pounds I had to drop out – the farm is a real drain just now.'

For a moment it was as if Isobel Sadler had left the room, so preoccupied was her expression, and Michael suspected that the farm was rather more than a drain. He glanced again at her rough hands. This woman was obviously having to work as a farm labourer herself.

But then, just as suddenly as she had left, she returned. 'I sat for

24

a few moments after the lot had been knocked down. I was sort of stunned, I suppose. I didn't know who had beaten me but it didn't matter. I know that sometimes, at big sales, the underbidder will offer the winner a quick profit after the auction proper has ended, but I was so far over my limit anyway that, in my case, it was out of the question. There was no possibility I could offer any more. I started to leave – and that's when a man came up to me.'

Michael leaned forward. 'Your rival?'

Again she nodded. 'I learned later that his name was Molyneux. As I got up and struggled to the end of the row he helped me out. I thanked him and he said he'd seen me bidding and asked if I was a dealer. I said no. Then I explained my interest in the documents, just as I've explained to you. He apologised, saying he'd bought them on commission for someone else, an American. He walked out with me, making small talk, asking me where I lived, what else I collected and so on. He was very tall and towered over me. He towered over everyone. There were creases in his cheeks, I remember that. Outside on the pavement, he said he or his partner might be down in Gloucestershire in a few days and could he call? That's when he gave me his name. He also promised to ask the man on whose behalf he'd bought the documents whether he could send me some photocopies. It would be better than nothing, he said, and he might be able to drop them off if he stopped by.

'Then I forgot all about it. I never imagined he would call – it was just small talk. But he did. He didn't phone in advance, just turned up late one morning. He said he'd been visiting a house sale near Cirencester and had taken time off to visit me. I was half impressed and half puzzled. He had no news on the documents; he said his client was abroad and he had to wait for him to return before he could do anything. But he was hopeful, he said. I gave him some coffee, we chatted and he asked if he could look round the house. I gave him a very quick tour since I had to get back to the farm.'

'You showed him the picture?'

She nodded. 'He actually laughed when he first saw it, pointing out how odd it was, just as you did a few minutes ago. He asked how long I'd had it. I told him it had been in the family for ever – I inherited it from my father, he from his father and so on. Anyway,

25

after Molyneux had examined the painting we went on round the rest of the house and he began to talk about the curiosities he himself collected. He said he was reviving the old tradition of the fifteenth and sixteenth centuries, when people like the Hapsburgs had curio chambers with things like stuffed dodos, pictures of bearded ladies or notorious murderers, perpetual-motion machines or gems that were supposed to have magical properties. He said he would love to have the picture for his collection and offered me a thousand pounds for it. He suggested I might use the money to make an offer to the man who had bought the "Bad Bill" documents. In effect I would be swapping the picture for the papers.' She brushed her hair away from her eye again. 'I nearly said yes. But then I thought: if the man didn't agree to sell the documents to me I would have lost both them *and* the painting. So in the end I said no. Molyneux was charming. He said he quite understood, and left soon after. Then came the coincidence. Three days after his visit someone tried to steal the same picture.'

She drank some coffee which by now must have been completely cold. Swallowing, she closed her eyes and bunched her eyebrows together. 'Too strong,' she gasped. 'Tell your boy not to brew it for so long.' Nonetheless, she drank again. The talk and the cigar smoke had no doubt made her throat dry. She waved the cigar smoke away again. Swallowing a second time, she went on. 'The more I thought about it, the more Molyneux's visit seemed odd. I even checked with all the estate agents in Cirencester – there aren't that many.' She placed her cup and saucer back on the tray. 'There hasn't been a house sale there for months.'

Michael went to interrupt but she waved him down.

'I think this man Molyneux came down to my house for a snoop. He was prepared to lie about the house sale, he was prepared to offer a thousand pounds for this picture, though you say it's probably not worth it, and now someone has been prepared to break into my house to steal the very same thing. I'll tell you something else. Molyneux is very tall, six feet four maybe. So was the burglar.' She looked intently at Michael. 'There's something about this picture, some mystery, that makes it worth stealing. It may have something to do with the documents I failed to buy and it may not. Anyway, Edward Ryan, who was a friend of my father when he collected

26

Far Eastern art, said it was a mystery just up your street. I don't know where it will lead or if there's any money in it – but I'm willing to go halves with you on whatever you turn up. Edward said that would appeal to your gambling instincts.' She rubbed an eyebrow with her knuckle again. 'Does it?'

Michael rolled the Havana between his fingers again. He blew out some smoke, but directed.it away from Isobel Sadler. He tried the coffee – yes, it *was* cold. He turned over in his mind what she had told him. For openers it was a crazy story. More, he rather thought that Ryan and Isobel Sadler were overrating his ability to search out a particular mystery – he had never encountered anything like this before.

She held her hand to her throat. The smooth skin of her neck contrasted strongly with the roughness of her hands – yes, she needed money all right. The farm must be a fight but . . . the picture just wasn't good enough to pursue.

At length he said, 'I admit it was a coincidence about this man Molyneux's visit and the burglary, but coincidences happen all the time. That's often all they are: coincidences.'

'Why should he lie about the house sale in Cirencester?'

'People lie all the time, often for no very good reason.'

'All right, then, I'll give you another reason to help me. I've lived alone for a year and a half now, since my father died. I'm hanging on to the farm, but only just. I've got a manager but that's all. I can't afford to hire any more labour, so I have to work the land myself. I've been scared since the break-in, though I never was before. I simply can't afford an expensive alarm system. So I'd like to get the damn picture away from the house, even if it isn't worth anything. On the other hand, if it is, even a few thousands, it would come in very handy.'

'But it *isn't* worth anything,' Michael said. 'I'm certain of it.'

'Bah! Don't you dealers ever make mistakes?' She coughed and batted a cloud of cigar smoke away from her. 'I seem to read about them from time to time in the newspapers. Isn't there *any* research you can do? Maybe Holbein painted a bit of it, or perhaps it once belonged to somebody famous. That would add to its value, wouldn't it? Please don't say no.' She suddenly looked much less composed than before. Her hair had fallen forward again and this

27

time she let it just hang there. 'I don't want to give up the picture, but I don't want it at home just now, either. *Please!*'

Was she acting? She didn't look the type to scare easily but being alone in a big farmhouse was, Michael supposed, very different from living in his own small house in the middle of Chelsea. He saw that her cheeks had flushed. They had a pink bloom like the woman's face in the painting which old Julius was restoring. That helped to make up his mind. The woman in Dover Street might well be an unsought-for bonus. If so, he could probably afford to spend some time on this other woman in front of him, even though Greg wouldn't thank him for taking on the extra burden.

'All right, all right. You walk in here out of the blue, you insult me, you criticise the coffee and make rude gestures about my cigars. Irresistible. Enbloodychanting.' But then he smiled and nodded. 'I'll take it off your hands – but at a price, and only for a week or so. If I can't find out anything in that time I'll have to hand it back. Is that a deal?'

'What do you mean, "at a price"?'

'Edward Ryan was not quite right. I'm not so much a gambling man as one who likes a wager. The difference matters, at least to me and my friends. I don't bet on the horses or play cards and I can't stand roulette, not for long anyway. That phone call you overheard just now was me practising my vice. Apart from this cigar, of course. And my whisky drinking and my chocolate habit.' He smiled. 'You won't have heard yet since we've been cooped up in here but it has just been announced that the film actress, Margaret Masson, has been divorced for the fifth time. Now, I belong to a small wagering club. Very small, only six members. Every January the first we each put up two thousand pounds, the money going to the one who, by the following Christmas, thinks up the most *amusing* wager. We don't do it regularly, only when something in the news crops up that takes our fancy. The stakes for the wagers are limited to a hundred pounds each, but at the end of the year we vote on who has had the best idea in the previous twelve months. The lucky man pockets ten thousand pounds – a nice Christmas present. That was a friend on the phone, a member of the club. His idea – and it's a good one – is that we wager on how long it is before Miss Masson announces her *next* engagement. You heard me opt for three weeks.'

'What you do in your spare time is your own business – but why are you telling me this?'

'Because I'm going to propose a wager to you.'

'I don't gamble.'

'Don't be such a prig. And I haven't told you the wager yet.'

Isobel Sadler said nothing.

'Don't worry, I have only mild vices.' He noticed that his cigar was going out and put a match to it. He rolled the leaves in the flame and flooded the room with billows of smoke. 'Dinner.'

She looked at him.

'If I find out *anything* about your picture that you didn't know and which increases its value, you agree to have dinner with me one of the times you are in London.'

'Do you often have dinner with strange women?'

'You're not that strange. Rita Hayworth wouldn't have worn that kilt, and you seem to like cold coffee, but no other oddities, as far as I can see.'

She smiled. 'I don't know whether I want to win or lose this bet – I mean wager.'

'Then you accept?'

'On condition that you don't smoke one of those filthy objects until the very end.'

'Done.'

'Thank you,' she breathed, quickly getting to her feet. 'I was beginning to think the picture was bringing me bad luck.' She began fiddling with her belt. 'I come up to London one evening a week – I have to get away from the farm one night or I'd go crazy. Shall I look in next week?'

'No.' He put the coffee-cups back on the tray. 'Give me a fortnight. There *are* other things I have to do, you know,' he said, smiling. 'I have a gallery to run, cigars to buy, wagers to win.' They shook hands.

'Very well. Two weeks it is. Expect me at the same time as today.'

He opened the door and showed her through to the main gallery. Michael pointed to a watercolour of some stone houses. 'That was painted not far from you, in Broadway, Worcestershire. It's a Sargent. He lived there for a while. Henry James used to visit him.'

They both looked at the picture, then Michael opened the gallery door. Isobel Sadler hesitated at the main entrance into Mason's Yard and said, 'It's a beautiful gallery, Mr Whiting.'

'Thank you.'

'Yes. How would I describe it?' She paused, an eyebrow raised in the sharpest angle he'd yet seen. ' "Well worth a detour"?'

2

In the next few days Michael and Gregory Wood were very stretched. There was a house sale in Yorkshire which had to be visited, an offer of some eighteenth-century portraits from Ireland, which took another forty-eight hours out of the schedule, and Michael had to dance attendance on an Australian collector who suddenly appeared in London and expressed a serious interest in the Gainsborough. That meant three breakfasts in a row at the Westbury Hotel.

Then there was Robyn's wedding. Michael's younger sister had so far led an itinerant life. A zoologist by training, she had spent her early twenties in some of the remotest spots on earth, studying the local animals. Now she was one of the staff at a safari park near Bath. Her husband-to-be was a young Oxford don and, since Michael and Robyn's father was dead, it fell to the brother to give Robyn away. The wedding was held in the local church in Somerset and Robyn, for once, was too nervous to tease Michael. He made her laugh when he told her that her old-fashioned lace dress made her look 'Ottobloodycento', and she was delighted with his present, a small oil by Rolandt Savery showing the animals entering the ark. His mother looked more relaxed than he had seen her since his father had died and he travelled back to London feeling very content and ready to make a few inquiries on Isobel Sadler's behalf.

When she arrived back at the gallery two weeks after her first visit, Michael saw her not in the inner sanctum but in his office on the first floor, above the main showroom. She was led upstairs by Elizabeth Allsopp, his secretary. This time Isobel Sadler had left her

31

raincoat downstairs to dry, and Michael thought the green dress she was wearing underneath did not entirely suit her colouring. He noticed that the plaster had been removed from her cheek. But her hair still flopped down one side of her face and she looked more Hayworth than ever.

'No more burglaries, I hope?' he said after she sat down.

'No, thank God. And just as well. With all the rain we've had since I last saw you, we're dropping behind with the silage.' She brushed her hair off her face in a gesture Michael was already fond of. 'Any news?'

Michael pointed up behind her head. She turned. His small office, which had two high windows looking out into Mason's Yard, was lined from floor to ceiling with art books and auction catalogues, save for one spot, opposite his desk, which he kept free to hang his favourite picture of the moment, or something he was researching. Isobel Sadler's picture hung there now.

'When we have dinner – ' He smiled and held his hand up to steady her as she turned back to him eagerly. 'There's good news – and there's bad news. On the one hand, yes, I think I have solved your mystery . . . on the other hand, it's a good bet that I've uncovered a more tantalising one.'

She put an elbow on the edge of his desk and rested her chin in her hand. 'Ryan was right; you *are* a good detective.'

Michael shook his head. 'Hold on. So far it hasn't been difficult. If I'm right, the real problems are just beginning.'

He took a cigar from the ashtray and wedged it into his mouth. He had taken off his jacket, revealing a pair of bright scarlet braces. He hooked a thumb inside one and rocked back in his chair.

'Let's get the Holbein thing out of the way first. I showed your picture to Frank Cobbold at the National Gallery – he's the top-ranking Holbein scholar in Britain at the moment – and he confirmed there is not even the *smell* of the master in your painting. So you can forget that.'

She moved slightly and bit her lip. She blew the cigar smoke back towards him. 'What else?'

'I can't rush this. I've got to give it to you in the right order or it's confusing.' He looked out into the yard. The weather had indeed changed: sluicing rain, bang on schedule to drench the rented morning-suits and fancy hats at Ascot races. He pulled on his cigar. 'Cobbold also pointed out what I should have remembered. There were almost no English landscape painters of the sixteenth century. Your picture may have been painted *in* England but the artist himself was possibly Flemish. I haven't actually been able to find out *who* painted the picture but, as I shall show you in a moment, that may not matter. In fact, let's forget the picture completely to begin with and concentrate on the documents you didn't buy. I know you didn't ask me to, but the first thing I did, after that quick check with Cobbold, was with Sotheby's. I thought I'd take a closer look at the documents in question. You may not have noticed but, according to Sotheby's catalogue, the documents you tried to acquire were the property of one Matthew Hope – does that name mean anything to you?'

Isobel Sadler shook her head.

'Since he wasn't bothered about anonymity, Sotheby's were happy to give me his address. Hope is a retired vicar living in Lincolnshire. Here I had a stroke of luck, since I had to go to Yorkshire for another reason. So instead of going by train I took my car and called in on the old boy. He was a talkative old chap and didn't mind in the least that Sotheby's had given me his address. At seventy-eight he still has all his marbles and was glad of the company. Like you he's interested in the sixteenth century but in his case, being a vicar, his main concern is in how English Protestantism grew out of English Catholicism. He was naturally very interested in the dissolution of the monasteries and used to have quite a collection of documents relating to the whole business. I say "used to" because he's been selling them off, bit by bit, to supplement his pension.'

Isobel Sadler nodded reflectively. Michael could see she identified with the poor man.

'The ones you were interested in were just the latest batch to come under the hammer. But – and this is the good news – he has kept photocopies of everything he ever had. I told him, quite openly, that I had come on a simple errand, on my way north to a house sale in Yorkshire. I said that a friend of mine whose ancestors were mentioned in the latest batch of papers which he had sold had wanted to buy them but had been pipped at the post, so to speak.

Yes, he said, they *had* fetched more than he expected. So I asked if he would be willing to let me take away a photocopy of his photocopy of the documents. He didn't mind at all and, after a couple of sherries and I had given him an opinion on a painting he had, off we went into Market Rasen together to the photocopying shop.'

Michael leaned forward, placed his cigar back in the ashtray and reached into a drawer in his desk. He took from it a folder with some sheets of paper inside. 'Here they are. They could be clearer but I think they are good enough for what we want.'

Isobel Sadler lifted her chin off her hand and took the folder. She opened it and scanned the papers. After a brief moment, she looked up. 'These aren't letters. And they're in Latin.'

'You don't read it?'

The eyebrows lifted. 'I'm a farmer.'

Michael nodded. 'I know you were mainly concerned with the letters. They are in a separate file in the drawer here. But the Latin documents are much more interesting.'

'Oh yes? Why?'

'The important one consists of an inventory, a list of things that were in a monastery in Somerset, near the village of Monksilver. Now, I've checked in the history books and that was indeed one of the monasteries that Bad Bill was involved with. Sir William visited Monksilver in November 1537 to assess its assets and supervise its break-up. That time, however, it seems that he was too late. Most of the more valuable assets had gone by the time he arrived. Two of the letters you were interested in relate to his arrival at Monksilver, to find only the lead roof intact and some of the stained glass. On the other hand, most of the other treasures – and there was quite a lot – had vanished. Salted away into the Somerset air.'

Michael took back the photocopied documents from Isobel Sadler and arranged them in front of him. 'Monksilver, I have found out, was a rich monastery. The monks were medical men, would you believe? And they had a number of wealthy patrons – patients, in effect, whom they had cured.' He noticed a puzzled look on Isobel Sadler's face and explained what he had himself learned only days before. 'This was before the age of medicine proper, don't forget. The monks were educated men and a lot of them were travellers: they picked up cures and treatments on their travels and learned

34

how to use herbs as drugs. There was another similar monastery at Evesham and that also became rich through medicine – it was by no means unheard of.'

'Rich monks?'

'The monks took a vow of poverty of course but the money they made went back to the monastery and not just into the fabric of the building – they bought books and manuscripts, commissioned candlesticks, reliquaries, jewelled crosses. It became famous for its treasures – most of which were silver. That's why the village is now called Monksilver.

'None of it was ever found, either then by Sir William or later. According to legend – I've checked this in the books too – the monks took the silver north, intending to hide it in one of the many caves in the Mendip Hills. Unfortunately, they were in so much of a hurry that they took a short cut across the estuary of the River Parrett north of Bridgwater. So weighed down were the carts they were using, allegedly, that they could only travel at two miles an hour. Hence the need for a short cut. Unfortunately, they made the crossing of the Parrett in October when the tides in the Severn Channel are especially strong.' Michael picked up a pair of scissors and dropped them on to the desk in front of him. 'They got caught halfway across the estuary and the whole lot sank in quicksand and disappeared.'

Isobel Sadler groaned, but Michael held up his hand. 'However, an inventory *was* found, a list of the most beautiful things that once adorned the abbey. Sir William even refers to it in one of his letters. Look – ' Michael took another file from his drawer. He drew out a sheet and turned it so that Isobel could read what he was pointing at:

Monksilver was as barren as a nun's belly. Deceiving Order! Roman Rogues! An Index of furnishings showed a dowry that the King, and I, had been jilted of. Monksilver wasn't worth a copper.

Michael rubbed the bridge of his nose with his thumb and forefinger and went on, 'The monks, obviously having good connections through their medical work, had been given a warning about Sir

William's visit. It didn't happen that often, but it happened. Now, look at this inventory.'

Isobel Sadler leaned forward. Michael turned another paper and pushed it across to her. 'This is a rough translation from the Latin. My sister's got a new husband who's an Oxford don. He helped.'

What Isobel read was:

'Oh Lord, protect us and all that is yours.
Grant us thy vision and a faithful spirit to follow thy
path in troubled times.
Lead us, Lord.
Those who seek the Kingdom of Heaven on Earth
shall surely find thee, for thou hast said,
"I am the Way."
The keys to the Kingdom of Heaven are thine alone.'

The Abbey of St Peter, at Monksilver

This Register was writ
in the year of Our Lord
1537

★One hand reliquary, in silver, with an emerald ring on the third finger. Ruby windows (no bones).

★One map of the True Cross, in silver with emerald stations.

★An eagle vase, in polished porphyry with a gold head and, as handles, gilt wings.

★An elephant-ivory crosier, showing three scenes from the Life of Christ. The knop set with cloisonné enamelled plaques representing the Blessed Virgin and Child. Silver-gilt panels show saints and angels.

★Four candlesticks, silver-gilt, showing fish, lions, dragons and griffins, overcome by man.

★Jewelled gospels from France, showing the Passion with the blood of rubies and a silver clasp.

★Incense boat and censer in German silver, a lion at each end of the boat, and the censer filigreed.

★Silver-gilt chalice from Spain, an ivory collar carved with leaves and, at the lip, the words 'From hence is drunk the pure flow of the Divine Blood'.

*Altar cross, silver-gilt, set with amethysts and cornelians, and bearing miniatures painted on vellum. Tablets of glass cover lists of relics inside the cross.

No key but this +

'What's a hand reliquary, and ruby windows?' said Isobel Sadler. 'And a map of the True Cross? The rest I think I understand. Just.'

'Yes, they confused me too, so I asked an old friend at the V and A. A reliquary, as you know, is some sort of device containing the relics of a saint. A hand reliquary means it is a statue in the form of a hand. This one is made of silver and originally contained the bones of the saint's hand – that's why it was fashioned into that shape. Ruby windows means that the little glass panels in the fingers of the statue, so you can see the relics, were in fact made of rubies. A map of the True Cross, I now know, means it was a silver map of Europe and the Middle East showing all the places where pieces of the True Cross were believed to exist. The holy places were marked by emeralds. Hand reliquaries are not that unusual but silver ones are. The map is rarer – there is only one other known, in the Rijksmuseum in Amsterdam.'

'Engrossing, and grisly. But what has this to do with the picture?'

'I was just coming to that. In the first place, there are apparently grounds for disbelieving that the Monksilver silver, so to speak, actually disappeared as legend has it.'

'Oh?'

'Yes. Reverend Hope told me about that. Apparently, the Monksilver legend is identical with the story of the loss of King John's state treasure, which disappeared in the sands of the Wash in October 1216. The details are exactly the same, down to the carts which could travel at only two miles per hour. The King John treasure really is in the quicksands of the Wash, for anyone to stumble across even today. So the Monksilver story may be just a smokescreen, to put Bad Bill and others like him off the scent.'

'Are you saying – ?'

'Hold on. Hear what else I have to say first.' He picked up his

37

cigar from the ashtray and pulled on it. 'Now, here's the hot news. There is a link between the inventory and your painting.'

'What?' She stared at him. 'There *is*?'

'How many objects are listed in the inventory?'

She looked down and counted. 'Nine.'

'And how many figures in the painting?'

She turned and started to count again. '. . . nine, but – '

'That's right. Now look closer. *Each figure in your picture is associated with something from this list*! The man in the funny tunic is standing next to the eagle vase, the skeleton is holding the crosier – see? – one monk has the gospels, and the other has the candlestick. They are all there, all nine.'

She turned back to face Michael. 'What does it mean?'

Now Michael got up and walked around his desk. He stood in front of the picture. 'From here on, it's guesswork. Pure theory. I haven't checked what I'm going to say with any authority so I may be completely off the rails. But see if I can convince you.' He paused and drew on his cigar. 'Okay, here goes.' He nodded towards the papers on his desk. 'Have another look at the inventory. It tells us one thing we didn't know before: the name of the abbey.'

'St Peter's.'

'Exactly. Now look at the very last words on that list.'

Isobel Sadler moved her eyes down the paper. ' "No key but this" - and then there's a – well, it looks like a cross.'

'Right! But a very special cross – '

The eyebrows were lifted, then lowered and bunched together as Isobel Sadler frowned. 'The cross bar is lower than it should be?'

'Abloodymazing! Ten out of ten. You've spotted it. Except that the bar is exactly where it ought to be – because *it's upside-down*. Start with the fact that Monksilver was dedicated to St Peter. In the Bible, Peter was given the keys to the Kingdom of Heaven by Jesus. That's why the papal insignia, at St Peter's in Rome, are crossed keys. Then, according to legend, at the end of his life Peter was crucified upside-down.' Michael loosened his tie and unbuttoned the collar of his shirt. 'Now move on to the possibility that these nine items were not lost in the sands of the Severn Estuary near Bridgwater but were hidden *somewhere else*. I think that the phrase "No key but this" followed by a drawing of an upside-down cross was intended as an indication of where the St Peter's treasures *had* been put. The writer of the inventory is saying, in effect: "Look for another upside-down cross." Now look at this.'

Michael turned and with the end of his finger traced the edge of the red curtain that partly shielded the chapel in the painting from view. Going from top to bottom, about half the way down, the curtain fell down a fraction to reveal, half hidden behind it, a small religious memento hanging on a wall. It was a metal moulding of a man being crucified upside-down.

'And you think – '

'Think is too hefty a word. If my sister were here she would say I'm playing Micawber again. But it is possible . . . *possible* that, taken with everything else, this upside-down cross links Monksilver Abbey, the inventory and your painting. The medieval mind adored riddles. They loved nothing so much as a session on the conundrums. They believed that secret wisdom was hidden in that way to keep it special. I reckon it is at least on the cards that the monks at Monksilver hid their treasures before Sir William arrived and that, not knowing what would happen to their order, whether they would be dispersed or imprisoned, or worse, the abbot commissioned this picture as a secret record of where the main treasures were hidden.'

'Micawber? Or Machiavelli?'

'Cruel – but hear me out. In the fifteenth and sixteenth centuries pictures were full of symbols, and educated people prided themselves on being able to "read" them. The abbot at Monksilver may have meant to keep the picture himself, or he may have intended to send it to another monk or abbot at a safer monastery. On the other hand, look at that prayer which was written as a preamble to the inventory. That's also the kind of thing they did in those days . . . but read it again, knowing what you know now. It's all about following paths, having a special vision, seeking heaven on earth, finding the key. Follow, seek, find: those are the verbs. Any other monk reading the prayer would also have known by then that the Monksilver treasures had gone. But no one else did get a chance to read it. Bad Bill got there first. Since it's been in your family for such a long time, the picture must have been among the few things that Sir William *did* confiscate at Monksilver.'

Isobel Sadler frowned. 'It's neat, I grant you that, Ryan was

39

certainly right about you – you do think like a detective. But you're a gambler too. This sounds like long odds to me.'

'Maybe. But there's something else. Cobbold inadvertently suggested it when I showed the painting to him. He was the one who noticed the half-hidden crucifix. He told me that, although your picture wasn't by Holbein, this device *was* borrowed from one of Holbein's own pictures – in the National Gallery here in London, as it happens. The picture, called *The Ambassadors*, was painted in 1533 and shows two men wearing furs and surrounded by astronomical and mathematical instruments. But it also shows a crucifix half hidden by a curtain – I went to look at it only yesterday, to refresh my memory.'

'You mean it's the same crucifix?'

'The similarity is marked, except that in Holbein's painting the figure isn't upside-down of course. Anyway, this device, according to Cobbold and all the textbooks, which I've also dipped into, is generally held to mean that the artist is saying that the truth, the Christian truth, is always hidden and that it can only be discovered through diligence and study. It all fits.'

He could see from the sparkle in Isobel Sadler's eyes that, despite herself, she was beginning to believe him and to share his excitement. The silvery sheen coming off the wet paving stones in the Yard outside was reflected in her eyes. But she had one more doubt. 'Why didn't Sir William make the connection you have made? He was there, alive at a time when, as you say, they thought in conundrums.'

'Good question. As a matter of fact I think Sir William *did* have some idea of what was afoot. That's why I think he confiscated both the inventory and the picture. I think he intended to look for the treasure himself at a later date but he never got the chance. The king kept him very busy, and Bad Bill had better fish to fry than go chasing off after hidden silver. There were plenty of other monasteries less well organised than Monksilver. According to the Reverend Hope, Sir William was in Gloucester later that same month and Worcester after that. And, as you well know, he died before the year was out. It may have been then that the inventory and the picture were separated.'

'But . . . wherever they were hidden, surely the monks retrieved them as soon as they could. You don't think they are still – well, buried or locked up somewhere, do you? This all happened over four hundred years ago.'

Michael shrugged. 'Now we get to the difficult bit. Do we go looking – or is that a romantic idea but a waste of time? Micawber mania, as my sister might call it. As you rightly say, it's been four whole centuries since these things were hidden.' He picked his cigar out of the ashtray and sucked the end. 'But works of art *do* go missing for very many years. There is a censer and incense boat in the V and A which disappeared for five hundred years before turning up in Cambridgeshire – discovered by a man who was hunting for eels. Every year there are half a dozen great old masters found in someone's attic or an old house in the country. The point is, so far as anyone knows, none of these nine very valuable objects has turned up anywhere. That means the odds are they are still in their hiding place – or lost for ever.'

'How valuable *are* they?' Isobel Sadler's eyes gleamed.

'Ah! Another good question. You may find your judgement even more muddled when you look at this.' Michael returned to his desk and dipped into his drawer again. 'It's not easy to value objects like these, you know, since no two art works are exactly alike. But my friends at Sotheby's helped out, checking against their computer records.' He retrieved another sheet from the drawer and handed it to Isobel Sadler. 'This is the best I can do, in the circumstances. The figures on the right are the auction records for objects as similar as I can find to those on the Monksilver list.'

Isobel Sadler put both elbows on the desk in front of her and leaned forward to look at the list. Almost immediately, she grunted involuntarily. What she read was:

1.	Hand	£2,000,000
2.	Map	£3,500,000
3.	Eagle vase	£750,000
4.	Ivory crozier	£450,000
5.	Candlesticks	£1,000,000
6.	Gospels	£4,000,000
7.	Censer etc.	£1,000,000
8.	Chalice	£450,000

| 9. Altar cross | £2,000,000 |
| Total | £15,150,000 |

'I don't believe it.'

'You should. The figures are, if anything, on the conservative side. For example, the world record for a manuscript, the Hughes de Lionne gospels, is $11 million, £8.1 million. But that was in 1983. The Monksilver gospels could fetch twice the value I have put on them.'

Isobel Sadler's gaze kept alternating between Michael and the figures in front of her. 'But . . . what I mean is . . . . if we found any of this, who would it belong to?'

'Yet another good question. That depends partly on where it was found and partly on what happened to the order which St Peter's belonged to.

'The law on trove is clear: the stuff belongs to the Crown, which cedes it to the Treasury, which cedes it to the British Museum. If they take it – and they'd almost certainly take this – they pay the full market value to the finder.' He paused. 'In other words we would split more than fifteen million pounds, fifty-fifty. You could buy a few tractors with that.'

For a while there was silence in Michael's office. The only sound was the distant hiss of traffic as it swished down Duke Street.

At length Isobel Sadler said, 'I just can't believe that something could remain hidden for so long without anyone finding it – or stumbling on it by accident.'

'I know. But if that had happened the world would certainly know about it. Some of the treasure is so important it would have ended up in museums. We know that isn't the case. Besides, aren't you forgetting one other thing?'

'Oh yes? What?'

'Your burglar. *He* was convinced there is something in all this. I've asked around the dealers who specialise in medieval things, and the auction house people, and no one has ever heard of anybody called Molyneux. So he may have given you a false name. He may read Latin and therefore spotted the significance of the inventory. By itself it wasn't worth a lot of money, of course, but it had academic interest, enough certainly for him to spend what he did

42

spend. Your presence in the auction room, however, was a bonus. When he found out you were a Sadler, he must have seen his chance immediately. He wouldn't have known about the picture, of course, not at that stage. He probably came down to your house hoping to spot one or more of the treasures from the inventory which, he hoped, you weren't aware were so valuable. That's how coups are made in the art world all the time. But when he saw the painting he must have noticed that the figures are holding the items from the inventory and he would have realised immediately how significant it was. That's why he wanted it and that's why he tried to steal it.'

'So you're convinced it was him, are you?'

Michael nodded.

'How can you be so certain?'

'For one very good reason, which I hope will finally convince you that we're on to something. Look at this.' He stood up again and walked round to the picture. He took a pencil from a jug and pointed to the part of the picture where the chapel altar was covered in a green cloth. 'Look at the white lace edging. It's very finely painted, see?'

Isobel Sadler turned and peered at the lace. 'Yes?'

'Now stand back a bit and look at the design overall. It's very like the lace edging in one of Van Eyck's paintings.'

'But I don't see – '

'There's some *wording*. Look, just here . . . three words picked out in lace.'

Isobel Sadler stared. 'Good grief, you're right! What does it say?'

'It's Old English. It says "Landskyp of Lees". "Landscape of Lies", in everyday English in the twentieth century. Your picture has a title, "Landscape of Lies". Ask yourself why that should be . . . ? Because, Isobel Sadler, this picture conceals the truth. Molyneux, or whatever his name is, may have spotted this when he came to visit you. He would have realised its significance straight away. That's why he wanted it, why he wanted to steal it. Landscape of Lies. Now do you believe me?'

It was past noon and Michael thought they both needed a drink. He reached for a bottle of Islay malt which was hidden behind some books on Raeburn, Ramsay and Peploe – all 'Scotch' artists, which Michael regarded as a huge joke.

Isobel Sadler shook her head as Michael offered her a whisky. 'I hope he *was* the burglar,' she said. 'Then I've maimed him.'

Michael had a glass in one hand and a cigar in the other. He was never happier. 'In fact he was very crafty. It was cunning of him to offer you a thousand pounds to "swap" the picture for the other documents. If he'd offered you any more you might have been suspicious and if you had agreed he would have had both the inventory *and* the picture. As it is, the boot's on the other foot. We have the important bit and he has nothing – what's the matter?'

Isobel Sadler had jumped to her feet. 'Oh no!' She coughed as she regained her breath. 'No, no. I didn't tell you before because I didn't know it was important. It didn't seem relevant.' She took another breath. 'When he turned up that day, when he said he had come across from Cirencester, and I showed him around, he brought a camera with him. I didn't see him use it and he didn't ask. But at one point I was called away to the phone. The vet, I think. For a few minutes Molyneux was alone and near the painting. *He probably photographed it!*'

There was a long silence in the room. It was still raining outside and pellets of water skidded down the windows, like tiny snails that left a hundred silver trails. At one point Patrick put his head round the door but before he could say anything Michael snapped, 'Not now!' Then, more softly, 'Not now, Paddy. Later.' The bow tie – today it was blue with yellow spots – vanished.

The silence resumed. Michael was again looking out of the window, down into Mason's Yard. A new gallery had opened up recently, selling Scottish art. He had never imagined there to be so much, but the young man who ran the gallery seemed to have an inexhaustible supply. Michael watched him now as he took a number of canvases from the back of a car.

The rain worsened. Gusts of wind rattled the windows, as if the building shivered. Michael alternated between sips of whisky and pulls on his cigar. The blue smoke dissolved as it drifted from him, slipping away like the wake of a ship. He got up and went round the desk, to stand in front of the painting once more. Isobel Sadler turned in her seat.

'So. Molyneux has a start on us. I don't know why he needed to steal the original when he had a photograph. To stop anyone else following him, I suppose. Still, that's not our main worry. The main thing is that he may be uncatchable, I'm afraid. It's a pity about the photograph. A great pity. That snap may have cost you nearly eight million pounds. Still, what's done is done, and we've either got to go forward or give up.' He brushed his hand through his hair. 'I'll show you what I've worked out so far and then we can decide what we're going to do. Whatever it is, the fact that Molyneux has a photograph means we have to decide today, now. He's got enough start on us already. We mustn't give him any more.'

Michael turned back to the painting and pointed the unlit end of his cigar at the canvas, at the chapel.

'This is the easy bit. This is where we start. See this column here?' He moved the cigar up and down a thick, red-brown marble column. 'At the top there's a scene carved into the capital – see?'

Isobel Sadler nodded.

'A naked man and a naked woman, an apple and a serpent in a tree.'

'Adam and Eve.'

'Mr and Mrs Eden. Genesis. The first book, the beginning. We start here.'

Isobel Sadler stood up for a closer look at the scene.

As they stood there together, Michael could smell the shampoo on her hair. Willowherb. He moved his cigar to the right. Here, because of the way the column was drawn, a second side of the capital at the top was visible. 'This isn't too difficult, either. It looks to me like a man holding a stick, descending some stairs – agreed?'

She nodded.

Now Michael moved back to the desk to where there was a thick, brick-shaped book with a piece of paper wedged as a marker. He set down his whisky glass, jammed the cigar into his mouth, and looked at the spine of the book. 'This is by an American named Rowland. It's called *The Classical Tradition in Western Art* and it's more or less an encyclopaedia of myths, gods and goddesses. I think I've found the right reference – tell me what you think.' He sat down and opened the book at the place he had marked. 'Here we are.' Speaking out of the side of his mouth, he began to read. ' "Wand: A red-hot iron wand, or staff, held by a figure, usually a man, is sometimes used to indicate the Truth. A long staff is used in classical tradition to fend off the Cloud of Unknowing." ' He looked up at Isobel Sadler. 'If I'm right, this figure with the wand represents the reader of the picture, chasing the truth. If that's the case, then the path the figure is following is important. Remember the prayer: follow the path.' Again Michael raised himself from his seat, edged around the desk and stood in front of the picture. He pointed to the top of the red-brown column. 'As you can see, the figure is descending some steps.' He took his cigar from his mouth and held it longways near the canvas so that it almost touched the tops of the steps and pointed diagonally downwards. 'Now look where the path leads.'

With her eyes, Isobel Sadler followed the line of the cigar. 'It points to that figure there, the one with the tunic, with what you called the eagle vase and a clock.'

'Yes, I think so too. Whatever your friend Ryan says, this detective work is new to me, but I think we're being instructed to start with this figure in the tunic.'

He returned to the 'Scotch' books and retrieved the bottle of Islay. 'Are you sure you won't have a drink? It's Laphroaig.'

She shook her head again. 'Not in the middle of the day.'

He poured himself another enthusiastic slug and splashed some water on top. 'As I said, that was the easy bit. Now I'm stumped. I don't recognise that first figure and, what's worse, I haven't a clue how to start finding out.' He checked himself. 'Well, that's not quite true. I *do* know my way around the art libraries. But the question is: do we want to pursue this now? Is the chase worth it? Can we overtake Molyneux and, even if we do, will there be anything at the end of the line?'

Isobel Sadler was still examining the painting. She said nothing and Michael continued. 'I haven't been in this exact situation before but I have been in others like it. For example, it sometimes happens that I get a suspicion that a picture coming up for sale at auction is more than it appears. It's more valuable than the auction house seems to think, and may even be by a quite different painter, someone who is much better known than the painter given in the catalogue.

'That's what this art game is all about. When that happens I have to drop everything and concentrate on just one thing for a few days before the auction takes place. I spend whole days in libraries, looking up books and articles in academic journals. I pore over countless photographs, comparing how this artist drew hands, or that one painted flesh. Sometimes that leads to the need to look at other paintings, in private collections – pictures by the artist *I* think painted the work to be sold at auction. That means I have to find out *which* collections and then persuade the owners to let me look. It's frenetic but a lot of fun . . . and what I'm saying is this: if we *are* going to follow this up, that's what it will be like. We have to give days – a week, two weeks – to the project. And we have to decide now, this minute. We have to get going today if we're going to make a start at all. Molyneux has over two weeks' start, which may mean it's too late already. But last time you were here you sounded as though the farm couldn't do without you, that you can't get away for more than one night a week . . .' He tailed off.

Again there was silence, if you could call the drone of a jumbo jet, two thousand feet above, and the hiss of driving rain, silence. At length Isobel Sadler took her gaze off the painting, sat down and put her elbows back on the desk. She seemed unaware of the way her dress strained over her breasts. 'I *do* have a farm manager – Tom. He's been an angel, especially since the break-in.' She bit her lip and went on quietly, almost as if talking to herself. 'If I take any days off at this time of year he may just leave.' And then, just as on her first visit, she was gone, preoccupied, busy in her own world.

'I understand – ' Michael began, but she interrupted him.

'On the other hand, what the farm really needs now is investment, new equipment . . . some more land would make the whole operation more cost-effective . . . my father never had the chance to do that but *I* do. Three hundred acres have become available right next to us.' She rubbed the back of her neck with a hand. 'If I can't raise the money to buy that land and some new vehicles, I'll probably have to sell the farm in a year or so anyway . . .' Absently, she waved yet more cigar smoke back towards Michael. 'A few days, you say?'

He shrugged. 'Probably more. If it took only a few days, that would mean Molyneux has already found it. I know how the art market works but, as I told you last time, my field is really late eighteenth- and early nineteenth-century English painting.' He drained the whisky glass and sat back in his chair. 'I am not necessarily the best person to decipher this picture for you. Possibly, I can find the right books and the right museums to help us with the clues, but it may be better, and much quicker from your point of view, to let someone else help you, someone who can read allegories better than I can.'

She shook her head firmly. 'No. I trust you, Mr Whiting. You told me about all this when you didn't have to. You could simply have taken a photograph of the painting, without telling me, and got on the trail yourself. Then you wouldn't have needed to split any profits with me. If we brought in another expert he could do the same to both of us. Not only that: if medieval studies are as small a field as you say they are, anyone we got to help would be known to Molyneux. We could never be certain that he might not know our every move. As it is, although Molyneux has a start on us, he can't be certain that we are on the trail. He doesn't know that we know, if you see what I mean. He may not feel there is any urgency. That's our one advantage.'

'You sound as if you've made up your mind.'

'I have. I won't say farming is fun but it *is* satisfying. This may be a wild-goose chase. But I don't have any choice. I've got to take my opportunities as they arise. This one is not exactly copper-bottomed but it's all I've got. I must ask one favour, though.'

'Yes?'

'A raincheck on dinner.' She looked at her watch. 'There's a train at two-thirty. That means I can't get back to the farm till around five, five-thirty. I'll need most of tomorrow to brief Tom on what to do at the farm while I'm away. I can be back in London, with a suitcase, by tomorrow night, ready for an early start the day after. I know it means more delay, but I can't just drop everything. Tom *would* leave then and I couldn't blame him.'

'That needn't matter. What matters is that *I* start today, digging in the libraries. Maybe, by the time you come back to town, I'll have some news.' A thought occurred to him. 'Where will you stay?'

'I haven't thought about that. A hotel could get very expensive, if this thing goes on too long.'

'You could stay with me; there's a spare bedroom in Justice Walk.'

She shot him another sharp glance. 'No, thank you, Mr Whiting. I do have friends in London, you know. I expect I shall be able to stay with them. I will have dinner with you soon, since you've won your wager. But that's all. Who do you think I am – Rita Hayworth?'

3

When Isobel Sadler arrived in Michael's office the next time it had been rearranged. There were now two desks instead of one, and, to make room for the second, several piles of books had been removed from the floor. Patrick Wood, in a bright red bow tie today, showed her upstairs. Inside the office, Michael was talking to a tall, thin, balding man who she guessed, from the similarity to Patrick, must be Michael's partner, Gregory. They were introduced.

'Let me have him back as soon as you can, Miss Sadler, please. He won't tell me what all this is about – but . . . well, we get these mysteries from time to time. The best security is ignorance, I suppose. Good luck with the project, anyway, whatever it is.' He smiled and went out.

Isobel Sadler looked around. On one desk stood a jug of coffee. Piles of books littered the other.

'Booty from the London Library around the corner,' said Michael, following her look. 'I rather fancy that a lot of our work is going to be done in books. These are the standard reference works on iconography. Arnold Whittick's *Symbols, Signs and Meaning*, Gilbert Cope's *Symbolism in the Bible and the Church*, John Vinycomb's *Fictitious and Symbolic Creatures in Art*, plus that stock over there. I asked a friend at the V and A and she gave me the titles – don't worry, I didn't say what I wanted them for.' He pointed. 'You can use that desk.' Michael was again in his shirt sleeves. The same bright red braces, like fairground ribbons, slashed across his shirt. The room was already filled with the fug of tobacco smoke. His hair was chaotic and without his jacket he looked slimmer and younger.

Isobel Sadler looked over her shoulder to the wall. 'Where's the painting?'

'Downstairs. I'm having it photographed properly, in full colour. Then we can put the real thing in our vault. If we have to travel around, as we will do if we get anywhere, it will be much easier to use photos than the picture itself.'

She took off her coat. Today she was wearing jeans and a sweater. Ready for work. She helped them both to coffee. 'Any luck yesterday?'

Michael shook his head as he relit his cigar. 'Our friend, the first figure, is holding, as you may recall, the clock in one hand with the eagle vase nearby. I looked up "clock". Obviously it's a symbol of time passing – but I can't see how that helps. Apparently it's also a symbol of temperance, that someone abstained from liquor or had a temperate nature. Again, I don't see what use it is. He's not Father Time, whose attributes are a scythe and an hour-glass. It could mean that the person holding the clock is a scientist – so I called the Royal Society. Unfortunately, they weren't founded until 1662.'

He sat down and drank his coffee. 'Not a good day at all, yesterday. I drew a blank on the picture, and lost a wager.'

She glanced at him sharply.

'Who are we today?' he asked, his mouth full of cigar. 'Not Zelda or Rita. They wouldn't be so disapproving. Victoria maybe, or Boadicea – you look ferocious enough.'

She smiled.

'That's better. It was a good wager – and harmless. Yesterday was the summer sale of Impressionist paintings in New York. We all had to guess how many pictures would sell for more than fifty million dollars. I said three but I was way out. One Van Gogh, three Renoirs, two Degas and a Monet. Amazing.'

'What other bets – sorry, wagers – have you got on at the moment?'

'Only two. The length of the longest traffic jam on the M25 this year. I have thirty-seven miles. And how many nations finally boycott the Olympic Games. I say twenty. As you know, seventeen already have.'

'What are the odds on us reading the picture before my farm goes bust?'

Now he smiled. 'Abloodypalling, and getting worse all the time we sit gassing about something else.' He sat up. 'Tell you what. I've been through all these books and drawn a blank. I *was* planning to have a dig in the National Fine Art Library. That's part of the V and A – want to come? It might be a relief – I can't smoke in there.'

Isobel Sadler was already on her feet. 'The answer's not here, as you say. Anything to get away from that filthy cloud. Let's hope we don't bump into Molyneux.'

They took a taxi to South Kensington. Michael was always rather overawed by the vast V & A building. To him it looked as though it had been designed by a mad Victorian architect who had adapted designs for either a railway station or an asylum. Bela Lugosi baroque, he called it. Walking through the sculpture gallery, they turned into a short corridor devoted to fakes and forgeries, past a beautiful golden screen, about fifteen feet high and showing the lives of the saints, then climbed some wide stone steps to the first floor, where the library was. They signed in. There was no sign of Molyneux.

Michael made for the subject index. There were eleven entries under 'clock' and he filled out a slip for each one. Then they sat at a desk waiting for the references to be brought to them. After some minutes an assistant carried over a pile of books and Michael divided them into two stacks. 'You look through these,' he said, pushing across one set. 'I'll take the others.'

For two hours they sat reading. Eventually, when Michael was beginning to miss a cigar, he said, 'Any luck?'

'I don't think so,' whispered Isobel Sadler. 'The only halfway relevant thing I've found is that in many still-life paintings a clock has the same meaning as a candle – to indicate the passing of time, as you said. I've also found that several individuals in history used a candle as their symbol.' Michael looked at her eagerly as she said this but Isobel Sadler shook her head. 'Unfortunately, all of them – Bridget of Sweden, Sybil, Genevieve, Isabella d'Este – were women. We are looking for a man. What have you found?'

'Zero. Zilch. Nix. Apparently the ancient Greeks confused their word for "time", *chronos*, with their old god of agriculture, Cronus, who had a sickle for his attribute. That's why Father Time carries a sickle. The Roman god of agriculture was Saturn – I suppose we might try him.'

Michael went back to the index to look up Saturn. This time there were fifteen references, and filling out the forms in itself took many minutes. When the books arrived they sat leafing through them for another hour, again with no luck. Michael sighed heavily. 'This is hopeless.' Just then a buzzer sounded – the library was closing. 'A complete waste,' he grumbled as they handed back the books at the main counter. 'And we are another day behind Molyneux.'

As they descended the stairs by the tall screen, Michael turned to Isobel Sadler and said, 'The men's loo is just along here; do you mind waiting?'

She shook her head and while he was gone drifted into the long gallery, browsing through its sculptures, medieval tapestries and gilt objects. She looked out at the new Italian garden. Wet cypresses buckled in the wind like the tongues of enormous vipers.

When Michael returned, he could not at first find her. As he stepped further into the long gallery, however, he recognised her jeans and sweater. She was half hidden behind a statue.

'Sorry to keep you,' he said. 'Getting a taxi in this weather will be as hard as gambling with Gabriel.'

Isobel Sadler didn't move. It wasn't that she was angry with him, though. She reached out with her left hand and grabbed Michael's sleeve. 'Look!' she hissed. 'Look at those.'

Perplexed, but shaken by her tone, Michael examined the statue she was standing near. It showed a male figure wearing a helmet with wings growing out of it. The figure also had wings on its heels. 'I don't see—'

'Forget the helmet and the damned clock! Look at his tunic!'

Michael followed her gaze to the bronze tunic which the figure had slung about its shoulders. 'You think there's a similarity? I don't see it.'

'The motifs, the squiggly things . . . they're the same as on the picture. Or as near as makes no difference.'

Now Michael saw what she was getting at. Scattered across the statue's tunic was a galaxy of feathers, or petals, curly somethings that certainly did recall the motifs in Isobel Sadler's painting. Quickly he searched the base of the statue for a title or an artist's name. There was none and he cursed the museum's administration for not being more helpful to visitors. Any other gallery, in Europe or America, would have had an identifying card prominently displayed.

'Follow me,' he cried. 'The shop! The catalogue will be there.' They hurried along the gallery, turned left into the medieval treasury, rushed by the stained glass and the bone carvings and came out into the entrance hall. The shop led off the hall.

'Quick!' said Isobel Sadler, pointing. 'They're closing.'

A woman was getting ready to put a cover over the cash register.

'Look at all those books,' Isobel Sadler whispered. 'We'll never find the right one in time.'

Michael thought fast, then ran to the woman by the cash register. 'Excuse me, ma'am,' he said in what he hoped would pass as an American accent. 'I'm flying back to Boston first thing in the morning. I'd sure like to take a museum catalogue with me – you know, the big one. Could you help me please, before you close?'

The woman gave him a furious look and for a moment he thought she was going to refuse. But no, she stopped what she was doing, moved out from behind her counter and went to the shelves. She returned with a box containing three big red books. All she said was, 'Thirty-five pounds, please.'

Michael winced, but the catalogue might save them a day. He reached for his wallet and laid seven five-pound notes on the counter.

'Keep the receipt,' said Isobel Sadler, as they walked back across the hall to the exit. 'I'll pay back half your expenses – once I have something to pay them with.' She grinned. It was the first really relaxed grin he had seen her make.

The rain was slackening at last but it still took them nearly half an hour to find a taxi. When they did so, Michael was livid to find a sign behind the driver that insolently thanked him for not smoking. Isobel Sadler grinned again.

On the ride back to Mason's Yard, Michael ripped the cellophane off the catalogue and flipped through it, searching for the statue. They saw everything except that – Indian miniatures, jewellery, costumes, old photographs. 'Where *is* it?' Michael gasped. He turned more pages, past German guns, Italian porcelain, Japanese lacquer.

'There!' shouted Isobel Sadler suddenly. 'Turn back!'

He riffled back. She was right. There was a small, single-column photograph of the statue, in black and white. Underneath was written:

Mercury. North Italian. Anon. 15th century (?). Mercury was a very popular god and often appears in art. As the son of Jupiter he was a god in his own right – the god of commerce and the protector of shepherds. He was also a messenger, the patron of travellers and inventor of the lyre. In allegory he personified eloquence and reason, the qualities of a teacher.

'A teacher,' said Isobel Sadler. 'Not a scientist but a teacher.'

'Hold on,' said Michael. 'This is only six lines. There must be more about him in the books back at the office. This doesn't even explain the design on his tunic.'

The taxi dropped them off by the archway leading into Mason's Yard. Before going to the office Michael stepped into the Chequers, the pub just next to the arch, and emerged with a couple of Havanas. Seeing the look on Isobel Sadler's face, he said, 'Love me, love my cigars. Look, I've been a good boy all afternoon. I'll be losing the habit if I'm not careful.' He grinned and led the way into the Yard.

The gallery was closed – Gregory and Patrick had gone for the day. Michael opened the main door, deactivated the alarm and led Isobel Sadler upstairs. He found some glasses and a jug in a tiny kitchen at the very top of the building, and took them back down to the office. Isobel Sadler was already going through the reference book at the top of the pile on the desk which Michael had given her to use. He poured the Scotch and topped the glasses up with water. This time Isobel Sadler accepted. 'It's after six,' she explained, smiling.

After a few minutes of reading solidly, she swallowed some whisky and said, 'This is it, I think. What we've been looking at are not feathers or leaves or petals but upside-down flames. I'll read it to you: "Upside-down flames may have one or more of three meanings. In his illustrations of Dante's *Divine Comedy*, Botticelli dots the spheres of heaven with upside-down flames where they are intended to represent individual souls burning like stars in the crystal sphere of the firmament. Second, in the painting entitled *The Virgin of the Book*, in the Museo Poldi-Pezzoli in Milan, the same flames in a badger-like formation appear on the shoulder of the Virgin's cloak. Here they radiate downwards from a star and must surely represent divine inspiration. It was, after all, tongues of fire which came down from heaven on the day of the Pentecost and sat upon each of the Apostles filling them with the Holy Ghost so that they began to speak with other tongues, as the Spirit gave them utterance.

' "Another use of the emblem in antiquity was as a characteristic of Mercury in his guise as guardian of secret knowledge. The inverted torch was in fact an early symbol of death, one of Mercury's roles being to conduct souls to the underworld of Hades. But the badge, the upside-down flame, eventually came to symbolise all of Mercury's functions, not just this gloomy one." '

Isobel Sadler rested the book on the desk in front of her. She took another gulp of whisky. 'Am I being defeatist, or does all that tell us what we already know, only more so?'

Michael sat back in his chair so that he wouldn't blow smoke into her face. She had a point. He was tapping ash into the lacquered tray on his desk when he suddenly noticed a folder that hadn't been there when they had left. He picked it up and opened it. Inside were the colour prints of the painting. He slid one across to Isobel Sadler and swallowed his whisky. Raw sand itched his veins. He gazed at the photograph as if for inspiration.

At length he said, 'We're obviously not reasoning like medievalists. Let's try thinking out loud. We've been directed to this figure who, we find out, is three things: a guardian of secret knowledge, a teacher and a messenger, a conductor of souls into strange lands. As you say, we knew a lot of that already . . . therefore this is a kind of underlining. Why would it need underlining?'

Isobel Sadler was only half listening, still scanning the figures in the photograph in front of her. 'What *I* find odd,' she said, 'is this man's hairstyle. Why is it shaved so high . . . It doesn't – well, it doesn't look very Greek or Roman, does it? It's hardly godlike; quite the opposite, in fact–'

'That's it! That's it!' Michael slapped the palm of his hand on the open book in front of him. 'Well done! Why didn't I think of it?'

He got up and went round to Isobel Sadler's desk and stood behind her, so they could look at the photograph together. He held the bottle of whisky in one hand.

'Look at the faces on the other figures . . . All of them are ideal-ised, some are hidden, none of them is carefully painted or properly drawn. The detail is coarse or simply not there. Yet this face, this first face as we can now call it, is painted very carefully. Not just the hair, which, as you say, is very real-looking, but the eyes, the nose, the lips, the jawline. Strong dark eyebrows, a thick neck, a cleft in the chin. Remember the first day you came to the gallery? I remarked how well this face was painted and how weak the rest was? Damn – I should have put two and two together right away. There was a reason for it! The reason this head is much better than any of the others is because, unlike the others, *this man actually existed*. He must have been famous in his day. People would have recognised him, either because they knew him or because he had been painted in other pictures, pictures where he is identified. That's it! You see! The identity of this man takes us to a *place*, where he lived, or taught, or preached, or died. *That* is where we start. He's both a guardian of the secret *and* the messenger – the man who can conduct us to it.'

'But how on earth can we find out who he is? He's been dead for four hundred and fifty years. And where are we going to look to find a likeness for him? There must be thousands and thousands of pictures still in existence from that time. And what about the clock? We still haven't explained that.'

'The clock's not a problem,' shouted Michael, still excited and puffing huge folds of blue smoke into the room. Isobel Sadler pushed his hand with the cigar away from her. 'It has nothing to do with Mercury, or this man, whoever he is. Dammit, again it's obvious.' He leaned forward, over Isobel Sadler's shoulder, again catching a brief smell of the Willowherb on her hair. With the neck of the upturned whisky bottle he traced the nine figures in the picture. 'Look at the composition as a whole . . . The people are arranged, very roughly, in a circle, a flat ring. Now think ahead. Say we do eventually find out who this character is, the one with

57

the shaved head and the cleft in his chin. What then? Which way do we go, where is the next clue? Along the top or along the bottom? I'll put it another way: do we go clockwise or anticlockwise? See? *That's* what the clock means.'

Isobel Sadler was impressed. She twisted in her seat to look up at him. 'Clever. I can see that nothing in this picture is going to be straightforward.' She looked at her own watch.

'Where did you decide to stay?'

'With a friend, near Harrod's. I shouldn't be too late on my first night. It wouldn't be polite.'

'Tell you what, then. Since I've won my wager, let me claim my reward straight away. Let's have a quick dinner together tonight. We can carry on trying to work this out over a bottle of something or other – and then I'll drop you off. I live that way.'

'Not the prettiest invitation I've ever had. But we might as well get it over with, I suppose. Is there somewhere I can wash my hands, please, and comb my hair?'

Michael showed her to a small bathroom at the top of the building, on the same floor as the kitchen. He put out the lights in his office and waited for her down in the main gallery. There was a fresh picture where the Gainsborough had been; the Australian collector who liked breakfast so much had taken it on approval. That meant he could have it at home on his walls for up to three months before deciding whether he wanted it. It was a nerve-racking way of doing business. The picture was worth about six months in overheads, which was fine if a sale went through. During that time, however, no one else was able to see the picture and fall in love with it. But Whiting & Wood Fine Art had no choice: everyone else operated that way.

When Isobel Sadler reappeared they both went out into the Yard, after Michael had set the gallery alarm. The rain had eased but the roads were still very wet. They threaded their way through the narrow streets of St James's. 'I love this part of London,' said Michael, as they walked. He pointed to one gallery selling old master drawings, another selling coins, a third with a small watercolour in the window and yet another with an eighteenth-century French chest of drawers in red lacquer and gold on show. 'There are more beautiful objects in these few streets than almost anywhere else in the world. Eggshell lacquer, ormolu, mahogany veneers, lapis lazuli, parcel-gilt, watered silk. Even the words are promiscuous. It's like a museum and all for sale.'

He took her to Keating's, a restaurant in a small mews behind the Ritz Hotel. It was an art-world favourite and Michael was known there; he didn't have to book in advance.

'Drink?' he asked as they settled into their seats. 'It's very arty here – so they do all those fancy Venetian cocktails, you know, "Bellini", "Tiziano", "Tiepolo" and so on.'

She pushed her hair away from her eye. 'I'll have a Bellini.'

He ordered two.

She looked around her and he saw her eyebrows lift in wonder.

'This place is called Keating's in honour of that old rogue and forger, Tom Keating. Every picture on the walls here is a fake. Some are Tom's but by no means all. It has become the practice in the art world that when a dealer finds himself landed with a forgery, or spots one and picks it up cheaply, it is given to this restaurant. Look,' he added, and pointed, 'that's a "Raphael" over there, with a "Titian" next to it and a "Picasso" on the other side.'

Isobel Sadler's gaze raked the room. There were a few pictures so famous that even she recognised them. 'Have you donated anything,' she said at length, 'or do Whiting & Wood never get caught out?'

Michael turned and pointed. 'That one is ours. It's a "Turner".' He shifted in his seat so as to face her again. 'The grand old man is always supposed to have produced a number of erotic drawings and paintings – but Ruskin, the art critic, who was a great Turner fan, destroyed them after Turner's death. They contradicted what he – Ruskin – thought a great artist should produce.'

A waiter brought the Bellinis and two menus.

'Some bright spark had the idea of "rediscovering" a few of the erotic Turners and brought them in to us. The style was quite good. The provenance was weak – but then you'd expect that. Sadly, the paper which the drawings were made on wasn't itself produced until the 1860s. Turner, of course, died in 1851. It was a nice try. The drawings would have been very popular if the hoax had come off.' He smiled. 'Let's order.'

After they had chosen, he said, 'No more art chat for a bit. If we give our brains a rest we're more likely to come up with a solution. Tell me about the farm. By the sound of it, you love it but find it hard – yes?'

She accepted a bread roll from a waiter. 'Yes and no. I love the land – yes. The countryside, the fields, the Cotswolds. And I love horses – I was a very horsey schoolgirl.' She brushed her hair away from her face. 'But I don't think I'm a natural farmer, not like my father was. He was a widower most of his life. My mother died having me so I never knew her. After he retired from the foreign service, he threw himself into farming, which I think he loved even more than diplomacy. If he had to get up in the middle of the night, even in the middle of a snowstorm, because a sheep was lambing, he loved it . . . it was all part of the adventure for him.' She swallowed her drink. 'That meant he was quite happy to get by, financially I mean. Farming was a way of life for Pa, not a means by which he could become a millionaire.'

'You don't see it like that?'

'No. I suppose I've kept on the farm out of loyalty. And because Tom and his family depend on us.'

'What would you rather be doing?'

The wine arrived before she could answer. Michael tasted it, a Volnay, and the waiter filled their glasses.

'Don't get me wrong; I don't want to be a millionaire either. Not especially. But if I were to sell the farm tomorrow I would probably spend the money on a boat.'

'What sort of boat?'

'A big one.' She laughed. 'Well, a fairly big one. Big enough to live on.' She drank some of her wine. 'I'd like to live in the sun – Florida or California, maybe. Or Australia. Where people could charter my boat. Where not many people smoke.'

Michael pushed down the Havana in his top pocket, so that it no longer showed. 'But you haven't done it, so far?'

'I'm stubborn. When I sell the farm – when, not if – I want it to be from a position of strength, as a going concern producing healthy profits, not because I have to. If I couldn't do that I'd feel like a failure for the rest of my life and I wouldn't be able to enjoy any boat I bought.' She leaned back in her chair. 'I'm talking too much. All this is such a change for me. A whole day away from the farm.

I must be a bit disorientated and you are a stranger, Mr Whiting, after all . . . I'm being more honest than I'm used to being.'

Oddly, Michael was hurt by this remark. 'I had hoped that we were about to get on to first-name terms,' he said softly.

Just then the food arrived and she waited for it to be served before replying. After the waiter had gone, she said, 'I'm not that easy with men, Mr Whiting – Michael – as perhaps you've noticed. I've not had very happy experiences. I'm sorry but I can't help it.'

Michael could not pursue this, not for now. He smiled as warmly as he could. 'My own experiences with women, in the last few months anyway, have been not so much unhappy as non-existent. If *I'm* not easy, it's because I'm rusty.'

She let this go. 'Tell me about Michael Whiting, and Whiting & Wood Fine Art. How did you become an art dealer?'

Since Michael had promised not to smoke until the end of dinner, he was nervously playing with his matches. 'By accident, really. I should have been a musician. I went to a school which worshipped music in general and the local composer, Elgar, in particular. I was one of those people who was naturally good at music – I played the cello – and with that went an ability in maths, as it often does. I loved numbers. I loved them for their own sake and I knew – and still know – how many pieces of matter there are in the universe, how many grains of sand there are in a mile-long beach, how many drops of water pour over Niagara Falls every minute. The love of numbers, of course, led to an interest in probability – odds – and *that* led to an interest in gambling.'

'Weren't you a bit young?'

'It was more an academic interest than a practical one. I became interested in gamblers and unusual wagers, as I told you.' Michael tugged the hairs on his eyebrow. 'There was a man called George Osbaldeston in the eighteenth century who was known as "The Squire". He found it was boring to be an MP and much preferred his "matches", as he called his wagers. There were women like Lady Archer and Lady Buckinghamshire, who played cards better than almost anyone, but still ruined themselves.

'I began collecting prints of all these people and their doings – artists like Gillray, Hogarth, and so on. I began visiting antique shops and local auctions. I found loaded dice made in the seventeenth century and an eighteenth-century roulette table with a special mechanism underneath, so that the croupier could control the turning of the wheel. When I had saved up a bit more, I started collecting proper portraits – oil paintings – of the people, and etchings of the great gambling clubs that no longer exist - the Cocoa Tree, Almack's, Goostree's and Arthur's. Without realising, I had quite a collection.

'Then, when I was twenty-one, I went skiing. Nowadays my sister is a great skier – goes all over the world – but then it was my first time and I suppose I was clumsy. I fell. Worse, I fell in front of someone else whose ski sliced into my wrist—

Isobel winced.

'The bones were all broken but on top of that the tendons were very badly cut. It took months to heal and by that time the place I had won at the Royal College of Music had, quite rightly, been given to someone else. I never played the cello again.

'The only other thing I knew was the world of seventeenth- and eighteenth-century British sporting pictures. Through Elgar, I had become interested in Englishness.

'So, with my left arm still not functioning properly, I applied to Sotheby's. In those days you used to start on the front counter, receiving pictures brought in to be valued. In my very first week someone arrived with a large picture – I'll never forget it – showing a man on horseback. They thought it might be worth a few hundred pounds, possibly five thousand if they were very lucky. Imagine how flabbergasted they were to find that it was a long-lost Guido Reni; and how astounded when it sold at auction, three months later, for one point eight million pounds. I was just as astounded, and, of course, that packed a million volts into my system. I've been wired ever since. My sister calls it *Anopheles arte*, the Bond Street Bug.'

'Have you worked anywhere else than London?'

'Oh yes. My break came when I was posted to Glasgow. It was in Glasgow that I acquired my taste for Scotch. Littlemill is nearby, so is Interleven and Auchentoshen.'

'What bugs did you catch in Scotland?'

Michael grinned. 'To cut the story short, in my first nine months in Glasgow I managed to discover not one but two lost masterpieces, a Canaletto and a Reynolds. That got me promoted to New York. I had three wonderful years in Manhattan but there simply aren't any paintings in America waiting to be discovered. On one of my trips back to London for a board meeting I sat next to Greg Wood on the plane. He was a banker who had acted for Sotheby's once or twice and had also got the bug. We got to know each other and, later on, when I said I was thinking of moving back to London, he asked whether, if he could raise the money, I would contemplate setting up shop with him. And that's what happened. In the trade I'm told we are known as "Fish and Chip" - Whiting and Wood - but they can call us what they like. He's brilliant with money and I've been lucky with pictures.'

'Ed Ryan says you've made some major discoveries. Tell me.'

Michael shrugged and chewed some fish. 'I suppose my biggest coup was a picture I spotted at a house sale in Hampshire. The family were originally French and had escaped here during the French Revolution. The picture was an equestrian portrait and was estimated at between fifteen hundred and two and a half thousand pounds. The bidding went up to six thousand five hundred - someone else probably had an idea it was more than it seemed. Anyway, I got it. Later, I was able to prove it was a Van Dyck painted here in Britain but taken to France in the eighteenth century. The end of the story is that I sold the picture to the Gilston Museum in Texas.'

'For how much?'

'I'm not sure I should tell you.'

'Ed Ryan says two million.'

'Halve it and you'd be closer. Greg's job's been easier since then.'

The food, and the wine, were finished.

'Coffee?' Michael asked.

She shook her head. 'As I said, I shouldn't be too late tonight. And you're about to set fire to that horrible object. I've kept my part of the wager - so let's go.'

While they waited for the bill to be brought Michael, undaunted, fished his Havana from his top pocket and lit up. Isobel covered her nose with a napkin. 'You don't know what you are missing,' said Michael, grinning.

When the bill came, Michael handed his credit card to the waiter and they got up and went out, waiting by the front desk for the credit card to be cleared.

'What's that?' asked Isobel as they waited.

He followed her gaze. 'It's a portrait of the owner – didn't you recognise him? It's not the best painting in the room, I agree –'

'I didn't ask *who* it was,' she cut in tartly. 'I asked *what*. That thing around his neck – what is it?'

'I think it's called a *tastevin*. It's a silver dish or cup which the wine masters in France use. They hang them round their necks on ribbons, or chains, when they are elected to the wine masters' society. It's a sort of honour. Have you lost something?'

Isobel was bent almost double, dipping into her bag. She took out the photograph of the picture. 'Look.' She pointed to the figure. 'He's got something hanging round his neck too.'

'You think Mercury was a master of wine, do you?' Even as he said this Michael wanted to bite back the words.

'No, don't be stupid! He was a member of some order or something. There's a coin or a medallion on the end of the chain – can you make out what's on it?'

It was fashionably dark in the restaurant, so Michael took back his card, signed the form, and they moved out to the lobby where there was more light.

'It's not very clear, is it?' said Isobel. 'I suppose a four-hundred-and-fifty-year-old picture picks up its share of grime. It *looks* like a man with a spear or a long rod . . .'

'The other thing, on the left, looks to me more like an animal. Cleaning the picture might help. Hold on! I've got it . . . it's a dragon. Look, little puffs of steam or smoke coming from its nostrils–'

'St George and the dragon!' said Isobel.

'He was a member of the Garter,' breathed Michael. 'Fanbloodytastic. Phebloodynomenal. At last, at last, at last! Dazzling Inspector Sadler, and thank God for Keating's.' He looked at his watch. 'Just after ten. If I drop you off now, what do you say if I pick you up in my car around ten in the morning?'

'To do what?'

'To get down to Windsor by the time the St George's Chapel

opens, that's what. That's where all the Garter ceremonies are held and that's where the complete list of Garter members will be.'

'But how will we know who our man is?'

'We won't, not exactly. But don't forget, there are only ever twenty-four members of the Garter at any one time. To judge from the painting, our Mercury was about fifty in 1537. That should narrow the field down considerably.'

'But that's not enough. We need to narrow it down to just one.'

Michael steered Isobel out into the street. 'You made the break-through tonight, Isobel. It took a gold-card brain to notice the pendant. But I have my uses too.' He tapped his temple. 'It's not just cigar smoke up here, you know. You're forgetting that there is in Britain such a thing as the National Portrait Gallery - with eight thousand pictures of famous Britons. Even if we get six poss-ible names from Windsor, we can then go on to the NPG and see, from the portraits they have there, who our man is.'

They walked north and found a taxi waiting outside the Ritz. As Michael held the door for her, she grinned and pointed. "Thank you for not smoking," she read out loud. Furious, Michael knocked the end off his Havana and followed her into the cab.

Isobel was staying in a small house in Montpelier Mews, near Brompton Oratory. Michael waited for her to be let in before he told the taxi to move off. He couldn't quite see who her host was, if it was male or female. As the taxi twisted back to the Brompton Road, then down Sloane Avenue towards Justice Walk, where he lived, he noticed against his will the smell of Isobel's shampoo, which lingered on in the back of the taxi. He was consumed with a sudden, and utterly useless, lust.

4

There was one thing to be said for bad summer weather. It kept the number of tourists down. By the time Isobel and Michael had fought their way down the M4, through sluicing rain, to be at St George's Chapel by 10.45, when it opened, there were already a few of the more dedicated tourist nations in evidence – Germans, Japanese, Dutch. But it could have been much worse.

Neither Isobel nor Michael had been to the chapel before. They stood for a moment looking up at the stained-glass windows, four rows of saints in scarlet and deep blue. On either side, the chicory-coloured wood of the gothic choir stalls stretched down to the altar, each one surmounted by the banner of its present Garter occupant – purple slashes, yellow squares, black eagles. The pageantry was perfect.

As she looked above her, Isobel said, 'Why do you think the painter gave Mercury a chain with St George on the medallion? Wouldn't a garter have made more sense? It *is* the Order of the Garter, after all.'

'That had occurred to me. I suppose a garter would have been too obvious, or didn't suit the composition. Look, there's a vicar or curate or something. Let's ask him where we can find a list of members.'

He crossed the nave and approached the man who had just slipped out from a corner door and appeared to be making for the organ. Isobel couldn't hear the conversation but she saw the man turn and point back to the door he had entered by. Michael waved her over, and they both converged on it. Through the door they found themselves in a small courtyard with a glassed-in cloister running around all four sides. The stone, thought Michael, smiling to himself, was whisky-coloured. They walked along one side, then turned left. Through an arch they came to a cream-painted building on their right. Over a doorway in black letters were the words 'St George's House'. They rang the bell and a woman came out to meet them.

'May I help you?'

'Hello,' said Michael, handing her his card. 'I am an art dealer and we are researching a painting. We need to identify a member of the Garter from the sixteenth century. I wonder if you could let us see the Garter records for the years 1500 to 1550, please.' In the car on the way down to Windsor, Isobel and he had worked out that if Mercury, as they referred to him for the time being, was about fifty in 1537 he could not have received the Garter before he was, say, fifteen, even in those days. That meant the earliest date they needed to look at was 1502 but Michael rounded down the date to be on the safe side.

'What do you know about this person?' asked the woman, showing them into an office.

'Just his appearance,' said Michael. 'Which gives us an approximate age, that's all.'

'This way, then.' She led them through the outer office into another corridor with windows down one side, looking out on to the Curfew Tower of the castle and the Thames beyond. They were quite high up. They were shown into a small room with a large window. The woman sat them at a large table and then took from a glass-fronted cupboard a large book, bound in blue leather. 'This is the blue book,' she said. 'I'm afraid there are no statutes of the Garter before Henry VIII's reign, 1509, so this is the best we can do. Also, in the first instance, I will have to ask you to use these. They are facsimiles of the original Garter ledgers. The originals are now quite fragile, as I'm sure you appreciate. Even so, I'll have to lock you in, I'm afraid – but when you wish to leave just press that buzzer near the door and one of us will come and release you.' She smiled. 'Not everyone gets locked in at Windsor Castle. How long do you think you might be?'

'An hour, two at the most,' said Michael. 'I'm hoping our task will be fairly simple.'

After the woman had gone, locking the door behind her, they sat side by side and opened the ledger.

'Oh Lord! This is treason,' said Michael, after a few moments. 'It's alphabloodybetical, not chronological.' That meant they had to work their way through the entire volume, which applied to Garter activities from 1509, the date of Henry VIII's accession to the English throne. Against each entry was a name, sometimes quite a long name, the date of the candidate's elevation to the Garter and a brief description of why the award had been bestowed.

The writing was not easy to follow. It was in English but not modern English. 'Much' was written as 'myche', 'duty' as 'duetie', 'audience' as 'awdiens'. Worse, the handwriting varied and the ink had faded patchily. Still, they made progress, and in about an hour and a half they had five names which, to judge from the dates of their elevation, might be Mercury. Two of them – Sir Ranulph Kenny and Sir Edward Whitlock – even came from the West Country. 'I'd lay odds on it being either of them,' Michael breathed, looking at Isobel.

But she shook her head and grinned. 'I still owe you for the V and A catalogue. I'm not getting in any deeper just yet.'

As instructed, Michael pressed the buzzer and they were released. They thanked the woman and were led back the way they had come, into St George's Chapel. An organ practice was now in full swing and many of the tourists, mindful of the heavy summer rain outside, were sitting in the chapel pews, enjoying the free show.

'Lunch?' said Michael, as they came out into the fresh air. 'There's a nice pub on the river here.'

'Let's get on,' said Isobel tartly. 'I'm surprised you want to stop now.'

Michael lit his cigar. 'Ah . . . well. I happen to think a mild celebration is called for.'

'What? Why?'

'Although Molyneux started with such a time advantage, I think we have already overtaken him.'

'Surely not. What on earth makes you think so?'

'That woman back there in the Garter office. If Molyneux was ahead of us, he would already have been here, on the same errand. Two people making the same unusual request within a few days of each other would be bound to arouse curiosity and that woman would almost certainly have mentioned it. The fact that she didn't must mean that Molyneux hasn't worked out what we have worked out.'

They reached the National Portrait Gallery, just off Trafalgar Square, at a few minutes after two. The head librarian was still at lunch, they were told, and only she could grant access to the study collection in the basement. This was the vast bank of 8000 portraits which the gallery held but which were not judged to be of sufficient interest or artistic quality to be put on permanent display.

Michael gave Isobel a wink, to rub in the fact that they could have had a quick lunch in Windsor after all, and the two of them strolled around the gallery, killing time. Michael took Isobel to see the portraits of Elgar, Delius and Thomas Tallis.

Just on half past two they presented themselves back at the library and were shown in. They gave their list to the head librarian, a glamorous Indian in a peach-coloured sari, who cast her eye over the names and dates and scribbled a note in pencil. She looked up over her spectacles and said, 'If you would care to wait at desks fourteen and fifteen, whatever holdings we have will be brought to you in a few minutes.'

'Thank you,' said Michael. 'Does it help if I tell you all those names were members of the Garter?'

'It might. If the names are not held separately, we may have some group portraits in which some figures are not identified. But let's see what we have filed by name first.'

They found their desks and sat down. 'You see,' Michael whispered. 'She didn't respond at all when I mentioned the Garter. Molyneux hasn't been on this part of the trail, either.'

They sat in silence for a few minutes, looking around the library and at the other people using it. There was a dealer Michael knew vaguely, several students and a few better-dressed people who looked like foreign academics.

Then a young woman in a dark blue tracksuit moved towards

69

them. Michael didn't realise at first that she was the assistant librarian – it was fairly casual dress, after all. But she was carrying two large green folders, boxes really, and slid them on to the desk. 'The others will be here in a moment,' she said.

On the cover of one folder the words 'Sir Ninian Greene' were typed on a white label. Gingerly, Isobel turned back the cover. Sir Ninian wasn't Mercury. He was fat, almost bald, and had onion-like eyes.

The second folder had 'Sir Edward Whitlock' typed on it. 'Aha!' said Michael, reaching for it and turning back the cover. Sir Edward had long flowing hair, a moustache and, to judge from his lace cuffs, was a bit of a dandy. He wasn't Mercury either.

The librarian in the tracksuit had reappeared and this time she brought 'Sir Wyndham Tyler'. Isobel pulled back the cover to reveal a blond, round-faced man with no chin at all, let alone one with a cleft in it.

'Two left,' said Michael. 'I'm getting nervous. It *must* be Ranulph Kenny.'

The assistant librarian was approaching again with more green folders, which she put on the desk. 'That's it. One of these last is a family group, not a single portrait, I'm afraid. I hope it's good enough.'

Isobel turned to Kenny first.

'Oh no!' cried Michael, but softly. Sir Ranulph was a pasty individual who also had a moustache – and red hair.

'Here goes,' said Isobel, reaching for the last folder. She read the label: 'Sir Francis Waterlow and family'. 'Cross your fingers.'

There were seven people in the engraving: Waterlow himself, his wife and, according to the note on the back, his brother, his brother's wife and three children.

'It's not him either!' whispered Isobel urgently. 'Or his brother, come to that.' She was right. Waterlow had a pronounced nose and very fleshy lips. His was a much more self-indulgent face than Mercury's.

'Dammit,' said Michael. 'Dammit, dammit, dammit. Where on earth have we gone wrong?'

Isobel was busy looking back through the folders but there was no way she could make any of the figures resemble Mercury. That shaven hair, those eyes of his, that chin – nothing on the desk in front of them fitted the face they were looking for. 'Thank God we didn't celebrate after all. It would have been a waste of money.'

Michael played with the cigar in his top pocket. Then he said, 'I'm certain our reasoning is correct. We must have missed a name.' He looked at his watch. 'Too late to get back to Windsor today. And in any case there's someone I'd like to talk to before we go back again – a man who deals in medals. He'll know all about the Order of the Garter and he'll be able to show us where we're going wrong. Look, you hand these folders back while I call him. I'll see you at the main entrance.'

Isobel checked in the five knights and found Michael waiting for her on the pavement outside the gallery. The rain had stopped and he had lit a cigar.

'We're out of luck,' he said. 'Willie's at a coin auction in Amsterdam today. But he'll be back over the weekend, so we'll go and see him on Monday, before going back down to Windsor.'

'Is there nothing we can do over the weekend? It seems such a waste.'

Michael shook his head. 'I can't think of anything. Galling, I know – but don't forget Molyneux will have the same sort of hold-up. At least it gives you a chance to go back to the farm. The cows must be missing you.'

'Stop being so bovine, Michael. It doesn't suit you. Now, what time shall we start on Monday?'

Michael brushed ash from his jacket. 'Not before ten-thirty. The majority of dealers don't get in very early. They don't need to. Most people are more responsive later in the day – that's why the biggest sales are held in the evening. Come to the office for coffee around ten.'

'You're sure there's nothing else we can do today?'

'Yes, I'm sure.' He took a step towards her. 'You look . . . unsettled. Is there anything wrong?'

'No. I don't know. I mean, yes.'

'Go on.'

She paused. A big red bus splashed up Charing Cross Road, spraying rainwater all over the pavement. 'You're the expert, Michael, but . . . but, the fact is, I think you're wrong. I think the

71

reason Molyneux hasn't been to Windsor or here to the Portrait Gallery is not because we're ahead of him at all. It's because we're going in the wrong direction.'

Willie Maitland's coin and medal gallery ('Maitland's Medals') was a bow-windowed shop, tucked away in Crown Passage, just down from the Golden Lion pub in King Street, almost opposite Christie's. Willie was a tall, rangy individual with wispy fair hair and a glass eye. Michael had met him a few years before when Willie bought a painting from him. Apart from his gallery, he had an extensive collection of pictures with coins or medals in them.

It took Isobel and Michael only a few minutes to walk down from Mason's Yard. Michael was itchy, prickling with outrage after attending over the weekend a film festival of old black and white movies which had been artificially coloured. 'You wouldn't add colour to a Rembrandt print,' he complained to Isobel. 'This is just as criminal.'

'You call *that* criminal? We had hail on Sunday. Hail! At this time of year. God himself is sometimes the delinquent one on a farm. Any more dampness and some of the cattle are going to get problems with their hooves.'

'Keep your hooves out of that puddle, and turn left here.'

Maitland's face broke into a smile when he saw Michael enter, though almost immediately his one good eye roved across to Isobel. The gallery was empty and Michael was able to make the introductions. He came straight to the point.

'On Isobel's behalf, I'm trying to identify a figure in a picture. I'm not going to show it to you, Willie – you understand why.' Maitland nodded. 'We have a rough date for it – early sixteenth century – and we have reason to believe that the man was a member of the Garter. Unfortunately, we've compared his likeness with those they have in the National Portrait Gallery for members of the Order in the sixteenth century and the faces don't match. We're going wrong somewhere and I'm hoping you can help.'

Willie loved this sort of problem. He put aside a medal he was cleaning and gave them his full attention. 'The Garter records are kept at Windsor, at Arundel Castle and in the British Library.'

Michael nodded. 'We went to Windsor on Friday.'

'Hmm. All Garter knights have banners designed for them when they are elevated, rather like coats of arms. Any arms in your picture?'

Michael shook his head.

'How do you know he's a Garter knight, then? Is he wearing it?'

'No, he's wearing the badge, on a chain around his neck.'

'St George and the dragon?'

They both nodded.

'Hmm. That's something anyway. Can you describe the chain? There are several types of Garter chain, according to the monarch of the day. That would at least confirm your dating. Early sixteenth century would make it Henry VII or Henry VIII, right? As I recall, the chain should be gold, showing little knots of ropes set between precious stones, garnets or rubies, I think. Does that ring any bells?'

Michael looked at Isobel. She shook her head firmly. 'It might be gold – it's difficult to tell – but there are no jewels. It's plain.'

Willie frowned. Before he could go on, however, the gallery door opened and a man entered. Michael and Isobel stood to one side as Willie attended to him. It appeared that they knew each other quite well. The other man was French and a collector of French coins. Did Willie have any new rarities in stock?

Just back from the auction in Amsterdam, Willie did indeed. 'I even have a louis d'or eight,' he said.

The Frenchman's eyes lit up and Willie went into the back of his shop, coming out again immediately with a small, black leather-covered case. He unlocked it and took out a coin. The gold glistened in the morning sun. Willie and the Frenchman then went into a huddle, lowering their voices and speaking in French. Michael and Isobel stood near the door, trying not to overhear the talk of money. After a few moments, the Frenchman straightened up, said goodbye to Willie, nodded to Michael and Isobel, and left the shop.

'A fish who got away?' said Michael.

'Oh, but no. He's gone to arrange the money with his bank.' Willie weighed the gold coin in his hand. 'Have a look at this, Michael; it will interest you. This is a louis d'or eight, made for Louis XIII. Only twenty were ever minted and none of them was circulated. One of the rarest coins ever. They were used as gambling

73

chips at court.' Michael leaned forward as Willie grinned. 'I bet you'd like one for your collection, eh? This little monster is worth forty thousand pounds. No one carries that sort of cash on him.'

Isobel whistled and stepped forward for a closer look. Willie let her handle the coin and she rubbed her fingers over it.

Willie suddenly cried out. ' "Eh bien!", as the French collectors say. I've had a thought. Describe the badge, will you? The badge in your picture.' He turned and looked behind him. 'Better still, draw it on this pad here.' He gave Isobel a pen. She handed back the gold coin and, looking mystified, took the pad which Willie now passed to her.

She spoke as she sketched. 'I'm not very good at this sort of thing but St George is standing in the middle – like this.' And she drew a stick-like creature. 'The spear goes diagonally down, from top right to bottom left – just so – pointing towards the dragon, which cowers at the bottom, looking up.' She put in a few final squiggles. 'You can just make out little puffs of steam or smoke, coming from the monster's nostrils . . . There, what do you say, Michael . . . is that a fair likeness?'

He leaned forward. 'You're no Holbein but it's good enough.'

Willie took the pad and inspected the drawing more closely. 'Hmm. There's no horse?'

'No,' said Isobel. 'Of course not. I might not be Holbein but I wouldn't forget something as big as a horse.'

'Is the horse important?' asked Michael.

'You could say that.' Willie was grinning. 'Without a horse this isn't St George.'

'You're kidding!' shouted Isobel.

'Joshua bloody Reynolds!' gasped Michael at the same time.

'It was that French collector who gave me the idea. Now I come to think of it, I can see it's an easy mistake to make if you're inexperienced. There are *two* dragon-slaying myths, not one. St George is always shown dressed in armour and riding a white horse. To the early Christians a dragon symbolised paganism. The St George legend was founded after he had supposedly converted the heathen country of Cappadocia to Christianity. Without a horse, the figure is not St George but the archangel Michael. In *his* case the dragon represents the devil, and Michael is vanquishing the devil

74

from the world. That's all the history I know, but what I'm saying is that your figure, the man you're trying to identify, isn't a member of the Garter but a member of the French Order of St Michael. As I said, it was that French collector who gave me the idea.'

Michael shifted his gaze from Maitland to Isobel. He felt himself blushing. And was that a slight smirk on her face? He had certainly been over-confident in reading the picture and his mistake had cost them time they could ill afford. No wonder Molyneux hadn't been to Windsor!

Michael sighed. 'Willie, top marks. You noticed more with one eye than we did with four. The old Maitland magic. You've done exactly what we hoped you would do. Set us straight on Orders. Not in quite the way I expected but – well, we now know where we're going, which we didn't when we came in this morning. I owe you one. Before we go, though, is there anything else you can tell us about the Order?'

'Not offhand, but I think I have a book in the back. Hang on.' Willie disappeared with the black leather case, the louis d'or now safely back inside it. He reappeared with a small volume. 'Here we are. I'll read the entry out to you.' He leafed through the book. 'Yes . . . Michael, Saint, Order of . . .' He twisted his head slightly, to make it easier for his one good eye. 'The Order of St Michael was instituted in 1469 by Louis XI and is one of the great Orders of chivalry in Europe, the French equivalent of the English Order of the Garter. . . The badge of the Order was supposed to be worn at all times . . . on ceremonial occasions it was worn as the "Grand Ordre", suspended from a gold collar of cockle shells linked by intricate chainwork. At other times it was worn as the "Petit Ordre", on a fine ribbon or chain . . . At any one time there were only thirty six members of the Order . . . a sketch of the medallion by Holbein is preserved in Basle.' Maitland snapped the book shut and looked up. 'That's it.'

'And where,' said Michael, 'do you think the records of the Order of St Michael are kept?'

'Hmm,' said Maitland. 'If it was founded by Louis XI and was closely associated with the court, it may have been abolished at the time of the French Revolution in 1789. The records might easily have been destroyed during the Terror. If they weren't, then I

75

should say they will probably be in the Bibliothèque Nationale in Paris.'

Isobel groaned. If the records had been destroyed, the search was over.

'You might begin at the French embassy,' said Willie. 'They will have a cultural attaché there who may be able to help. Or you could try the university; their department of French will have a historian who might know something.'

Just then another customer came into the gallery so they quickly thanked Willie and got out of his way. 'Give my regards to your sister,' he called out, as they left. On their walk back to Mason's Yard, Michael looked sheepishly at Isobel and said, 'Sorry about the false start. I got carried away.'

'Let's just keep our fingers crossed that the French records were not burned in the Revolution.' Her tone told him that she was not the type to dwell on past mistakes. 'Your sister seems popular.'

Michael snorted. 'She once had a famous rock star as a boyfriend. She turned him on to collecting and he bought up most of Bond Street. Of course she's popular.'

Isobel threw him a glance. 'But he didn't fancy anything in Mason's Yard – right?' She went on before Michael could protest. 'Shall we divide the labour? One do the embassy and the other the university?'

They were just passing Dalmeny's, a small but expensive gallery that dealt mostly in French furniture and a few paintings. They had passed it two nights before, on their way to Keating's. Michael brightened. 'No,' he said. 'Not yet, anyway, I'll call Jumble Jacques in Paris.' When Isobel turned to look at him, he added, 'Jacques de Selve, if you want the grown-up version. He's an old friend, and a colleague of sorts. He tells me about any English paintings that come his way, and I let him know when any French art or furniture is included in the contents of a house sale I'm offered here. It's not a regular trade, but enough for me to be able to ring him and ask his help.'

At the gallery there were several messages for Michael but before doing anything else he took down a large book from the shelves in his office. It was heavy and he dropped it on to his desk with a thud.

'This is Chamberlain's *catalogue raisonnée* on Holbein. Everything the painter did is in here.' He turned to the back where there was an index of places where Holbein's work was kept. He looked up Basle and flipped the pages until he reached it. There in black and white was a small photograph of the master's drawing of the medallion. Michael showed it to Isobel. 'The answer was in this very room all the time. Maddening. But at least we know we're on the right track now. There's no doubt . . . the designs are identical.'

Isobel nodded. 'Why would someone living in England have a French Order?'

'That had occurred to me too. I don't see it as a problem, though. Presumably, if and when we find out Mercury's true name, we'll also find what he did to merit the honour.'

He reached into a drawer for his address book and found de Selve's number in Paris. When his call was put through, it turned out that the Frenchman was at a sale. 'Damn!' hissed Michael, putting his hand over the receiver. He left word that de Selve should call him back as soon as possible. 'All right,' he said to Isobel. 'You call the embassy and I'll try the university. It's better than sitting here, waiting.'

But it wasn't. At the university Michael was told, in so many words, that the department of French did not exist to answer queries from the general public. Isobel was referred by the embassy to the French Institute in Belgrave Square but they said that, although they had books on chivalry, they had no records relating to any Orders.

Michael's insides felt as if they were being ploughed over by the frustration – and he lit a fresh cigar to calm himself. Then Jacques called back. How different he was! Gentle, considerate, friendly. He couldn't answer Michael's query personally, he said, but there was a coin and medal dealer just across the street, the rue de Seine. The man was a good friend, would surely know the answer, and Jacques would call again the moment he had spoken to him. Just as Michael was about to hang up, de Selve added, 'Michael, is this something you might have for me?'

Carefully, Michael replied, 'I haven't bought it yet, Jacques. But if I can identify the man, and he's of more use to you than he is to me, you shall certainly have first refusal.'

'*Bon. A bientôt.*'

They waited. It was lunchtime but neither of them could even think about eating until Jacques had called back. If the records had been destroyed . . .

Michael looked at his messages. One was in Greg's handwriting and said simply: 'Call Ed.' Ed McCrystal was an Irish member of the gambling syndicate, and had a big job in a firm of Dublin stockbrokers. Michael was put through straight away. 'Yes, Ed? Are we under starter's orders?'

'We are indeed, my boy, we are indeed. You may not have heard it on the news yet – Greg says you have better things to do with your time than listen to the radio – but late last night they finally netted a large object in Loch Ness –'

'No!'

'I'm Irish, remember, I exaggerate but I do not lie. The object, the organism as it is being called, is being towed ashore even as we speak. Unhappily, the TV screens in the office here show only what's happening to the price of coffee, tin and bauxite. Otherwise I could watch it. Anyway, it's too good an opportunity to miss.'

'I agree. What's the idea?'

'Length.'

'Of what?'

'The entire object, the whole organism, Michael. Don't be crude.'

'All right, all right. Good idea. I'm in. Who's got what, so far?'

'Greg has thirty feet, Charlie has fifty, the fool, Doug has fifteen, one-five. I haven't spoken to the others yet. You?'

'A ton.'

'A hundred feet!'

'That's what it usually is. In the civilised world.'

'This is the last chance to change your mind.'

'No thanks. If they are towing it in, and haven't already hauled it aboard, it must be pretty big.'

'Done!' cried McCrystal. '*Rien ne va plus.*'

Michael put down the phone.

Isobel had been frowning during most of this exchange. Michael's cigar had gone out and as he relit it he smiled and explained the wager.

'Your bets are your own business, Michael. But what if de Selve has been trying to get through?'

Michael buzzed the secretary. There had been no calls from Paris.

So, again, they waited. For each minute that passed without de Selve calling back, Michael grew more apprehensive. He drew hungrily on his cigar. He tried to think of old Julius Samuels, working on the woman in Dover Street. The old man should be finished soon. Michael looked at the cigar between his fingers, inspecting semi-consciously the brown leaves, intertwined like the scales of a crayfish. He was one of a dwindling band. Who smoked now? Widows, the French, prison inmates, who still rolled their own, so he'd heard. That made sense. Widows and prisoners had little else to do. Why the French? But that only brought his mind back to de Selve. Why hadn't he called back? Had Jacques been told the records had been destroyed, and was hesitating to give them the bad news? Was the coin dealer away?

After more than half an hour the phone eventually rang and, when Michael snatched at it, Jacques was at the other end of the line. 'Michael, I am sorry to be so long but Eclier, the dealer I must speak with, he had a client with him and was not free until a few moments ago.'

'I understand, Jacques.' Michael tried to keep the edge out of his voice. 'What did he say?'

'Good for you, I think. Eclier has a book that goes back to 1643, the reign of Louis XIV. All the members of the Order until the Revolution are in it.'

'No, Jacques. I am interested in an earlier period – 1500 to 1550.'

'*Eh bien*. In that case you must go to the Bibliothèque Nationale, here in Paris. It is the old Palais–Mazarin. You know it?'

'No.'

'It is a little like the reading room in your British Museum.'

Michael's pulse was racing now. He gave a 'thumbs up' sign to Isobel. 'The Bibliothèque is open normal hours?'

'For sure. But Michael, can I help? My French is better than yours, I think.' Jacques laughed. 'And it will save the air ticket.'

'Thank you, Jacques. But for the moment I must respect the confidence of the present owner of the painting. She is an English-woman and doesn't want any information about her picture to be widely known before she is ready.' It was only a white lie, he told himself. 'I am sorry – but don't worry. If I think France is the place

79

for the picture, Jacques, you'll be the first to know. I promise. And thank you for being so helpful, I knew I could rely on you.'

He put down the phone and sat back. 'So, the Bibliothèque Nationale it is.'

'Are we both going?'

'Nnno . . . I don't think so. One ought to be enough. How's your French?'

'Not brilliant.'

'Then I'll go to Paris tonight, so I can be in the Bibliothèque first thing in the morning, when it opens. I'll get the names, then phone them through to you here. You can check them out at the National Portrait Gallery –' He saw Isobel's eyebrow rise quizzically and explained, 'There must be a French equivalent of our National Portrait Gallery, which we may be forced to use later. But I've been thinking: this is an English picture, it must relate to someone who, whether he was French or Florentine or Finnish, was famous in England. So let's stick with the NPG for the time being. Now, I'd better get on to Air France.'

It was raining in Paris. Away from the main boulevards, as the Bibliothèque Nationale was, the streets were narrow and the wind had less chance to whip the drops into cutting edges than it did in the wider thoroughfares. And, despite the wet, the smells of Paris, half forgotten yet immediately familiar, were welcoming. Michael felt invigorated.

The Bibliothèque was tucked away in the busy, clogged area of Paris just to the north of the Louvre and the Palais-Royal – an area full of pâtisseries and stationery shops, of coffee merchants and print sellers, small squares, dogs and, Michael was delighted to observe, cigar wholesalers. The entrance to the Bibliothèque Nationale was nowhere near as imposing as the British Museum's. It was a simple gate on the east side of a small, leafy square. Michael took a quick coffee, bitter and black as the clouds above, in a café on the corner, before passing through the gate, which was plastered with posters of forthcoming exhibitions. He crossed a courtyard to a large glass porch, inside which was the dark entranceway to the Biblothèque proper.

Jumble Jacques had been right; it *was* rather like the reading room of the British Museum. The work tables, each with a bright green glass lightshade, radiated out from a central circular issue desk like the spokes of a wheel. Whatever the weather outside in Paris there was always a kind of winter fug in here.

Michael gave his order at the central desk and waited for more than an hour before the documents arrived. Naturally there was no smoking in the library. When the documents were placed in front of him they turned out to be two large piles of scarlet, leather-bound books. No facsimiles this time: this was the real thing. Michael looked at the spines of the books: nothing. Opening one he was dismayed to see that it was handwritten in a flowery, ornate scrawl which he found very difficult to read. 'Bibliobloodythèque', he whispered to himself. At the same time he was relieved that the names were laid out chronologically. One book, he found, ended in 1518 and the next, beginning in that year, contained names up to 1556. So he just needed to concentrate on those two volumes.

After about an hour, he found that he was reading the handwriting much more easily and within another hour he had completed what he had come for. Between 1500 and 1537 only fifteen awards of the Order of St Michael had been made. He therefore wrote down all fifteen names: he was taking no chances. Like the British Museum, the Bibliothèque Nationale had a system whereby, if someone wanted the same books two days running, they were not returned to the main shelves but held in an 'overnight stack'. Michael used this facility now, just in case he needed to consult the ledgers again. Then he found a telephone in the corridor and phoned London. Isobel, at the gallery in Mason's Yard, was soon on the line and writing down the names he gave her.

'I'm staying at the Saint-Simon,' he said after he had finished dictating the list. 'It's a small hotel on the left bank near a marvellous one-star restaurant and the Beaux-Arts area.' He read the telephone number out to her. 'But I also have a reservation on the seven-thirty Air France flight tonight, in case we make progress. Call me the minute you're through in Trafalgar Square. Good luck!'

Isobel was more nervous today than she had been on their previous visit to the National Portrait Gallery. Owing to Willie Maitland they had been given a second chance; they wouldn't be given a third. This trip to the gallery had to succeed, or they were lost.

She pushed her way through the main glass doors and mounted the staircase. To her right there was a poster of a woman who vaguely resembled the friend she was staying with. She wore an off-the-shoulder dress and advertised an exhibition of portraits by John Singer Sargent, the American artist who painted all the fashionable people of his day. The dress in the poster was red, like Michael's braces.

The head librarian nodded and smiled – she was on her way *out* to lunch this time. But the assistant took the names Isobel gave her and disappeared through a door. Isobel sat at a different desk this time feeling that, unless she did so, their luck might not change either. After a few minutes, the assistant came back. To Isobel's alarm she saw that the woman was carrying *no* folders.

'Some of these names look French,' the assistant said softly.

'They all are,' Isobel replied.

'Which means there may be some we don't have – you realise that, don't you? Only if someone came to England to live, or on a mission to the court, or was perhaps distinguished in his own right, so that they were painted or drawn while here – only then would we have them.'

'I understand,' said Isobel. 'Just do what you can, please.'

Twenty minutes elapsed. The library was not as busy today, but Isobel recognised the dealer whom Michael knew vaguely. He was seated at the same desk as before and nodded.

When the assistant librarian reappeared, Isobel immediately noticed with relief that she was carrying a number of green folders: at least her mission wasn't a complete wipe-out.

As the assistant put the folders on the desk, she said, 'According to our master index, we only have four of the fifteen names you are interested in. The rest you would have to check out in France. Sorry.'

Isobel smiled, though inside she felt anything but cheerful. Four names only! She reached for the folders, her hands clammy from nerves.

The name on the first label said 'Albert Martres'. She opened the folder. Albert Martres was tall, grey-haired, a slim and slender figure, a graceful-looking priest, and he didn't fit. The second was Jean Duquesne, a man with a squashed-in face and large ears. Isobel sighed. Two down, two to go. The third was Philippe du Croix. Her body told her what she saw moments before her mind registered it. She felt a pleasant rubbing sensation at the back of her eyes. She stopped breathing. Her spine itched. Du Croix's haircut was familiar, the nose was identical, the gaze was the same gaze. But it was the jawline, that and the cleft in his chin, that clinched it. Those features gave the face its character and it was the same character as in the painting – without a shadow of a doubt.

They had their man.

Isobel started to breathe again. Her sigh was audible. She turned the print over. On the back was written: 'Philippe du Croix: du Croix came to England in 1528 to marry Elizabeth Goodwin, the eldest daughter of Sir John Goodwin, after which he anglicised his name to Cross.'

And that was all. Nothing about what sort of life he had led or where he had lived. Isobel got up and moved to the main desk. The assistant librarian looked up and smiled. 'This man, Philippe du Croix, Philip Cross,' said Isobel. 'How can I find out more about him, please?'

The assistant took the print from her, turned it over, and read what was on the back. She pursed her lips. 'You might try the *Dictionary of National Biography*,' and she nodded across the room to a long row of brown volumes.

Isobel moved over to the shelf, took down the volume marked 'CAG-DRE' and carried it back to her desk. She riffled through the pages – yes! – here was a bit more at least. The entry read:

CROSS, Philip (1485–1536), born Philippe du Croix, was a French nobleman who achieved prominence as a diplomat, devoting his energies to a reconciliation between Catholic and Protestant countries. From 1514 he travelled in Germany and the Low Countries. In 1525 he crossed to England on a diplomatic mission and while in London met Elizabeth Goodwin, daughter of Sir Thomas Goodwin [q.v.], of Godwin Magna in Dorset. In 1526 du Croix narrowly escaped death when engaged on a mission for the French king in Spain. The Spaniards, believing that du Croix was a favourite of the French king, held him hostage in Seville, pending settlement of a number of matters disputed between the two countries. But du Croix escaped and made his way to Paris, undergoing a series of adventures *en route* when he was pursued by Spanish forces. Twice he escaped death only narrowly. In Paris his loyalty and bravery were rewarded, the king bestowing on him the Order of St Michael, then France's highest honour.

The following year du Croix, who seems by then to have had enough adventuring, returned to England and married Elizabeth Goodwin. On condition that he anglicised his name, Cross, as he became, and his new bride were given extensive lands in Dorset and, when Sir Thomas's only son died young, without marrying, to be soon followed by Sir Thomas himself, Cross and Elizabeth succeeded to the entire Goodwin estate. In his later years Cross wrote two books which returned to his earlier interest of trying to reconcile the Catholic and Protestant faiths. His books, for example, are chiefly notable for Cross's enlightened discussion of divorce. He was buried in the Goodwin family chapel at Godwin Magna, near Dorchester.

With growing excitement, Isobel took the opened book and the print to the main desk where she was directed to a small office with a photocopying machine. She needed several copies made: Michael would want to see the likeness and the dictionary entry for himself.

'Going to be an exhibition on Cross, is there?' said the girl who operated the machine.

'No. I don't think so. I haven't heard. Why do you ask?'

The machine flashed green as the copies were made. 'There was someone else in here the other day. He wanted copies of the same man. I remember the haircut – '

'When was that? Can you remember?' Isobel felt her heart race in her chest. Every time they took a step forward, there was always a step back soon after.

The girl stopped the machine and handed Isobel the photocopies. 'Can't say exactly . . . some time last week, probably. Yes, it must have been, because the photocopier was out of order . . .

Isobel paid the girl, took the photocopies, returned the print and the dictionary, and hurried out of the library, anxious to telephone

Michael in Paris and tell him the news. She ran down the stairs, reached the mezzanine landing and turned, ready to descend to the marble tiles of the entrance hall. As she did so she noticed, coming through the glass doors, a tall, stringy, grey-haired man with creases in his cheeks, and a thin upper lip. Molyneux.

Isobel halted. Feeling her skin go clammy, she turned and retreated back up the stairs. What was Molyneux doing *here*? She had to think. As she did so she climbed the stairs back to the first floor, as far away from Molyneux as she could. Had he seen her? She thought not. She had stepped back instinctively and could not have been on view for more than a few seconds. She reached the corridor which led to the archive. That was it! Molyneux had come for his photocopies. Thank God, she hadn't bumped into him in the archive, or the photocopying room. Isobel hurried on past the archive, beyond the entrance to the Sargent exhibition and on up to the top floor, where the Tudor and Georgian portraits were kept. She didn't dare look round.

When she reached the top floor she followed the gallery as it wound round, deeper into the building, and found a small room with a green-painted beam-engine. It was full of complicated levers and was about eight feet high. She hid behind it and began studying a series of small silhouettes on the wall.

How long should she give Molyneux, she asked herself. She had been in the library herself for about forty minutes. It would take about fifteen minutes for his order to be fetched up – that was the safest time to leave. She looked at her watch.

'Bit sinister, silhouettes, don't you agree?'

Isobel's blood seemed to jerk in her veins. He'd seen her and followed her! She turned.

'Miss Sadler, what a pleasure. I thought it was you downstairs, but you turned suddenly and came up here. Did you forget something?' His eyes moved to the photocopies she was carrying. 'Are you a regular visitor to the gallery?'

Isobel was filled with alarm. Gripping the photocopies in her right hand, she let her arm fall and half hid the papers behind her back. Molyneux mustn't see what she had.

She searched her brain for an answer to his questions. She must look, and sound, as natural as possible. 'I . . . I was visiting the

Sargent exhibition . . .' Thank God she had noticed the poster on the way in. 'Then I thought I might as well come and see the rest of the gallery while I'm here. I'm sorry, I didn't see you downstairs. Any news about those documents yet? Has your client stopped travelling?'

'You are interested in Sargent?' Molyneux ignored her questions.

Isobel suddenly felt out of breath. He didn't believe her. She looked about. There was no one else in this small part of the gallery and the levers of the beam-engine were like bars in a surrealist prison. She searched her memory for something Michael had said. What was it? Yes. 'He spent some time near us, you know? Broadway in Worcestershire. I've always been interested in his work.'

'Hmm.' Molyneux pointed to the photocopies in Isobel's hand. 'Have you been taking notes?'

She gripped the photocopies more tightly. 'No.' Now her voice was growing unnatural. She knew it but she couldn't help it.

'Have you seen these over here?' Molyneux walked to the other side of the gallery. 'These are life masks which Benjamin Haydon made of Wordsworth and Keats. Bit grisly, don't you think?'

Isobel looked at the masks.

'I have some similar ones, except that mine are death masks, taken from corpses.'

Isobel tried not to shudder. He wasn't going to frighten *her*.

'Did you like Sargent's portrait of Lady Eden?'

Now completely out of her depth, Isobel could only say, 'Is that the woman in red?'

'Maybe you preferred Miss Cicely Alexander?'

Isobel felt as if she was melting. She could feel the sweat from her hands making the photocopies greasy. She nodded her head uncertainly.

Immediately there was a change in Molyneux's expression and she knew she had made a mistake. He had caught her out, as he intended. She had lied to him and he knew it. He couldn't be certain of her reason for coming to the gallery but he must have a good idea.

Isobel wanted to scream at him but knew that she had to act as relaxed as she could. And she had to leave quickly before the situation got any worse. She ought to carry the fight to him, to ask him what *he* was doing in the gallery, to press him on the documents, where his gallery was if he had one. At the back of her mind was the thought that she might confront him and ask his real name. But she realised they couldn't be certain he was using a false one and she would look very foolish, and very suspicious. No, she had to get away. She looked at her watch again. 'Mr Molyneux, my train leaves in forty minutes. I'm afraid I must dash. Please forgive me.'

He looked hard at her and stepped aside. Isobel shot him the briefest of smiles and hurried by. Outside the gallery, she turned south and forced herself to stroll towards Trafalgar Square as if she was looking for a taxi. Once she reached the square, however, and was out of sight of the entrance to the Portrait Gallery, she ran most of the way back to Mason's Yard.

Michael cheered loudly into the phone when Isobel told him what she had found at the Portrait Gallery. 'Specbloodytacular.' Then, immediately more serious, he asked, 'Where exactly *is* Godwin Magna?'

'I've checked. It's about three miles east of Dorchester.'

'Right. there's a hotel in Dorchester called The Yeoman. You'd better book a couple of rooms there for tomorrow night.' He looked at his watch. 'I'll make the seven-thirty back to London tonight. I'll pick you up at Montpelier Mews at eight o'clock tomorrow morning, in my car. Not too early, is it?'

'I'm a farmer, remember. That's the middle of the day for me.'

'Well, it's quite early enough for me. That way we'll be down in Dorset by eleven. That should give us enough time.' Michael smiled again into the phone. 'That was a great piece of detective work today, Inspector Sadler. Marvellous. Now, I'd better make a move. The traffic on the way to the airport might be heavy at this time of the day. Anything else before I dash?'

'Well, yes, there is – '

'What is it, Isobel? What is it?'

She repeated her conversation with the girl in the photocopying room at the Portrait Gallery.

'Molyneux!'

'Yes, and that's not all.'

'Go on.'

'I saw him as I was leaving the gallery. I tried to avoid him but he followed me up the stairs where I was trying to hide. He must have come back to get his photocopies. I had our photocopies in my hand but I pretended I had been to a show, the Sargent exhibition That's on at the moment.'

'Good. That was quick thinking.'

'Hold on.' Isobel shook her head at the phone. 'He was very suspicious and I'm sure I put my foot in it. He asked me about some paintings of Sargent's. I think one was called Lady Eden and the other was something like . . . Sister Alexander? Does that sound right?'

'Cicely Alexander?'

'Yes, that's it. What's wrong with them, Michael? Are they not in the exhibition?'

In Paris, Michael groaned into the phone. 'No, they are not in the exhibition, Isobel. There's no reason they should be. They are both by James Whistler, one of Sargent's main rivals.'

5

By 8.30 the next morning they were leaving on the M3, heading west. The rain had started again and the windscreen wipers of Michael's small Mercedes 190 swished back and forth in a steady 'Du – Croix', 'Du – Croix', 'Du – Croix'. Michael, who was driving was feeling elated. There was no news yet on Margaret Masson's marriage plans, but the Loch Ness monster, which had finally been landed the evening before, just as Michael was flying back from Paris, had proved to be a form of eel. More important to his mood, it was eighty-nine feet long and Michael had won the wager. Today he was £500 richer.

Isobel had a book of maps open in her lap. 'It looks to me,' she said, 'that the quickest way to get to Dorchester is to turn off the motorway just before the end, then take the A303 until we see the sign for Sherborne. It's duel carriageway mostly until then. We turn off south there. That eventually takes us on to the Sherborne – Dorchester road. Out of Dorchester we take the Wareham road. The turning to Godwin Magna is a few miles beyond. Two and a half hours more, I'd say.'

'You managed to book us into The Yeoman – yes?'

Isobel nodded.

Michael was relieved that they had now got beyond library research and were out of London *doing* something. For him, getting out of town was always associated with excitement. All the best art dealers subscribed to the maxim that 'Anyone can sell; it's the buying that counts.' That was more and more true, especially in the old master field. Provided you could find the first-rate pictures, they would walk out of the gallery all by themselves; but you had to find them in the first place. As Michael did his best deals in private, with the owners of country houses who did not care for the glare of the auction rooms, a drive such as the one they were now making was invariably associated with an acquisition: good news. If only it would be like that today.

'You think Molyneux went back to the NPG just for photocopies?'

'I can't think of any other reason, can you? The girl did say the machine had been out of order.'

'Bad luck bumping into him like that.'

'Hmm. I was in so much of a hurry to call you, I didn't have my wits about me.'

They drove on, watching the rain, listening to *The Dream of Gerontius* on the tape deck. The deep, mellifluous tones and the majestic rhythms contrasted warmly with the iron rain outside. 'This was Elgar's favourite as well as mine,' said Michael. 'He once admitted, "This is the best of me." '

'I know people who are mad about Wagner, or Mozart – but you're the only one I've met who's so keen on Elgar.'

'I told you, it was school that did it. But Elgar is so romantic for an Englishman, don't you think? So romantic for a *Midlander*. When I was a boy and first had to play his cello concerto in E, I liked to think that the E stood not just for the key but for Edward and Elgar himself, England and English, epic and elusive, evaporate and eternal, erupt and erotic – '

'Ease up, ease up . . .'

They drove on in silence for a while, listening to the music. But then they switched their attention to the next clue in the picture, the next figure in the ring, in a clockwise direction. Isobel had had the foresight to take back with her to Montpelier Mews as many of the reference books as she could carry, and these were now on the back seat of the 190.

They reached Salisbury Plain, where the wind was worse, gusting the rain in huge sheets. The chalk showed through here and there in the landscape, wet scoops of white, like ice-cream. The second figure in the picture was every bit as puzzling as the first, albeit in a different way. It was certainly much odder – a small, plump, rather dumpy man, lying on the ground. Even more strange, he had what appeared to be a bush or a tree growing out of his stomach. He was holding the hand reliquary. Now, as they swished past Stonehenge, barely visible in the rain, Isobel reached back for the reference books.

She opened one after the other.

Under 'Tree' she could find only that it was associated with ancient fertility rights, and that Adonis, the Greek god, had been born from a tree. But the dumpy male in the painting was clearly not the beautiful Adonis, with whom the goddess Venus had fallen hopelessly in love. Next, Isobel looked up 'Tree of Knowledge' but found that it should be either an apple tree or one with serpents entwined around it. Neither fitted the tree in the painting, nor, so far as she could tell, was either plant ever depicted growing out of someone's stomach.

'Look up individual species of trees,' suggested Michael. 'Ash, beech, oak.'

'I *do* know what a tree is,' said Isobel, raising an eyebrow and looking across at him. She was quiet for a while, reading. The car descended from the plain and the visibility improved a fraction. Presently Isobel said, 'Ash, nothing. Beech, nothing. Olive equals peace, of course, and stands for Minerva and wisdom. The oak is sacred to Jupiter and to the ancient Druids – that might mean something. A bishop in the act of baptising while his foot rests on a fallen oak symbolises the conversion of the pagan, Boniface.' She looked up Boniface. 'Maybe this is relevant. "Boniface was an English martyr born at Crediton in Devon" – that's right next to Dorset and not too far from Monksilver. "He became a missionary and travelled abroad, became Archbishop of Mainz in 744 . . ." no, all this stuff is irrelevant. Damn!' She went back to oak. 'An oak was the badge of certain popes . . . no, it doesn't look like oak either.' She tried palm. 'Nothing.'

'Leave it,' said Michael. 'We're coming to the turn-off. We'll be at Godwin Magna in just over half an hour. Let's find the tomb, look around and see what we see.'

Isobel threw the reference book on to the back seat. 'Fine by me. And, if you see anywhere we can get coffee first, that's fine too.'

They stopped for a late breakfast in Sherborne and both felt better for it.

The rain was easing as Michael turned the 190 off the Dorchester—Wareham road at around 11.15. Once away from the trunk road, he slowed to negotiate the many twists leading to Godwin Magna. The lane rose till they were riding a ridge with a view of the rolling Dorset hills on either side. To their right the countryside sloped away in a graceful green shoulder. A clutch of beeches, their barks dusty with mould, flashed by. The rain hung in black nets out over the sea.

Michael slowed still more to squeeze around a tractor coming in the opposite direction, then picked up speed again. They passed one hamlet which appeared to consist only of a pub, the Quiet Woman, three grey stone houses and an orchard. Then they were back amid the hedges of the countryside again. They skirted a small reservoir, disturbing a heron, grey as water. A small village was to be seen below them.

'That must be it,' said Michael.

'And there's the church,' said Isobel, pointing. 'Turn left when you can.'

The rain hereabouts was fiercer and, as Michael drew the car to a standstill at a T-junction in the village, the water rattled heavily on the roof. They turned left, followed the road round to the right as it curved past some copper beeches, cowering in the rain, and came to the church. Before getting out, they both manoeuvred into their raincoats as best they could. Then they ran for it, up the stone path that led to the porch.

The church was open. Inside, it was surprisingly light, thanks to the white walls. There was no one else about so they could take in what the building had to offer in their own time. The stained-glass window at the east end was modern, an abstract design in crimson and blue. But the rest of the church was very old. A Cromwellian-type helmet was displayed at the north side of the nave together with a pre-war photograph of the church, now rather brown and faded.

Presently, Michael said softly, 'Here we are.'

Isobel crossed to where he was standing.

Off the north transept was a wooden screen, through which could be glimpsed a small chapel. He pointed to the stone lintel above the screen. Inscribed faintly was one word: 'Goodwin'.

Michael motioned for Isobel to step forward into the chapel and then followed her. It was tiny, containing barely enough places for a dozen people. There was a small altar, with a simple brass cross, and a number of tomb plaques set into the walls. But by far the most dominant feature of the chapel was the enormous window which made up almost the whole of the north wall. This window, which must have been nearly twelve feet high, flooded the chapel with light. The rain, driving against it, drowned the chapel in sound.

'Here's Philip Cross's tomb,' said Isobel, pointing to a slab on the floor. 'With his wife's next to it.'

The pair of them stood at the foot of the slabs, looking down, reading the wording carefully. It was the usual details – dates, names, a Latin legend: *Crux crucem sequitur.*

'It beats me,' said Isobel, after a while. 'There's nothing here that has the slightest thing to do with trees.' She looked around. 'There's the screen, of course. That's made of wood. Do you think that's relevant?'

Michael shook his head. 'It looks fairly new to me.' He poked around gloomily. 'Quite a bit looks new, actually. The cross on the altar, the cloth it's standing on, the glass in the window.' He took out a cigar.

'Not in here, Michael. *Please.*'

'But I think better when I smoke.'

'Rubbish. That's silly.'

'Okay, okay. Let me play with it, then. I promise I won't light it until we are outside.' He looked down at the tombs. ' "*Crux crucem sequitur.*" Cross follows the Cross. Neat, eh?' He put the cigar into his mouth and sucked it. It was better than nothing. He looked down again. 'I wonder . . .'

Isobel reached across and took the cigar from his mouth. 'Speak clearly. I can never understand you with that thing in your mouth. What did you say?'

'What I was *about* to say was: the True Cross was made from a tree. Cedar, according to tradition, unless I'm mistaken.'

Isobel handed him back his cigar. 'You're right. You *do* think

93

better with this. Clever, Inspector Whiting. Very clever. All we have to do is find a cedar tree or some cedar wood.'

They searched the chapel for any reference to cedar. Nothing.

'Could the original screen have been cedar?' Isobel wondered aloud.

'Possible, possible. I suppose it could have been carved in such a way as to contain further clues.'

'If that's true, then we've had it.'

'Let's go back to the car and look up cedar in the books,' said Michael. 'That way I can have a smoke. Cigar boxes are made of cedar, you know. Keeps them fresh.'

She glared at him.

He led the way back to the car. The rain – large, pewter-coloured pellets – bounced off the yellowed, crusty paving stones. Michael fished an umbrella out of the boot of the car and spread it open. As Isobel dipped her head inside the car and retrieved the reference books, he put a match to his Havana.

'That's better. Larranaga, Corona, Aguiles Imperiales – even the words take you out of yourself. You must have *some* sins, Isobel? There must be some fault, some blemish, some stain on your character, as the courts put it?'

'Oh yes. I've garrotted three people who blew cigar smoke in my face, quartered several gamblers, and guillotined at least two men who kept the umbrella to themselves. I'm getting *wet*, Michael! Stand closer, turn your head the other way and listen to this.'

He did as he was told. The rain on her hair had released the smell of her shampoo. He turned his head halfway back, so as not to give up that pleasure entirely.

' "Cedar. A blond wood from a sacred tree, traditionally the tree from which the True Cross, on which Jesus was crucified, was made. In the Middle Ages, alleged splinters of the True Cross appeared all over Europe and were venerated as holy relics. According to Professor Polkner of Tübingen University, if all known splinters were brought together in one place, they would weigh three tons and comprise a cross that would measure fifty feet high and thirty feet wide." ' Isobel turned her face to his. 'Do you think they had a splinter of the True Cross here, Michael? Perhaps Godwin

Magna was itself shown on that silver map - the one with the emeralds?'

Michael shook his head. 'To the medieval mind, a relic of the True Cross was much more valuable than emeralds or rubies or silver. Bad Bill would have mentioned it in his letters or it would have been in the inventory. No, I'm beginning to think that this blond wood is a red herring.' He stared into the churchyard. 'I don't see any cedars out here either. Copper beeches, yews, oak - but that's all. Let's scout the graveyard, just in case. Here, you take the umbrella.'

There was little to see. Gravestones, pitted and septic with black and yellow lichen. The carved names, scathed by centuries of wind and rotted by the rain, meant nothing to them, even when they were legible. They drifted back to the car.

'We should look for the local vicar,' said Isobel. 'He might know something about the chapel that we don't.'

'Snap,' said Michael. 'My thoughts exactly. The vicarage must be that large house over there. Any chance of the starboard side of the umbrella?'

The house – a flinty structure with sharp gables and a thicket of chimneys – was the vicarage but they were out of luck. The vicar, they were told by his housekeeper, was in Bath all day but would be back tonight. They told the housekeeper where they were staying and asked if the vicar would mind contacting them when he returned. Michael left his card.

'Now what?' said Isobel. 'It's nearly one and I'm starving. How about you? A pub lunch at the Quiet Woman?'

'Hmm,' said Michael. 'No, why don't we drive over to Dorchester, check into the hotel, have lunch there and then, instead of trudging around in the rain, put in some systematic research with the reference books? There'll be a library in Dorchester, in any case. We might make use of that.'

Isobel saw the sense in Michael's suggestion and they set off, reaching Dorchester within half an hour. The Yeoman was an old-fashioned hotel with an archway through which they could drive the car to a courtyard at the back. They checked in but before going to their rooms decided to have lunch. At Isobel's suggestion, they each ate a ploughman's, washing the cheese down with cider. Then, around 2.30, they settled in Michael's room, taking the reference books with them.

'Let's not rush things,' he said. 'The answer must be in here somewhere, if only we know where to look. The person who painted this landscape would have been educated by the standard of his day, or else instructed by someone who was. But he would not have had massive libraries at his command. I remember reading somewhere that the average noble in the late Middle Ages had something like twenty books in his library. The answer *must* be here.'

They had brought their coffee upstairs with them and they sat in silence as the rain beat against the bedroom windows. The room had a view of the red-tiled roofs of Dorchester, which resembled an uneven piecrust, some slopes more highly baked than others. After half an hour Isobel got up, stretched and went to the window. She stared down at the main street of the town. She was watching a crocodile of schoolchildren, a line of dark blue raincoats being led along the pavement like so many goslings, when, behind her, she heard Michael breathe out.

'Eubloodyreka!'

She turned. 'Any luck?'

'Gloss among the dross, my dear.' He held up Gertrude Saxl's *Iconography of Christian Art*. 'Under "Tree", it says, among many other things, "See Jesse". So I saw Jesse.' He rolled his eyes, imitating Isobel's eyebrows. 'Jesse . . . joy . . . jubilation . . . *jackpot!*'

She leaned back against the window-ledge.

He read aloud. ' "Jesse, Tree of (Stem of). The prophecy of Isaiah, chapter eleven, verses one to three, that a Messiah would spring from the family of Jesse, the father of David, was interpreted visually in the Middle Ages as a genealogical tree. A tree rises from Jesse's loins on the branches of which appear the ancestors of Christ. The theme also occurs in Renaissance painting, especially of the early Netherlands." '

'You know, I think I prefer you when you drink cider – it gives you more fire. That was pyrobloodytechnic,' she added, mocking him back. 'That's our man, all right. There must be a Jesse buried in the church somewhere.'

So back out into the rain they went, retracing their steps and tyre tracks, to Godwin Magna. By four o'clock they were back in the church. In the chapel they examined every plaque, every tomb, expecting one to refer to a Jesse. None did. Undaunted, they tried the rest of the church, the walls of which were covered in plaques of every description. There were Jameses, there were Jeremiahs, there was a Jason and five Johns. But no Jesses.

'Nothing for it,' said Michael, nodding at the window, where the rain still buffeted. 'Let's try outside.'

Back into the long wet grass they went. They already knew how hard it was going to be to read some of the names. 'Trace the letters with your fingers, if you can't read them,' said Isobel. 'It might help.'

It would also look very odd, Michael thought, if they were observed fondling gravestones.

The rain and the wind kept up, making it difficult for Isobel to wield the umbrella. Cold trickles of water sneaked inside Michael's collar and scored down his back. Systematically, they covered every tomb. It took them until half past five. There were five names they couldn't read but in each case the dates on the headstones were much later than the sixteenth century, so they were at least certain that Jesse, wherever he was, was not in the cemetery.

Michael thrust his hands into his pockets and stared at the church. The rain dripped from his eyebrows to his face. Even his cigar, which had gone out again, was wet. 'I don't know about you but I feel slow-witted. I'm sure our next move is staring us in the face, if only we knew where to look.'

'Do you think the next figure, the next clue, might help? It might guide us back to Jesse.'

Michael nodded. 'Worth a try, certainly. Let's go back to the car, out of the rain.'

They sat in the Mercedes and looked again at the photograph of the painting.

'Hmm,' said Michael. 'Here we go again. I don't understand this at all. The next figure looks like a ghost.' He rubbed his hand over his face, to brush away the rain. 'I wonder if we did the right thing, not employing an expert.' The figure they stared at was by far the most insubstantial of the bunch: a grey man, ghost-like in appearance, as Michael said, with flesh that was deathly pale. A badly

97

drawn animal, what appeared to be a three-headed something, sat at his feet. He was holding the chalice.

'If this figure *is* a ghost,' said Isobel slowly, 'that too would point to a tomb or cemetery, don't you think? Maybe the church has been rebuilt since the sixteenth century and a crypt or undercroft has been covered over:'

Michael didn't reply but instead got out of the car again and went back to the church. He was inside for several minutes before returning, running through the rain. 'Extraordinary,' he said, settling back behind the wheel. 'I looked at the back of the nave, in the choir, even in the pulpit, everywhere . . . but nowhere is there any literature about the church. Usually these country churches have a pamphlet or two about the history of the building. That might have told us whether you are right, whether the church has ever been changed or rebuilt.' He bounced the ball of his hand on the driving wheel. He looked at his watch. 'Six o'clock. The local library will be closed now but that had better be our first stop tomorrow. There must be some sort of local records there, which might help.' He looked across to Isobel. 'We'll take a break here, as they say on the chat shows. Let's go back to the hotel, have a nice hot bath, a big whisky, an even bigger cigar, and treat ourselves to the best dinner they can offer.'

'Three out of four will suit me, thanks. I'd better call Tom, too. I hope his day has been better than ours.'

It was just on eight o'clock when Isobel joined Michael at the hotel bar. They sat together as the barman poured their drinks and placed them on the counter. Ceremoniously they both lifted them to their lips, then sighed in pleasure.

'What news from Château Sadler?' Michael said. 'All okay?'

'Yes, thank God. The drainage system worked very well after the hail and the meadows are drying – so the problem with the cow's hooves isn't serious. It damaged some of the early crops too but not permanently. A little sunshine wouldn't go amiss, though. Lord, I'm famished.'

Michael looked about for a waiter and signalled for him to bring the menus.

'Steaks, I think, don't you?' said Michael. 'After the day we've had, the redder the meat the better.' When she nodded, he added,

'And a nice heavy burgundy.' He dipped into his top pocket and removed a cigar.

Immediately, Isobel reached across and laid her hand over the book of matches lying on the top of the bar. 'Do you have to? Haven't you sinned enough for one day?'

Michael snipped the end off the tube of tobacco and took a second book of matches from another pocket. He held a match to the cigar and made several silent sucking movements with his mouth, soon enveloping them in smoke. 'Lady Bracknell didn't think it was a sin. She described it as an "occupation". At least you didn't say "Thank you for not smoking." '

Isobel put her hand over her nose and mouth in protest.

Undaunted, Michael said, 'I have a goddaughter – Clarissa, would you believe? Such an old name for a seven-year tot. Anyway, she's always saying things like, "Pink is my fifth favourite colour", "Seven is my third favourite number", "So-and-so is my fourth favourite doll".' He drew heavily on his Havana. 'After painting and the cello, after whisky and' – he looked at Isobel and grinned – 'after sex, cigars are my fifth favourite thing. Now you want to take them away.'

'They're bad for you. You're putting your life at risk.'

He spoke while gripping the cigar with his teeth. 'Would you miss me?'

'I wouldn't miss the ash, or the smoke, or the smell. Now sit a bit further away and tell me if you had any luck in the books.' She sucked the ice from her drink. 'I'm afraid I was too busy phoning Tom to do anything else.'

'Not sure,' said Michael. 'I looked up small animals, starting with cat. Nothing; but under dog there is a three-headed monster mentioned, which is part-dog, part-human. It symbolises Prudence. And there is a many-headed dog, Cerberus. But I was too badly in need of a drink by then. Also, I was listening to the news on the radio – and guess what?'

'What?'

'The government has announced that it is to legalise brothels. A good wager, eh? Predict the number who register in the first year.'

'Michael!'

'Or the number of customers an average establishment receives on an average night.'

'Stop it.'

'Or the average price.'

'You're disgusting.'

'Or – '

'Mr Whiting?'

Michael was astonished to hear his name spoken and both of them turned to see who it was. The mystery was easily explained, however, for the man who stood next to them wore a dark suit and, at his throat, a white dog-collar.

'Anthony Fleming, vicar at Godwin Magna,' he said, holding out his hand. 'And at Godmanstone, Eddleston and Hesketh, come to that.' He smiled. 'I phoned home before I left Bath and my housekeeper said you were staying here. There's a meeting of the county library committee at the town hall in about – oh, seventeen minutes. Rather than telephone, I thought I'd drop in. Nothing else to do until eight-thirty anyway.' He smiled again. 'How may I help you?'

Michael introduced Isobel, then said, 'Thank you for taking the trouble. May I offer you a drink?'

'Splendid, splendid. A dry sherry, if I may.'

Michael caught the barman's eye, ordered the sherry and turned back to the vicar. 'I'm an art dealer in London and I've been offered a picture that may have something to do with the Goodwin/Cross family. I'm researching the Goodwins and the Crosses, so naturally I'm interested in the family chapel at Godwin Magna. When it was built, why it was built, whether it was added to, what sort of family it was. Details.'

The sherry arrived and Fleming took a sip. 'Splendid. Yes, well, we're rather proud of the church and the chapel. The church is originally fourteenth century, the main door is later and the oak screen at the edge of the chapel is eighteenth century, of course, though donated by a late member of the Cross family. The font is the oldest font in the county and dates from the sixteenth century, when of course the church became Anglican at the Reformation. The east window is by Wystan Cadie, an English pupil of Chagall's and very modern, as I'm sure you noticed. Pity about the Jesse window in the chapel, of course, but you can't have everything. Those are the main features of the church. Now as to the family – '

Michael was in the middle of swallowing his whisky, so Isobel got in her reply first. 'What do you mean, Jesse window?'

'You can't have missed it. That tall window in the chapel. Dominates everything else. In the Middle Ages it used to consist of the most beautiful stained glass, showing Jesse at the bottom with a tree growing out of him and the ancestors of Jesus on the branches. The story started at the bottom and read upwards, as with all stained glass. There's one at St Jude's in Exeter by the same artist which still exists, and there's a drawing of ours in the British Museum. But the glass itself, of course, was all destroyed in the civil war – the family was royalist, of course. Later on it was replaced with the plain glass you see today. Such a shame.'

Michael, his heart pounding, said: 'When exactly would the window have been destroyed? Can you remember the date?'

Fleming blinked. 'Of course. Never been asked that question before though: 1640s, something like that. Anyway, it's all in the pamphlet . . .'

'Yes, where are the pamphlets? I looked for them but there didn't seem to be any.'

Fleming blinked again. 'What? None at all? That's very odd.' He fixed Michael with a rather baleful glare as he finished his sherry. 'I suppose I can just understand people stealing paintings from churches, or silver chalices – in those places lucky enough to have them. But pamphlets! – who on earth would do such a thing?'

Michael looked at Isobel. Molyneux! Trying to stop anyone following him again.

'Are there no other pamphlets? In the vicarage, say?'

'I only wish there were. This is most distressing. All the spares we had were kept in a box under the table in the church. Has the box gone as well?'

Michael nodded.

'What is the world coming to? The worst is, the man who wrote the pamphlet – old Toby Clark – is dead now. I shall have to do the new one myself, when I get the time. It won't be as good, though. Toby was a real historian. Published books.'

'What else can you tell us about the family?' Isobel asked.

'The Goodwins were traders, originally, from Bristol. They imported wine from France. Because of their links with the French the early generations were not at all popular with Henry VIII. The Crosses, as they became, found favour with Charles I – though that did them no good in the long run. They died out at the end of the eighteenth century.' Fleming paused, 'Is that enough detail – or is there anything else you want to know?' He looked at his watch. 'I see it's nearly eight-thirty. I suppose I should be cutting along.'

Michael smiled and held out his hand for Fleming to shake it. 'No, thank you. You have been very helpful. Thank you for telling us about the window. We shall go and look at it again tomorrow. And,' he added, 'with fresh eyes.'

'Splendid!' said Fleming. 'Goodnight to you both. Thank you for the sherry. Splendid!' And he was gone.

Later, after they had finished dinner, Michael said, 'Molyneux is damned cunning and doesn't miss a trick. Those pamphlets obviously mentioned the Jesse window and by stealing them, he has gained a day on us.'

Isobel rubbed an eyebrow and brushed her hair away from her eye. 'We'll have to go back and look at the window again in the morning, of course. But will it tell us anything? I mean, perhaps the design of the window was important. Does that mean going back to London straight away, to the British Museum? Maybe there was something in the window itself that won't even be in the drawing . . .'

Michael snorted. 'Pessibloodymist! Don't be so windy! We'll worry about that if and when it turns out to be true. At least we've made a bit of progress today. We're not exactly on the fast-forward button, I agree, but we know more than we did.' He poured the last of the burgundy. 'Actually, you can explain another mystery to me. You, Isobel Sadler. Thirty-ish, I would guess, very beautiful, I know, a farmer, so she says, though her heart isn't really in it. And the only man in her life seems to be a farm manager called Tom, who depends on her. Something missing there.'

Her plum-black eyes gleamed like wet rocks on a beach. She picked up a knife and dug a furrow in the tablecloth with it. 'You ought to mind your own damned business.' But then she dropped the knife back on to the table. 'Sorry. I agree, we can't keep going

102

in circles around the Jesse window.' She paused. 'What I've told you is all true, so far as it goes.

'What shall I add? Well, I was never very ambitious when I was young, so I never had much idea what sort of career I wanted. I knew I *wanted* one, but until I was twenty-one I never knew what exactly. Then, one Easter, I was in Rome. Like all the other tourists I was in St Peter's Square to see the Pope as he walked in procession. As it happened I got quite a good view from where I was. The procession, and the Pope himself, came very close to where I was standing.

'I had my camera out and was clicking away happily, when suddenly there was a commotion nearby. Someone raised his voice, and then a gunshot cracked out. It was so close I went cold for a moment. You really do wonder for a moment whether you've been hit. But when I turned, just a fraction, there was the man with the gun. I photographed him just as he was taking aim the second time and before the police could get to him. He fired. I can remember his arm, sticking out, very clearly. I remember thinking how ugly the gun looked. Short and squat, like one of those blind, blunt animals you get on the bed of the ocean. The first time he fired people weren't sure what they had heard, but the second time there was no doubt. There were screams and a whole wave of people fell on the man.'

'You must have been terrified.'

She shook her head non-comittally. 'By then I had turned back to the Pope. He had been hit, of course. His cassock had turned red under the arm. His skull-cap had slipped off. That made him seem more human, somehow. I photographed him as he fell, then as he was carried away. The blood was turning black – amazing how quickly that happens. I took more pictures, twenty at least. I have never been so cool in my life. While the Pope was carried away and the people all around were still screaming and shouting and comparing notes on what they had seen, I slipped away. I found a bar with a phone and a directory. I called the Rome office of one of the Fleet Street dailies. I explained what had happened and that I had it all on film.

'I wasn't interested in the money. But I'd been there when some-

thing important had occurred and I had a record. I was interested
to see what would happen next.'

'And . . . ?'

'My pictures *were* used. Oh, how they were used. The front page
of one of the Fleet Street papers next day, the rest of the world the
day after, and again in Fleet Street the following Sunday. More
surprisingly, perhaps, the paper behaved very honourably and actually paid me a share of all the syndication. I bought a better camera
with some of the money. With the rest of the cash I travelled. As
happened to you, I got the bug.'

'*Anopheles* . . . what?'

Isobel smiled. 'The picture editor at the paper which had bought
the photographs was very helpful. He said he could not employ me
on the strength of my Rome pictures – I'd just been in the right
place at the right time, so to speak. He said I'd have to do what all
budding photographers do – get on the road and find the stories. If
I sent my photos to him, he said, he would give them his personal
attention.

'So that's what I did. It was election year in America so I started
there. I didn't get anything particularly newsy or dangerous but I
did get a picture of one of the candidates' wives weeping when he
was beaten and that was used.'

'I think I remember. So that was you, was it?'

'At the end of the campaign I was in Washington when that
aeroplane crashed on take-off. If you remember, it plunged into a
river. I took a taxi to the bridge and photographed survivors swimming in the waters. It was very dramatic and after that the paper
did offer me a job.'

She drained what was left of her wine.

'To begin with it was a disappointment – photographing people
being interviewed, party political conferences – faces, faces, faces.
But then, when President Marcos was forced out of the Philippines,
I was sent there for weeks. That was exciting. I must have done
well because I started to work abroad much more. Ethiopia, Korea,
Nicaragua, Afghanistan, China once. And, inevitably, the Middle
East.'

Michael noticed that Isobel's fingers were wrapped tightly around

104

her fork as she dug its prongs into the tablecloth. He refilled her glass.

'By then I had teamed up – emotionally, I mean – with one of the foreign correspondents from another paper who often worked on the same stories as I did. He worked for a Sunday. We were both sent to Beirut. It was very dangerous then – I'm talking about a few years ago now. People were being abducted all the time and you never went anywhere alone.

'Well, Tony did. He left the hotel one night without telling me, without telling anyone. Something you just didn't do. He must have had a tip-off of some sort.' She swallowed some wine. 'I say "must have" because we never knew.' She looked at Michael. 'Tony was never seen again. Never seen and never heard from. No body was ever found. There were all sorts of rumours – that the Druze had got him, or the Iranians. Or that he was really a British spy and the Syrians had taken him out. I never knew what to believe. To begin with I thought he would be released eventually. I stayed in Beirut for a while but after a month the paper, though understanding, wanted me to go somewhere else on another story. That felt as though I was abandoning Tony, so I left the paper instead and lived in Beirut as a freelance.'

'That was brave.'

'After a year there was still no news of him. I didn't know what to do. If there had been a body then at least I would have been able to grieve – but there wasn't. He wasn't there, I missed him terribly but I couldn't even say goodbye. After another month or so I received a letter from his parents, saying I should give up and come home, that I'd done enough. It was a terrible wrench and I felt like a traitor. The one tribute I could pay him, if he *was* dead, and maybe even if he wasn't, was to give up journalism, just as he had been forced to give it up. I'd lost a lot of my appetite anyway. I went back to the farm, and, I suppose, moped for a while. Then Pa died. Mercifully, that was quick – a heart attack – and having to look after the place by myself has certainly kept me occupied.'

'And have you grieved for Tony yet?'

'I don't know. There's been no *focus*. I can't believe he's dead but I don't think he's alive, either. I don't talk to him any more – inside my head I mean, as I used to – I haven't put him *behind* me yet.

I've been out with other men a few times, but it was like flying a plane on a simulator. It wasn't for real.'

Michael spoke softly. 'Look, you don't have to go on. I didn't realise my question would be so painful. I'm sorry.'

'No. No. Funnily enough it's rather comforting to talk about it. I never have before.' She gave him a rather sad smile. 'Tony smoked cigars.'

A waiter came and took away their plates. Michael toyed with the idea of a cigar but thought, just this once, that he'd wait. The waiter set the coffee-cups in front of them.

'It's been a grim three years, frankly,' Isobel went on. 'I think I told you that my father was not a serious money-maker. But I hadn't realised that things were quite so bad. He had a large mortgage. That was paid off with his death, of course, but the interest payments had prevented him from modernising. On top of that he had never been able to afford to leave any of our land fallow so that it was not producing as well as it should.'

Suddenly, she shot him a blinding smile, not sad at all this time. 'Are you sure you want to hear all this?'

'And photography? Did you ever go back to that?'

She shook her head. 'All my things, all my photos of Tony, the box of cigars he left in his hotel room, are locked away at the paper I worked for, where I can't stumble across them.' She drank some coffee. 'You've no idea how I felt that day you told me about the mystery of the painting. It has offered the first chance in three years for me to get away from the farm.' She bit her lip. 'Every time it has looked like coming to a full stop, my heart has been in my mouth.' She tossed back her hair with a shake of her head. 'To be honest, I couldn't face going back to the farm just yet.'

She sat back and, Michael judged, had talked as much as she wanted to. He suggested a game of cards but she surprised him by saying she preferred chess. They moved back into the bar and he soon saw why: she beat him easily.

'This is one thing I *have* been doing, these last three years. You can play yourself and improve – that's one of its attractions.'

They went to bed at about 11.15.

'One thought,' said Isobel, her fingers gripping the handle of her bedroom door. 'If Molyneux stole all those pamphlets, that must

mean he's certain he's being followed. I didn't fool him at all yesterday. We've lost our one advantage. Oh Michael, I'm sorry.'

6

Next morning the rain clouds had gone, sunshine splashed along Dorchester High Street and what puddles were left shimmered like sheets of bitumen. After an early breakfast – a 'Thomas Hardy Special' of 'Egdon Eggs' and 'Brockhampton Buns' – Isobel and Michael drove across to Godwin Magna for the third time. Raindrops were still trapped in the hedgerows and sparkled like a thousand silver spoons. Michael opened the sun-roof and put Delius on the tape deck.

'What's this?' asked Isobel.

'*Brigg Fair.*'

'Summer morning music.'

'To begin with, yes. All Delius ends in tragedy. He knew things didn't last.' Michael smiled at her. He felt good, and Isobel also seemed easier, as if the rain storms, or their dinner conversation, had taken away some of her stiffness. On the back seat of the car were stacked all the reference books they had brought with them, just in case. And a box of Havanas that Michael had bought before they left The Yeoman.

At Godwin Magna the copper beeches were ablaze in sunshine. The church was open and Michael and Isobel hurried forward to the chapel. Michael had with him the photograph of the painting and, once they were installed within the chapel, took it out.

After a moment, he murmured, 'No, I don't get it. Do you?'

'Let's be systematic,' said Isobel. 'We don't know what the window design was, and until we go back to the British Museum, we can't know. So let's assume that we were referred to the window

108

for the most natural of reasons – to look *through* it. Why don't you climb on that ledge and see what the view is.'

He did as she suggested. It wasn't too difficult to climb from pew to window-sill. Balancing as best he could, he described what he saw. 'The cemetery, of course. A line of trees . . . I can see some poplars beyond the oaks. Fields beyond that, then a dip or valley that I can't see into. The ground rises beyond that – and I think there's a village up the slope. The trees are in the way, though. There are hardly any houses you can see.' He got down.

'Now let's go back to the books,' said Isobel.

They returned to the car. Michael leaned against the boot and lit a cigar. He had not had a chance to follow up his discovery of the night before, that the tiny animal at the foot of the ghostly figure who was the next clue was either Prudence or Cerberus. He plumped for Prudence first. He shook his head when he found it. 'Prudence was a three-headed monster but with *human* heads. Not ours.' He turned to Cerberus. 'Now that's more like it. Listen to this: "In Greek mythology, Cerberus was a many-headed dog, commonly with three heads and perhaps with a serpent's tail. He was the guardian of the entrance to Hades, the underworld, in both classical and Christian themes. He sometimes accompanies Pluto." ' Isobel began to turn the pages of her book but Michael said, 'Don't bother. I *do* know about some classical gods. Pluto was the god of Hades, the underworld.' He held his cigar downwind of Isobel.

'I've just thought. Could the underworld refer to the undercroft of the church, do you think?' said Isobel.

Michael looked across to the church. 'It *might* have had an undercroft at one point, I suppose, but I doubt it. We know that the Goodwin/Cross chapel has been here for centuries and there's no sign of any rebuilding. The vicar didn't mention it. That sort of thing might be mentioned in the church pamphlet, of course. I could stone Molyneux for stealing them!' He looked at Isobel. 'Can you face going back into Dorchester yet again? The library must have the church pamphlet and other documents on the building. If there *was* an undercroft that's the only way to find out without making the vicar suspicious.'

She shrugged. 'As I said last night, I'm not ready to go back to the farm just yet.'

Michael turned the 190 and they set off back to Dorchester. Isobel sat with the photograph of the painting in her lap. Occasionally she looked out at the countryside. Orchards flashed by: apple and pear trees. It was the end of the blossom and the leaves looked as though they had been tied on to the branches with ribbon. 'Tell me,' said Isobel after a while, 'was it this figure of Pluto that convinced you the painting wasn't by Holbein? Is that what your friend Cobbold, at the National Gallery, said?'

'Not at all. It was the subject matter, and the general quality. Why do you ask?'

'It's so badly drawn, don't you think? Not only is his cloak vague, but he's much less well formed than the others. The hands are ghostly, the face is cadaverous. It's almost as if the painter wasn't very interested in the character – *careful*! Why are you stopping?'

Michael was braking hard. He pulled the car off the road near a gate at the side of the lane. He put on the handbrake, snatched the photograph from Isobel and studied it for a moment. Then he looked up at her, grabbed her hand and kissed it. 'Brilliant,' he said. 'Hallebloodylulah! You don't have to go back to the farm just yet.'

'Michael! Give me back my hand. What have I said? Tell me!'

He pointed at the photograph, at the first figure, of Mercury or Philip Cross. 'You learn fast, thank God. Zero to zoom, in no time. Look at how well Mercury was drawn. Fantastic detail, his tunic with those flames, his medallions so we could know which Order it was, his facial features and hair so accurate we could recognise the likeness from another picture. Why? Because, as we now know, he was important in himself, the gold-card character – Philip Cross. Now ask yourself why, as you just said, Pluto is so badly drawn, flimsy and dull-looking? *Because he's not important in himself!*

'Now ask yourself about Pluto's function – king of the *under*-world. Isn't that drawing attention to the *over*-world – the part of the painting *above* Pluto? Remember, too, what the vicar said, about stained-glass windows: they are read from the bottom up. I knew that but had forgotten it.' Michael was looking excited, almost bouncing in his seat. 'Now put all that together. Pluto himself isn't important, not directly, but read up, above him, like in a stained-glass window, a Jesse window. What is there *above* Pluto in our picture?'

'A window.'

'More than that, Isobel. Come on, look at it again. It is the *only* window in the painting. It *opens* on to the landscape, with buildings in the distance. What clinches it is the shape of the window. Look at it, tall and thin– '

'You mean– '

'Yes. It's the same shape as the Jesse window in Godwin Magna church.'

Isobel was growing excited now, as Michael's argument began to convince her. 'But . . . you said you could hardly see any buildings when you looked out of the window.'

Michael pointed to some lines on the painting, in the window. 'Those are branches of trees, right? With no leaves. I keep noticing things about this painting that I hadn't noticed before. Look, the landscape seen through the window is a winter landscape, whereas all the rest, over here by the river, is a summer landscape. See?'

Isobel nodded.

'In other words, what we are being told is that these buildings are probably visible from the window only in winter. But it should be easy enough to find them – if they still exist, of course. Remember, I did say there seemed to be a village beyond the trees, at the other side of the valley? The buildings in the picture must have been there once. Let's hope they still are. There can't be many medieval buildings still standing.'

Michael reached into the glove compartment and took out the book of maps. He scrabbled through the pages until he came to Godwin Magna. 'Here we are. Now, the Jesse window is in the north wall of the church . . . so the village we want is even further north, across a valley . . . That's it, Higher Lewell. We can get there if we take the next right.' He passed Isobel the book of maps, quickly put the car into gear, and they moved off.

They found the road to the right and descended into a valley. Beech and ash trees crowded the lane, throwing green shadows, like smoke, across the road. They crossed a narrow stone bridge, wet with pelts of moss, and ascended again. As they reached the crest of the hill they came out into the sun. On the road ahead, black flecks of melting tar glistened like toffee. Their spirits had rapidly revived.

111

Higher Lewell was an even smaller village than Godwin Magna. It boasted a row of houses, a post office, shop and garage all rolled into one, a pub, the Chalk and Cheese, and the village's only claim to fame: its ruin. This was located at the far end of the row of houses and within sight of the pub.

Michael drew up the car near a green notice-board which announced that the ruin was, or had been, Lewell Monastery. Before he got out of the car he looked again at the photograph of the painting.

'This is getting easier,' he said. 'Look at that next figure. He's dressed as a monk. Besides the fact that he is carrying the gospels, he also has three knots tied in the rope round his waist. Even I know that signifies him as a Franciscan.' He pointed at the green board. 'And, as that board says clearly, this is, or was, a Franciscan monastery. Let's have a look round - but bring the photograph. We'll need it.'

They got out and followed a path into the ruins. There were the remains of a chapel – most of the walls but no roof – a cloister, a walled garden where the monks had grown fruit, and some small dark rooms which, they read on a board, had been cider breweries.

They also read on the main board that Lewell had once been one of a thriving community of monasteries in the area – Shilling and Monksilver were others, said the notice – which had specialised in ancient forms of medicine, as well as brewing. The monasteries had all thrived, commercially and spiritually, until the middle of the sixteenth century, when they had been abolished and their assets seized.

'Let me look at the picture again,' said Michael.

Isobel passed it to him.

The next figure after the monk was an old man, with a long beard. He had a pole and a kind of boat. Behind him could just be made out what appeared to be a bird with a human face. At his feet was the map of the True Cross. 'Here we go again,' said Michael. 'I think another session with the books is called for. I haven't a clue who this next character is.'

'Well,' said Isobel. 'Now that the weather has changed there's no need to go back to the hotel. Why don't we find a nice secluded spot in the corner of a field and do our research in style?'

'That's the second best idea you've had today,' replied Michael. 'After spotting Pluto's lack of substance, I mean.'

They grinned at each other and returned to the car. 'Look,' said Isobel as they were getting in. 'There's a sign along there saying "Public footpath". Why don't we see where it leads?'

So, each taking a couple of reference books, they locked up the Mercedes and made off. The footpath cut across some fields until it reached a small beech wood. The beech leaves, shiny on one side, powdery on the other, intercepted the sunlight, perforating it into a thousand silver battens. As they came out at the other side of the wood a broad vista of rolling fields opened up before them, acrid yellow acres of rape, dusty green patches of unripe wheat or barley, and, above, a straight white furrow chalked by an aeroplane in the sky.

'Here suit you?' said Michael.

'Perfect, I can do my first sunbathing of the year.' To Michael's consternation, Isobel then set down her raincoat, took off her shoes, and hiked her skirt well above her knees. Her legs were not disappointing.

He had brought a blanket from the car and now rolled it out. He invited Isobel to choose her spot, then flopped down himself next to her, turning his back on her legs. He took out a cigar and lit it.

'Where the hell do we start?' she said to the fields in general. 'We can't look up "man" or "old man", or "beard".'

'Styx.'

She looked at him. 'Sticks?'

'We didn't only do Elgar at school. I'm sure this figure is the ferryman of the classical world, the old man who shipped souls across to the underworld. I've forgotten his name but I remember the river was called Styx.' He spelled it out.

But after a minute, Isobel said, 'No, nothing under Styx here.'

'Nor here . . . try Hades.'

Another silence, save for the birds quarrelling above them in the sky.

Isobel held up her hand to shield the page from the sun. ' "To the Greeks, Hades was a grey region inhabited by ghosts; it was also the name of the god who ruled the underworld. The entrance to Hades is guarded by the three-headed watchdog, Cerberus" –

113

that we already knew, right? – "and it is located on the further shore of the River Styx, or the Acheron, across which the souls of the dead are ferried. Mercury, in the role of psychopomp, the conductor of souls, leads the spirits of the dead down to Hades from earth above . . ." No, everything but the name we are looking for. I'll look up Cerberus–'

'I already have . . . Listen: "In Greek mythology a many-headed dog, often three in number and perhaps with a serpent's tail, stands guard at the entrance of Hades in both classical and Christian themes. Cerberus is sometimes the attribute of Orpheus." '

'Orpheus, here I come. Orpheus, Orpheus, Orpheus,' she repeated to herself as she riffled through the pages. 'Yes, here we are . . . "Orpheus, the legendary poet, famous for his skill with the lyre. Orpheus married Eurydice, a wood nymph, and when she died he descended into the underworld in a vain attempt to bring her back to earth . . ." Then there are some themes featuring Orpheus and Eurydice . . .' She muttered to herself, ' " . . . Orpheus charming the animals with his lyre . . . Eurydice bitten by a snake . . . Orpheus in the underworld . . ." Now, what does it say . . . "Orpheus descended into Hades where, because of the beauty of his music, Eurydice was allowed to follow him back to earth on condition that he did not look back. At the last moment he did so and Eurydice vanished for ever. The loss made Orpheus despise women." Hmm . . . "Hades is usually shown seated on his throne, Cerberus sits beside it, snarling, and a fire-breathing dragon may be seen in the background. Sometimes Sisyphus, Tantalus or Tityus are also portrayed, their torments in the underworld temporarily eased by the beauty of Orpheus's music." No . . . nothing we want. It also says: "See Hercules and the Descent into Limbo." '

'My turn,' said Michael. 'I just wish I could remember the ferryman's name . . . it would save so much bother.' He turned the pages of his book while Isobel rolled over on to her back and stared up at the sky. Sparrows and swallows and grey and white pigeons swooped about in the air.

'Oh Lord,' Michael groaned a moment later. 'There's pages on Hercules. No . . . I take it back . . . there's just a paragraph on the underworld . . . "In *Alcestis*, by Euripedes, the queen, who loved her husband deeply, agreed to take his place in the underworld when he was about to die. Hercules went after her, fought with death, and brought her back to earth . . ." No, that's no good.' He thumped the book with the flat of his hand. 'Why can't I remember the ferrybloodyman's name!'

'I'll have another go.' Isobel rolled over again and picked up her book. This time, however, she didn't even bother to read out loud what she found. She just said, 'No go in Limbo.'

They lay in the sun a little longer. The high wisps of cloud were being burned off as the day grew older.

'Michael,' said Isobel, 'does it really matter if we don't have this character's name? After all, whatever he's called, he's still a ferryman. Surely that means the next clue lies along a river?'

Michael cupped his hands over his eyes so he could keep his eyes in shade as he looked at her. 'Not necessarily. We don't know whether the ferryman is leading us to the river or across it to the underworld, whatever that might be.'

'No, look at the next clue. A merman. Surely that's a gross hint that we go down the river towards the sea, rather than *up* the river or across it.'

'You're right. We're wasting time, all over a name.' He got up and held out his hand, to pull Isobel to her feet. 'Let's go to the pub. A little drink might clear our heads.'

He led the way back through the beech wood and up the slope of the fields. The sun was now blazing high in a sky wispy with cirrus clouds, and Michael took off his jacket and slung it over his shoulder. When they reached the road they turned away from Michael's Mercedes towards the pub. A postman's van came towards them and they stood to one side to give it room to pass. Isobel's eyes followed the van as it went and she glanced back behind them to the monastery.

'Michael!' she suddenly shouted. 'Michael, look! Look at your car!'

He swivelled. 'Good God!' he cried. As he spoke he was already running. The car boot, which they had left locked with their cases in it, was wide open, its lid yawning up like the jaw of a large snout. Isobel rushed after him.

Michael reached the car and peered into the boot. He rummaged through the papers and maps he always kept there.

Isobel caught up with him. 'What's been taken?'

Michael didn't reply immediately. He continued sifting and rummaging, moving the luggage about. Then he straightened up. 'Nothing, so far as I can tell. Odd.' He felt relieved until he pulled down the boot lid and examined the lock. The paint around it was badly flaked and scratched and the metal was severely mangled. 'Somebody wrenched it open –'

'And took nothing? After all that trouble?'

'Perhaps we disturbed them.' He looked again at the damaged bodywork. 'They must have been very strong. Perhaps there was more than one and they kept watch on us. They would have had the chance to escape very easily.'

'But they would have taken something, surely? It was a long walk from the end of the beech wood to the road. They would have had time to take out our cases.'

'Conjecture,' said Michael. He moved round to test the main doors. They were all locked, the windows all intact. 'Let's put the cases inside the car. I'll tie the boot down so it doesn't flap about and we can have our pub lunch in peace. Come on, get in.'

Slowly, he drove the few hundred yards to the Chalk and Cheese and parked as close to the main door as he could, so he would be able to keep an eye on the car from the bar. Isobel went on inside to order lunch while Michael fished out the rope he always kept in the boot for emergencies. He transferred their luggage to the back seat, locked all the doors, then tied down the lid of the boot and threaded the rope through the tow hook on the underside. Then he joined Isobel.

They sat in a small bay window where they could see the 190. In honour of the local monastery, they both drank cider. Michael raised the glass to his lips and took a hefty swallow. 'Aahhh. The sun makes this taste all the better.' He smiled at Isobel. 'Now, where are we?'

'Not as far ahead as you think, Michael.'

'Oh?' He swallowed more cider. 'And why not?'

'Listen to this, first. While you were fixing the car, I ordered drinks but I also looked up "River". I'll read it to you.' Isobel already had the book open at the page. ' "According to Babylonian tradition, Paradise was watered by the Euphrates, Gihon, Pison and

116

Tigris, four rivers which the Middle Ages made into symbols of the gospels. The four rivers of Hades were the Acheron, Cocytus, Phlegethon and Styx, which Dante made into stages of punishment of the soul in hell. The classical ferryman of the Styx was Charon–" '

'Charon! Of course, of course. How could I have forgotten it? I never knew that bit about rivers being associated with the gospels. Gospels mean "good news" of course, so that confirms our thinking, to go *along* the river, not across it. We follow the waters to get the good news. It all fits, Isobel, so why are you being so pessimistic?'

'Because I also asked the man behind the bar where the nearest river is. And there isn't one. Not here, not for miles. The nearest, funnily enough, flows through Godwin Magna. But there isn't one in this village. It's dry.'

Michael frowned at his drink. Instinctively, his brain was calculating the cost of repairing his car boot. It would certainly cost him his no-claims bonus on his insurance. That virtually wiped out his winnings on the Loch Ness monster.

Isobel was speaking again: 'Perhaps the Charon figure has a different meaning. A crossover point, a boundary of some sort, between one world and the next, so to speak.'

'No, I don't think so. Charon has a specific meaning: river ferryman.' He fished out the photograph. 'And don't forget the next clue – the man with a fish's tail – the merman. That certainly means we're looking for a river.'

Just then the landlord appeared with two plates of cheese, bread and salad. 'I ordered for you,' said Isobel. 'I hope a ploughman's lunch is enough.'

'Perfect,' Michael replied. And to the landlord, 'Same again please. Two halves of cider.'

While the landlord was pulling the drinks, Isobel said, 'Michael, there's something else.'

He was just finishing his first cider and had his glass to his lips. He nodded.

'I don't think it was any ordinary thief who broke into your boot.'

He swallowed. 'What are you getting at?'

'Think, Michael. This is not the first time that we, you and I, have suffered a break-in when nothing has been taken.'

'You mean –'

'Yes. I think it was Molyneux who broke into your car this morning –'

Michael frowned again. 'That's reading too much into what's happened –'

'Is it? Those church pamphlets were stolen. That means Molyneux knew we might be right behind him on the trail.'

'No, it doesn't, not necessarily. It might have been a general precaution. True, he saw you at the National Portrait Gallery. True, you lied to him and he probably guessed as much. But it's a long way from there to assuming that he has just burgled my car. It is *my* car, remember, so how did he link you to me?'

'He could have followed me to Mason's Yard. He could have looked in the register at the National Portrait Gallery. Your name was next to mine.'

Michael swallowed some cider. 'Now you're being fanciful.'

'Am I?' She waved a spring onion at him. 'When Molyneux bumped into me at the gallery he was, well, not threatening exactly, but . . . wary. He saw the photocopies in my hand. He must have realised then that, one way or the other, I had found out about the Landscape of Lies. That must have worried him, enough for him to follow me, I would say. If he did follow me, or checked in the gallery register, he would have realised he had a race on his hands. That his cosy, leisurely pursuit of the secrets within the painting had been transformed into a scramble. That would explain the missing pamphlets.'

The landlord brought the fresh ciders and Isobel waited for him to set them down before going on. 'As to the business of your car, that may need no explaining. All we have to assume is that Molyneux saw us, earlier today, when we arrived at the monastery. Maybe he was having a drink in this very pub. If he did see us, and then watched as we went along the footpath, he would have realised he had the perfect opportunity to break in–'

'But *why* did he break in? Okay, I admit your reasoning so far is pretty impressive, Chief Inspector class, even. But I still don't see why Molyneux should break into my car and not take anything.'

'Michael! It's obvious. He was looking for the picture. He could see it wasn't in the main part of the car, which is why he didn't bother to break the glass or force the doors. And that explains why, once he had broken into the boot, he still stole nothing. The one thing he wanted wasn't there.'

Michael stared at Isobel. She ate some cheese. The dimples in her cheeks appeared as she chewed. Her eyes were aglow.

'That could mean one of two things,' said Michael after a long silence. 'Either . . . that he simply wanted to take our "map", so to speak, away from us, to stop us following in his tracks and maybe even getting ahead of him. Or . . .' He paused, the implications of what he was about to say still sinking in. 'Or . . . Molyneux has come to the conclusion that his photograph of the Landscape is no longer good enough to pursue this puzzle.'

'Exactly,' said Isobel, picking up her fresh glass of cider. 'Absobloodylutely.'

She drank and then helped herself to more cheese. She balanced it on some bread and added pickle. She looked at Michael as she chewed. It took some time for Michael to register emotionally what Isobel was saying. He had never met Molyneux, didn't know what kind of man he was. He had been burgled in London once before and he now relived the sense of invasion he had felt on that occasion. Slowly, as he sat there, staring at his cheese and cider, and as he considered again the damage that had been done to his car, damage inflicted in full daylight, he started to boil. This time, however, it wasn't just fury. There was also alarm, worry, a tinge of real fear. Michael had a sharp tongue when he needed it. He could use the language of violence. But the real thing! He had never even considered it and it shook him now that he had come so close to someone who *was* prepared to use force. Molyneux made Michael apprehensive. No, dammit, he wasn't apprehensive; his feelings were stronger than that. He supposed he felt much as Isobel had felt when she had interrupted Molyneux in her home that night – except that she must have gone through even more. No wonder she had wanted to move the picture somewhere else for a while.

Isobel sliced through an onion and said, 'Assume that he has reached the same point as we have. That the next clue lies along a river – but there's no river here. That must mean we have both missed something, some minor but crucial clue that is not present in the photographs but *is* in the painting itself.'

119

Michael frowned at his cider again. He cut some more cheese. He dragged his mind back from Molyneux to the picture itself. 'I don't see how anything could be in the painting but not in the photograph. Unless the colour is important. Paintings are often quite different in the flesh compared with how they appear in photographs.' Suddenly, he put his knife down with a clatter. 'That's not it. Of course. *Of course*! The painting conceals the next clue, just as the photograph does. *But the picture can be cleaned*! Yes, that must be it.'

He looked again at the photograph, his eyes raking the detail. After a few moments, during which he chewed his bread and cheese, he pushed the photograph across to Isobel. He picked up a spring onion and pointed with it. 'Look at this. Look at the monk one clue back. The Franciscan. The figure before Charon.'

Isobel leaned forward to examine the photo as Michael went on. For the moment he had forgotten Molyneux and squashed his fear. 'See how the monk is looking down. I had assumed that was just his attitude of humility, as it should be in a holy man. But he could be looking at something on the ground, something at his feet. Pluto and Jesse are all looking at exactly the same point. See!' Michael tapped the photo with the end of the onion. 'The painting *does* look fuzzy all around that area.' He finished the last of his cheese. 'I suppose we'd better get a move on, back to London, I mean. If Molyneux would contemplate breaking into my car, he might just break into the gallery.' It was a thought that had only occurred to him as he had been speaking. Now Michael was truly alarmed.

As they finished their cider he said, 'Molyneux can't have got to London yet, so we're relatively safe, but better to be doubly sure.'

While Isobel hurriedly paid the bill, Michael rushed to the telephone. He dialled the gallery and waited for the phone to ring out. When it did so, he was concerned that there was no reply. He let it ring and ring but still no one answered.

'Puzzling,' he said to Isobel when he joined her, outside by the car. 'I know Greg's out. But Patrick should be there, and Elizabeth. What's happening?'

Michael double-checked the rope holding the boot lid down and, satisfied that it would hold all the way back to London, got into the driving seat.

They stopped at a service station on the M3 and Michael tried ringing again from there. Still no reply and, although they both knew that Molyneux could not yet have got to London, their fears were mounting. What if Molyneux had a partner in London whom he had telephoned?

Michael drove fast, very fast, hurtling the Mercedes along at more than 95 miles an hour. There was Vaughan Williams on the tape deck but neither of them was really listening. Around half past four, as they were coming into London, he stopped and tried to phone again. Still no reply. Now beginning to stiffen with fear, Michael used every trick he knew, tried every back street he could think of, to cheat his way around the traffic into town.

Even so, it was nearly six when they arrived at Mason's Yard. Everything *looked* all right as he parked outside the gallery. The lights were out, the windows were intact, the door was locked and the pictures which had been on the walls when he left were still there. There was no sign at all of a forced entry. He inserted his key into the lock. It turned exactly as it should have done. He pushed at the door. The alarm pulsed out in an entirely normal way. He went to the back of the gallery, stepped behind a desk and switched off the whine. The noise died exactly as it always did.

They went upstairs to Greg Wood's office, which was at the back where the vault was located. Michael locked the outer door, swung aside a real bookcase to reveal the vault and inserted a key into the first of two locks. His heartbeat cannoned around in his ribcage like a berserk bull. The key turned normally. Michael tried the second and held his breath. His pulse throbbed in his ears. But the second lock also rolled back as it should do. Finally, feeling a trickle of sweat percolate down the side of his neck, he pulled back the vault door.

The picture was there.

'Thank God!' breathed Isobel.

Michael wiped his neck with his handkerchief, took out the Landscape and propped it on a table which Greg used to keep old catalogues on. He examined the area near the Franciscan's feet. 'Yes,' he said after a moment. 'There *is* some grime here. Something is hidden – I hadn't noticed it before. There's a yellowish gold poking through in a few places. See?'

121

Isobel bent forward and looked at where he was pointing. 'What can be done about it?'

Michael had been so intent on driving fast that he hadn't smoked at all on the way back to London. Now he lit up. Isobel took a step away from him. He stared at the picture, then at his watch. It was nearly 6.30. 'It's too late to get to the restorer's tonight. But we'll do it first thing in the morning. Then we have to wait a few days.'

Isobel groaned. 'How frustrating.'

'I know. I know. But remember. Molyneux will be even more frustrated. He has no picture to clean.'

'That only makes him more dangerous. Michael, we have to be very careful, right now. I feel it in my bones.'

'I agree. I don't think I'll leave the painting here overnight. I'll take it home with me.'

'Is that wise? Don't you live alone?'

'Yes, but Molyneux won't burgle me while I'm there.'

'I'm not so sure. He tried it with me, remember.'

'He doesn't know where I live.'

'You're in the phone book, aren't you?'

When Michael nodded, Isobel went on. 'Don't underestimate him, Michael. Think what he's done so far: broken into two places, stolen those pamphlets and been alert and cunning enough to spot that we are following along behind him. He's not fooling around.'

'Are you saying you want to take it with you? To an address he doesn't know? I don't think – '

'No, I'm not. It wouldn't be fair on my hosts to put them at risk, however slight.'

'There you are – '

She interrupted him again. 'But what I'm also thinking is that two people are a whole lot safer than one. We can stay awake in shifts throughout the night.' She looked at him without blinking. 'I am inviting myself to stay for the night.'

Michael swallowed. He thought she was being melodramatic. At the same time, he acknowledged that it was possible Molyneux might come looking for the picture. The man had now tried unsuccessfully to get his hands on it twice, and without it he was stymied. There was no doubt that the man was capable of violence. Michael felt sick just thinking of the damage to his car. He spread his arms

122

and, without taking the cigar from his mouth, said, 'Be my guest. You can sleep in the smoking-room.'

They carefully wrapped the painting in a black leather portfolio which Whiting & Wood kept to carry pictures in. They closed the vault, slid the bookcase back into place and went downstairs. Michael turned off the lights, reset the alarm and placed the portfolio with the luggage on the back seat of the car.

On the way back to Justice Walk, they stopped off at a Chinese restaurant in Ebury Street. 'Living alone,' said Michael, 'I never keep a lot in the fridge except booze and chocolate. This means we won't have to go out again, once we are locked in at home.'

Everything looked calm and safe at his house. Michael explored all the floors, while Isobel sat in the Mercedes in Lawrence Street with the engine running and the doors locked. They had talked themselves into a fine state of nervousness. And, after all, there was still no explanation why the gallery had been deserted that afternoon.

Michael's house seemed safe. They hauled the suitcases out of the car, together with the portfolio and the Chinese meal. They locked the front door behind them.

Over noodles and crispy beef, Isobel said, 'I suppose I'd better check in with Tom.'

'Good idea,' said Michael, and after dinner they spent half an hour on the telephone. At first Isobel brought herself up to date on the farm. Then Michael called Greg and his secretary, Elizabeth. He had no luck though: all he got was Greg's machine and no answer from Elizabeth. They would have to remain in ignorance about what had happened in the gallery until the morning. Although they had the Landscape of Lies with them it was disturbing.

Michael showed Isobel his collection of gambling knick-knacks. He took down from a wall a piece of yellowed paper framed in gold wood. 'If we had time, which we don't, we could count the pin-pricks in this piece of paper. They are the most notorious pinpricks in the history of gambling.'

'Why?'

'At the beginning of the French Revolution one nobleman, who didn't exactly have the poor on his conscience, bet another nobleman that he could prick half a million holes in a piece of paper before his friend could ride from Paris to Versailles and back. As you can see,' Michael said, hanging the paper back on the wall, 'the man won his bet.'

Isobel stared at the paper and shook her head. 'I don't believe it,' she breathed. 'So dumb.' She looked at the paper again. 'I *do* believe it.'

Michael next pointed to a print which showed a grinning fat man in a three-cornered hat. 'Jeremiah Austin. One of the slimiest Englishmen ever. He was a member of that great gambling club, White's, in the eighteenth century and one day, when one of the club servants collapsed, Austin bet a thousand pounds – a great deal of money in those days – that the fellow was dead.'

'Charming.'

'Hear the rest. Another servant sent for the doctor . . . but Austin wouldn't let him near the collapsed man – because it would spoil the bet.'

Isobel peered at the print. 'I'd like to stick half a million pins into him.'

Michael chuckled. He started to light a cigar. While he had his hands full, coping with his cigar and some matches, Isobel reached into a half-open drawer and picked up a pack of playing cards.

'Don't!' cried Michael urgently. Then, more calmly, 'I mean, they're not very interesting, artistically, that is.'

But Isobel had opened them. Something in Michael's tone told her he was lying. She slid the cards out of their box and turned them over so that she could see the faces.

Bodies would have been a better word. The cards were porno-graphic, all the picture cards being naked kings, queens and knaves. As she passed the cards from one hand to the other, she cocked her head to one side and stuck her tongue in her cheek. 'Whatever these people are doing, it isn't playing cards.'

'They're French,' said Michael nervously. 'They belonged to the Regent, Philippe, Duc d'Orléans. You know, the dissolute one, who had those *petits soupers* . . . orgies . . . he was a great gambler . . . sorry . . .' He tailed off.

Isobel put the cards back into the box and replaced it in the drawer. She looked at Michael. 'When I was in Afghanistan, I photographed a dead Russian soldier who had had his heart cut out of him and stuck on a pole in the ground. In Argentina I saw pictures of torture victims with cattle prods in their vaginas. In Beirut I photographed the bodies of women who had their breasts cut off. None of the pictures was ever used, of course. They were too horrible. But don't treat me like a child, Michael. I've seen *real* obscenities. You think a pack of dirty playing cards is going to make me throw up – or think any the less of you?' She leaned forward and took the cigar from his mouth. 'Look at this,' she said, holding it in front of him. 'Wet as a worm at one end and reeking like Rangoon at the other. That's what I call obscene.'

That night one of them kept the portfolio in sight at all times. Michael let Isobel go to bed first, while he lay on the sofa in the living room and watched videos of old movies to keep him from going to sleep. He still smoked, but sheepishly, even though there was no one watching him. He had come across anti-smokers before but Isobel's style was a bit too much, he thought. No doubt his cigars reminded her of that man – Tony? – in Beirut. Did she feel guilty, he wondered. Guilty that she was alive and he, presumably, wasn't. Was it something else? Was she fond of him, Michael? He thought of her body upstairs, in his spare room. He had never made love in that room. No, not tonight. Maybe not any night. She had given him no hints, unless her attacks on his smoking were hints – a bloody funny way to show your feelings. But it was too late at night to think it all through. He switched off the light and shifted his attention to the real Rita Hayworth on the video.

When the film was over, Michael decided to make himself some coffee before watching another. In the kitchen he used the last of a jar of instant coffee and threw the empty jar into the waste bin. That was nearly full, so he lifted it out of its container. Justice Walk was a passage that linked Lawrence Street with Old Church Street. The house had no back garden and no traffic was allowed in the walk. Michael's dustbins were therefore kept in a cupboard at the front of the house. Without switching on the hall lamp, he quietly opened the front door and peered out. He looked right, to Old Church Street. An amber light shone down the street, casting the walk into shadow, but the street itself seemed clear. Michael looked left to Lawrence Street – and just glimpsed a figure slip out of view in the direction of the river.

Michael's blood started to race again. He looked at his watch:

125

1.30. Late, but this was Central London. Being abroad at that hour wasn't in itself out of the ordinary. Michael hadn't convinced himself, though, and was already moving. Leaving the rubbish where it was in the hall, he closed the front door behind him, double-locked it, and ran to where Justice Walk opened into Lawrence Street.

He looked towards the river. Nothing – or was that a figure disappearing into the little park that lay between the houses and the embankment?

He looked back to his house. There was no one in sight. He ran down Lawrence Street, paused at the junction that led to Cheyne Walk and looked to his left. No one. He knew that the pub to his right had a yard at one side. He was sweating now. He peered into the yard. That too was empty.

He ran the rest of the way to the park but when he reached it he found he was alone? Or was he? Wasn't that a figure on a bench? It was lying down, as if it was trying to hide behind the back of the bench.

A car flashed by on the embankment, sending light and shadows raking through the trees of the park. For a split second the bench was lit up. Yes! there *was* a figure lying on it. It might be a tramp, of course, or a drunk. But if it was Molyneux Michael wanted to know. He felt both frightened and foolish at the same time. A sleeping tramp might be very angry when disturbed. Yet Michael had to know. He *wanted* to face Molyneux, to have some idea of whom he was up against. And he wanted to frighten the other man too, just as he was frightened himself.

He moved closer. Noiselessly. When he was five yards from the bench he had his answer. The stench which the horizontal body gave off could only mean that the figure was a sleeping tramp.

Now Michael's fear took another turn: he had left the house, and the picture, unguarded. He turned and ran back up Lawrence Street, his heart bucketing in his ribcage. He skidded into Justice Walk. His front door was locked, just as he had left it. He turned the key and let himself in. The rubbish bag lay in the hall as he had left it. His pulse boomed in his ears. He checked the picture: it was safe. He sat in the kitchen and reached for his coffee.

Had that really been Molyneux he had seen in Lawrence Street?

126

It had certainly been a tall figure but he had not registered any features. As he lifted his mug, Michael realised his hand was shaking. It had been quite a day – first his car mangled, now this. Nearly two o'clock in the morning and he was chasing shadows in Chelsea.

He sat, sipping his coffee and listening to the night outside. A motor bike started up in Old Church Street; footsteps passed along Justice Walk; someone ran in the distance. They could all have been Molyneux. Twice he looked out of the window in Justice Walk. Nothing – nothing, that is, except shadows.

Around four o'clock, armed with a big mug of tea, all he had left, he awoke Isobel. He showed her how to work the video, drew her attention to the rare old movies he had which she might not have seen, then took himself off to bed. He slept at the top of the house in a room with a huge bed and a single painting, the most beautiful picture he had ever been able to afford for himself. It was a small Cozens watercolour of Lucca in Italy. The lines were no more than hints, the washes were only suggestions, yet he had counted at least fifteen yellows in it.

He didn't mention his nocturnal prowl, deciding that he was doing enough worrying for both of them. But he took the Landscape upstairs with him and slid it under the bed. He tried to sleep but the image of that figure, slipping out of view towards the river, kept floating before him in the dark.

7

When he awoke, around eight o'clock, it was to the smell of fresh coffee. Parabloodydise. He quickly shaved, showered, dressed, and went downstairs.

'Sit down,' said Isobel, as Michael entered the kitchen. The table was laid for breakfast. 'You seem to have run out of instant coffee but there were some beans in the fridge. And some eggs. Some tomatoes but no bread. I'm making us an omelette.'

He drank some coffee, contemplated a cigar but thought he had better not. Not if he wanted an omelette. He watched as Isobel expertly slid the yellow and brown mass from the pan on to two plates. 'You appear to be as good with kitchen gadgets as you are with a camera.' Too late, he realised what he had said. 'Sorry, sorry. That was tactless.'

She gave him another of her looks and banged his plate down on the table in front of him. 'Eat that.' Meaning: and shut up.

He did both for a while. 'Mmm. This is *good*. Light and it needs no pepper or salt. Twenty-two-carat cooking.'

'What's our plan today?'

He drank more coffee. 'I have some calls to make before I can be certain, but, during the night, I decided it's too dangerous to send this picture to my regular restorer. For a start, he's not far away, in Dover Street, and very easy for Molyneux to get at. Also, he's known throughout the trade, so he's hardly the most secure person to send it to.'

He ate the last of his omelette and ostentatiously licked his lips. 'Wonderful. Four knives and forks, as Michelin would say. I'll bet

128

Rita Hayworth couldn't cook like that. There's another restorer I have been trying out, for when old Julius retires, which can't be far off. Her name's Helen Sparrow and she lives in East Anglia. That's safely out of the way. If she's free and can do this job for us over the weekend, then I can be pretty sure Molyneux will never find her.'

He looked at Isobel. She was nibbling a burnt piece of omelette. He held his fingers around the cup to warm them. He had, in fact, done quite a lot of thinking during his 'watch' earlier on that morning. 'Isobel, today's Friday. You said you didn't want to go back to the farm just yet. Say we go to East Anglia today and give Helen the picture. There's nothing else you or I can do until she's taken away the grime and our next move is revealed. But we needn't come back to town. We could spend the weekend on the coast, or looking at churches. East Anglia is where many English painters did their best work. I could show you. Constable country. Gainsborough gulch. We could pick up the cleaned picture on Monday morning and come back then, ready to take up the trail again. What do you say?'

A level stare.

'Cotman, Turner, Cozens. They all painted some of their best works near where we have to go.'

She drank some coffee but still didn't speak.

'Too much art? How about fish, then? Helen Sparrow's studio is barely thirty minutes from Lowestoft, as the crab scuttles. Fresh halibut, whitebait, sole, mackerel, lobster, herring, haddock, oysters, shrimps . . . I can't think of any more. I'm fished out.'

Was she laughing at him? She still hadn't spoken but her expression seemed to have changed. The flint in her eyes shimmered.

'Okay, I'm going to play my trump card.'

'I hope it's not obscene.'

'Ah, I thought my eloquence had knocked you speechless. No, it's not obscene. Quite the opposite, in fact . . . Are you ready?'

Now she *was* smiling at him.

'Come with me and I promise not to smoke before dark.' The idea had come to him from nowhere. He only hoped he could keep to it. If she agreed.

Isobel reached across and took his empty plate. She stood up. 'An almost ash-free weekend. Days without a cough. The unadulterated smell of fresh air. What woman could resist?' Still smiling, she turned and started to put the cups and plates in the dishwasher.

Michael looked at his watch: 8.40. Time to call Greg Wood at home. Greg, who sometimes stood in for Michael at house sales, had had a good day up in Warwickshire, he said. He had bought two of the three paintings Michael had wanted but the other had gone for way over its estimate to a Dutch dealer. That they had acquired two paintings was very good news. One had been catalogued as a James Ward but Michael believed it to be by Ward's brother-in-law, George Morland, a much better painter and a better-known name. If he was right the picture was worth at least five times what they had paid for it.

Though Michael was pleased by Greg's news, this morning it wasn't his main concern. 'Greg, what happened yesterday? I knew you were going to be out of the gallery. But what happened to Patrick and Elizabeth? I called in all afternoon and no one ever answered.'

'You mean you haven't heard? Elizabeth's mother was rushed to hospital. In Aberdeen. Touch and go, I hear. Patrick drove her to the airport. He didn't bother to come back afterwards, since it was the day for his Italian lesson in High Street Kensington. He went straight there.'

Relieved, but worried on Elizabeth's behalf, Michael said, 'Which hospital is the mother in? I should send some flowers.'

'Don't worry,' said Greg. 'I'll do it. How's your hunt going? Any luck?'

'Luck? Yes. Bad as well as good. It's moving, Greg but – well, there's a long way to go. I'll fill you in on everything when we get back.'

Michael had to wait another hour for people to get to their offices – as he had told Isobel, there weren't many early birds in the art world. He occupied his time by opening his mail and reading the newspapers. The government's proposals to legalise brothels were receiving their fair share of criticism, not least from the cartoonists. But the plan, even if it came off, wouldn't be brought in for more than a year so it wasn't worth a wager just yet. Something else, however, caught Michael's eye. The managing director of a large

130

sugar-refining company, a millionaire and a knight to boot, was just going on trial for fraud, attempting to manipulate the stock market. Michael knew that many people doubted the man would be sent to gaol, even if found guilty. He felt strongly on the issue, believing the man *should* be gaoled, but he knew others in the syndicate disagreed. It was, therefore, a perfect wager.

He phoned around. Everyone liked the idea and the sentences ranged as high as seven years. He himself opted for a fine of £100,000 but no prison sentence. Then, if he lost the wager, at least he would have the satisfaction of seeing the man go to prison. The trial was expected to last a month.

Around 9.30 he went to his desk. In a pigeon-hole there were a number of invoices from Helen Sparrow, for work she had done cleaning some of Michael's own pictures. The invoices had her phone number printed on them. He called her. Yes, she said, she had nothing she couldn't put off and would be pleased to help. She knew as well as Michael did that she was 'in waiting' for when old Julius retired and it was a boost to her career to be taken on by a London gallery. She said she would expect him some time that afternoon.

He hung up. 'Now,' Michael said, motioning Isobel to a seat. 'We need a little planning. Molyneux's a foxy snake and we can't afford to let our guard slip. See what you think of this. We've got to have the picture cleaned – right? Either we sit with it the whole time, which will be very tedious, or we have to make sure Molyneux doesn't know where we leave it. Which means making sure he's not following us when we get to Helen's. What I suggest is this. The frame I have over the fireplace, the one with half a million pinpricks, is roughly the same size as the Landscape. I'll pack it into the portfolio and give it to you. I'll then pack the Landscape into my large suitcase along with the clothes I will need for the weekend –'

Isobel looked mystified but Michael raised his hand. 'Hear me out. We both leave the house together and take a taxi. I drop you off with your case and the portfolio at Liverpool Street station, where I wait and watch you take a train to Cambridge. Then I get back into a taxi, cross London to King's Cross station, and take a train to Peterborough.'

Still Isobel looked perplexed, but Michael grinned and said, 'This

131

is the clever bit. You do not get off at Cambridge but at Audley End, about half an hour before. Why? Because Audley End is a tiny station and you can easily see if Molyneux gets off with you. If you are being followed it doesn't matter because you don't have the picture. Just smile at Molyneux, cross the line and catch the next train back to London and come here – I'll give you a key. If he's not following you, take a taxi from the station at Audley End to the Royal Garden Hotel in Cambridge and wait there in the bar for me to join you.'

'Where will you be?'

'Running roughly parallel. At King's Cross I shall catch the Peterborough train but get off at St Neots. Just like Audley End, it's a tiny station and I shall be able to see anyone else leaving the train. If Molyneux has followed me, I shall tell him he's been duped and that you've taken the picture with you. But my bet is that, if he does follow us to Liverpool Street, he'll be torn between which one of us to pursue – and will opt for you because you will have the portfolio and are the weaker person – physically, I mean. He doesn't know you've been to more wars than I've had cigars. If Molyneux doesn't follow me, I shall take a taxi from St Neots to Cambridge – it's not much further from there than it is from Audley End. If you're not there, I shall go to Helen's alone, leave the picture with her and meet you back here this evening. If we do meet up in Cambridge we shall be certain we're not being followed. We can leave the picture with Helen and enjoy the weekend. What do you think?'

'How do we get from Cambridge to Helen's?'

'By hired car. Which I shall now arrange, if you approve the script.'

Isobel was impressed by Michael's idea and couldn't think of a better one. He therefore telephoned a car rental company and reserved a medium-sized vehicle at its Cambridge office, for later that day. He then telephoned the Harbour Inn at Southwold, on the Suffolk coast south of Lowestoft, and reserved two rooms for three nights.

They took down the frame with the half a million gambling holes and exchanged it for the Landscape in the portfolio. Michael wrapped the painting in tissue and put it at the bottom of his suitcase, packing fresh shirts and shoes and other things on top. He phoned for a cab.

On their way to Liverpool Street, they kept looking back but, if Molyneux *was* following them, he was being very clever about it. The traffic behind them appeared completely anonymous.

At the station Michael queued with Isobel while she bought her ticket. They had forty minutes' wait before the next Cambridge train and passed the time having coffee. Then Michael watched as Isobel boarded the train. To begin with he watched all the other passengers too – but he didn't know Molyneux so he quickly abandoned that and went off to catch his taxi to King's Cross.

As he paid the driver at the other end, Michael now began to feel very alone and he guessed Isobel was feeling that way too. Without being aware of it, they had begun to rely on each other very much.

He hurried across to the ticket office. He had to kick his heels for another half an hour before the next Peterborough train left. When it did so it was seven minutes late and Michael was beginning to fret. He paced along the train's corridor looking for very tall, grey-haired men. There must have been four candidates at least. As the train moved off he walked back through the carriages, carrying his suitcase. To be on the safe side he spent the entire journey in the buffet car. It was always busy there and he felt safer surrounded by lots of people.

The train arrived at St Neots at about twenty past twelve. Michael did not leave the train immediately. If Molyneux *was* aboard, Michael wanted to give him as little opportunity as possible to observe that this was where he was getting off. Michael waited until he could hear doors being slammed and the train was ready to leave again. Only then did he open the door where he was standing and jump on to the platform. A guard was standing nearby and moved forward aggressively to close the door after him. 'You asleep?' he growled at Michael.

Michael had never been more alert and hurriedly cast his gaze along the platform. It was bigger than he had anticipated and had an old-fashioned, ornate glass roof – the kind which people wanted to destroy fifteen years ago but now campaigned to save.

No one else had jumped down from the train since he had done so. Someone else was getting on to the train as it began to move off. He counted five other people on the platform, two of them women and one of them the guard who had grumbled at him. The other two consisted of a soldier in uniform and a thin man with a briefcase, no more than thirty. He couldn't be Molyneux either.

Michael gave a silent cheer but then thought: maybe Molyneux was already outside. This didn't make sense because Molyneux could not have known Michael was going to get off at St Neots until he did so. But Michael was so worked up, he believed anything was possible and would not be happy until he saw outside the station.

He lifted his case and strode in the direction of the 'Way Out' sign. Before he had reached the ticket barrier the train had all but left, its back half disappearing. He inspected the platform again: it was deserted. He handed in his ticket and went through into the small booking-hall. He could see no one who would fit Molyneux's description. The solitary taxi outside was a big white Ford and Michael clambered in. 'Cambridge, please,' he said, and looked back to the station as the driver sped off. The station forecourt was empty. His plan had worked.

It took about thirty minutes to reach Cambridge and as they approached the city Michael began to feel on edge again. There was no possibility that Molyneux could have followed him but Michael didn't relish going to Helen's all alone, should Isobel have had to turn back. He was slightly surprised at how disturbing he found this thought.

The taxi turned into Downing Street, then along the Parade. Another left turn and the Royal Garden Hotel was in front of them. Michael quickly paid the fare and got out. He hurried into the hotel, lugging the case with him. The bar, he knew, was on the right. It was a big room but he immediately sized up that Isobel wasn't there. Jesus bloody Christ. They had been right to be careful. He looked at his watch: just on one. She wouldn't be back at Justice Walk yet, so he was stymied—

'Michael? *There* you are. I'd nearly given you up.'

He pivoted. Isobel came towards him from the direction of the hotel shop, where she had obviously just bought a newspaper. She held it up. 'This is the fifth paper I've read. I know more about yesterday than any day in the history of the world.'

'Molyneux?'

'Not on my train. You?'

'All clear.'

'So, Detective Whiting's plan worked.' She grinned. 'An ash-free weekend after all.'

'Don't remind me. I'm dying for a smoke.' He took a cigar from his pocket, smelled its leaves and replaced it.

Isobel threw the unopened newspaper into a waste bin. 'I shan't need that. Let's get going.'

The porter at the front desk showed them to a phone in the lobby which was a direct line to the car rental firm. Michael arranged for the vehicle to be dropped off for them at the hotel and was told it would take about twenty minutes. That allowed time for a sandwich in the bar.

The car, when it came, was more like a minnow than a Mercedes but at least its boot was intact. Michael completed the formalities, they packed away the portfolio and the suitcases and drove off.

Outside Cambridge, the countryside became flatter. It was not the kind of landscape that appealed to Michael 'in the flesh', so to speak, but he loved it in the paintings of Constable and others of the Norwich School. Low horizons in a picture, he believed, made the rooms where the pictures hung more airy and spacious. People liked that.

They joined the main London-to-Norwich road, turned off at Thetford and headed towards Bungay, where the road then followed the River Waveney until they turned north and headed for Aldeby. The road was narrower now and their speed was much reduced. There were few hedges hereabouts and the sky came all the way down, like a backdrop which reached to the stage. Lines of loam lay out to their right, deep furrows in the plum-coloured earth. Buckled trees, oak and ash that had spent years labouring against the cold Russian winds, leaned east, giving the landscape a lop-sided look. Isobel and Michael arrived at Aldeby just before three o'clock.

Helen Sparrow's studio was in a converted stable, just off the High Street. She lived on the ground floor, and there was an outside staircase up to where she worked. There, they could see, part of the slate-tiled roof had been removed and replaced with glass, to give added light. Michael noticed Helen's van in the garage one stable along.

Hearing their car, Helen Sparrow came down the stairs to greet them. Michael made the introductions. She belied her name, being a tall woman, though she was rather awkward and jerky in her movements, like a bird. Somewhere between thirty-five and forty-five, she had a long face with a surprisingly ruddy complexion for someone whose job was so sedentary. She had long thick hair that had gone grey very early on. It swooped down on either side of her forehead, like curtains, and was held at the back in a long pony tail. She wore a red smock over a faded blue dress and what had once been very white espadrilles. Her fingers gave away the fact that she was a restorer; they were long and supple. She led the way back up to her studio while Michael hauled his suitcase up the steps. Inside the studio there was a wooden easel all ready to receive the picture. Michael opened the case and unpacked it. He placed the canvas on the pegs.

Helen Sparrow returned from a kitchen off the main studio, carrying a tray with three mugs. They stood sipping tea and surveying the picture.

'It's an unusual composition,' said Michael. 'The landscape is English, part of Dorset, I think. The figures are religious, mythological, and real. Where I need your help is just here.' He indicated near the monk's feet. 'It looks to me as though there is something under this grime.'

Helen leaned forward. 'Yes, it looks like dirt, or discoloured varnish, rather than overpainting. Is that all you want me to do?'

'Well,' said Michael, who had examined the picture in detail the night before, while Isobel was sleeping, 'there *are* one or two other areas we might as well have cleaned.' He pointed to the flesh on one of the faces and a patch at the foot of one of the columns, at the top of which was the carved Adam and Eve scene where it had all started. 'I don't know if there's anything concealed in these areas but, just in case and provided you can have it ready by Monday morning, you might as well clean them too. This is not my usual type of picture, Helen, as you can see, and this time speed is all important.' He stood for a moment looking at the picture and drinking his tea. 'Can you have it done by Monday morning?'

'Hmm. There's something I ought to get out of the way today. But I can work all day tomorrow and on Sunday. Do you want me to bring it down to London?'

'Oh no. In fact, we're planning to stay in the area over the weekend, in the hope that you can finish it quickly. There's more than the usual urgency in this.'

Helen thought. She knew better than to ask, with a dealer, what the urgency was. 'I shall have to charge you extra for working on Sunday. Is that all right?'

'Of course,' said Michael. 'A rush job is a rush job.' He took his pocket-book from inside his jacket and, tearing a slip of paper out of it, he scribbled some names and numbers. 'If there are any problems, I have checked into this hotel for the weekend. It's at Southwold, not far from here. You can always call there.'

Helen took the paper and pinned it to a board on the wall. Then she took their cups from them and showed them to the top of the outside staircase.

'How's Julius?' she asked.

'Fine, so far as I know,' said Michael. 'I saw him last week, as a matter of fact.' Then, responding to her unasked question, he added, 'But Jules won't last for ever, Helen. He's still the best there is at the moment, but you're getting there. There'll be more to follow after this, I promise.'

'Should we have told her about Molyneux?' said Isobel, once they were in the car again and heading for the coast.

'The fewer people who know the better, don't you think? Even though she lives out here, and is discreet, Helen still knows plenty of people in the trade. There's always the risk of gossip. We must keep this to ourselves as much as we can.'

They reached Southwold around six, having stopped off to look at the church of St Edmund, King and Martyr, which was also in the village. It had a magnificent two-storey porch. Then they checked into the Harbour Inn.

At dinner that night, which they took in the hotel, Michael said, 'At last we can relax. Without the picture, Molyneux's had it. However slow we are at deciphering the Landscape of Lies, it doesn't matter any more. We have the only key that fits the lock. So let's enjoy our weekend. Let's forget about your farm and the picture.

We'll head south tomorrow – to Constable territory. Then come back north, take in Gainsborough's house, and end up at the museum in Norwich. How does that sound?'

'I think it's a lovely idea, Michael. But first, you've got some making up to do.'

'What do you mean?'

'Last time we had one of these dinners, I did all the talking, about the farm, about Tony. Now it's your turn.'

'Oh yes, the night I thrashed you at chess, you mean?'

She smiled. 'Now it's not late, there's plenty of wine left. Last time, you said you were interested in English*ness*. What did that mean?'

Michael took out a cigar. 'Am I allowed one of these now?' She nodded, and for a moment he played with his matches. 'Have you never noticed how, with many people, to be English is not enough? They have to have some Scottish blood, or Welsh, or French. Or more important than being English is being a Yorkshireman, or a northerner. Being just English is too negative for many people, too wishy-washy, too . . . zero. Everyone else is proud of being Irish, say, or Indian, or Italian. But the English are rather – well, reserved, embarrassed almost. Yet England has as colourful and important a history as most places. There have been just as many famous – and notorious – English men and women as there have been French or Germans, and a good deal more than the Welsh or Swiss, say. Yet it appears to make no difference. If you have to describe a Frenchman, an Italian or a Scot, you can do it in a very few words. But an Englishman? Impossible.

'Now, look at all the activities of mankind, especially all the creative, artistic activities that reveal things about their authors . . . There's only one thing which the English do well and which other nations hardly do at all.' He held the cigar low down so she would not be disturbed by the smoke. 'Care to guess what it is?'

She smiled and shook her head. 'Make gin? Hardly art, I suppose. Play cricket? Except that others do it better now, don't they? Foxhunt? Overcook beef? Drive on the left? Come on, tell me.'

He drew on his cigar and breathed out, turning his head away from Isobel as he did so. 'Watercolours. We paint in watercolours. Only the English do it superbly. The French tried it in the eighteenth century – but they simply produced pale oil paintings. The Americans had a go in the nineteenth – but they were never very original. The Japanese do it – but again their watercolours are scarcely any different from their paintings in other materials. No: English watercolours are unique, in subject matter, in technique and in quality. It must therefore be a distillation of Englishness.' He tugged at an eyebrow. 'Next question: what does it show?'

Isobel said nothing.

'Delicacy. A concentration on landscape. Few firm outlines. Impressions. Few people. The English are always called literary, cold, unemotional. Not true. The colours in watercolours are promiscuous – look at Turner or Constable. But everything else is hinted at. Nothing is rubbed in. The forms have few outlines – and are indistinct anyway. The pictures capture a *mood* but within the picture nothing has any real substance. It's as if nothing is trusted. The lack of people in watercolours is the biggest give-away of all. They prove that the English look outwards, not inwards, and we only do that with the minimum conviction. Art, whether it's painting, literature or music, seeks to give comfort. Or at least it thinks it does. Some people think that the comfort of art is only transitory – that the beauty of a phrase or a tune vanishes as soon as it's uttered. They are more right than everyone else but still wrong. The truth is that there is *no* comfort. Riffle through any book of quotations – you can find hundreds of occasions where one fine epigram cancels out another. Oscar Wilde said that was the definition of truth – when the opposite was true also. I think that, just this once, Oscar had it upside-down. Both epigrams may *sound* beautiful but they can't both be true. Without truth there can be no comfort. Bleak, eh?

'The English are not so much cold as solitary, suspicious and disdainful of groups. The reason there are so few people in English watercolours is that the English have no psychology, no *collective* psychology anyway. That's why you can't sum them – us – up as easily as other nations. That's one reason why psychology as a medical discipline – psychiatry – has never caught on here as it has in other countries. We are not cold so much as *unformed* emotionally. We don't need comfort as much as other nationalities.'

'You can tell all this from watercolours?'

He grinned. 'I'm exaggerating, of course. But watercolours are an odd, wonderful art form and they *are* peculiarly English. They need to be explained. Now, I've been talking too much.'

'No, no, not at all. I can't be truly English, though, because I *am* interested in people. Your family, for instance.'

'I've an older sister who married a New Zealand eye specialist. I have two nieces, one of whom is my goddaughter. She says I'm her second favourite godparent. The younger sister, I told you about. My father died five years ago and my mother lives in War- wickshire now, just outside Stratford-on-Avon.'

'And women?'

'One. One serious woman, anyway, apart from the varnished vamps who seem to gravitate to the art world.'

'Tell me about the "serious" one. How long did it last?'

'Five years. Her name was Sylvie and she was half French. She was an archaeologist – but she was a scuba diver too so she specialised in underwater excavations. Sunken ships off Italy, Greece, Turkey mainly.'

'How did you meet?'

'A lunch party at Bodrum in Turkey. I was on holiday and she was working there. We were put together at the table because the hosts thought we would get on. Then we met by accident at the opening of an exhibition back in London. Three weeks later, Sylvie moved into Justice Walk.'

'That was quick. Why did you split up?'

'There wasn't one reason. Is there ever? Just lots of little reasons. We did have a big disagreement, though. At the time I was working in the auction business, as I think I told you. There was a sale of antiquities which included some vases from southern Italy. Sylvie said they had been stolen and smuggled out of the country.'

'How did she know?'

'That was the point. Though she was certain, she couldn't prove it. Apparently there's a big catalogue published by an Oxford scholar which lists and illustrates all legitimately excavated vases. Thousands of them. By definition, if a vase is not in the catalogue, it must have been illegally excavated – and smuggled.

'Sylvie thought the auction house should refuse to sell the vases. She wanted me to lead a campaign to stop it. She said an auction house couldn't be seen to condone theft and I agreed. I even raised it in the office. But it wasn't my department and I was overruled. Sylvie got very angry, with the auction house and with me. She thought I should have resigned, but I didn't. Things were never the same between us after that. It was the beginning of the end. She moved out about a month later. She's living in Greece now, so I hear.'

He looked at Isobel. 'The funny thing is, I don't really know why she went. I don't think there was someone else. She never explained and we never discussed it. I never understood.'

'Perhaps you never put yourself in her skin enough. Women *like* to be understood, Michael. They find it comforting. You say there's no comfort. That may be true of art but it's not true of relationships. Men too often think of control. If they give it up from time to time, they think they're diminished, in the eyes of others as well as in their own. Maybe the vase auction was a test.' Isobel leaned forward. 'This *is* a wager I'll make with you. I'll bet that, if you *had* offered to resign, Sylvie would have told you to withdraw it. She just wanted you to feel your way into her skin for a moment, for as long as it took to show that you knew how to comfort her.' Isobel sat back again and gripped the stem of her wineglass. 'You're like many men, Michael. You enjoy your job but I wonder if you actually *like* women. You probably think that you want equality from a woman when in fact what you want is compliance.'

'You can tell all that from old vases?'

She smiled.

Michael was silent. What she had said hurt. Did that mean she had guessed right? He *did* think he treated women as equal, had always prided himself on it. He pulled heavily on his cigar and then breathed out long and hard, trying to relax himself. Relax? He hadn't realised he was keyed up. Isobel had really got to him. He looked at her. She was smiling very faintly but her expression was really a quizzical one and that angle in her eyebrow was more sardonic than ever. She was wondering whether she had hit home. Michael wasn't sure he enjoyed being understood so well. Then, with a jolt, he realised that was what equality was all about.

Whether or not Isobel could see his discomfort, she helped him out. 'Do you miss not having a regular woman in your life?'

141

'Sometimes. Being an art dealer carries with it, if you want, a heavy social life. It would be nice to share that. On the other hand, a spare man is always in demand.'

'And children? Do you miss not having them?'

'No. Not yet. I'm only thirty-three, you know. My "sell-by" date hasn't expired just yet. You?'

'I *do* miss them a bit, mmm. But with Tony . . . it's been difficult.'

Later that night they played chess again. Though Isobel won for the second time, it wasn't such an easy victory – Michael learned fast. There was a new easiness between them now. They sat up late, talking in between moves, laughing at each other's mistakes on the chessboard, having an extra calvados. When they went upstairs, it was just after one. They said goodnight in the corridor and Michael leaned forward and kissed Isobel lightly on the cheek. She did not resist.

8

Next day they started slowly. A long breakfast was accompanied by all the newspapers. But then, around 10.30, Michael steered the hired car south, into Constable country.

They made for East Bergholt, and Dedham, and the Stour Valley, scene of so many Constable landscapes. They found Gun Hill and looked down to Flatford Mill and Judas Gap. The river looped its slow way east, black as liquorice. Next they headed west and slightly north, to Sudbury, where they visited Gainsborough's house. After lunch they headed north to Norwich, to visit Cotman's house and gallery in the castle, where scores of Norwich School paintings were on view. They returned by way of Lowestoft, where many of Turner's coastal abstractions and cloud studies were produced. Today, however, there were no clouds. The sunny weather continued and the uninterrupted light, sweeping across the fens, brought with it a luminous magic that not even Michael had seen before. Every blade of grass, every stem of corn, every feather of every bird, seemed brighter than before, clearer, as if seen through some magical magnifying glass. Waves beat on the beaches in an explosion of sunlight. For the moment even Molyneux was forgotten.

On their way back, they crossed the River Waveney at Beccles Marshes. On either side, the Broads stretched away, shimmering black, glazed with honey.

'Michael!' Isobel cried out suddenly. 'Why don't we do that tomorrow? You've taught me such a lot today. It was marvellous.

Why don't we hire a boat for the day, and I'll take you boating? As a thank you?'

'Terrific – if it's sunny. But if it's raining, forget it.'

'Done!' she said, thrilled by the prospect.

That night they did not eat in the hotel but at a small fish restaurant by the harbour. The halibut, which they both chose, was very fresh and simply grilled with butter and parsley. Michael was delighted to find that the restaurant had an excellent cellar and chose a Pouilly-Fumé to go with the fish. Afterwards they decided to return to the hotel for more chess and calvados but not before they had strolled around the harbour and watched some of the fishing boats putting out to sea to catch the tide. Out along the jetty it was breezy and Michael took off his jacket and put it around Isobel's shoulders. He lit a last cigar. In the night air its smoke was quickly lost in the sea breeze. That night, when they parted, Michael kissed Isobel's cheek once more.

Next morning, Isobel knocked on Michael's door at eight o'clock.

'It's Sunday, for God's sake!'

'And it's lovely!' she shouted back. 'The Broads – remember? Hurry up, slowbones. I'm going down to breakfast. I want to be on the water by ten. If you're not ready, I shall go without you.'

Shaking the sleep from his head, Michael dragged himself out from under the sheets, shaved, showered, and was in the breakfast room by half past eight. 'Banshee!' he said, his face set in a mock-serious frown. 'I was having such a sexy dream.'

She ignored this. 'I ordered for you. We had fish last night, so no kippers. And no eggs – we had an omelette on Friday. Bacon, sausage, tomatoes, that's what you're getting.'

'What I need is some juice.'

'Over there, on that table. Help yourself.'

He went to a sideboard where the jugs of juice were kept. He poured a glass, drained it and filled it again. He returned to their table. 'I'm not used to being organised in this way,' he said, enjoying every minute. 'Is this a side to you I haven't seen before, Field-bloodyMarshal Sadler?'

'Probably. But if we *are* going on a boat there's no point unless we make a reasonably early start. Boats move slowly, don't forget, so if you want to see the countryside you need more time than in a car.'

She forced the pace throughout breakfast so that they were out of the hotel by five to nine. They reached Lowestoft before nine-thirty and soon found the basin where the boats for the Broads were berthed. Michael was only just beginning to wake up.

At the office there was already a small queue of people who had had the same idea and had beaten them to it. Michael was forced to admit that Isobel was right about one thing. By the time they reached the head of the queue, the line behind them was three times as long as when they had arrived.

Since there were only two of them, they didn't need a large boat. 'Still, we might as well get one with a cabin and a loo,' said Isobel. 'You can never tell with the English weather.'

Michael was amused by Isobel's ferocious energy and her organis-ing capacity. 'I can now imagine what you're like, down on the farm,' he said, grinning as he clambered down into the boat. 'Is this how you treat the animals?'

'Only the goats and the donkeys. Now hold this,' she said, hand-ing him a rope. 'When the engine has been started and I give you the word, unwrap it from that metal ring and just let go.'

In conjunction with the boatman, who was explaining everything to her, Isobel got the engine going and, with a skill that even the boatman admired, had the craft free of the jetty and the other boats in no time and with the minimum of fuss.

'You'll be all right, miss,' called the boatman from the bank. 'See you tonight.'

Isobel steered gently out of the basin, juggling her way cleverly in and out between other boats that were moving in the same general direction. Then came a section of river, a sort of canal, which ran through the less attractive parts of Lowestoft. It was narrow just here, with the backs of houses and small workshops or factories on either side. Since it was still relatively early, the canal was mostly in shade and cool.

Isobel shivered. 'Can you look out the map? The man said there's one in the main cabin.'

'Going below,' shouted Michael, laughing. Isobel's bossiness was

145

quite new but he liked it. He found the map and went back to where Isobel stood by the wheel. They were now coming out of the town and into open countryside. Sunshine flooded in on all sides.

'Isn't this relaxing?' said Isobel, holding her face to the sun. 'That sound of water slapping against the boat. Comforting, being the centre of all that attention.'

'Any duty-free on this tub?' Michael asked. 'I've only got two cigars.'

'No, but we can make for Havana, if you like.'

They examined the map and decided to sail in a big circle, following the River Waveney as far as Haddiscoe, then along the New Cut to Reedham, where there was a swing bridge and a pub where they might have lunch. After that, they would sail through Reedham Marshes and look at the windmills, as far as Burgh Castle, where Breydon Water started. Finally they would return past Waveney Forest and the remains of St Olave's Priory.

By now the traffic was spreading out as some of the other boats turned down different reaches of water. Soon they had long stretches of the Broads to themselves.

'It beats roads,' said Isobel. 'No traffic light, no cones, no jams, no police.'

'No pubs yet, either.'

'Philibloodystine.' She laughed. 'Like some coffee?'

'What? This tub has Pullman service?'

'You bet. It's in my bag over there. I brought a thermos from the hotel.'

With the coffee Michael finally came round. Afterwards he lounged on the seat watching the flat countryside go by, listening to the ducks and moorhens, feeling the sun on his face and the backs of his hands. He watched Isobel steering and imagined her body moving under her shirt.

They chugged past an old construction which Michael saw from the map was known as Black Mill. Some words of Constable came to mind: 'Old rotten banks, slimy posts, and brick works. I love such things.'

The golden morning passed slowly by. The soft breeze, carrying with it the smell of the sea, not so far off, kept the day from becoming too warm. Michael was given a turn at the wheel, during which time Isobel took off her shoes and hitched up her skirt again to give her legs some sun.

Shortly after twelve they sighted the swing bridge at Reedham. As they passed underneath it, Michael saw beyond, at the end of a bend, a ferry and a white-painted pub, The Ferryman. 'Aha! Right on cue. Rum break.'

Isobel supervised the mooring. Then, when they were safely tied up, Michael jumped ashore and went to buy some drinks. He came out to find Isobel sitting on the bank, her legs again displayed to the sun.

'I bought cider. It brought us good luck last time.'

'Mmm.' Isobel had her eyes closed. She opened them, took the glass, drank, then closed her eyes again and lay back. 'Amazing how a day like this bleaches all your problems.' She spoke to the air.

Michael lay alongside her. 'Don't get used to it. Monday tomorrow; back to Helen's.'

She reached over to slap him. Michael caught her wrist and held it. For a moment they lay, with him holding her arm. Then, but not immediately, she disengaged herself.

They lay in the sun till Michael ordered lunch, sandwiches and cold chicken drumsticks. Isobel hadn't moved when he came back. In fact, he thought she was asleep until she said, 'God, I feel lazy.'

He knelt down by her and held a drumstick over her, just above her mouth. 'Here you are.'

She opened her eyes, then parted her lips.

Michael lowered the drumstick till she could grip it with her teeth. For a moment she nibbled at it while he held it. Then, when the grease from the chicken began to settle around her lips, she lifted a hand and took the remains from him.

During the afternoon the sunshine continued and they wound their way sleepily past Berney Arms Mill, Churchfarm Marshes, Howard's Common, Seven Mile House. They saw eel fishers at Somerleyton and a kingfisher in Oulton Dyke. They saw two huge, white carthorses drinking water. Near Wheatacre Marshes, Michael inspected the map. 'You know, in about a mile we shall be very close to Aldeby, where Helen Sparrow's studio is. I wonder how she's getting on, whether she's come up with anything yet.'

In reply, Isobel accelerated. 'Let's get past as quickly as possible. I don't want to think about tomorrow until tomorrow.'

Around six, they found themselves in Oulton Broad and entering Lowestoft. Other boats were heading in too and they had to slow down. They were both sitting by the wheel now.

When they reached the basin, the boatman saw them coming and moved forward to direct them where to berth the boat. 'You can't get next to the jetty,' he shouted. 'Pull alongside those boats there, then climb ashore over the other craft.'

Isobel brought the boat very neatly alongside, so slowly that Michael was easily able to clamber on to the other boats between them and the jetty. He handed the boatman the rope which Isobel had given him, then he went back to help her.

A bigger launch was now nosing into the basin but its helmsman had little of the skill Isobel had shown. Just as she was climbing from one boat to another, the launch nudged the outside deck of the boat she was leaving. Isobel was surprised – she had her back to the basin – and she missed her footing.

'Watch out!' Michael cried, seeing what was happening. He leaped forward to catch her. Just in time he managed to grab her as one of her legs slipped against the gunwhale of the middle boat of the three tied alongside each other. One arm grabbed Isobel's elbow, the other he threw around her waist and pulled her to him. At that moment, and while he was still trying to keep his own balance, Michael was suddenly filled with an immense sexual longing, stronger than he could remember. The full impact of touching Isobel, feeling the muscles of her stomach under her shirt, the smell of her, released inside him a burst of sensual energy that only now he realised had been held in for so long. He wanted to ravish her.

Instead, now that the danger was over, he bent to examine her leg which had slipped on the gunwhale and scraped the skin. It was painful and unsightly but not serious.

'You'll live. What you need for that is more halibut, I'd say. Shall we go to the same restaurant tonight?'

Isobel nodded. 'But I'd like to bathe this first.'

That night, at dinner, she had a surprise for him. 'There's really only one thing more peaceful than what we did today.'

Michael was tempted to respond in his own way, but held his tongue. 'Oh yes?'

'Mmm. Parachuting.'

'You've done it?'

'Eighteen times.'

'Don't you need to be just a little bit crazy to do that sort of thing?'

'I hope you're wrong. I knew a man before Tony who had been in the parachute brigade. The first two or three times were a bit scary – and my father was very much against it. But that only made me more determined.' She grinned. 'But nothing ever went wrong. Drifting down on a sunny day like today, feeling the breeze swish past you . . . I suppose that most of the time we associate a sinking feeling with bad things. But when you parachute you just go on sinking and sinking and sinking. It's not like flying at all. You're amazed at how much air there is, at how high the sky can be.'

They left the restaurant to find that, as on the night before, the air had turned quite cool. Isobel had brought a sweater with her this time, but even so she shivered.

'Shall we walk to the end of the quay, like last night?' said Michael. 'Or are you cold?'

'I'm cold. But let's do it all the same. You can smoke there without doing too much damage.'

They strolled along the quay without speaking. Michael took out a cigar and licked the end. His thoughts drifted back again to Isobel's fall earlier in the day. He wanted to lick her. Cables slapped on the masts of moored yachts as if applauding his thoughts. With difficulty, he got his cigar going: the breeze coming off the sea was now quite strong. Isobel shivered again and Michael put his arm around her shoulders.

The end of the quay had a small lighthouse. They stood near it and watched as a ship steamed steadily out of the harbour, the dark, mysterious silhouettes of its crew already busy, bending and pulling and winding.

'Look,' said Michael, pointing. 'They don't seem at all aware of how romantic they are. Where do you think they're going? Leningrad? Santiago? Piraeus?'

Isobel looked up at him. 'Newcastle?' She smiled.

149

Michael kissed her as she smiled. He kissed her more forcefully than he had meant to, but all the longing he had been feeling earlier was there, and now saw its chance.

Though surprised by the force of his kiss, Isobel soon responded. She kissed him back but she also began to run her fingers over his shoulders, beneath his jacket. 'I'm not trying to undress you,' she said after a moment. 'But could I borrow your blazer. I'm freezing.'

He laughed, took it off, and wrapped it around her shoulders. Then they walked back down the quay and round the harbour. Two more ships were preparing to leave, the men shouting to each other, operating winches and clanging and banging on metal. The smell of sea water and fish was now mixed with diesel oil and cigar smoke.

Outside the hotel they stood for a moment, watching again the lights of the fishing boats as they moved out to sea. Isobel stroked Michael's hand. 'Tonight,' she whispered, 'even Newcastle seems romantic.'

Michael leaned his body against hers and kissed the top of Isobel's head. Then he led her into the hotel.

At reception he was handed his key but was surprised to find a piece of paper with it. 'A message for you, sir,' said the man at the desk.

Michael unfolded the paper and stared at the writing.

'What is it?' asked Isobel.

Michael began moving to the hotel stairs. 'It's from Helen,' he whispered. 'It says to call her. Urgently.'

'The painting's gone!'

'Helen, no! Please God, no.' Michael groaned into the phone. 'You mean stolen?'

'Michael, I'm so sorry. It was all my fault. I finished what you asked around teatime this afternoon. It was such a lovely day . . .'

Yes it was, thought Michael. But not any more.

'. . . and one of the local gardens is open to the public. Just today, I mean. I went for a quick peek. I was gone an hour, no more. And I locked up. But when I got back this man had broken in – '

'You saw him?'

150

'Yes, and no. Yes, he was still here when I came back and I disturbed him. But I didn't see his face. He was wearing a motor-cycle helmet – '

'Helen! Stay there, we're coming over. Tell us the rest then. We'll tell you what it's all about. I'm sorry, too, for putting you at risk. Very sorry . . . There's something I should have told you . . . Look, it will take us ten minutes to check out, twenty-five minutes in the car. Hold on!'

Michael banged down the phone and started to grab his clothes. As he did so he relayed to Isobel what Helen had told him.

'A helmet!' gasped Isobel.

'How on earth did he find us?' Michael growled through his teeth as he stuffed shirts into his suitcase. 'We were so damn careful. Did he follow you, or me?'

'I'm certain he didn't get off the train with me,' said Isobel, thinking back. 'There were only three others, I remember it clearly. You don't think he was in disguise, do you? Oh, Michael!' Isobel brushed his cheek with her fingers but then went to her room to pack her suitcase. Michael wracked his brains for the weak link in his plan. He was certain Molyneux hadn't been on his train.

Downstairs, the receptionist was surprised they were checking out so late and assumed they had had a fight. They had to pay for the night they were going to miss but neither of them gave a thought for that. They were soon in the car.

Michael headed north on the Lowestoft road, then turned off at Wrentham. The rented car wasn't anywhere near as nippy as his Mercedes but at that hour – nearly 11.30 – there was little traffic, the road was flat and straight and they made good time. They arrived at Helen's just before midnight.

The stables were a blaze of light and, as soon as she heard the car, Helen came out to meet them.

'This has never happened before,' she said without preamble as they climbed the stairs. 'I'm so sorry, Michael.'

'What happened, Helen? Are you all right? He didn't hurt you, did he?' As he said this, Michael was startled to see, beyond the doorway, that the studio was in chaos. 'You had a fight?'

Helen nodded. 'More of a scuffle, really. He was hiding behind the door when I came back, and grabbed me. He was very tall and

151

strong. He was wearing big motor-cycle gloves and gripped my flesh – here.' She held out her forearms for Isobel and Michael to see a row of purple bruises.

'What happened then?' Isobel looked drawn.

'We struggled. I kicked him. I got one arm free and threw some turps over him.'

'Did you see his face at all?'

'Not really. His helmet had a dark visor. I grabbed some brushes and tried to poke him where it might hurt.'

Despite themselves, Isobel and Michael smiled

'And . . . ?'

'It didn't work. He forced me back into the kitchen and locked me in. Then he left with the picture. That was about five o'clock this afternoon.'

'So how long were you locked up?'

'Nearly four hours. I had to unscrew the entire lock and dismantle it with a knife. The screws were old and rusty and the knife kept buckling. I phoned you as soon as I could.'

Michael took out a cigar but didn't light it. Instead, he fingered it as he explained to Helen about the Landscape and Molyneux. She listened, growing more intrigued as the story wound on. 'So you see why I'm sorry, Helen. We thought it was good security not to tell you anything. But if we had done you might not have gone out and you would never have been hurt.'

Helen waved a hand. 'I'm still in one piece, Michael. If I'd been here the whole time, it might have been worse. He was a very strong man.'

'How did he find you? That's what I don't understand,' said Michael. 'We were so careful, we even came on separate trains as far as Cambridge.'

'I think I can answer that,' said Helen, moving to the mantelshelf. She picked up a piece of paper. 'He dropped this in the scuffle.' She handed it to Michael. 'It's an invoice I sent you. It has my address on it.'

Michael took the paper and stared at the heading. In black capitals it said, 'HELEN SPARROW FINE ART: PICTURE RESTORATION AND CLEANING', and gave her address, phone number and VAT number. Michael breathed quietly. 'He could only have got this by breaking

152

into Justice Walk.' His mind went back to that late-night figure he had seen in Lawrence street. Oh no!'

They stood in silence, staring at the remains of the picked lock on the kitchen door.

After an interval, Michael said, softly, 'Have you called the police?'

'No.'

'I'd better do it now. Burglary, assault, theft. That must constitute an entire crime wave in Aldeby.' He moved to the phone.

'Michael, hold on.' Isobel spoke in barely more than a whisper. 'Helen, why didn't you call the police? That would have been *my* first reaction.'

Helen hesitated, then smiled sheepishly at Isobel. 'It's your picture, your property that's been stolen. So if you want to report it I can't stop you. But, from my point of view . . . well, if I go to the police, it might get out . . . other people might not send me pictures if they think I'm a security risk.' She looked across to Michael. 'I know you have lost a painting and I'm mortified about that. I know you'll never send me any more business . . . but . . . but I'm not really hurt. A few scratches and bruises. I can tidy up the studio in a couple of hours. The kitchen doesn't really need a lock anyway.' She looked at Isobel, then was silent for a moment. 'Unless you have to report the theft, I would rather not report the break-in or the assault.'

Helen sank into a chair, not meeting anyone's eyes. There was silence in the room.

Michael was the first to break it. 'I'm sorry, Helen. I sympathise with what you say. But we must report the theft. Two thefts, one here and, almost certainly, one at my house. I don't know if he took anything else but we've to get that picture back. That's what the police are for – '

'I agree with Helen,' Isobel cut in.

'What? But – '

Isobel interrupted again. 'Listen, Michael. It's late, you've had some drinks and your brain's not in fast-forward, as you would say. In the first place, we exposed Helen to this attack. She was put at risk, bruised and locked up because of *us*. Therefore, if she wants us to do something for her in return, the very least we can do is listen to her. But forget her problem with the bad publicity. You can forget the burglary in London too. Molyneux broke into your car and took nothing, so I bet all he stole from your house was that invoice, that tiny piece of paper with the information he wanted – ' Michael tried to interrupt but she waved him down. 'Listen to me for a moment. Don't forget that the painting is mine and, if I don't want to report it missing, it's my decision. In any case, what are we going to tell the police? Will they believe us? The picture is only valuable theoretically. We don't know if Molyneux is his real name and neither Helen nor you has ever seen him.'

'They'll believe all this chaos. They have records of the aliases that criminals use.'

'Michael! You know perfectly well that Molyneux is no ordinary thief.'

'We have a picture of the painting. The police could circulate it.'

'But Molyneux's not going to sell it, is he? He can just sit on it until we lose interest. Assume he *is* a known criminal, that Molyneux is even an alias known to the police. Say they question him. He was wearing motor-cycle gloves so there are no fingerprints here, we can't identify him and he will simply hide the picture until everyone has forgotten this business, then quietly start up all over again.'

'But we can't just do nothing.'

'That's not what I am suggesting,' said Isobel. 'We haven't asked Helen the most important question yet.' Isobel turned. 'When you cleaned the picture, what did you find?'

Helen was relieved to be talking about something else. 'I started on the patch of grime at the foot of the column just so I could get used to the picture. Then I cleaned that face you mentioned, with spirit . . . it was interesting because there was a small pear-shaped tear under the grime, tiny but an exquisite pearl of water. Then I had a go at the area you specifically asked to be cleaned.'

'And . . . ?'

'I found two things. The first was very curious. The monk, the monk with no face, in fact didn't have feet either, or not ordinary feet. They were furry with sharp bits, pointed, like claws really.'

'And second?'

'In front of this monk, directly in front of the sharp toes, was a stone slab, a floor-tile really. Hexagonal, with a design on it.'

'What sort of design?'

Helen shook her head. 'It was too vague to make out. Sorry.'

'Damn,' hissed Michael.

'No, that needn't matter,' said Isobel. 'Think. Maybe the vagueness of the tile is deliberate. Remember, the monk is dressed in a Franciscan habit, Michael. It directed us to Lewell Monastery. That must be where the tile is. There must be a floor-tile at Lewell which has the design clearly etched. That design contains the next clue. Don't you see, Michael, Molyneux has to go *back* to Lewell.'

Michael stared at her. He was experiencing a mix of emotions he had never felt together before. Admiration, for Isobel's cleverness. An unease at her disregard for the police – she'd picked that up as a journalist in foreign parts, he assumed. And the way that she stood in the studio, her skin aglow with the fire that now burned inside her, as she thought it all through, brought back the sexual longing that had been extinguished with the message to call Helen.

Isobel continued. 'Which means,' she said, half smiling, half grimacing, 'that *we* have to leave for Dorset right away. Molyneux has a four- or five-hour start, maybe a bit more. He won't know exactly how much time he has over us because he won't know how soon Helen freed herself or how quickly she got on to us. That's our one chance. He can't have got to Lewell before dark and, if he feels safe enough, he may prefer to leave his search for the tile until daylight tomorrow.' Isobel looked at her watch. 'It's now coming up to half past midnight. From here to Dorset will take . . . what? . . . five or six hours in the dark?'

Michael nodded.

'Are you ready?'

'Just like that? You want to leave, just like that? We arrived barely half an hour ago, Helen's been attacked and locked up, for God's sake . . . we can't just leave her.'

Isobel looked at Helen and smiled. 'Helen's in better shape than you are, Michael. At least mentally. And the best thing you can do for her is not sit here and mollycoddle her. All she wants from you is an assurance that you don't need to go to the police. Right?'

Helen smiled and nodded. 'Your man Molyneux's not going to

155

come back here, is he? I'll go to bed and tidy up tomorrow. Don't worry about me, Michael. I'm exhausted and I'll sleep like a baby. I just hope you get your picture back. Go on, Michael, get going. Isobel's right. It's your one chance to catch him now. The more you delay, the more likely it is that you'll miss him. Phone me tomorrow some time and let me know what happened. *Move!*'

Reluctantly, Michael allowed himself to be led outside to the top of the stairs. 'If Molyneux were to come back, I'd never forgive myself – '

'He won't,' hissed Helen, and gave him a gentle shove.

Inside the car he flashed the headlights as a farewell and nosed out into Aldeby High Street. There was no sign of movement. Michael judged that it was quicker, at that hour, to stick to motorways, rather than cut directly across country. By twenty to three they were west of London, had reached the M3 and were hurrying past Runnymede. It began to rain. Then it began to teem – so bad it was dangerous to travel at more than seventy. Michael managed eighty for most of the way. They were both on edge and barely spoke. Stonehenge flashed by, barely visible in the rain. Around Sherborne it began to get light. They approached Higher Lewell just after half past five. It was still raining.

They pulled up alongside the monastery. 'No sign of anyone?' said Michael, twisting round in his seat to survey the ruin. 'Are we too late or too early, I wonder.'

'Let's hide the car,' said Isobel. 'Then find a place where we can keep a lookout while one of us hunts for the tile.'

They drove on a little. About a third of a mile beyond the village there was a barn set back slightly from the road. Michael was able to manoeuvre the car behind it. The farmer who owned the land would hardly be pleased, if he were to notice, but at least the car couldn't be seen from the road.

They walked back.

'What's our plan?' said Michael.

'One of us keeps a lookout, in case we *are* ahead of Molyneux. The other searches for the stone slab or tile.'

'Okay. You do the searching.'

They reached the entrance to the monastery, where there was a stone arch standing all by itself. Michael hovered there, where he could see the road in both directions. The rain gusted against the walls of the monastery, forming dark, whisky-coloured stains of damp. The wind whipped tiny waves on the puddles in the road. Michael used the arch for what shelter he could but even so the rain had soon numbed his cheeks. He glanced at his watch. He had been waiting nearly fifteen minutes. How many stone slabs could there be, for Christ's sake –

Suddenly, he heard a car engine.

He looked west, in the direction of the sound. In the distance, a dark blue van was coming towards him. He turned and swiftly followed the path inside the monastery, calling softly, 'Isobel! Car!'

He hid in what was left of the nave. There was no sign of Isobel.

He heard the blue van approach. Then it stopped. Michael couldn't see where but it must be nearby. Had Molyneux seen him as he ran to hide? Was he coming the rest of the way on foot so as to take them by surprise? Didn't Molyneux travel by motor-cycle anyway? Michael shivered, not simply from the cold.

He heard footsteps. They stopped. They started again. Then the van door slammed and its engine sprang to life. It seemed very loud in the morning air. Moments later the van flashed by and Michael was just able to read 'Devon & Dorset Dairy' on the side. It was the milkman.

Relaxing, he took out a cigar. He was just about to light it when he heard more footsteps, much closer this time. He tensed. A voice said, 'Michael?'

It was Isobel.

He stepped forward and looked to his left. She was standing half obscured by another doorway and she was beckoning. He walked towards her. As he approached, she retreated beyond the door and he followed her across what had once been the north transept. She stopped, her head bent and her eyes looking at the ground in front of her feet. Michael stood at her side.

'There,' she breathed, pointing.

Michael looked down, 'You're right,' he said. 'Shhhit! We've been left at the gate.'

The floor of the transept was covered with stone slabs – except that one had recently been dug up. The earth it had covered was still fresh and the scratch marks at the edges of the adjoining stones were only too visible.

'That's what our monk was looking at.'

'And it contained a clue.'

'Yes. Whatever was carved on it helps with the next figure.'

They both stood in the rain, staring at the ground.

Isobel said, 'He came straight here.'

'Yes. We should never have doubted that. We're dealing with an obsessive mind here. He takes no chances. And he dug up the stone, like he stole the pamphlets, so we can't follow him '

They trudged silently back to the car. The summer rain still fell, clattering on the barn roof like stampeding horses.

As he nosed the car out from behind the barn, Michael said, 'A slow trip back to London, I think. I don't know about you but I'm feeling fairly whacked. We can have breakfast on the way and think about what we're going to do now. It's still not too late to call in the police, though I think we might as well leave that till we've seen what damage Molyneux did at Justice Walk.'

'Who *is* Molyneux, for Lord's sake? I wonder how many Molyneuxs there are in the phone book?'

'What's the point? We don't know that he lives in London and, as you yourself said, we don't even know if it's his real name.'

'Didn't I read somewhere that criminals give themselves the same initials and the same first name, so that, if they bump into someone they know, that other person won't give the game away?'

'Maybe you did. But I can't see what use it is.'

'No, I'm just thinking out loud in case it provokes an idea in your head. If his name isn't Molyneux, why did he choose it? Isn't it an Irish name? Maybe he's Irish.'

'Hmm. Could be. We could ask around along those lines, I suppose. Might do some good. I can try Sotheby's again.'

'It's so frustrating, not knowing what sort of person you are up against. It's like jungle warfare.'

'No bacon and sausage in the jungle,' said Michael, turning into the car park of The Lamb at Hindon. 'Breakfast.'

They were both ravenous and devoured everything that was put before them. They felt better physically but that was as far as it went. On the rest of the way back to London they were quiet. The

158

rain was clearing, the day was brightening, but it looked as though their adventure was over. Isobel was thinking about going back to the farm and didn't want to do it. The mood of the previous evening, when they had both been preparing to spend the night together in Southwold, had entirely evaporated.

Michael switched on the car radio, so that they could catch up with the news. Save for one item it was the usual diet: Beirut, Belfast and brothels still making the headlines. The exception was an announcement from Los Angeles that the actress Miss Margaret Masson was to be married again. This time the lucky man was Dr Edward Whicker, a plastic surgeon. A wedding in a matter of days was anticipated.

Michael cheered in a lacklustre way. He was £500 richer. 'That's fifty of my favourite cigars,' he said, trying to make a joke of it.

Isobel punched him on the shoulder but her heart wasn't in it. The good news only highlighted their plight over the Landscape of Lies.

Isobel went with Michael to Justice Walk. She wanted to see what damage Molyneux had inflicted when he had burgled the house. She had been right. There was no damage save for a window in the basement which had a small hole cut out of it and by means of which Molyneux had got in. Inside the house the only signs of disturbance were at Michael's desk. 'He knew we had to have the painting cleaned,' said Michael, staring at the invoices from Helen which were scattered over the study. 'If he did follow us on Friday and saw us leave by train he knew he had a clear run here. He out-thought us. Once he found these invoices, it was a fair bet that's where one of us had gone. He probably got to Helen's a few hours after we did and let her finish the cleaning before he broke in. More snake than fox, eh?' Michael looked at Isobel. 'I'll bet there are no fingerprints on the window downstairs and that he let himself out by the front door. He's messed up my papers but nothing is missing except one slip of paper. You're right, it's not even worth mentioning to the police.'

She retrieved her suitcase from the hire car and took a taxi to Montpelier Mews. They were both exhausted and she wouldn't let him drive her. They planned to sleep until evening, then have a late supper together and decide what to do.

After Isobel had gone, Michael found the house very empty. He recalled fondly the breakfast of Isobel's which he had enjoyed the previous Friday. Feeling sorry for himself, he turned to the only comfort available. He lit himself a cigar and, despite the early hour, poured a Laphroaig.

Then, with his hands full in the way he liked, he sat by the telephone answering machine and played back his messages. His mother had called. The Australian collector had phoned from Sydney, wanting to discuss the Gainsborough. Ed McCrystal had called to congratulate him on winning the Margaret Masson bet and adding that another wager was in the wind – would he please call back soonest. And Julius Samuels had rung. The portrait was ready, he said. There was no coat of arms in the picture but plenty of jewellery. That was good news. The bad news was that Julius's daughter had given birth to a son in Australia and he was taking six weeks off to visit the child. He might even retire when he got back.

Involuntarily, as the Landscape of Lies project appeared to be going off the boil, Michael found his mind turning back to the other deals the gallery was involved in. The Gainsborough, for instance. If the Australian was calling all the way from Sydney that seemed to indicate he intended to buy – good news. And, now that Julius had finished the nineteenth-century portrait, maybe Michael could put a name to the face. It was a pity there was no coat of arms but you couldn't have everything and the jewellery would help. If he *could* identify the woman that would boost the price significantly – more good news.

Before he went to bed he called Helen. There was no reply. Probably having lunch somewhere, he thought. Trying to pretend that nothing had happened.

He went up to bed. He stared at the Cozens for a few moments. As he put out what was left of the cigar, Michael reflected that it didn't look as though he was going to know Isobel Sadler any better. So far as their relationship was concerned, nothing *had* happened.

He was wakened by the peal of the phone. At first he was perplexed by the light. It didn't *feel* like morning. Then he remembered: it wasn't.

He groped for the receiver. He hated sleeping in the afternoon and, on holiday, always tried not to, however much he had drunk at lunch. Waking up in the early evening was almost as bad as going to bed in the early evening, as he had been made to do as a child, at just the moment when his parents were getting ready to entertain.

'Hrrgh?'

'Ah! I'd recognise that speech defect anywhere.'

'You sound cheerful. What time is it?'

'Just after seven.'

'Hrrgh.'

'I love it when you talk dirty.'

'I hope no one's listening to this conversation.'

'Is this what passes for conversation in the art world?'

'Did you call for a reason? I know you're bossy on boats but – '

'I want to ask a favour.'

'Hrrgh.'

'Exactly. Michael, can we have a night off?'

He reached for a cigar.

'I've stayed several nights in the mews and I've hardly seen my hosts. They've asked me out to dinner tonight and I ought to accept. I ought to take them out. Otherwise I'll leave tomorrow without repaying any of their hospitality. Nothing is lost if you and I make it lunch tomorrow instead. I don't know what to suggest anyway – do you?'

Michael swung his feet out of bed and on to the floor. 'I'm not awake yet; I don't know.' He couldn't admit he had no suggestions either. He wanted to see Isobel.

'There you are, then. I'll come to the gallery in time for lunch tomorrow.'

Michael reached for the matches. 'I suppose that's all right. I must take the car back – the rental people will be missing it by now. And I should fix the window in the basement.'

'As your friend Lady Bracknell said, "A life crowded with incident".'

'Hrrgh!'

'Have you called Helen yet?'

'No reply.'

'Oh dear, I hope she's okay.'

'I'll try her again, as soon as I've finished talking to you.'

'I'll let you get on then. See you tomorrow, around one.'

Michael hung up feeling unreasonably lonely. Isobel sounded so goddam *cheerful*. Was there some man around that he didn't know about? That only made him more gloomy.

He lit a cigar and drew on it, reflecting on the Cozens as he did so. It usually had a wonderfully settling effect on him but not this time. It was one of the pictures that had been cleaned by Helen. The invoice was among the wad downstairs, one of those Molyneux *hadn't* stolen.

He dialled Helen's number. This time he was relieved to hear her answer on the third ring.

'Helen? Michael Whiting.'

'Oh, it's you. Good. How did it go?'

Michael told her.

'So you're no further forward. Oh, Michael, I'm *so* sorry. I feel it's all my fault – '

'Now you are not to feel that way, Helen. It *wasn't* your fault at all. If anybody is to blame, I am. I underestimated Molyneux. I knew he was cunning and I knew he was nasty. I knew that he had broken into Isobel's house and I should have guessed he might break in here. But I didn't.'

'Will you . . . Michael, will you still be giving me work . . . ?' Helen said it so timidly that Michael realised how important his business was to her.

'Of course I shall. Of course. In fact, I learned this afternoon that Julius has just become a grandfather again. He's off to Oz for a while to see the baby. So I'll be sending you *more* stuff, not less. Don't worry about this Molyneux business. It doesn't change our professional relationship at all. Next time you're in town, though, it wouldn't be a bad idea if you popped into the gallery and took a look at this portrait which Julius has just cleaned. You can see what varnish he has finished it off with. I like the way he does it and so do the punters. If you can do the same I'll be very happy.'

'Fine. I'll come as soon as I can. No problems with Julius, eh? Unlike me.'

'Don't be so down on yourself, Helen. As a matter of fact this picture wasn't at all straightforward. Julius found a Victorian portrait of a woman under a sickly saint and we had hoped to find a coat of arms or a banner which would help identify her. We were out of luck, though. No heraldry at all, unless the jewels she is festooned with are a clue. But that research is my job, not Julius's.' He changed the subject. 'You're sure everything is all well with you? No after-effects? And is the studio all tidied? I called at lunchtime and there was no reply.'

'Yes, everything is straightened out. Don't worry, Molyneux hasn't been back. I had to go out earlier on to deliver a picture to Ipswich museum and that took a couple of hours. So relax, Michael. I'm fine. I've recovered my nerve already, so I can't have been that badly affected. Just keep sending the work.' She laughed, to make light of it.

Michael hung up and got dressed.

The rest of the evening was the most tedious he had known in a long while. First he tackled the basement window. The best he could manage in the circumstances was a cheap print roughly the size of the window-frame tacked on to the wood. Provided it wasn't examined too closely it should be a deterrent.

Returning the rental car to a location where it was not expected did not prove at all easy or at all cheap. In fact, had he had more time it would have been less exorbitant to have driven the damn thing all the way back to Cambridge and caught a train back, first class.

His mood was not improved when he returned home shortly after ten to find a message from Isobel on the answering machine. 'It's eight-thirty and we're at a restaurant near – where are we? – oh yes, Chelsea Wharf. My hosts said they would like to meet you and had you been in you could have joined us. But you're out, too bad. You'll probably go "Hrrgh" when you hear this – sorry. See you tomorrow.'

Michael did not say 'Hrrgh'. He said something else. He then stormed into the kitchen, took a bar of chocolate from the fridge and a bottle of Tormore from the cupboard. He selected a number two Montecristo and an old black and white Rita Hayworth movie. He switched on the movie, kicked off his shoes, poured a whisky

163

and broke off the first of the chocolate. He soaked the chocolate in the whisky and slid it on to his tongue. He stretched himself on the sofa, lit the Montecristo and proceeded to get gloriously, seriously drunk.

9

As often happened when he had drunk too much, Michael awoke very early next day. That also had something to do with the fact that, in his stupor the night before, he had fallen asleep in front of the video, woken, stumbled upstairs and flopped on to the bed without closing the curtains. From soon after 6.30 sunshine streamed into the bedroom.

He dressed, ate a fairly ancient grapefruit, cooked himself some eggs and settled down to read the paper. At a quarter to eight, itching to do something, he washed up, found his jacket and went out into the King's Road in search of a taxi. Only one person in the entire art world was awake and at work at such an hour: Julius Samuels.

As Michael walked up Dover Street, the pavements glittered with the previous day's rain. The pools of water reminded him of his happy Sunday on the Broads. He'd like to drown Molyneux! He climbed the steps to Samuels's studio. It was just after eight o'clock. The old man was already there, his palette, white coat and cigar in place.

'Come for breakfast, have you?' Julius was just pouring the first whisky of the day.

Michael winced but he knew he couldn't refuse. 'Actually, I came to visit a lady,' he said, taking the proffered glass.

'Behind you,' said the old man. 'And she's a cracker, if you ask me.'

Michael turned. She was indeed beautiful. The mane of red hair, which was now revealed in its entirety, was rich, vivid as a vixen's and reached down to the woman's breasts. These too had been lovingly painted, in cream with a hint of honey. Her cleavage was now a scoop of blue glaze, so wispy you wanted to touch it with the tips of your fingers. The bodice of her dress, crimson with a fine gold line running through it, suggested watered silk. The way the dress fought what could be seen of the woman's flesh suggested a frank sensuality. However, the expression in the face was reserved but with an ironic twist in the mouth, suggesting that the woman was well aware of her charms, her powers to disturb men. This series of paradoxes Michael found very erotic and he immediately liked the woman. That was important. It meant he would devote whatever energy it took to research who she was. And Julius's work showed that she *was* somebody. The face showed more than character; it showed a sexual *presence*. No wonder the Victorians had wanted to cover her up.

Michael turned and lifted his glass in a toast to the old restorer. 'She was no saint, Jules. Thank God you spotted her underneath everything else. It will be fun finding out who she is.'

Samuels replaced his whisky glass on the shelf. 'There was no coat of arms, so it won't be easy. But look at what she is holding between her finger and thumb. That might help.'

Michael studied the object in the woman's hand. It looked to him like a small turret. 'What is it?' he asked.

'It looks to me like a chesspiece,' said Julius. 'A castle or a rook.'

'She was a chess player?'

'Maybe. Odd, eh? And no wedding ring but a big bracelet with emeralds.'

Michael examined the bracelet. It was gold, embedded with what appeared to be six emeralds, the size of olives. Samuels might be right. Some old families *were* identified with stones. He'd have to check it out at the College of Arms.

Michael moved near to Julius, to look at the new painting the old man had on the easel. It was a large Canaletto, on its side. Few people saw pictures this way up but for a restorer it often made sense to turn a painting on its side, or even upside-down, if in that way it was easier to treat a piece of sky or the top of a building.

'Nice,' said Michael, sipping his whisky and looking down. Protocol dictated that he could not ask whose painting it was. But he

166

could make an educated guess as to which dealer had sent it to be restored. It sometimes helped to know who had what. Canaletto had worked a lot in England and so Michael needed to know something about him.

He stood for a while, watching the old man at work. Every so often, Julius stopped and wrote down what he was doing in his notebook, or made a tiny drawing. Michael watched as Julius made a little sketch of some chimneys.

'These were painted over,' said the old man. 'Someone in the nineteenth century didn't like the skyline of this picture, and had it changed. I've put them back by removing the sky that was painted over them, and then I touched them up. This drawing shows anyone exactly what I did.'

'Who do you like restoring best?' said Michael, as always full of admiration for Julius's casual demonstration of superb skill.

'The Venetians are the most difficult. They actually mixed their paints on the canvas, unlike the Florentines, who did it on the palette and then put the mixture on with a brush. So it's hard to get the colour *and* the texture right with the Venetians. My own first love is for Reynolds. He prepared some of his colours so badly that a lot of them, especially the flesh tones, have faded.' He looked up at Michael and winked. 'I've put more carmine into more Reynolds portraits than I've had whiskies. Want another?'

Michael patted the old man's shoulder. 'No thanks, Jules. I'll take the picture now, if I may. You'll send the bill?'

Samuels nodded. There was no haggling. He was the best there was and dealers either paid his price or Julius didn't do the work. He knocked a little bit off for Michael because he paid in whisky and because he was a regular customer. But not much.

Out on the street Michael once more found himself smiling. Every encounter with Julius was a joy. He carried the picture easily but didn't walk too fast. It was still only 8.30 and he didn't want to collide with anything or anyone while he had the portrait under his arm: it would damage all too easily.

Turning from Jermyn Street into Duke Street, he stopped to look in Myer's Gallery. They specialised in Italian pictures and there was a Bellotto in the window. Michael admired it. In some ways, he thought, Belloto – Canaletto's nephew – was better than the master.

He reflected that the Canaletto old Julius was treating could have come from this gallery.

He turned into Mason's Yard, let himself into the gallery and took the woman with the cleavage up to his office. Amazingly, Julius's whisky had revived him. Michael lit a cigar and stared at the picture. It was important to *look* at pictures. Too many dealers were too busy to spend time looking at the objects in their charge. There was something about this picture that didn't add up . . .

He had got nowhere in his thinking by nine o'clock, when, feeling suddenly very hungry, he took himself up the road to Fortnum and Mason for another breakfast. The kipper lasted him until nearly ten, when he strolled up Piccadilly and across Leicester Square to the National Portrait Gallery. He wanted the main gallery, not the archive. Conveniently for his purposes, it was laid out chronologically, with the earlier portraits on the top floor and the more recent ones lower down.

He found what he was looking for – the Regency pictures from the late eighteenth and early nineteenth centuries – and stared at the portraits, one by one. There was Nelson's mistress, Emma Hamilton, the various Georges, the poets and writers of the time. And there were some of the great women – Maria Edgeworth, the Gunning sisters, the Countess of Sutherland. Michael concentrated on their jewellery and anything they held in their hands. He was looking for any similarities with the woman old Julius had uncovered, but for his purposes the portraits were inconclusive.

Michael left the gallery and took a taxi to Portman Square. There he entered a building on the north side. This was the Witt Library, room upon room stacked with photographs stored in green box-files. The files contained reproductions of paintings and were arranged alphabetically by schools. Each painter had a box to himself and famous painters had several. Michael climbed to the first floor where the English schools were located. He wasn't sure what he was looking for but that was often the way. He had to start somewhere, so he took down a box which was marked: 'Sir Thomas Lawrence: Portraits, Women, Single'.

Michael spent all morning in the Witt. He looked at box upon box, at works by Hudson and Reynolds, Ramsay and Gainsborough, Cotes and Romney, Fuseli and Etty. By 12.30, when he had to leave for his lunch with Isobel, he was weary and in need of a cigar. But he was beginning to have some idea who had painted the woman with a cleavage. He still had to find out who she was.

Isobel was already in his office when he arrived. She looked spectacular, in a mustard-coloured sweater and dark green pants. As Michael planted a kiss on her cheek he noticed her suitcase by the door. 'Back to the farm?'

She brushed the hair off her face. 'Yes, but I don't give up without a fight. I went to Sotheby's this morning, to try to find out who bought the documents.'

Michael stepped back and stared at her. 'That took some pluck.'

Isobel grinned but grimly. 'No luck, though. They wouldn't play ball. Isn't there anyone there you could bribe?'

Michael shook his head. 'They're quite tricky about that; they don't want dealers poaching their customers. Besides, Molyneux may have paid cash and used a false name. Nice try, though. Very impressive.'

He led Isobel out of the gallery, to lunch. This time they went not to Keating's but to Wilton's in Jermyn Street. The service there was exquisitely slow and Michael wanted to stretch out this meeting with Isobel. He couldn't be sure but it just might be their last.

'I hate just giving up,' she said after they had ordered. 'It's not like me at all.'

'You didn't have any suggestions last night. Got any today?'

She tossed her head so that the hair swung back off her face. 'I suppose we could drive down to Dorset and just cruise around, hoping to bump into him.'

'Dorset's a big place . . . and in any case we don't know that the rest of the trail stays there. Cross was French originally. Maybe that's where the other clues lead.'

'Mmm. You're right.'

They were silent for a moment.

'What about the Irish connection?' Isobel said.

'We don't know that there is one. We can't ring around all the dealers and ask if there's a Molyneux on the staff.'

'We can't just give *up*!'

But, try as they might, over the fresh asparagus, over the grilled sole, over the raspberries, they could think of no way forward.

169

'Maybe you were right,' said Isobel as she finished her berries and spooned the last of the cream into her mouth. 'Maybe we should have gone to the police. Maybe we still should.'

Michael shook his head. 'Much too late now. Helen's tidied up her studio, got back to a normal life. So have I, almost. It would look very odd, suspicious even, if we went to them now. We know no more about Molyneux than we did days ago and if the painting were to turn up, at an antique shop, say, it would almost certainly mean that he had no further use for it. Meaning he had found the treasures. I'm afraid,' he said, signalling to the waiter to bring some coffee, 'that we have been beaten. We may as well get used to it.' He smiled.

She would not be jollied. 'Do you think we'll ever know, if Molyneux finds whatever is hidden?'

'I don't want to think about it.'

Isobel pummelled the table. 'God, it's galling.'

Michael didn't reply but instead examined the bill, which the waiter had brought. He paid by cheque, turning over in his mind the topic *he* most wanted to discuss: when they could meet again. He sensed that right now was not the time. Isobel was keyed up. Maybe he could mention it back in the office, as he kissed her goodbye.

They left the restaurant and walked back to Mason's Yard. On the pavements the puddles from yesterday's rain had all but gone. Michael's memory of his day on the Broads was evaporating too.

They entered the gallery and climbed the stairs to Michael's office. He picked up Isobel's suitcase, intending to give her a hand with it, but as he did so he noticed a piece of paper wedged under his phone. He plucked it from where it was lodged. 'Look,' he said, lowering the suitcase to the floor and handing the note to Isobel.

She took it from him. It read: 'Ring Helen Sparrow. Urgent.'

Michael punched Helen's number on the phone. It seemed to take ages to connect.

'Please God, no,' said Isobel, scarcely audible.

The call went through and, down the line, they could hear the phone ring out, once, twice, three times. It was answered on the fourth ring. 'Helen? It's Michael, in London. What is it?'

'Michael – good. Look, Michael, I've had an idea. I still feel terribly guilty about your painting being stolen from my studio. You said something last night, when you were talking about the picture that Julius has been cleaning for you. You said you'd been hoping for a coat of arms but hadn't found one. That rang bells in my head and today I tried out an idea. There's a famous priory between here and Ipswich, with a marvellous gatehouse. Butley Priory it's called. I went there again this morning – I wanted to check if my idea was feasible before I called you.'

Michael looked at Isobel and silently shook his head. He had no idea what Helen was going on about. Presumably she would get to the point soon.

'The gatehouse is covered in carved stones. It was once part of an Augustine priory founded by someone who travelled with Richard the Lionheart on the crusades. It has the arms of England cut in stone and the three crowns of East Anglia, the Passion and the Holy Roman Empire – '

'Helen – '

'But *below* all that, also carved in stone, are the arms of the great families around here, the Stavertons, the Suffolks, the Hadleighs. Michael, you didn't see the cleaned painting but I did. Although the design on the stone slab was vague, I'm convinced now that it was a coat of arms. It certainly could have been. It may have been divided into quarters. I'm trying to help, Michael. The design or motif you are looking for is a coat of arms.'

Michael frowned. He was touched that Helen had gone to so much trouble to be of help but he couldn't immediately see if it took them forward.

'Great, Helen. Thanks.' He tried to sound as enthusiastic as possible. 'That might help, really. Let me try it out on Isobel. That was very thoughtful, Helen. Thank you very much.' He hung up and relayed the conversation to Isobel.

Like him she was touched that Helen had travelled several miles and back to check out her hunch. 'Thank God she wasn't calling to say that Molyneux had returned. It makes sense, I suppose. A coat of arms would lead to another family, at another location.' She bit her lip. 'A location where, no doubt, damn Mister Molyneux is even now unearthing what should be ours.'

They were both silent for a moment. Then Isobel looked at her

171

watch. 'Nearly half past three. I'd better go, I suppose, if I am to catch the four-seventeen.' She moved over to where Michael had placed her suitcase.

Michael still hadn't raised the subject closest to his heart. It had to be now. 'Isobel – '

'Michael!' Isobel suddenly shouted. She had lifted her case but now set it down again. 'Michael, how much heraldry would Molyneux know?'

'Search me. Why?'

'How would he find out who the coat of arms refers to?'

'If he didn't recognise them, you mean? Books, I suppose, or the College of Arms.'

'How many colleges are there?'

'One, I think.'

'In London?'

'Yes, Queen Victoria Street, in the City. Why?'

Speaking quietly, Isobel said, 'You remember when I was at the National Portrait Gallery and ordered a photocopy of the portrait of Philip Cross? And the girl asked if there was to be an exhibition about him? Because I was the second person to make that request within a few days? Our path crossed with Molyneux's. The same might be true of the College of Arms. If there's only one College of Arms and Molyneux is not an expert, he's got to go there. We can cross his path, so to speak. Why don't we go to the College right away and ask the people who work there if someone like Molyneux has been making inquiries, and, if so, what about?'

Michael stared at Isobel and grinned. 'Brilliant. Dynabloodymite. It might take a bit of bribery.' He tapped the wallet in his breast pocket. 'But it's only money. Let's go.'

They found a taxi easily enough at the Cavendish Hotel but, to their intense frustration, got ensnared in traffic in Trafalgar Square.

'What time does the college close?' asked Isobel.

Michael shook his head. 'I haven't a clue but normally these sorts of institutions don't stay open late. Five or five-thirty, I guess. Now what story are we going to concoct?'

Isobel was fiddling in her bag. She took out a comb and mirror and tidied her hair. She applied lipstick to her mouth and powder to her face. She doused herself in more scent. Seeing Michael watching her, she grinned. 'We might need this warpaint.'

They arrived at Queen Victoria Street just after 4.15. They mounted the steps of the College of Arms where a board announced that it was open until 5.30. Inside was a cloakroom, where Isobel was instructed by a security guard to leave her bag. They signed in and were directed to the library, a large room with a gallery around the edges. 'Look purposeful,' whispered Isobel, taking command. 'Pull a book down and pretend to read. Let's see the lay of the land.' All of a sudden she was as busy and as bossy as she had been on the boat.

Michael did as he was told and they sat at a polished pinewood table facing each other and pretending to dip into various books. Fifteen minutes passed. Isobel got up once or twice, ostensibly to get more books, but used the opportunity to move about the room. After a while, she came back and whispered, 'There seem to be two librarians, a woman and a man. Give me your wallet.' Michael looked at her but she hissed, 'Give me your wallet!'

He slid it across.

'How much is inside?'

'Three stamps, two opera tickets, my London Library membership card, three credit cards – oh yes, and about two hundred pounds.'

'Good. Let's hope we don't need it all. Now, in a moment, the next time the male librarian leaves the issue desk to put a book back on the shelves, go and engage the woman in some sort of conversation. I don't care what, just do it, and make it last long enough so that I can collar the man. Understand?'

Michael gave her a mock salute.

The librarians, however, did not play their part. The man and the woman sat at the central desk talking in near-whispers. For ten, fifteen, twenty minutes, Isobel had no opportunity to put into effect whatever it was she had in mind.

'We need another plan,' said Michael, as five o'clock approached. 'We've only got half an hour.'

As Michael spoke, the male librarian rose and moved over to a section with some very big, heavy boxes, Michael pushed back his chair and got to his feet and approached the issue desk. 'I wonder if you could help me,' he said to the woman at the counter. 'I'm an art dealer and I have a painting with some unusual jewels in it. Emeralds, I think. I am trying to identify the woman wearing them. I was wondering, are there any coats of arms with jewels in them? I'm very ignorant about these matters.'

As he said this he was aware that Isobel had now also risen from the table and had approached the male librarian, standing by the shelves at the far end of the room. That was all Michael had time to notice, however, as the woman to whom he had addressed his remarks now took him to another area of the shelves where there were indeed books on jewels and heraldry. He asked her to explain to him how they were organised and she seemed pleased to do so.

After that the woman moved back to the main issue desk, Michael was relieved to see that Isobel was still deep in conversation with the male librarian. Michael turned his attention to the books in front of him. He found a great deal on emeralds and, though he tried to keep an eye on Isobel, he soon discovered that the green stone was closely associated with three families in Britain: the Berners of Chester, the Duttons of Ripon and the Haskells of Henley-in-Arden. At least he was killing two birds with one stone, he told himself. Maybe the emerald bracelet in the portrait old Julius had cleaned indicated that the woman was from one of these three families. It was worth following up. He was about to turn his attention to chess and heraldry when he noticed that, across the room, Isobel was glaring at him. He moved over and sat down at the table opposite her.

Isobel looked flustered. 'The worm wouldn't help.'

'What do you mean?'

'I told him I worked for a newspaper. I asked if a tall man with grey hair had been here inquiring about a particular family. I said we thought he was trying to pretend he was a beneficiary of a will, trying to find out all he could about them. I said the paper was convinced he was a fraud.'

'And?'

'He wouldn't play ball. I offered him fifty pounds. It made no difference. He loathes the press. God, what a lizard.'

'What were his exact words?'

'He said that no one had been here who could possibly have been a fraud. They were all faces he had seen before.'

'Did he indeed?' Michael looked around the library. He took out his pocket-book and tore off a piece of paper. 'We haven't got much time: the place is closing. Follow me out and, when you get your bag at the cloakroom, make a fuss. Spill the contents on to the floor, drop your umbrella or something – '

'I don't understand. I don't *have* an umbrella, you donkey – '

'Isobel! It's nearly five-thirty, I'll explain after. *Please.* Just do it.'

To forestall any more discussion Michael got to his feet again. Isobel followed him out of the library.

Along the corridor by the cloakroom the guard was already standing by the door to stop newcomers entering. When he saw Isobel he moved forward, took her ticket and went into the cloakroom to fetch her bag. Michael motioned for her to follow. He spread his hands to remind her again to tip the contents on to the floor.

Isobel stepped into the cloakroom. 'Yes, that's mine,' she said as the guard came towards her. 'Let me just check if my pen is inside.' She took the bag, opened it and thrust her hand inside, smiling at the guard as she did so. Deftly she swivelled the bag so that it upturned. Then she dropped it on to the floor, the contents spilling on to the guard's feet. Make-up, coins, pieces of paper and boiled sweets scattered everywhere. They both stooped to pick them up, Isobel apologising profusely as she did so. Even after everything had been put back she made a fuss of looking for her pen. Eventually she contrived to find it in an outside compartment of the bag with its own zip. She smiled again at the guard, thanked him, and went back out. Michael was not there.

She stepped outside. He was waiting about fifty yards down Queen Victoria Street, towards Blackfriars Bridge. He had lit a cigar. He came towards her.

'Bossy on boats, a litterbug in libraries. Very talented, Inspector Sadler – '

Before he could go any further, Isobel had snatched the cigar from his mouth. 'You'll get this back when you've told me what you were up to in there. Stop talking in jingles and get a move on.'

He smiled. 'I was copying out the names of all the people who signed in on Monday. All the men, that is.'

She stared at him.

'The librarian you spoke to said all the people who came here were known faces. If Molyneux did come here, and was known, that means two things. One, he is in some way mixed up in the world of heraldry, or history, someone who perhaps does research here from time to time.'

'And? . . .'

'And, two, *because* he was known, he had to use his real name.' He reached out and took the cigar from Isobel's hand. The rush hour traffic zoomed past them so that Michael had to raise his voice. 'Nine people used the library on Monday, six of them men, possibly seven because one person signed in with his or her initials only.' He waved the piece of paper at her. 'The names are all here. It's too late now, but tomorrow we can start ringing round the dealers and museum people I know to see if any of these names mean anything – if any name belongs to a tall, grey-haired man who has been seen limping lately.' He grinned. 'Now who's a donkey?'

The first place Michael tried, next morning, was *Who's Who*. The London Library opened at 9.30 and he and Isobel were there on the dot. None of the seven names checked out. Then he tried friends and ex-colleagues in the auction houses. No good. He rang around the dealers he knew in the fields that might be relevant – antiquarian books, arms and armour, miniatures, jewellery. One of the names, George Grainger, rang a bell with one of the dealers in stained glass but, maddeningly, he couldn't be more specific than that.

The day wore on. Instead of lunch, they hunted through the London telephone directories. They found three of the names. None of the addresses meant much and two of the people answered when Isobel rang them. She could tell from their voices that neither man was Molyneux.

'He's two days ahead of us,' hissed Michael to no one in particular. 'Nearly three.'

'We're so close. Isn't there somewhere else we can check?'

Michael called a book dealer he had already tried, and asked him to suggest colleagues in the West Country. He was recommended

176

to a firm in Bath. But that did no good either. None of the names meant anything in Bath.

Four o'clock approached. Isobel paced around Michael's small office, her impatience visibly growing. He tried a gallery in Lower Sloane Street which, he knew, had once held an exhibition of heraldry and naval flags. The gallery sold maps with coats of arms on them. No, none of the names meant anything there either.

Four-thirty. Isobel had sat down and now Michael was pacing the room. He stopped opposite his books on Holbein. 'Hold on a minute,' he said. 'Remember how the Order of St Michael was right under our noses?' He tapped the spine of a book. 'Inside this very volume.'

Isobel looked across to him.

'Come with me.' He led the way downstairs and out of the gallery. They walked to the end of Mason's Yard where Michael pointed across Duke Street. 'Look.'

'It's a bookshop.'

'Not just any bookshop,' said Michael. 'Oliver Quartermain, the art world's bookshop. Lots of expensive books in all languages, books of which there are only forty-nine copies printed, books so academic you'd fall asleep before opening them.'

'So?'

'They have a section on stained glass. Remember that one name – Grainger – which rang a bell with the stained-glass dealer? Maybe he was a customer, maybe he was an authority who had written about it. Let's see.'

They crossed the road and entered the shop. Michael was known and they were left to browse. The books on stained glass were one of the smaller sections, at the back, high up. Michael reached up and ran his finger along the spines of the books. They were alphabetically arranged: Barbier, Broglie, Chadwick, Fleming, Fouquet, Friedrich, Goody, Grainger! He reached up quickly and took down the book. It was entitled: *Northern Light: Stained Glass of the British Isles.* Michael turned to the back flap.

'It's him!' Isobel stared at the author's picture, a small square in black and white. The silvery hair, a long jaw, creases in the cheeks, a sharp wariness about the eyes.

'Odd,' said Michael. 'It looks to me as though he was photographed in Oxford or Cambridge – that's an old-fashioned quad-rangle behind him. Yet it says underneath that he is Reader in Medieval Studies at the Royal Institute of History, here in London.'

'So he changed jobs. People do.'

'An academic. We should have thought of that before. I should. You were right. I *have* been a donkey.' Michael reached into his pocket for his wallet. 'Better buy this. Maybe it will tell us something about the man.' He paid for the book and they went out to the street. Michael flipped through the pages but the book was very academic, technical even, and revealed very little of its author.

'We know who we are up against, at last. This still doesn't help us with our next move.'

'It might, Michael. Where *is* the Royal Institute of History?'

'Search me. The Tower of London would be appropriate for Grainger, don't you think?'

'Michael! Go and look it up.'

They crossed back into Mason's Yard. The phone books were by the secretary's desk on the ground floor.

'Gordon Square,' said Michael. 'I know that . . . It's up behind the British Museum . . . where the Courtauld Gallery was before it moved.'

'Come on then.'

'Come on where? And what for?'

'You'll see.'

Back in Duke Street, Isobel raised her arm and waved down a taxi that had dropped someone off at the Cavendish Hotel. She got in and Michael followed. it was just after five o'clock.

They reached Gordon Square about twenty minutes later. After paying the taxi driver Michael pointed across the square. 'There we are. But – '

'All right, leave this to me. Grainger – as we can now call the snake – broke into my house, broke into your car *and* your house, and burgled Helen. It's time he was on the other end – '

'Isobel – '

'You don't have to come. In fact, it's better if you wait here. Now you've got that book jacket, you know what he looks like. I'm going inside, to find his office. I don't know what I'm going to do if he's there but if he's not . . . we'll see. You wait here and, if by chance he comes back, detain him somehow.'

'Isobel! This isn't our style. This isn't primetime TV either, you know. You can't do it.'

She looked at him. 'He's got two days' start on us – nearly three. You said it yourself. Now stay here.'

Isobel half ran across the square so that Michael couldn't hold her back. She approached the entrance of the Royal Institute of History. A posse of students stood outside. Michael watched Isobel push her way past them, climb a few steps and disappear through the glass swing-doors.

Inside, there was plenty of bustle and so she went unnoticed as she examined a board on the wall. From this she learned that Dr George Grainger was to be found in room 216. That, she realised, meant his office was on the second floor. She found the stairs and climbed to the second landing.

She stopped when she reached the landing and tried to compose herself as best she could. She didn't dare think of meeting Grainger. Grainger? She still thought of him as Molyneux.

It was quiet in the corridor. Isobel marvelled – and worried – at how short the interval had been between her first notion to come here, outside Quartermain's bookshop, and this moment, when she was on the verge of doing something illegal. It was only evening the score, she said to herself over and again.

She set off down the corridor. As she passed room 212 she heard voices, but no one appeared. Room 214 – silence. It was now nearly 5.45. She reached room 216. Quickly she glanced behind her; she was, for the moment, alone.

She gripped the door handle and squeezed it gently. Noiselessly the door swung open. Isobel followed the sweep of the door, as if she was part of it, and closed it behind her. She breathed more easily, though she knew that if she was found here, by a cleaner or – perish the thought! – Grainger himself, she would have some explaining to do. She looked about her, then moved across to the desk. As she did so, she glanced through the window, down into Gordon Square. There was no sign of Michael. She prayed that didn't mean Grainger had been spotted.

At that moment she heard voices. Some people further up the

corridor must be leaving. Surely they wouldn't look in here? What if one of them stopped by to leave a note? What could she do? Footsteps were approaching and there was absolutely nowhere to hide!

The voices were outside the office now. Had the people stopped walking? Were they coming in? Isobel stared at the door handle, watching for any movement that would precede its opening. She held her breath.

Being near Grainger, she remembered, always made her hold her breath.

The voices stopped. *They were coming in!*

But then the voices started up again and the footsteps moved down the corridor. Still, Isobel didn't dare breathe. Only when the voices started to fade, as they descended the staircase at the end of the corridor, did she began to relax.

Now she turned back to the desk and began to search around. Grainger's desk was covered with papers. Books and academic journals stood in stacks, like models of skyscrapers. One journal had a ticket stuck between some pages and Isobel opened it. Several lines were highlighted with yellow marker: it seemed to be about horse breeding and she closed it. She tried the desk drawers, marvelling at her new-found ability as a burglar.

The drawers were all locked and she turned her attention back to the desk top. The other books were unhelpful – dry academic works, some of them in French. She tried to remember how the books were stacked before she had disturbed them. In rearranging them, she noticed that another book had a marker between the pages. The book was a university library book, about divorce in the Middle Ages. Wasn't that the subject which Philip Cross was so concerned with? She read pages of the book at random. They were no help. Then she noticed that the marker was in fact a receipt from the National Portrait Gallery. She examined it. It was printed faintly in crimson ink. The date was illegible but the amount wasn't: 35p. What could have cost so little? Not a book or a poster or a slide. A postcard perhaps – or, she realised with a shiver, a few sheets of *photocopies*.

She searched the rest of the desk for other things that might help. There was nothing. Yes, there was. By the phone a number had been scribbled. Isobel looked at it and grunted. She snatched the NPG receipt from the book, took a pen from a holder and copied the number. Then she replaced the pen and left the room, taking the receipt with her. An NPG receipt more or less equalled a Helen Sparrow invoice, she told herself.

Isobel closed Grainger's door behind her and quickly marched down the corridor to the stairwell. Breathing more easily all the time, she descended to the ground floor and went out by the glass swing-doors.

Michael had bought an evening paper and was leaning casually against a car. She crossed to where he was. 'Quickly, let's get out of sight. Then I'll explain.'

Isobel scurried off, south to Russell Square. Michael followed. When they reached the square Isobel turned left towards the Russell Hotel. She found the phones. 'Got 50p?'

Mystified, Michael searched his pockets. A long-distance call?

Isobel inserted the money and dialled the number she had scribbled on the Portrait Gallery receipt.

'Good evening,' she said when someone at the other end answered. 'Can you tell me, please, are either Dr Grainger or Dr Molyneux still with you? . . . Oh, I see. Tell me, where are you exactly? Yes . . . yes . . . thank you. Goodbye.'

She turned to Michael and showed him the receipt with the number on it. 'Look at this number. I found it scribbled on Grainger's desk. The code is the same as for Dorchester, except that one digit is different. I know because I had to phone The Yeoman, to book our rooms, remember?'

Michael nodded.

'It's another hotel, called Peverell Place. They just confirmed that "Dr Molyneux" left yesterday morning. We've done it, Michael. We're back on the trail. Two days late, but we're not out of the race altogether.'

Michael smiled. 'And where is Peverell Place?' He took out his matches to light a cigar.

'Stoke Hembury, midway between Dorchester and Bridport on the Dorset coast. Do you have to light that filthy object?'

'Another early start, then. Don't be so disapproving, Inspector Sadler. Remember, you're the burglar.'

10

The A303, Michael thought, was a nice enough road. No big towns, mostly dual carriageway, faster than the A30 these days. Some heavy-duty traffic but not like the main motorways heading north from London. Just lately, however, he had seen quite enough of the A303 and was becoming bored with it. It was 9.30 the next morning and they were already approaching Sherborne. They had left London before seven, stopping for breakfast at a roadside café on Salisbury Plain. Vivid fried eggs awash in fat that was so deep it was navigable. Lethal and wonderful.

Over breakfast Michael had handed Isobel a sheet of paper, a photocopy he'd had made the evening before in his club. After their adventures in Gordon Square, Isobel had gone off to the mews to call Tom and tell him she wouldn't be coming back to the farm after all. Michael's club was the only place open at that late hour where he could consult the *Dictionary of National Biography*. The entry on the Peverells was not long. It read:

PEVERELL, Sir Harold (1485–1549), was a key figure in English horse breeding. The son of Henry, an ambassador to Venice, who brought back a number of horses from his travels, Harold Peverell crossed the animals with native stock to produce a sturdy but good-looking strain, now known as the Stoke Chaser, named after Stoke Hembury, the estate where they were first bred.

Harold Peverell had two sons, Charles, who became bishop of Poole, and Percy, who became a naval captain and perished in 1568 when his ship, the *Weymouth*, sank in heavy seas off Ireland.

'That explains one thing,' said Isobel. 'The book about horse breeding on Grainger's desk. It all fits. Why would an academic lie about his name and burgle houses? It's not exactly donnish behaviour.'

'Maybe living in ivory towers gives you a taste for ivory. And fifteen million pounds, don't forget, is apt to turn even the most level of heads. Here's something else that fits. I called a friend at Oxford last night, a man who's an assistant keeper at the Ashmolean Museum there. I asked him if he knew anything about Grainger. It wasn't much but it was enough. Apparently he was involved in a bit of scandal a couple of years ago when he authenticated an allegedly rare piece of stained glass, so that it was bought by a German collector for quite a lot of money. Grainger was paid a fat fee, dependent on the sale. Later it turned out that the glass was a clever forgery. Completely modern. When that happened, Grainger lost his fellowship at his Oxford college. He wasn't sacked exactly, he just wasn't re-elected, but in that world it amounts to the same thing. He may still be smarting from the humiliation. It could be that he needs to make an academic comeback and he thinks the discovery of the Monksilver silver is it.'

'Pay the bill,' Isobel had said. 'All he's going to discover is that we are back on the trail.'

Stoke Hembury, which Michael had found on the map only with difficulty, was further south and west than the places they had already visited in Dorset, and it was very close to the sea. To reach it, they had to travel to Dorchester, then west along the Bridport road. The landscape was more windswept here: wide expanses of green wheat, rolling slopes of lemon rape. After Winterbourne Abbas and Black Down, they turned south again through Litton Cheney. The roads got narrower and they descended rapidly, nearing the sea and the cliffs. The earth turned redder. They passed an old fort and the remains of a chapel.

Suddenly the Channel came into view. Michael stopped the car and wound down the window. Dimly they could hear the roar of the waves. A brisk breeze blew off the sea. Michael always forgot the smell of salt water but it always brought back memories of childhood holidays in north Cornwall where the sea went out for miles and where, once, out boating with other children, they had come across a school of basking sharks – entirely harmless, though they didn't know it at the time and had been terrified.

Slowly, he eased the car forward. Stoke Hembury was only half a mile down the road now. For once, as they came into the village, their next step was easy. 'Look,' said Isobel. 'That must be it.' She pointed to a blue sign with red lettering, partly hidden by some rhododendron bushes. The lettering announced: 'Peverell Place Hotel'.

Michael stopped the car opposite the entrance. From here they could see past a thicket of trees to the parkland inside and, at the centre, the house itself. 'A lot of that must have been added after Harold the horseman,' said Michael. 'It's no older than seventeenth or eighteenth century. Some is even Victorian.'

Isobel followed his gaze. 'We'll have to go in. Maybe we should stay the night. That would be the most natural way to look around.'

Michael turned off the road into the drive. As they emerged through the line of trees, the drive curved left and made a shallow arc around the building.

'Lord, how beautiful!' cried Isobel as they saw the point of this. A view of high cliffs and beyond that the sea stretched out before them in a magnificent panorama. 'It's like being on the bridge of an enormous ship.'

Besides the Channel, another part of the house came into view, on the seaward side. It was much older than the rest, with gables and stone mullions.

'*That's* the Tudor part,' said Michael. 'And very fine it is too.' The drive ended in a wide gravel sweep and he pulled the car around before stopping. They both got out and waited a moment, enjoying the breeze and the vast horizon, before they entered the hotel.

They found themselves in a large panelled room with a huge stone fireplace in the middle of one wall. On either side of the fireplace, where suits of armour might once have stood sentry, were enormous bunches of flowers, massive splashes of colour in an otherwise dark hall. At the far end, through an arch, they could make out a reception desk, or rather a dark oak table with desk things on it.

As they went through the arch, they could now see a young woman to one side. She was hunched over a filing cabinet, red

184

metal and rather out of place. When she saw them she smiled, straightened up and asked, 'May I help you?'

'If you have any free rooms, you may,' replied Michael.

The woman moved around to the table and riffled through a number of cards in a box. She frowned, but then brightened. 'I have a double room in the Jacobean part of the building,' she said, looking up. 'That's not the oldest part of the house, of course, but it does have a view of the sea. Will that do?'

Flustered, Michael hesitated. If they had only one room, what should they do? However, Isobel said quickly, 'May we see it, please?'

'Of course. This way.'

The woman turned, retrieved a key from a cupboard on the wall behind the stair, and led them back through the hall and beyond. Here the house grew lighter, the wood pannelling paler and the ceilings higher. She took them up a large staircase, which doubled back on itself. On the first-floor landing the woman turned right and stopped opposite a pale oak door. 'Here's the room,' she said. 'I hope you like it. You're lucky. Most days at this stage of the season we're booked solid for weeks at a time. This was a late cancellation.' She opened the door. 'The rooms aren't numbered. They're named after local landmarks. This is Old Priory.'

It was more like a pyramid than a priory. The room was very large, with a high, vaulted ceiling. There was a bay window overlooking the cliffs and the sea. There was a four-poster bed, a desk and a sofa in the bay window. There were also a number of portraits on the walls. 'These aren't originals,' said the woman, following Michael's instinctive gaze. 'They are copies of the pictures in the main lounge downstairs. The house once belonged to the Peverell family, as perhaps you know. One of them was an English ambassador to Venice. There are books and pamphlets in the library, if you are interested. By the way, at this point in the season we insist that all our guests accept the demi-pension plan – that is, you must take either lunch or dinner here, as well as breakfast. For that the rate is eighty-five pounds.' She smiled at them. 'I think that's all. Would you like to take the room?'

Michael looked lamely at Isobel. She said firmly, 'We'll take it. For one night, perhaps two.'

'Good,' said the woman. 'I'm sure you will enjoy your stay. Perhaps you will just come back downstairs and check in properly.'

Downstairs, Michael completed the formalities. Then he joined Isobel, who was unloading their cases from the car. As she heard him step out on to the gravel, she turned and whispered, 'Did you notice the big sofa under the bay window? That's why I wanted to inspect the room. That's where *you're* sleeping.'

'I'll wager you for it.'

'No, I don't gamble, remember. Try to be a gentleman about this.'

Back in the bedroom, as they were unpacking, Isobel said, 'What's our plan?'

'Lunch here, afternoon in the library and a tour of the house and grounds in the early evening. Casual conversation with the bar staff, the waiters, the owners, tonight.'

Isobel looked at her watch. 'It's not even twelve yet. Let's go and look at the cliffs and the sea. It's such a lovely day. We can get the lay of the land.'

'Fine. It will give us an appetite.'

They set off. As they went down the drive, Michael slipped his hand in Isobel's. At first she shied away but he hissed: 'It looks more natural. If we look like we are lovers, sofa or no sofa, people will be off their guard.'

She shot him a glance that was none too loving. Still, she left his hand where it was.

The walk achieved exactly what Michael had said it would. The sea breeze, the steep climb and a brief trudge along the shingle on the beach primed their appetites perfectly. And, after all, they had been up very early. Michael noted the slope of the cliffs, the small inlets here and there, places where the shoreline had crumbled dangerously. The sea looked waxy and cold.

Back at the hotel, after lunch, they settled in the library. They found only one book and one pamphlet about the Peverells. Michael opened the book, which was entitled *Dorset to the Doge*. Isobel concentrated on the pamphlet, 'The Peverells of Stoke Hembury', and for an hour there was silence in the room, save for the rustle of pages being turned.

After a while, Michael yawned. 'God, this is boring. Henry Peverell, the ambassador, was a pompous, self-important, heavy-handed phoney, so far as I can see.'

'Never mind that. Are there any clues in the book?'

'You tell me. So far as I can tell, he was appointed ambassador at a young age – thirty-four-ish, as this account goes. Before that he had a fairly undistinguished career. He was in Venice for four years where he met his wife, Elisabetta Dagaiole. Her family emblem – a mask – apparently occupies part of the Peverell coat of arms. It says here, in typically pompous style, that the Dagaiole arms were doubly appropriate – masks being very common at all the masked balls in Venice, but also suitable to the trade of diplomacy, in which the Venetians were so adept, and where deceit is the most useful skill. Then there's a lot of stuff about horses, how he purchased a number of Arabian ponies from the Turks at a special market in Venice and appointed a Turk to oversee their shipment to England. After his four years were over, a great ball was held in his honour, given by the Doge, the elected ruler of the city. Then Henry and Elisabetta travelled back overland, stopping at the great courts and being entertained along the way. His son was the one who decided to cross the Arab ponies with local stock.'

'Perhaps the clue is in the horses, Michael. That seems to be his most notable achievement.'

Michael shook his head. 'You're forgetting the next clue – Charon, the ferryman. Either there is a river hereabouts, which I haven't seen, or there is some other link with water or the underworld, or death, which we haven't spotted yet. What about your pamphlet – anything there?'

'Not much. It's much shorter, of course. There's a bit about Venice but very skimpy. It does mention the horses, though, and says that when Henry came back two of the seven horses he had bought died *en route*. Apparently, the king was so thankful for the job Peverell had done in Venice that he held a great feast of swans in his honour and gave the Peverell family the singular distinction of being allowed to eat swan, normally a royal prerogative, for a whole year. That's why, with the masks, swans became part of the Peverell coat of arms. Then there's a lot of technical stuff about horse breeding.'

Michael got to his feet. 'Back to the books, I think. I'll get them from the car and meet you in the room. We don't want to advertise what we are up to.'

Upstairs in the room he handed some of the books to Isobel. 'You try horses, I'll look up swans.' He sat down. 'At least the view is better here than in Mason's Yard.' He sighed.

After a while Michael went to the phone and ordered some tea. When it arrived, Michael filled two cups. He handed one to Isobel and said, 'Right, where are we? You go first.'

Isobel pursed her lips and shook her head slowly. 'Nothing obvious. A horse is the mount of warriors, kings, nobles, either in battles or on their travels. The horse is an attribute of Europe, Europe in this sense being one of the four parts of the ancient world. Then there are lots of individual horses which signify different things. A white horse, for instance, is the mount of Alexander the Great. A fallen horseman is Paul or pride.' She looked up at Michael. 'Doesn't seem like the right tack to me.'

'I agree,' said Michael. 'Mind you, what I have isn't much better. Swans are mute, of course, but in classical times, apparently, people believed that they used to utter a beautiful song at their death. For some reason, they thought that meant the soul of a dying poet had entered the swan. Romantic, but I can't see what good it does us.' He stood up and poured more tea. He looked out at the sea beyond the cliffs.

Presently, Isobel said, 'I feel a bit like a donkey now. We're not making sense of all this. We need outside stimulation. Let's go and look at the house. Also, remember how that vicar, in the pub in Dorchester, just happened to mention the Jesse window. That set us off again after we thought we'd run into the sand. Let's find the owner and talk to him.'

Michael agreed. He put on his jacket and followed Isobel down the stairs. The owner, they were told by the woman at the desk, had gone into the village and would be away for about an hour. They therefore explored the old part of the house, that part which would have existed when the picture was painted.

It had been well restored. All the stonework looked good and *looked* original, more or less. The Peverell coat of arms, the masks and the swans, separated into quarters were everywhere – over doors, set into the fireplaces, carved on the balustrades of the staircase, adorning the portraits in the main hall. There was even one set into the paving stones of the formal garden.

'A proud, as well as a pompous, family,' said Michael. He examined the paintings carefully but there was little value in them, he thought, so far as their quest was concerned. They were all bust length, shown against green, brown or browny-red backgrounds. They were all Peverells and included the Venetian beauty whom the ambassador had brought back from Italy. She was blonde, with heavy-lidded eyes, rather buxom, dressed in crimson and a lot of lace. In one hand she held an elaborate mask. There was a dog in her lap and a horse in the background.

'I don't think she's very beautiful, do you?' said Isobel.

'That was the Venetian style. They loved buxom blondes, just as they loved crimson. That dye – Venetian red – was so popular, and made the Venetians so much money, that its formula was a trade secret for years.'

'And the mask?'

'Very common in Venice. I don't know how it began but it was always popular. Venice was never the most religious of Italian cities and, among other things, the masks allowed men of the cloth to attend balls where loose women were also invited. The dog means she was married and faithful to her husband.'

The owner was still not back when they had finished going round the house. Isobel decided she would like to call Tom at the farm and then take a lingering hot bath before dinner. So Michael took himself back to the library for a while. He intended to look through the pamphlet before it was his turn in the bath. But there was nothing in the pamphlet that Isobel hadn't mentioned except a reference to the ambassador's 'annual retreat'.

Before going up to the room, Michael slipped into the hotel's television lounge to catch up with the news. He was surprised – and pleased – to see that, on the third day of his trial, the tycoon who was accused of fraud, the knight from the sugar company, had changed his plea from not guilty to guilty. There had obviously been a lot going on behind the scenes. Sentencing was expected the following day; if he won this wager, all Michael's costs in this current venture would be wiped out.

When he thought Isobel had had long enough to soak, he went

189

to the bar, ordered a couple of whiskies and a cigar for himself, and took them upstairs. As he let himself into the room, he discovered Isobel sitting in front of the mirror, wrapped in a huge cream-coloured towel. The sight of her white shoulders, slightly damp from the bath, brought back all his old longing. Instinctively he stared ferociously at the sofa.

Isobel turned, saw what he was carrying, and her face lit up. 'Is that for me? How did you guess? Just what I was longing for.' She smiled at him, took the glass and swallowed hard. 'Let me run your bath in return.' She got up and disappeared into the bathroom.

Michael found a clean shirt and took it with him into the bathroom when she came back.

'Any sign of the owner?' shouted Isobel as he got undressed.

'No,' he called back. 'But he's expected at any moment.' He told her about the trial.

She snorted. 'You're sick, Michael Whiting. Hoping to profit from someone else's misfortune.'

He laughed. Lounging in the bath, in the early evening, with a drink, a book and a cigar, was one of the best ways Michael knew of relaxing. Tonight he had with him a new biography of Gainsborough, which threw fresh light on the great man's rivalry with Reynolds. Michael lay full length in the bath; it was an old-fashioned type that went on for ever. Endless luxury.

Isobel knocked on the door after he had read about ten pages. 'You can come out now. I'm decent.'

By the time Michael had dried himself, dressed and brushed his hair, it was nearly eight o'clock. Isobel was wearing a red dress and, for the first time, a pair of dark red earrings – they looked like garnets. They enhanced the darkness of her eyes perfectly.

'You look magnificent,' Michael said.

'Thank you.' She smiled. Their relationship was edging back to what it had been in Southwold, before Helen Sparrow's assault. Michael reflected that they seemed to get on best in hotels. Perhaps there was something about the anonymity that relaxed Isobel.

In the bar they had another drink and ordered dinner. A sandy-haired man, who appeared to be the owner, was talking to some other hotel guests. He nodded and smiled across at them. Michael studied the menu and the wine list and had just finished ordering

190

when the owner came over. 'Hello. I'm Rupert Walker. I gather you wanted to see me.'

Michael stood, shook hands and introduced Isobel. 'Have a drink?'

'Thank you. A glass of wine, please. Red.'

They all sat and Michael began. 'We're down here on holiday but I'm an art dealer in London so we're naturally interested in the pictures, the Peverells, the house. We just wondered if you could tell us anything that isn't in the books. It's a lovely location.'

'Yes, it is, isn't it? Costs a packet to keep up, of course.' His wine arrived and he drank some. 'Well, let's see . . . what else can I tell you? . . . The books about the Peverells are all designed to flatter them, of course . . . so they don't mention the numerous rumours that the family had a big hand in the smuggling hereabouts . . . The quarry which provided the stone for the house is still in use, about two miles away . . . This isn't very interesting, I know.' He suddenly looked brighter. 'You say you're a dealer. Maybe you can help us with the pictures. The one thing we are not certain of is who painted them.'

Michael shook his head. 'Is there no documentation?'

Rupert Walker frowned. 'No. Funnily enough, someone was here yesterday, who thought they might be by someone called Michael Sittow. I had never heard of him but I gather he was quite a well-known court painter in Tudor times. The man said he would let us know.'

Michael looked at Isobel. Then he said, 'Maybe I know him. Did he leave a name?'

'Yes – Robert . . . Robert Molyneux – yes, that's it. Tall chap, very thin, silver hair. Know him?'

Michael shook his head but looked again at Isobel. Her expression said it all. He turned back to the owner. 'It says in either the book or the pamphlet in the library that the ambassador used to go into an annual retreat.'

'Yes, that's right. He suffered from erysipelas, St Anthony's fire. He was apparently cured, or his condition eased, by a monk who specialised in medical affairs. As a result he used to go to the monastery which the monk came from for two weeks every year, in the spring, when St Anthony's fire is at its worst.'

'You don't happen to know which monastery, do you?'

191

Walker looked at Michael intently, as if to say: What *is* this? These aren't casual questions.

So Michael added: 'Some monasteries had their own painters. It might help explain who did your pictures.'

That seemed to satisfy the other man. 'How interesting. I can't say offhand, but I've got the answer somewhere. Look,' he said, pointing, 'I think your table is ready. I'll go and rummage in my things and if I find the answer I'll come and let you know.' He got up. 'Thanks for the drink. Enjoy your dinner.'

'That was nifty,' said Isobel, smiling, once they were seated at their table. 'About the painter, I mean.'

'Hmm. Not nifty enough. We're still a day behind. Grainger's as slippery as a greased guillotine.'

Before they could go any further, Rupert Walker came back over to them. 'I haven't had a chance to go through my papers yet but I talked to my wife and she said she thought the monastery was at a place called Monksilver – that's not too far from here, in Somerset. Does that help?'

Michael nodded. 'It might. Thanks. I'll have to check it and let you know.' Walker retreated again, so they could start their dinner. But, later on, when they were back in the bar playing chess – another return to their relationship in Southwold – Michael managed to say to the owner, 'When this man Molyneux looked at your pictures, did he offer any help?'

'Yes, yes, he did. He asked if we had any photographs that he could take with him, to help his research.'

'And?'

'We don't have any photographs as such, but there's an old black and white brochure for the hotel that has four portraits on one page. They are not very big but it was the best we could do.'

'Do you have any more left? The other man sounds as though he knows what he's talking about, but I'd love to help if I can.'

'Sure. I'll get one from the office.' He disappeared but soon returned.

Michael put the brochure in his pocket. As he did so, he said, 'They can't be by Sittow. He was too late . . . Tell me, Mr Walker, is there a river near here?'

The owner shook his sandy head very firmly. 'No, none at all.

As you can see we are on the top of some cliffs. The nearest rivers are at Bridport, six miles west, and Abbotsbury, nearly two miles in the other direction. Are you a fishing man?'

Michael nodded, aware that Isobel's arched eyebrows were turned on him. 'And where are the Peverells buried?'

'The ambassador was buried at that monastery . . . Monksilver, I believe. One of his grandsons drowned at sea, of course. All the others are in the local churchyard.'

'Where is that?'

'Abbotsbury. There's a beautiful abbey ruin there. The Peverells are buried in the grounds.'

'Doesn't look hopeful, does it?' said Isobel, when they were back in the room. 'No river nearer than Abbotsbury, and no graveyard associated with the house. Perhaps Charon means something else?'

'Hmm,' murmured Michael. 'Grainger found it, whatever it is. He didn't stay long. We're being slow-witted again. I feel as though I'm in a video and someone has pressed the "still" button.' He took out the brochure and looked at the portraits. 'Rum bunch, the Peverells.' Then he smiled. 'One of these looks as though he has a hunchback. Do you think he got it from sleeping on the sofa?'

'You're about to find out.' But she was smiling too. Michael couldn't be sure but the prospect that it wouldn't always be the sofa was, he felt, back in her eyes.

Upstairs in their room they continued to talk after the light had been turned out. 'The link between here and Monksilver, the ambassador's retreat, it's too much to be just a coincidence,' said Isobel. 'Maybe Charon has a different meaning.'

Michael wasn't convinced. 'This all started with a picture. Now we have four others. Has it occurred to you that maybe your picture, and the four in this house, were by the same hand?'

'It hadn't. But surely one painting would not have referred to another – that would be too risky. Paintings could be moved or destroyed.'

'Yes, you're right. But why then did Grainger take the brochure with him?'

'Maybe he was misleading Rupert Walker, like you were.'

Michael could sense Isobel smiling in the dark. But when she spoke she was serious. 'Let's sleep on it, Michael. We're going round in circles again. Goodnight.'

But it was a long time before Michael dropped off. He lay in the dark for over an hour thinking back on how they had squeezed ahead on earlier occasions after being blocked. It did no good. The room smelled of Isobel: her hair, whatever perfume she was wearing, her body. The glimpse he'd had of her wet shoulders, earlier in the evening, danced before him in the dark. He imagined what it would, be like to touch her skin, pass his lips down the dip of her spine, score his tongue across the muscles of her stomach. Without noticing, he fell asleep.

His slumber was disturbed – the sofa *was* uncomfortable and he awoke around six, immediately aware that he would not go back to sleep again. He got up and crept to the bathroom, where he dressed as silently as he could. He went downstairs and outside.

It was a glorious morning, the fields and the cliffs and the lanes spilling sunshine. In the distance, the sea glittered like a million louis d'ors, making Michael think back to Willie Maitland. He started out down the drive. He didn't know what he was looking for, but if Isobel was right, and the answer lay in the place and not in the paintings, it had to be somewhere nearby. He walked west, rather than south to the cliffs. Almost immediately he came to a stream but it was so small, so insignificant, that he dismissed it. Indeed, there was no guarantee that the stream had even been here 500 years ago. Further on, he found the quarry. It was about fifty feet deep but it was perfectly dry – he'd had the idea that the quarry might also be associated with a pond or lake. No. It was a red blemish on a shallow hill and, as Rupert Walker had said, was still in use, as three ugly lorries, parked near the road, testified. He walked on for another mile but saw no trace of water, no sign at all of anything that might have meant something.

He retraced his steps, arriving at the hotel at about 8.30. Isobel was already downstairs, eating breakfast. Michael told her where he had been and what he had not found.

She grinned at him. 'You look as though you need water a lot nearer home.'

194

He felt his chin. Yes, he badly needed a shave. 'But first, breakfast. After that exertion, I need it, I'll shave later.'

Once his order had been taken, Isobel asked, 'Abbotsbury this morning?'

Chewing his toast, he nodded. 'Worth a detour, certainly. The river, the local museum, if there is one.' He waved a hand. 'But don't expect a power breakfast performance from me. After a night on that sofa, I'm fizzing like a flat spritzer.'

While Michael shaved, Isobel went for a rather shorter walk in the hotel grounds. Then, having told the girl on the desk that they *would* be staying another night, they drove into Abbotsbury and found the local museum. 'What happens here?' said Isobel, as they got out of the car. 'I've never done this sort of thing before.'

'Search me. Anything on the Peverells, parish records, old newspapers, whatever there is. The librarian might know something about the river here, too.'

The museum was a single, small, airy room with large windows and local maps all over one wall. The curator was a busy-looking woman with wiry blonde hair. Her spectacles hung down on her chest, held by a rope of glass beads that went around her neck.

'Hello,' said Michael. 'We're down here on holiday and staying at Peverell Place. It's a lovely part of the world and we wondered if you had anything of interest about the building or the family or the estate? We've read the pamphlet and the book at the hotel, of course. But we thought you might have something else.'

The woman smiled. 'Yes, it's a lovely house, isn't it? I'm afraid, however, we don't have much that will be of any interest. There are the parish records, but they aren't very interesting. They've been gone over a great deal and I don't think they've ever been considered exciting. The only other thing we have is Henry Peverell's will. A copy of course. The original is in the Public Record Office.'

'Thank you,' said Michael. 'We might as well look at that. We're in no hurry,' he lied.

They sat at a table, overlooking an estuary. The water had changed colour from gold to green. Brown reeds worried in the wind.

The woman brought the documents. 'Which will you have?' said Michael to Isobel. 'Parish records or the will?'

195

'You're dying for the will. Give me the records.'

Once again, as so often before, they sat side by side, reading quietly. As they read, the rays of the sun came round and spilled on to the table where they were sitting. Michael moved his chair so as to remain in the shade.

Isobel was the first to speak. 'Nothing here, Michael. Baptisms, marriages, deaths. What you would expect.'

Michael grunted. 'There's one thing here. Henry Peverell bequeathed a hand reliquary, inlaid with rubies, to the monastery at Monksilver.'

'There you are! We must be in the right place. Maybe the monks returned it, along with everything else, to hide here. We know now that they had strong links with the Peverells.'

'It's plausible, yes. But Grainger hasn't been here – or the woman would have mentioned him. And we are nowhere near the end of the clues yet. We still haven't got past Charon, damn him.'

They rose. As they handed back the documents to the curator, and thanked her, Michael said, 'The estuary . . . which river comes out there?'

'Two streams. The Abbot and the Nun, on account of the fact that one runs through the abbey, the other through the nunnery. They flow into the swannery and there's an old legend that the reason the swans are mute is because they observed so much mischief between the monks and the nuns, and were rendered dumb so they could never tell what they had seen. A charming story, don't you think?'

Michael and Isobel emerged smiling into the sun. 'I love those kind of stories,' Isobel said. 'Who dreams them up, do you think?'

'Probably the swannery PR people. Last year.'

She turned and punched his shoulder. 'Beast!' It was the first time she had willingly touched him since Southwold. 'What about the swannery?' Isobel added. 'There were swans in the Peverell coat of arms.'

'Yes, yes . . . I'd noticed that too. But the swannery is on the estuary, slap-bang next to the sea. The merman seems to suggest that the next clue is on a river, somewhere in the direction of the sea –'

'Or along the coast?'

'No. Charon is, specifically, a man who conducts souls across the *river* Styx, not the sea.' He tapped his temple. 'It sticks up here too. Cerebral stasis.'

They walked along the main street of Abbotsbury, towards the abbey. It was built from a crumbly, corn-coloured stone, the crust shot through with gunmetal. They turned into the local pub, The Ilchester Arms, where, to Isobel's delight, the house specialised in several kinds of cider. While Michael drank he took out the Peverell Place brochure and again scrutinised the portraits and read the legends.

Isobel looked over his shoulder. 'Just thinking out loud, Michael, could Charon stand for anything else than river? Maybe he stands for the underworld in general. Meaning, perhaps, a cave or a passageway that runs under the house, to the cliffs maybe. Remember that story about the Peverells and smuggling?'

Michael sipped his cider. 'Possible. A definite maybe.' He smiled at Isobel. '*I* like the effect cider has on you.' He braved her wrath and took out a cigar. 'Tell you what, we'll try the cliffs this afternoon, and if we get nowhere we'll go back to London first thing tomorrow and research this Sittow character. Maybe there's something in his life that will help.'

They decided to take lunch in the pub. Over the cheese and onions, they examined the map to see exactly how Peverell Place related to the coast and where the likeliest location for a cave would be. With mounting excitement they noticed that, in fact, a set of caves was actually marked on the map.

'Pity you weren't around to help Bad Bill,' said Michael. 'He might have had more luck.'

In the car they could not get very close to the top of the cliffs near where they wanted to be. They had to traipse across a large field. At this point of the coast the cliffs were quite high – a couple of hundred feet – and so they had to trudge some distance more along the edge before they could scramble down safely to the beach. The sun made it hot work but, once they were down on the shingle, the breeze coming off the sea was cooling.

Isobel and Michael were far from being the only ones on the beach – it was summer after all – but it was not crowded.

They tramped on. After about half a mile the cliffs became less sheer, with small dips between the peaks that were more accessible. Michael stopped and fished out the map. 'According to this, the caves are about here. They are set back a little and come out, not in the face of the cliff but at the side, into a kind of hanging valley.' He led the way off the beach, scrambling up the sandstone and turning to give Isobel a hand. At about twenty feet the grass began and gave them something to hold on to. Another thirty feet up and, to their surprise, the ground levelled out and they found themselves in a hollow which could not be seen from the beach.

'Perfect,' said Isobel, looking round and up. 'A perfect smuggler's patch. We're almost totally hidden.'

Michael pointed over her shoulder. 'And that, unless I'm very much mistaken, is a cave.' About fifty yards away and some ten feet above the line where they were standing was a dark opening.

'Pity we don't have a light,' said Isobel. 'We're not exactly equipped, or dressed, for this sort of thing.'

The cave was high, taller than a person. As they entered, it became suddenly very cool and smelled of damp. Isobel rubbed her fingers against the sandstone walls and felt the wet crumbs come away on her hand. They had the consistency of cheese.

As their eyes became accustomed to the gloom, they could see that, despite its height, the cave was not deep, forty or fifty feet at most.

'Look!' hissed Isobel, her words skidding around the enclosed chamber. 'Another passage – it's been bricked up.'

It was true. Off the main chamber led a smaller one but not for more than ten feet or so. There, a wall of grey breeze-blocks ran from floor to ceiling.

'That figures,' said Michael. 'These things are probably quite dangerous the further you get into the cliff.' His voice boomed back and forth across the cave. 'My guess is that we're at the wrong end. These caves aren't like those remote ones near the Dead Sea. England has been heavily populated for centuries. We're never going to find anything here; this ground has been gone over for too long. If your theory is right, what we're looking for will be at the other end, much nearer the house, on private property. But, thanks to Inspector Sadler, we *have* established that there *is* an underworld which may be associated with Peverell Place. It may be only half a step forward, but it's something.'

They left the cave, crossed the hollow and scrambled back down to the beach, earning some curious looks from others strolling on the shingle. It was harder walking back, against the wind and then back up the cliff. By the time they reached the car they were very tired.

Michael drove back to the hotel but, when he reached the main entrance, he stopped on the road outside, just as he had done the day before, when they had first arrived. 'This is the difficult bit,' he said. 'We can't ask about secret passageways without appearing a bit odd, and we can't go snooping either—'

Isobel put her arm on his. Physical contact again. 'Oh yes, we can, silly. We just make a joke of it. Drive in and leave this to me. Come on!'

Michael did as he was told. He pulled up outside the main door, got out and followed Isobel, who had already marched into the hotel. Rupert Walker was just crossing the hall, carrying a bowl of flowers.

'The very man,' boomed Isobel in her loudest voice. 'You can settle it for us.' Rupert Walker set down the flowers and turned to look at her. 'We were just walking off our lunch on the beach and we saw some caves. I remember you saying last night there was a rumour that the Peverells made money from smuggling. That *must* mean you have a secret passageway that links the house to the cliffs. Am I right? Michael thinks I'm just being romantic.' She laughed as she said this.

Rupert Walker smiled back. 'It's interesting you should say that. The same thought occurred to me when I first bought the hotel some years ago. A secret passage would add to the mystique of the house and we could publicise it. If you *can* find a secret passage here, I will personally pay your bill. The caves fell in years ago, well before they bricked them up for safety. So no one can get in from that end.'

As soon as they reached their room, Isobel voiced what both of them were thinking. 'If the passageway *is* the clue we are looking for, if that really is the underworld which Charon refers to, we've had it. We've come to the end of the road properly this time. Maybe that's why Grainger left so quickly. He realised how useless this all is.'

Michael shook his head. 'Not a chance. Were you listening hard to Rupert Walker then? No mention of "Molyneux". If Grainger had asked him about an underground tunnel, Walker would have mentioned the coincidence. But he didn't. Which means that our dear rival was not at all interested in it. We're on the wrong lines again, Isobel. A re-run of St George versus St Michael. Grainger left this place knowing something that we don't.'

At dinner that night, neither had much to say. After two days at Peverell Place, they had made no progress. Grainger was now three days ahead instead of one. For Isobel and Michael, tonight looked like the last of their adventure. To make matters worse, Michael had heard on the evening news that the tycoon in the fraud case had been sentenced to three years' gaol and a fine of £200,000. The man intended to appeal but that didn't count in the wager. Michael had lost. It wasn't the money so much as the fact that his luck had turned. It seemed like a bad omen. As usual in such circumstances, Michael comforted himself with his favourite wine, a heavy red burgundy. 'If I have enough of this,' he said to Isobel, 'I'll be able to sleep, even on the damn sofa.'

Rupert Walker came over to them during dinner. 'Before you go, will you leave me a card? You never know, I might want to have the portraits valued, for insurance. Perhaps you could help me?'

'Of course,' said Michael. 'But what about this Molyneux man?'

'He was an academic, he said, not a dealer. He did say one thing, though, that did indicate he had some idea who the pictures were by.'

'Oh yes? What was that?'

' "The mask reveals all," he said. "The mask reveals all." I assumed it was a signature of some sort, or a sign that some painter always used. Like Toulouse-Lautrec's monograph.'

'What do you think?' said Isobel, after Rupert Walker had left the table. 'Could that be right? About the mask being a sort of signature?'

'If it's true, then it's not anything I know about. Some painters,

Dürer and Toulouse-Lautrec, for example, used monograms. There was a German Romantic painter, Friedrich, who used to put moons and planets in his landscapes as a kind of identifying device. But that's all I know about. There are no painters, so far as I know, whose names sound like mask. What did Grainger mean, "The mask reveals all"? Grrrainger! I thought I'd sleep tonight. Now I won't.'

'Have a whisky. It will make you sleepy. And a cigar.' When she saw the surprised look on his face, she smiled. 'There's method in my madness. It will help unwind you. Once you're asleep I'll feel safer, and less guilty. Oh, and by the way, you can have the bed tonight. I always intended to take my turn on the sofa.'

Michael followed her suggestion with the malt and the cigar. They even played some chess. But his mind wasn't on it and he lost easily. As they went to their room after midnight he was still wide awake. Despite what she had said, when Isobel came out of the bathroom in her nightdress Michael was already tucked up on the sofa with a sheet and blanket around him. 'I know it's my turn in the bed, but now you know I'm safe *and* a gentleman. Maybe I've even earned a goodnight kiss.'

He was surprised when, very swiftly, she complied.

11

Isobel, on the other hand, was even more surprised when she was roused next morning by a kiss from Michael. She was immediately wide awake and wary. 'What are you playing at? And what time is it?' Her eyes were growing accustomed to the light, and to the fact that there was no sun yet, just a chalky bloom in the high, braided clouds.

'It's just after five-thirty – '

'What!'

'Yes, and you've got to get up. I'm not playing at anything, I'm as serious as a sermon. That sofa is bloody uncomfortable, especially on the second night. I couldn't sleep again and so I've spent the whole night sitting bolt upright and thinking. And I think I've sorted it out, our little problem, I mean. We've got to get a move on.'

'What? What do you mean?'

'Just what I say. I'll explain as we go.'

'Go? Go where?'

'Godwin Magna.'

'But why –?'

'Get dressed! I told you. I'll explain as we go.'

It took twenty minutes. Fortunately, though it was early, Rupert Walker was up so that Michael was able to pay while Isobel got dressed. Otherwise it might have looked as though they were trying to leave without settling their bill. He also used the opportunity to give Walker one of his cards.

'You drive,' Michael said, as Isobel came out of the hotel into the

202

cool morning air. The salt smell of the sea mingled with that of warm bread from the hotel kitchens. The sun was just beginning to bake the gravel in the driveway. 'You've had some sleep in the last forty-eight hours.' Defiantly, he showed her his lighted cigar. 'I need this, after the night I've had.'

Isobel started the engine, setting off a couple of dogs they hadn't noticed before, and no doubt waking the entire hotel. They both giggled. Quickly, she sped the car down the drive and east on the road to Abbotsbury. 'Now,' she said, as the car gathered speed along the empty lane. 'For the second time, *what* are you playing at?'

'At being a brilliant amateur detective. Almost on a par with some of Inspector Sadler's bright ideas.'

'Explain!' she hissed through clenched teeth. 'Or I'll drive your bloody car off that cliff.'

But Michael had the map open on his knee. 'We'll cut across country. Turn left in Abbotsbury. It'll be signed to Portisham and the Valley of Stones. It's quite a steep hill.'

'Michael!'

'Oh, I'll explain, don't worry. Just don't miss the turning.'

They slipped into Abbotsbury, as still as a tomb. The liquid sun at that hour washed over the yellow in the stone, so that the whole village seemed gilded for a moment. When they had found the road to the Valley of Stones and Isobel was accelerating along it, Michael went on.

'One thing I've learned in this little caper is that if you're getting nowhere you must start again, clock in, make your pre-flight checks, all over again, leaving all your assumptions to one side. That's what I decided to do about Peverell Place at - oh, roughly a quarter past two this morning.' He hesitated. 'Ask yourself this question: what is the most important attribute of Peverell Place, what is it that drew us here in the first place?'

'The coat of arms?'

'Exactly. It's obvious, very obvious. Next question: what does the coat of arms consist of?'

'Michael!'

'Okay, I'll answer for you. Swans and masks. Again, it's all very obvious. Now to the important bit: why swans and masks? I don't mean all that stuff about Venice and the king giving the Peverells the swan concession. Remember, we're dealing with an ecclesiastical mind here. Medieval grey matter. What would masks and swans have meant to the painter of the picture?'

Isobel was silent for a moment. They swept through a high beech wood, just beginning to glitter with gold and green. They passed a sign to Helstone. 'I don't know,' she said.

'You do – you've just forgotten for the moment. I was alerted by what Rupert Walker reported Grainger had said. Grainger said that "The mask reveals all." But a mask *doesn't* reveal all, does it? Quite the opposite, in fact. A mask is a disguise. A mask is the symbol of deceit. And the chief characteristic of a swan is its mute-ness, its silence. Deceit and muteness: that's two things. Third, going back to the picture and what Helen found when she cleaned it, there's something else we've overlooked. The figure of the monk gazing down at the tile isn't a monk at all – '

'Yes it is – '

'No. You're driving so you can't see, but in fact the monk has no face. It's hidden by his hood. I didn't think that mattered but I now think it matters very much. When Helen cleaned the grime away from the tile, she also uncovered the monk's feet and they aren't human feet at all – '

'She said he had pointed toes.'

'Correct. Well done. Your memory is waking up too. Helen said they were like claws. At about four o'clock this morning I found out what a beast, a lion, cloaked in a large garment and with no face, stands for. I simply went through one of the reference books from A to Z. A.M. to zzzz . . . Fortunately, I found it under "D", so it didn't take a fortnight.'

'D for . . . ?'

'Deceit. A lion dressed in a monk's habit is the medieval symbol of deceit. Don't ask me why at the moment, just take my word for it. Anyway, that makes two deceits and one mute, if you see what I mean.'

'What are you getting at?'

'Hold on. I want to give you all my reasoning, so you're con-vinced. We've just passed the Hardy monument; you should turn right soon . . . look out for the sign.'

They were coming into a small valley, descending. Ahead of them were some electricity cables. There was a village in the folds of the hills. 'Martinstown – yes?' said Michael. 'There's the sign. Turn right here.'

Isobel swung the car round. The sign said 'Winterborne Monkton 1½ miles'.

'Once I started thinking about deceit, I started looking at the monk figure again. And at about five o'clock this morning I finally registered something else we haven't noticed about him – it. Something so obvious we never thought it important. But it's crucial.'

'And that is . . . ?'

'Want to guess?'

'Michael!'

'No, seriously. There is a very simple, very obvious way the monk is different from some of the other characters in the picture.'

She started to brake, annoyed by his teasing.

'Okay, okay. Some of the figures in this puzzle face to the right, others face to the left.'

'Yes, of course I noticed that. It's obvious but . . . you think it matters?'

'I do now. Like you I had noticed it before, but never imagined it was important. However, just before the "Deceit" entry in the book I was reading throughout the night, there was another paragraph, headed "Dance". There was a drawing which made up part of the entry, a drawing of a picture that looked familiar, except that the layout artist for the book had split the figures in his drawing according to whether they faced left or right. I had only skipped the item as I waded through the entire book, but now I went back to it. I suppose I only noticed that the figures in our "Landscape" were facing different ways because my subconscious had seen this other entry, for "Dance". Anyway, when I paid more attention to the "Dance" paragraph, I immediately recognised the picture it was using to illustrate the point – Botticelli's famous allegory, *La Primavera*, "Spring". Everyone knows it – it's in the Uffizi in Florence. Now there are seven figures in Botticelli's picture, almost as many as in yours, and what I didn't know, but the book told me, was that they are laid out to symbolise a musical scale. The figures

205

facing right represent all the notes that are in harmony whereas those facing left represent discord.

'Now apply that to our picture. What *I* think it means is that all the figures facing right are proper clues, designed to produce a harmonious solution to the mystery. Whereas all the other figures, facing left, are – quite simply – red herrings.'

'You mean . . . you mean they were put there deliberately . . . to confuse us?'

'Yes. That's exactly what I *do* mean. The medieval mind was like that, as I keep saying . . . I also think that Grainger, grrreasy Grrrainger, who's more used to this than we are, twigged what was happening almost as soon as he arrived at Peverell Place. That's why he didn't stay long, and that's what he meant by the cryptic statement, "The mask reveals all." The Peverells were chosen by the person who painted Landscape of Lies because they were known at the monastery of Monksilver and anyone getting on the trail would automatically assume that Peverell Place, with its smuggling associations, and its undoubted links through Henry the Horseman, was a perfect hiding place. But whoever painted the picture, or designed it, also knew that their coat of arms was perfect. It underlines the point: like the masks, Peverell Place was a deceit; like the mute swans, it has nothing to tell us. We've been on a wild-goose chase. A wild-swan chase. That's why we couldn't find a river or anything else that fitted with Charon, the next clue. Philip Cross faces right. The next three figures face left, leading us astray. But Charon is a real clue – see, he turns to the right. And that's not all. The figures which face right also face the upside-down crucifix and, as we learned right at the start, the crucifix, in this context, stands for wisdom, for truth. Don't forget also that Helen told us she uncovered a tear on the face of one of the characters. He is facing the wrong way and, if you examine the faces of the other figures facing the wrong way, they all have tiny tears on their cheeks. Extraordinary detail – and why? They are sad because they know they are liars, they know they are misleading us.'

Isobel slowed the car to negotiate a blind corner, then picked up speed again.

Michael paused. 'Then, I looked up "sad" – it was a subheading under "Emotion". In medieval times certain colours represented sadness, brown especially. What do we find in the Landscape? All the figures facing the wrong way are wearing something in brown.'

Isobel took her eyes off the road and glanced at Michael.

'There's more. Their lips, for instance. All the real clues have their lips parted, as if they are speaking. They have something to say. All the false clues either have no lips at all, because there is no face showing, as with the lion, or their lips are closed. They can tell us nothing. All the wrong clues are wearing jewellery – rings mainly, or gems sewn into their clothes. Jewels are a symbol of vanity, or corruption – what could be more of a red herring? I've said it before, Isobel, once you know how to read this picture it hits you like Laphroaig. And now I'm certain: we've been on the wrong tack. Betamax, not VHS.'

'I can't believe – '

'There's one other thing. But first we're coming into Winterborne Monkton. We turn left, then right almost immediately, towards Winterborne Herringston.' He waited while Isobel negotiated the turns. They saw a milk lorry but that was all.

'When we started, right at the beginning, remember there was a design at the top of the marble column?'

'Adam and Eve?'

'No, no, the next design. A man with an iron rod, descending some steps which lead towards Mercury, the figure who turned out to be Philip Cross – remember?'

'Yes, of course. Why go back to that now?'

'This is something I noticed at a quarter to six this morning, when it all fell into place and, like Prince Charming, I woke you with a kiss.'

'If Prince Charming doesn't get a move on with this story, he's going to sleep for rather more than a hundred years.'

Michael grinned. 'I could use it, after the night I've had.' He pulled on his cigar. 'I should have thought of this before, but the man with the wand is descending five steps. I will wager tuppence to a Turner that means there are five clues to be negotiated before we get to the treasure.'

'Ah! Then your theory *doesn't* work. There are nine figures in the ring and, if my memory serves me right, five of them are facing left. That only leaves four clues.'

'Very observant. Prebloodycisely. But again I'll bet that means the last figure also contains the fifth step within it. Let's tackle that when we come to it. The main thing for now is that Peverell Place and Lewell Monastery play no part in all this. We have to go back to the last real clue, back beyond Higher Lewell, to Godwin Magna, and start again from there. The best news of all is that, according to the map, there is quite a large river flowing through Godwin Magna but we never saw it. It's called the Frome. The Charon clue obviously refers to that and, as we agreed the other night, the next figure, the merman, means we have to travel downstream, towards the sea.'

The road east of Winterborne Herringston wound down a gentle valley and was caked in mud from the hooves of cattle which, even at that early hour, had already been taken in for milking. The sun was higher in the sky and beginning to burn off the stretches of cloud.

After a short silence, Isobel looked across to Michael and said softly, 'Are you shattered? Two nights without sleep – I feel very guilty.'

Michael grinned back. 'Good. I like that. But don't feel too badly – after all, it paid off in the end.'

'I'll pay you back for the hotel room, and all the rest of our expenses, if ever we do find this damn stuff.'

Michael reached across to pat Isobel's thigh reassuringly. Quickly, she lowered her left hand and gripped his wrist, stopping him from touching her. But she held his hand for a moment longer than was necessary and, when she replaced it in his lap, stroked it for a moment before changing gear as they came to a crossroads.

'Just over a mile to Godwin Magna,' Michael said, reading the sign. He looked at the map again. 'According to this, we go through this village, then there's a sharp, left-hand bend that leads down a steep hill. At the bottom of the hill, the road curves round sharply to the right and crosses the river. Let's make for there.'

Isobel slowed as they came to the village. This time they came in from the south, the opposite direction to before. They passed the church on their left, and the copper beeches. By now there were signs of life – dogs, one or two people on bicycles, a postman's van. But the village shop, where Michael had hoped to buy some chocolate, for breakfast, was still closed. It was just on 6.30.

They descended the hill and, at the bottom, turned a corner. A low stone bridge, liverish with damp, lay ahead. Isobel drove slowly across the bridge to a gate on the far side. She pulled up beside it so that most of the car was off the road.

They got out and walked back to the bridge. They stood in the sun and leaned over the parapet to look at the brown waters below. Near the banks, the river was streaked with lines of sedge, green and black. In the middle, however, the water was too brown and too deep to see the bottom and ran swiftly.

'So that's the Frome,' said Isobel. She bent to pick up a twig from where it had fallen. She threw it into the waters and they both watched as it sped downstream.

'And we follow that,' she added. 'But how? And what are we looking for?'

'I left the map in the car, but from what I remember the river doesn't go anywhere near a road for two or three miles. And, in any case, in the sixteenth century river traffic was much faster than roads when they had them. I fear therefore that this is where we abandon the 190. Let's go back to the car and look at the next clue in the photograph.'

Isobel leaned against the side of the car, enjoying the sun, which was getting stronger all the time. She looked at the photograph. 'Look,' she said. 'The Triton, the merman, is wearing what looks like a string of flowers around his neck – just like Philip Cross had the order of St Michael around his. That must be a clue, don't you think?'

'I'm sure it is. I'd noticed it too. The details are what have counted so far – the upside-down flames on Mercury's tunic, the number of steps the man at the beginning was descending, the half-hidden upside-down crucifix. Everything in this picture has a meaning, so I'm sure the flowers do too. You don't recognise them, do you? The flowers, I mean. They aren't something you have growing on your farm?'

Isobel smiled. 'A farm is a farm. Not a market garden.'

'Well, there must be a market garden or a garden centre some-

209

where near here, where we can get help. Let's go back to the village and ask.'

They got into the Mercedes. Michael wound back the sun-roof and they returned up the hill into the village. By now it had gone seven and the shop was open. They bought chocolate and found from the shopkeeper that there was a garden centre seven miles away, in Laycock.

As they drove out of Godwin Magna, Isobel said, 'We'll have to show them the picture, I suppose.'

'I don't see that we have much choice. We'll have to think up some excuse that sounds perfectly natural. Any ideas?'

'Not yet. Look, do we need to do this? The flower is clearly painted – white petals with pink stamens and a small yellow spot at the end. If we found a boat somewhere and slowly explored the river, I'm sure we would recognise it. That way we need involve no one else.'

'Hmm. Our problem is time. Grainger is well ahead of us. The flower may be well known – and there may be well-known places around here where it grows in profusion. An expert would know all that and be able to guide us straight to where we want to go. On the other hand, the flower may no longer exist. It could easily have been cut down or the site where it grew built over. In that case it would help us to know what *sort* of place it grows in, so that we can search for somewhere it might have grown.'

Isobel was only half convinced. 'You may be right,' she said. 'We're nearly at Laycock anyway, so let's keep going.'

Laycock was bigger than Godwin Magna and boasted a school and, on that morning, a market. It was nearly eight o'clock when they arrived, and the main square was already choked with stalls selling cheese, homemade jams, vegetables, fish and flowers. Isobel, who was still driving, edged the car through the throng. Michael got out at one point to ask at a flower stall where the garden centre was. He was directed to the Slapstone road and told that the centre was about a mile along it.

Around Laycock the countryside was scrubbier than the lusher fields of Godwin Magna. Michael was always amazed at how, in England, the countryside could change so quickly. It was one of the things he loved.

'Nora's Nurseries' were announced by a big, bright, red and gold sign. Though it was not yet a quarter past eight, they were already open. The gate was pulled back and boxes of flowers, bright splashes of scarlet, were stacked near the entrance, ready for sale. They turned off the road into a dusty courtyard surrounded on three sides by greenhouses. A large, handwritten sign said, 'Geraniums – one free with every 4 U buy.' Next to it was a note which read, 'Please ring for attention.' An arrow pointed to a bell.

'Leave this to me,' said Isobel. 'You look too much the city slicker to be real in this part of the world. At least I've got farmer's hands.' She got out of the car and rang the bell. Almost immediately a voice from deep within one of the greenhouses shouted back, 'Coming!'

After a short delay a woman dressed in blue dungarees and wearing a red scarf around her head marched out through a door. She had ruddy cheeks, a huge chest and mud on her hands. A dog yapped at her heels. 'Bloody animal!' she said, playfully trying to kick the creature. 'Good morning. Lovely day.' She had a loud voice.

'Are you Nora?' said Isobel.

'Bloody awful name, isn't it? Still, I should be grateful it's not Edna or Ethel. Do you want flowers, or fruit?'

'Fruit, please, and some help.'

'Of course. This way.' She looked across to Michael, sitting in the car, then led Isobel back into the greenhouse.

Both women were gone for about ten to fifteen minutes. Michael switched on the radio in the car and started to listen to the breakfast-time news. In America no fewer than seven candidates had announced that they would be running for President, even though the contest was more than a year away. Michael wondered how many would survive the now regular media hunt for skeletons in their respective closets. He was just turning over in his mind whether to suggest a wager on the subject when Isobel reappeared. She shouted: 'Michael, come and give me a hand, please.'

He slipped out of the car and followed her. They walked down between rows of chrysanthemums, with high, dark green leaves, clammy from the thick atmosphere inside the greenhouse. At the end was a clearing, in the forest. Here Nora had her office, a stove

211

pipe which provided heat in winter, a chair, a phone and a primus stove to make tea.

He smiled hello to Nora, who nodded back. She held some money in her hand and was obviously in the process of giving Isobel change. Isobel motioned to a box of apples. 'Make yourself useful, Michael, please. Take that to the car.'

Michael lifted the apples and carried them back to the Mercedes, thankful to be back in the fresh air and out of the warm wetness of the greenhouse. He put the apples on the back seat with the reference books. Isobel was a few paces behind, still chatting to Nora. This time Michael sat behind the driving wheel. Isobel waved goodbye to the other woman and got in alongside him. 'Turn back to Laycock,' she said and then swivelled in her seat to wave again.

'Well?'

'I bought the apples as a sweetener – and it will be nice to have one every so often. I told her we were on a rally, one of those treasure hunt things, and that the flower was the next clue. I thought that would arouse the least suspicion.'

'At half past eight in the morning? Oh, well, so long as she believed you. Go on.'

'She recognised the flower – it's a problem, I'm afraid. It's almond.'

'Almond?'

'Yes. The good news is that almond grows near water. The bad news is that almond is almost unknown in Britain.'

'That needn't be a bad thing. If it is almost unknown, then the few places where it *does* exist might be quite famous locally. Could she help on that?'

Isobel shook her head. 'No. She said she only recognised it because her brother lives in Italy, where *he* has a garden centre, and almond is very common there.'

Michael steered the car back into Laycock, back through the crush of people in the market. As he came out on the other side, he said, 'Maybe I'll have an apple now. Pass me one, will you?' He chewed for a while, then said, 'So, we have to get down on to the river. We need to rent a boat. Once we are actually on the water, we may see all sorts of things we can't see from anywhere else. I can't say I like the idea, though. Some trees last for hundreds of years but a

212

rare one that doesn't normally grow here . . .' A thought struck him. 'Hold on. If it is a rare tree maybe that means someone in the area, someone with a property that adjoined the river, was very keen on gardening and brought back rare plants from abroad, just like Peverell brought back rare horses. That happened a lot.'

Excited now, he pulled the car to one side and reached for the map in the back of the car. Opening it he laid it on both their laps. He found the River Frome and traced its meanderings with his finger.

'Yes . . . See! There seem to be three places where formal gardens or woods come down to the river. Here at Sayers Heath, then at Quarr Wood and finally Warmwell Green.'

'But they could be eighteenth-, nineteenth- and even twentieth-century gardens.'

'True, but there's a chance that newer gardens, or woods, were built over earlier ones, because the micro-climate, or drainage, made it ideal for growing things. In any case, once we are actually on the river we can survey the whole bank, to be on the safe side. You didn't by any chance ask that Nora woman where we could hire a boat?'

'No. I thought it would sound odd.'

'Yes, you're probably right.' He tugged at an eyebrow. 'It will be in Dorchester, I expect. That's the only big town around here.'

It took about half an hour to get to Dorchester. Since it was still not yet nine o'clock, they stopped off at The Yeoman for another Thomas Hardy breakfast. 'We can find out from the hotel where the boatyards are,' said Michael.

Around ten they nosed the Mercedes behind County Hall, as they had been directed, down around the local prison to where a number of small, red-brick industrial buildings huddled on either side of the river. There were warehouses, a small gasholder, a ship's chandler's, a railway siding that hadn't been used in years and now led nowhere. They came to a dead-end road, and right at the bottom they saw a sign which read, 'Waddon Wharf: Boats for Hire.'

Michael pulled the car half off the cobbled road and on to the pavement. 'Let's take the rest of the apples,' he said. 'In case there aren't any pubs on the river. Leave your handbag in the glove compartment– we don't want it falling into the river.'

They crossed the street and walked into the dock. 'Now's your chance to be bossy again,' said Michael, grinning at Isobel. 'Boats are your business.'

A youth of about eighteen was sitting on a tin and slapping paint on to the upturned hull of a small boat. He was listening to a radio but looked up as they approached.

'We'd like a boat, please,' said Isobel.

'Oars or powered?' He didn't move or stop painting.

'Oh, with an engine of course.'

'It's three pounds an hour.'

Michael stepped forward, taking his wallet from his jacket. 'How long would it take to get to Wareham, do you think?'

The youth shrugged. 'Four hours. Maybe five.'

'And how late do you stay open tonight?'

Only now did the youth stop painting. 'We're open until eight all through June. But if you want the boat all day you have to pay in advance. Ten hours – that's thirty pounds.'

Michael handed over two £20 notes. The boy put the paintbrush on the top of the hull, got up, took the money and disappeared into a brick, lean-to shed which appeared to be the office. He brought back the change and then led them by a twisting path around several other upturned boats in the dockyard. This brought them to a short pontoon. The boat which the youth selected for them looked reassuringly new, though it was nowhere near as big as the craft on which they had sailed the Broads. In fact, it looked to Michael like little more than a rowing boat with an engine fixed to the back. The boy said it was called a skiff.

He showed them how to start and stop the engine. He checked that there was a full tank of petrol, and filled a spare. He stowed it away, with some ropes, in a compartment at the prow of the boat. A square piece of board fitted loosely in the top of the compartment to keep out the rain and spray. A single oar, for emergencies in case of engine failure, lay along the bottom of the skiff. 'This juice should last you all day,' the youth said. 'If it doesn't, or if you have any problems, you can get petrol and technical help at Wool and at Wareham. Or you can phone us on the number painted on the engine casing.' He pointed it out to Isobel. 'And, don't forget, rivers aren't like roads. You keep right.'

214

He held the boat steady as Isobel and Michael, carrying the apples, got in and settled themselves evenly. The small craft was much less stable than the bigger boat they had used in East Anglia. The youth pushed them off, waited for a moment to see how accomplished they were in boats and then, reassured that Isobel at least knew what she was doing, disappeared back to his paintbrush.

At first the river was quite narrow and ran quickly. Also, since they were still upstream from Godwin Magna and therefore on a part of the river they were not interested in, Isobel gave the engine full throttle. The sun was now high enough in the sky for its rays to beat on their skin with a good heat, though the breeze coming off the water was pleasantly cooling. It was shaping up into a perfect day.

They had the river more or less to themselves, though as they passed Dorset College of Agriculture they watched one or two rather larger boats drawn up along the bank, being loaded with bags of fertiliser.

It took them about forty minutes to get to Godwin Magna. As the familiar bridge, with its damp patches, came into view, Isobel slowed the engine so that they were moving through the water barely faster than the current. The hill to the village rose on their left, while on the other side a wide watermeadow, treeless, ran down the edge of the Frome for about half a mile.

For the next hour and a half Isobel and Michael moved slowly downstream. Sometimes the road was in view, though more often it was not. In the flatter parts of the valley the watermeadows were marshy, stippled with reeds. In other places the trees came all the way to the edge, making the water dark and the air cool. As their eyes became accustomed to river life, they saw fish, moorhens, different types of ducks, sly water rats just nosing the surface.

They came to Sayers Heath first but didn't bother to stop. It was a modern pine forest, regulated and dense and probably no more than forty years old. There was no house associated with it, which might relate back to earlier times. There were no flowers of any description.

They motored on, occasionally munching apples. Grainger might still be ahead of them but Michael found it was difficult not to relax in such idyllic surroundings. The sun, reflected in the water, was beginning to hurt their eyes. They passed a few boats but nowhere near as many as there had been on the Broads. They chugged by clouds of cow parsley with their acrid tang, wild rhododendrons, once crimson but now over, swags of dark blue berries they couldn't put a name to.

Quarr Wood they reached just after noon. This looked much more promising and Michael's pulse quickened. The wood lay just beyond a very old stone bridge and below a meadow which had a number of curious, curved dips in it. Isobel noticed these and recognised what they were.

'That's where the river used to run,' she told Michael. 'There are places like that near the farm and all over Britain. In the thirteenth and fourteenth centuries the monks straightened the rivers so that the water ran faster and turned their mills more efficiently. That means we should find a very old mill, or at least the site of one, at the end of this straight stretch. This is a medieval area now, just here. Keep your eyes peeled.'

When they came to it, Quarr Wood actually straddled the river. The water here was wide with shingle banks. Two swans patrolled the shingle. To Michael, the trees looked like a mixture of the old and the new. There was a profusion of nettles, but what caught his attention was an old stone weir to one side of the river, where a tributary joined it, and an old wall which looked as if it had once enclosed a garden.

Michael pointed to the weir. 'That's marked on the map as Blood River – see how red the water is, from the local soil. Let's put in to the shingle bank.'

Neither of them was exactly dressed to forage in the jungle of nettles and trees which lay beyond the shingle, and the going was hard. Nonetheless, they followed the broken-down wall as best they could and found that, at its far end, there were a number of other walls, equally ancient. Trees and undergrowth sprouted up everywhere.

Breathing heavily from the exertion, Michael said, 'I remember on the map that there is a Quarr Abbey marked in old-fashioned gothic type, meaning it's a ruin. This must be it. If we could find a link between Monksilver and Quarr then this is the place where the almonds might have bloomed at one time.'

216

'Look, there's a lane over there, and a notice.'

It was true. They had reached the road.

They broke free of the nettles and undergrowth and emerged on to the tarmac. The sign was dilapidated but legible. 'Quarr Abbey' it read:

Quarr Abbey was a thriving institution in the fourteenth century but fell into disuse after a local woman, who had given birth to a child by one of the monks, killed her infant, committed suicide and was secretly buried in the abbey graveyard. Under ecclesiastical law, the abbey grounds immediately became deconsecrated. When the scandal became public, no one could be found who would exhume the body. The monastery thus gave away the land to the local village of Quarton but no one wanted it and it was never used. In time, other bodies which, for one reason or another, could not be interred in consecrated ground, were buried here at Quarr. These were mainly suicides and for that reason Quarr Wood was known for a time in the Middle Ages and up to the Reformation as the Wood of Suicides. The abbey could not survive the scandal and closed in 1467.

'Grisly,' whispered Isobel with a shudder.

'So the abbey was already a ruin by the time our story started. And no one would go near. That could make it an ideal hiding place.'

'What do you want to do?'

Michael hesitated. 'We've made so many mistakes so far, I don't want to make any more. This is a good bet but there's plenty of river for us to see yet. Let's go on, simply so that we can rule out any other sites. Then we can come back and study Quarr more carefully.'

They retraced their steps through the undergrowth and along the side of the wall and returned to the boat. Isobel started the engine and they moved off. They stopped at Wool, where the Wise Virgin pub adjoined the river, and bought some sandwiches. But they were soon on their way again.

Below Wool the river became very winding, almost doubling back on itself at several places. They passed another pine forest at

217

Stoke Common, but this did not come near the river. Warmwell Green, when they came to it, was an eighteenth-century house and park, well tended, with horses and grazing cattle, all standing about as if they were waiting to be photographed for a postcard. Michael noticed some Roman remains here and there, and a very old stone bridge, called Holmebridge. There was also a priory at Holmebridge but its grounds did not come down to the river.

Beyond that they passed under a railway bridge, chugged passed an oil tank and came to the playing fields of a school. They had reached Wareham. Isobel slowed 'Shall I go about?'

'You mean turn, I suppose.' He grinned and looked at his watch. 'Three-thirty. Yes. It has to be Quarr Abbey. It's the only place that fits. Let's get back to Dorchester and drop off the boat. If they have room at The Yeoman we can stay there tonight and start in the museum tomorrow morning. There must be old plans of Quarr somewhere, which might help.'

Going back, upstream, Isobel asked Michael to steer so she could sunbathe. They swapped positions – with difficulty – and she hitched up her skirt again to brown her legs. Michael tried hard to concentrate on the river banks. He lit a cigar.

The breeze blew the smoke towards Isobel and she waved it back to him. 'You make so many clouds, Michael Whiting, it's a wonder you don't make rain.' She turned away.

Sitting in the stern and watching the river more closely now that he had to steer, Michael was amazed at how unfamiliar it looked going upstream, compared with coming the other way. The over-hang of trees was quite different, bends looked different, the approach to bridges was unexpected.

They passed Quarr, Michael now convinced more than ever that that was where they would be coming back to. They passed Cranes Moor. At Woodsford, Isobel again took over the tiller and Michael sat near the bow of the boat, looking at the map. Woodsford was one of the villages where the church was on the river.

Suddenly, Michael shouted. 'I've got it! It's not Quarr at all. Pull over, Isobel, let me show you. It's on the bloody map!'

It was easier said than done to stop, but Isobel managed to steer towards an overhanging tree which Michael could grab hold of. She

218

didn't switch off but put the engine into neutral and took the map from Michael as he held on to the tree trunk.

'Find Woodsford on the map,' he said excitedly. 'Follow the river down from Dorchester . . . got it?'

She nodded.

'Right. Now go back upstream. What is written next to the village name in gothic type?'

'Woodsford Castle.'

'Correct. Now, look at what is written on the other side of the river, opposite Woodsford Castle.'

'Frome Mead?'

'No, next to that.'

'White Mead.'

'Yes!'

'So?'

'Isobel! White Mead. White Meadow. Why is it called *white* meadow? Because white flowers used to bloom there. Because, when it was given its name, the white colour was notable. Why was it notable? Because it came from a rare tree, a foreign tree, a tree that no one else had.'

'Why didn't they call it Almond Mead?'

'Maybe they did, some of the time. But it was White Mead that stuck. And the clincher is: where better to hide something than in a castle? This has to be the place.'

'A minute ago, you were convinced it was Quarr.'

'Isobel! It must be one of these two places. But my betting is on the castle now. Come on, let's get back. There's bound to be material on the castle in the local museum. We're only four miles from Dorchester.'

Isobel handed him the map, put the engine into gear and Michael let go of the tree. The boat surged forward. After a few hundred yards, the river wound to the right. 'White Mead should be just round this bend,' said Michael. 'Keep over as close to the bank as you can. Maybe there's still a trace of almond somewhere.'

There were bushes sticking out from the bank now, rather than trees, and they had to proceed quite far around the bend before White Mead opened up in front of them. The mead was indeed flat and stretched back several hundred yards to where a forest started.

219

There were, however, a few smaller trees clustered at one end of the meadow, and Michael was just about to ask whether Isobel thought they could be almonds when she cried out, in a half whisper, 'Look! Another boat.'

It was true. A launch, much larger than the boat they were in, was drawn up by the bank.

Michael stared ahead. As he did so, a figure appeared, walking across the meadow towards the launch. It was a tall thin man with greying hair and, from Isobel's earlier description and the photograph on the book jacket, Michael realised it could only be one person.

'Grainger!' whispered Isobel, voicing Michael's thoughts. 'Has he seen us?'

'Not yet, but he soon will. There's nowhere to hide in the middle of a river.'

'Oh God! Now he'll know we've caught up with him.'

'It had to happen, sooner or later. He's not finding this any easier than we are . . . It's been three days since he was at Peverell Place . . . He may have been cruising the river ever since, looking for a likely spot.'

'Do you think he's found anything?'

'He can't have, if I'm right and the answer is at Woodsford Castle.' Michael peered forward again. 'He doesn't look as though he's carrying anything. It *has* to be the castle.'

'It will take us nearly two hours to get to Dorchester and back again. If Grainger discounts the meadow, he might try the castle next – and we could be too late. Why don't we put ashore now and go straight there? I know we wouldn't have the car but it's better than – he's seen us!'

Michael peered across to the figure in the field. Grainger had stopped on the bank, in the act of untying the rope which tethered the launch. His face was stony and fierce.

By now the skiff was passing the launch. As it did so, another bridge, one used only for farm animals, came into view. Michael looked at his watch. It was nearly seven. 'Make for the bridge,' he said as softly as he could and still make himself heard above the engine noise. 'We can get ashore and there'll be a track of some sort leading to the main road. Easier than having to cross fields.'

The bridge was perhaps 500 yards away. Isobel opened the throttle as far as it would go and the engine pitch rose to a whine. The bow lifted as the propeller dug deeper into the river.

Michael looked back. 'Stampede time,' he breathed. 'He's following!'

It was true. Grainger had started his launch and had turned it to head back upstream. As Michael watched, he saw the bow of the launch lift, as Grainger also put his engines on to maximum power.

For thirty tense seconds, Michael watched. Then he yelled, 'He's catching us! Christ, he's much faster than we are.' The bridge was still a couple of hundred yards away.

Isobel looked back over her shoulder, and shuddered at how close Grainger was all of a sudden. 'I can't go any faster,' she cried. 'The throttle is full open!'

'Try for calmer water,' said Michael, pointing to a stretch of smoother river in the middle of the flow.

Isobel nudged the tiller and the boat moved over.

It was a mistake, Grainger's launch, moving up all the time, now slipped in between Isobel's wake and the bank, making it impossible, as the bridge approached, for them to put ashore as they had planned.

'We're going away from the castle,' shouted Michael. 'Can you stop and turn?'

Grainger was drawing level. And he was edging closer.

Isobel throttled back. Immediately, the boat settled in the water and Grainger's launch shot ahead. Quickly, Isobel thrust the engine into reverse. Their small boat might have been slower than the launch but it was much more manoeuvrable.

She took the boat's stern close to the bank – it was high and lined with nettles just here – then threw it into forward gear again and steered back down the river.

'See where the church is,' cried Michael, pointing. 'You can see the steeple. There's a graveyard between it and the river. It's flat and I saw a wooden landing. Let's try to get ashore there.'

But Grainger had also turned by now and was again in pursuit. Worse, it was further to the churchyard than it had been to the bridge going upstream, so he had more time to catch them. This time Isobel made no attempt to alter course; she simply set the boat's prow downstream and held it there, cutting as close to the bank as she dared when they came to the bend. With three hundred yards to go, Michael could see the landing but Grainger was only thirty yards behind them. At two hundred he was a boat's length away.

The waters of the river gleamed in the afternoon sun. The wake from the two boats rocked the reeds by the banks, flushing out the moorhens which bobbed up and down in angry disarray.

There was a hundred yards of water between the skiff and a safe part of the bank. Grainger's launch rocked in their wake.

They came to the final bend before the church landing. Isobel took the skiff very close to the bank, hoping Grainger, with a bigger boat, would have to take a wider course. The rattle of the engines bounced back off the bank, emphasising how close the two boats now were. The river straightened.

Then Grainger rammed them.

The first sensation Michael had was that they were being pushed faster through the water. But then Isobel was knocked forward and she fell into the well of the boat, rocking it wildly. The launch again rammed the engine and suddenly the whine died, fuel spilled everywhere, as the tank was burst and the feeder pipe snapped. The boat suddenly yawed to the left, away from Woodsford and the graveyard. The bitter tang of petrol filled the river and Michael noticed patches of it, purple and yellow, catch the sun on the surface of the water.

The launch, under full speed, rushed on past them but already Grainger was preparing to turn. Michael checked that Isobel was not seriously hurt, then reached for the oar which the youth had left in the boat for emergencies. He could at least steer with that. The skiff was so unstable, however, that it took Michael vital seconds to get the oar in position. By then, Grainger's launch had turned and was now aimed upstream, coming straight towards them.

'Where did he get that launch?' gasped Isobel. 'Do you think he has to give it back by eight o'clock, just as we do?'

Michael grinned grimly. He was now trying to use the oar to make contact with the bank, to steer them nearer so that they could scramble ashore. For some reason he noticed that he still had his cigar in his mouth. It hadn't even gone out. But then the launch was upon them.

Grainger was clever. Since they no longer had any power, he approached them below full speed. Then, about twenty yards away, he accelerated so that the bow of his launch rose in the water. Finally, at the very last moment, he throttled back so that the launch not only rammed them but dropped down *on* to their skiff.

The grating sound of cracking wood was louder than Michael expected. Splinters flew everywhere, and cold, cold water began to fill the boat. The force of the collision threw Michael and Isobel outwards, back into the centre of the stream and away from the launch. Michael gasped as the cold, raw water closed around him. His nostrils filled with river and the rank odour of sedge and petrol swamped him. He surfaced and gasped for air. Jesus, the water was cold! And it was June. He was a good swimmer – in a pool – and waited a moment before trying to strike out. He didn't know how strong the current would be. He watched himself being swept down-stream and immediately decided that the water flow was much too swift to fight.

Now he looked about for Isobel. He saw her head, her hair plastered to her skull. She was a few yards upstream but further from the bank. 'Don't fight the current!' he yelled. 'Swim with it and try to get over to the other bank – look out!'

Grainger had turned the launch and was coming back downstream again. He was about fifty yards away.

Michael struck out for the far bank. He tried to get himself downstream of Isobel so that eventually the current would bring her to him.

Grainger must have sensed that Michael was the stronger swim-mer, for no sooner had Michael taken a few strokes than he saw that the launch was making for Isobel. Worse, he could now see that Grainger had something in his hand. A pole. No! It looked like a boat-hook.

Isobel was helpless. From her movements it was clear that, though she could swim, she was not really at home in the water. Grainger would be able to spear her as easily as a leaf on a lawn. He was by now only thirty yards away and moving fast. There was no hope that Michael could get to her first and, even if he could, what would he do?

Michael could also see that Isobel was tiring – their clothes made

223

movement difficult. Frantically he looked about him. There was nothing he could throw at Grainger, nothing he could use as a missile. There were pieces of wood from the splintered skiff floating nearby but they were all too big to throw far. Now Grainger was only twenty yards from Isobel! The boat-hook in his hand looked vicious, an eighteen-inch stiletto at the end of a ten-foot wooden shaft. A curl, a hard metal twist, jutted out halfway down the spike. It transformed the spear into a barb. As Michael watched, the hook glinted in the sunlight.

Suddenly, to his right Michael saw the square piece of wood that had covered the compartment in the prow of the skiff, the compartment where the extra fuel and ropes were stored to keep them from getting too wet. The square must have been dislodged when Grainger's launch had rammed them. It was bright blue and floated a little downstream from Michael in the middle of the river. He took three swift strokes and grabbed at it.

'Isobel!' he called. As she turned to him, Michael gave a huge kick with his legs under water, forcing the top of his body above the waterline. As he rose he threw the square of wood towards Isobel. He spun it flat, just as, when he was a boy, he had thrown stones on the surface of the sea, skimming them along the top. The square of wood hit the water about five yards short of Isobel but skidded on, settling where, without a second thought, she grabbed it.

She didn't need telling what to do. But would she have time? Grainger was now no more than ten yards away. With one arm he was steering the launch straight for Isobel, intending to crush her as well as spear her.

Isobel took the square of wood with both hands and held on. Grainger was now five yards away. He lifted the boat-hook.

Just as the prow of the launch seemed as if it would sweep over Isobel, she did as Michael had done moments before. She kicked with her legs. Her body surged sideways and the launch missed her - but only just and, as he swept by, Grainger, in the stern, stabbed down at her with the boat-hook. The movement of the launch added to Grainger's own strength and the hook flashed down faster than a guillotine. Isobel twisted in the water. After the effort of kicking herself out of the launch's path, she was more exhausted than ever and lay virtually horizontal in the river, presenting a large, unmissable target.

From where Michael was it seemed that Grainger had aimed at Isobel's heart, though it might have been her neck. At the last second, however, she managed to lift the square of wood which Michael had thrown. She held it above her, a square blue shield about an inch thick.

There was no time to spare. The black, gunmetal spike slammed into the wood.

The sound, a thud mixed with a loud crack as the wood split from the force of Grainger's thrust, shot back across the river towards Michael. It was sickening in its intensity.

Michael didn't wait to see what Grainger would do next. He struck out directly for Isobel, fighting the current. She had a similar thought and was swimming towards him. 'No!' he shouted. 'There!' He pointed towards a part of the bank where a tree leaned out over the river. 'There!'

Grainger was slowing again, but the current had taken him further downstream and he would now have to come back against the flow.

Michael reached the tree first. Some of its branches hung down almost to water level but they were too thin to take a person's weight. The more sturdy trunk, however, was three or four feet above the waterline, out of reach. As Isobel approached, Michael gave another kick and his body rose in the water. His shoulders and arms lifted free. His clothes, wet and heavy, clung to him, hampering his movements. His hands reached the trunk but couldn't hold on, they were so wet and cold. He slipped back and the river closed over his head. The stench of algae and petrol again filled his nostrils.

As he surfaced, coughing and sneezing, he looked downstream and saw Grainger beginning to move towards them again, no more than fifty yards away. Michael realised with horror that Grainger had not turned his boat this time. *He was reversing upstream!* The boat was hardly slower in reverse, but that wasn't the point. The point was that Grainger was coming for them screw first! The propeller could cut their legs to bits below water. Michael looked at the tree above him. He had to get up there. Grainger would get one of them this time.

Michael struggled in the water, kicking with his legs as he

shrugged off his jacket. He curled his knees up to his chest and yanked off his shoes. They floated away though he barely noticed. He looked up at the tree again. He took a deep breath. Grainger was thirty yards downstream. Michael kicked. His body lifted and this time his hands closed over the top of the trunk. For a moment his body hung there, his skin showing through his dripping shirt, and his trousers clammy against his legs. Grainger was twenty yards away.

Michael heaved and pulled his legs out of the water and shoved his right knee over the trunk. Through his trousers, its bark burned his flesh. He pushed his knee further, until he could hook his foot over the other side. Then, using that, he levered his body horizontally along the tree. Grainger was barely fifteen yards from Isobel.

Michael reached down. Isobel's hands were wet and cold and her grip was not strong. Michael jerked her up, let go and, as she fell back, grabbed under her armpits. As he took her full weight he gasped. He thought his own arms would be dragged from their sockets. Water, cold heavy water, poured off Isobel, though her sodden clothes squelched with still more river. Ropes of sedge clung to her hair, her shirt, her belt. Ten yards away the propeller from Grainger's launch was churning the water a foaming white.

Michael pulled. And pulled. Isobel's body rose a few inches out of the water. He yanked again. She rose higher. The twisting propeller was five yards away. 'Hold the tree with your arms!' he yelled. She did as she was told. Michael grabbed her legs and pulled them clear of the water and on to the trunk. They both gasped for air, shivering and sobbing as their clammy clothes stuck to them, making every movement, even breathing, uncomfortable.

Below them a change in sound signalled that Grainger had shifted gear. The launch slid back into midstream and then, turning, moved ever faster as it caught the main flow of the river and surged with it downstream towards Wool and Wareham. Having missed Isobel a second time, Grainger was getting out.

For a moment Michael and Isobel lay shivering on the tree, getting their breath. Then, slowly, with Michael leading the way, they inched backwards to the more certain safety of the river bank.

Michael backed gingerly off the tree. Here the bank was covered with nettles. He looked about him. Were there any witnesses to the dreadful attack they had just endured? He could see no one. It was a perfect English evening. The countryside was serene, a landscape of lies in itself. He picked wet weed out of his hair, broke off a heavy branch from the tree and used it to sweep a path through the nettles to the flat meadow beyond. Then he went back for Isobel. She had edged herself to the foot of the tree trunk but she now leaned against it, sobbing. Her hands, her lips, her shoulders were all shaking.

'Michael . . .' she gasped, 'Michael . . . he tried to kill me. If that hook had . . . oh!' A sound, purely involuntary, escaped from her throat as she relived the moment and a shock reaction set in. She shook and cried inconsolably.

Michael put his arms around her. He plucked the wet sedge from her hair and her shirt. He peeled some of it from where it clung to her neck and cheeks. For a long while, he said nothing. He just gripped her tightly and felt her shaking inside his arms. Then, very softly, he said: 'Isobel, it will pass. You are in shock. Perfectly normal. It will pass. Don't forget, we're alive. Grainger lost this round. We beat the bugger.'

'But he'll come back. And – '

'Don't think about that now. I think we should move away from the river, don't you? It's bad luck. I've made a path through the nettles. Come on.'

Gently, he took her hand and led her into the meadow. They were both shivering badly now. 'I see some roofs over there.' Michael pointed. 'Let's hope the natives are friendly. I think we're safe from Grainger for a while.'

There was still no sign of anyone else. It had now gone seven and the day was no longer as warm as it had been. Michael made Isobel hurry as much as she could, even though they were both racked with exhaustion, and Michael had no shoes. The meadow was pitted with thistles, spiky branches and half-hidden stones. In no time, Michael's feet were bleeding. When they came to the gate, things did not improve. The lane beyond was made up of rough stones that helped a tractor's tyres but still bit into Michael's feet. Worse, when they came to them, the roofs turned out to be cow-sheds and a barn. There was not a human soul in sight. More exhausted than ever, they were forced to trudge on up the farm track towards the road. Their clothes clung to them as if they had been vacuum-packed to their skin and their joints felt cold and stiff. They walked awkwardly, like robots, their clothes squelching in time to their steps.

After another ten minutes they came to the tarmac road and Michael could tread more easily. There were no signs but instinctively they both turned left, towards Dorchester and away from Grainger. A car passed them going in the same direction. Michael waved at it and the driver, a woman, slowed, but as soon as she saw their appearance close up she accelerated hard and was soon out of sight.

Isobel was still shaking, still in shock. Her mind was still focused on the moment when Grainger hurled the boat-hook at her. Michael gripped her arm to guide her along the road.

After a few hundred yards, they reached a pine forest on the right. Young trees, straight and thin as boat-hooks, stretched upwards by the thousand. At the end of the trees they saw three or four houses. 'Thank God!' growled Michael.

Leaving Isobel at the gate, Michael tried the first house. He rang the bell. There was no reply. He knocked hard on the door. There was no reply. He tried again. Silence: the house was empty. Coming back down the path, however, he saw that he was being eyed from across the way by a large man who was just wheeling a bicycle down the path from the house opposite. Michael walked across to him.

'We had an accident on the river,' he said. 'Our boat sank. As you can see, we need a place to dry off and to make a telephone call.'

The man inspected him hard. He looked at Isobel, still standing where Michael had left her. Her shaking seemed to convince him that Michael's story was true, for he said, 'Hmm. That river's trouble. Flooded last year and drowned thirteen sheep. Missy there looks poorly.' He leaned his bicycle against the hedge. 'Come on.' He walked back to the house, opened a side door and looked out through it. 'This way.'

Michael had fetched Isobel from the far side of the road and they followed the man. The door led into a conservatory that had soaked up sun all day and was wonderfully warm. Immediately Michael felt his body respond. The man had some towels in his hand. 'There's a bathroom in there.' He pointed into the house. 'You can wear these if you like.' He fetched two old raincoats from behind the door. 'Better than nothing.'

'You go first,' said Michael to Isobel, gently shoving her inside the house. He turned back to the man. 'You're very kind. If I could just use your phone . . . ?'

'No . . . This has to be reported first. I'll call Frank Hilton – he's our local PC. He'll know what to do. Then you can phone. Hang on here.'

While he was gone, Michael started to dab himself dry with the towel. He took off his shirt and squeezed the water out of it. The conservatory was doing a wonderful job of reviving him. Michael had not been a direct target of Grainger, as Isobel had, and so his reaction to their ordeal was not as extreme. The image of her shaking, out there in the road, flashed into his mind. Her shoulders, her lips, her chin . . . tiny, rapid tremors. It brought back for him the vibrations he had felt in the water as Grainger had reversed towards them, the propeller of his launch twisting the water into white fury. Michael tried to think ahead but couldn't. All he was aware of was that Grainger's violence was getting worse. Money, big money, even the prospect of it, did that to some people, though he had never come across it personally before. Grainger's viciousness gave him only one piece of comfort. They must be very close to the end, very close indeed.

The man returned before Isobel. He had a bottle with him, and some glasses. 'Frank's coming right over. Five minutes. Here, you'll need this.'

Michael smiled as the welcome whisky was splashed into a glass. He swallowed hard and felt the familiar itch as the firewater warmed his insides, matching the effects of the conservatory on the outside.

'I'll show you to the phone.'

Michael followed the man, taking the glass with him. He found the number of The Yeoman in Dorchester in a book beside the telephone and called the hotel. Yes, they remembered him from before and, yes, they had two rooms. He sighed and finished his whisky as he put down the receiver. He could sort out everything else from there.

Isobel reappeared. She wasn't shaking so much now, but she wasn't recovered either. It was too soon for that. She accepted the whisky and sipped at it. The raincoat swamped her but at least it was dry and warm and, in a curious way, Michael thought it looked quite sexy. He didn't say so, though, and went off to the bathroom to change himself.

While he was gone, he heard a car pull up outside: the policeman had arrived. When Michael returned to the conservatory it was to find the policeman writing down details of the 'accident'.

Isobel spoke shakily, and scarcely above a whisper. As the constable was scribbling, she added, 'We're sorry to put you to this trouble. We were very foolish, trying to change places in midstream. Our own silly fault.'

Michael stared at her. What *was* this? But Isobel swallowed some whisky, glaring back at Michael over her glass, a fierce expression that dared him to contradict her.

The constable finished writing and looked up. 'So there was no one else in this . . . skiff . . . with you?'

They both shook their heads. That was true, as far as it went.

'And did the boat sink?'

'Most of it,' said Michael. 'Bits and pieces floated away.'

'Did anyone else see the accident?'

Again Michael shook his head. 'I don't think so. Mind you, we scrambled ashore along an overhanging tree. We weren't looking out for spectators.'

'What else did you lose? Personal things?'

'I had to take my jacket off. My wallet, credit cards, pen, cheque-book, were all inside. I took my shoes off too.'

The constable continued writing in his book. 'How did you get here?'

'We walked. Up a track, past some cowsheds, then along the road by the pine wood. A woman in a car saw us, but didn't stop. Can't say I blame her.'

More scribbling in the book. Then the policeman closed it and put it away in a pocket.

'If it's all right with you, sir, I think I'll drive you into Dorchester. Just to make sure all this has a tidy ending.'

'Fine,' said Michael. 'I don't know what my credit is like at The

Yeoman but, if they will allow me, I'll give you a bottle of whisky to bring back for this gentleman here.'

'This way, then,' said the constable.

Michael gathered up their wet clothes. He thanked the man whose house they had used and shook his hand. 'We'll need the raincoats as far as Dorchester. But the constable here can bring them back.'

The man nodded and they all got into the police car. The constable thoughtfully put the heater on so that the drive to Dorchester was both speedy and comfortable.

At The Yeoman, there was a certain curiosity about a couple who arrived wearing raincoats, and nothing else, but the receptionist recognised them, the hotel records confirmed the names and addresses which they had given to the policeman, so he was reassured. He said that next morning he would inspect the river near where the accident had taken place, just for form's sake. Then he added, 'How are you going to get home from here?' asked the policeman.

'With difficulty,' said Michael. 'I left my car near the boatyard, but my car keys were in my jacket. Isobel's handbag is locked in the car. And it's Sunday tomorrow.'

'If you have any problems, give me a ring.' The policeman handed Michael a card with a phone number on it. 'You'll probably have to ring your bank on Monday and they may need some convincing. They may trust me.'

Michael thanked the constable, gave him the whisky for the man whose house they had used, and then he and Isobel were shown upstairs. The hotel staff provided two towelling dressing-gowns and took away their wet things, promising to have them cleaned and pressed by the next morning.

They both took lingering baths, then climbed back into their towelling robes. Not having proper clothes, they could not eat in the dining-room. Dinner, plus the whisky and wine which Michael ordered, was brought up to them. They ate it in Isobel's room. Michael swallowed ravenously, though Isobel only picked at hers.

As soon as she had eaten enough, she asked him to turn his back. She slipped out of the bathrobe and got into bed. It was not yet eleven o'clock.

Michael sat drinking his whisky. 'Isobel?'

'Hmm?'

'Today wasn't pleasant. We could stop now. We *should* stop now. We should have told that policeman about Grainger. Why didn't you?'

She was lying on her side, her back to him. She pulled the sheets and blankets about her. 'Get into bed.'

He hesitated, unsure what to do.

'Get in. I'm cold.'

He took off his dressing-gown, put his whisky on the table at the side of the bed and slipped between the sheets. Isobel was indeed very cold. She pulled his arm around her, until his body cupped hers.

After a few minutes she said, 'Put out the lights, please. Then come back.'

Michael finished his whisky and switched out the bedside lamps. Then he put his arm around Isobel again. When they had settled, and their breathing was regular, Isobel whispered, 'Michael, I was scared today. Terrified. Terrified like I've never been before.'

As best he could, with one arm, Michael gave her a hug. Their bodies pressed together. Isobel was now not so cold. He was aware of the smell of soap on her skin.

'I really did think, when I was floundering in that river, that . . . that he was going to kill me. I even imagined what it would feel like to have a boat-hook in your chest – '

Her body jerked involuntarily as the memory came back, and Michael tried another hug.

'All the time I was in Beirut, I was never as frightened as today. Not in Nicaragua, the Philippines, Afghanistan. What got into Grainger?'

Michael, who had never had any ambition to see war, secretly thought he lacked the qualifications to comfort Isobel. His sister Robyn would be better; at least she had been to unusual places. Instinctively, he spoke softly and slowly, trying to reassure Isobel as much by his tone as his words. 'That's the wrong way to look at it. We don't know him and, obviously, he's a very violent man. Several million pounds are quite enough to make even the wisest owls cuckoo. He had several million pounds of cordite in him today. He was Megaton-mad.'

For a moment they lay quietly in the dark. Not that the room was very dark once their eyes became adjusted. Amber light from the streetlamps outside streamed around the edges of the curtains. Michael didn't so much kiss Isobel's shoulder as press his face into it.

Then Isobel said, 'I've never known any really violent people. I mean, when you are a journalist and you go to places where there is a lot of *political* violence, you see the end results, the damage, the bodies, the blood. But you hardly ever see the people who *do* all that. When you meet the terrorists, you meet the leaders, people who may *condone* bloodshed but don't exactly set off the bombs themselves. There must be a difference, too, between killing people at a distance with a bomb or gun and . . . well, like today.'

She paused, and Michael gave her another one-armed hug.

'To kill someone, to *stab* them, close to, in the countryside, on a summer's day, in England . . . disregarding the consequences . . . have you ever met anyone like that, Michael?'

Michael thought back. 'No, not personally. But Greg has. When he was younger he was in one of those crack army units – you know, all parachuting and unarmed combat. He talked about it once. The most remarkable thing he said, the thing I remember most, was that violent people often have a remarkably good grasp of the psychological aspects of rough stuff. He said, for instance, that even quite stupid people, when they get into a brawl, will not spend any time arguing. They hit the other person straight away and as hard as possible. Violence is so rare in most people's lives that when it happens to them their first reaction is *surprise*. They can't believe that it's happening and that it's happening to them. By the time they do, it's too late.'

'Yes, I can understand that. But what makes people erupt, like Grainger did today? What makes some people violent in the first place?'

'Genes? Drink? Then again some people seem to have violence bottled up inside them. Maybe Grainger's like that. Don't forget what happened to him at Oxford. It must have made him very bitter and angry and it's been slowly coming out. He broke into your house but didn't do much damage. He damaged the boot of

233

my car. Then he attacked Helen and knocked her studio about. Then today . . .'

He left it unsaid. He waited and then whispered, 'Talking might soothe you tonight, Isobel. But Grainger isn't far away, don't forget. He's probably in some other local hotel, just like us. We may be equally close now but he's got the advantage of being vicious. We can't fight fire with fire. We *need* the police.'

'Damn him! He's not going to win! If we told the police, it would be out of our hands. The police would take ages, just to ask questions. We'd have to tell them everything, about the picture and the missing things. We'd have to – or they wouldn't understand Grainger's motives. He's a respectable academic, after all. Unless we tell them everything, they might easily not believe us. Yes, we were in the river – they'd believe that. But no one saw Grainger attack us.' She sighed. 'If we did make them believe us, then the police would have to broadcast the details to other police forces . . . Who knows what would happen then? They might alert the papers. The picture would be evidence . . . Lots of people would get to know what we know.'

'Better than a repeat of today – '

'No!'

Michael had felt Isobel's body tense. Now it relaxed and she spoke more softly. 'No. After today, Michael, after today especially, this is personal. Between him and us. I was forced to give up in Beirut, over Tony. Not this time. I want revenge.'

Michael felt Isobel tense again. 'It frightened me, Michael. Grainger terrified me. But you don't know me very well. I don't give up. I stayed in Beirut, remember? No, we're going to catch Grainger and then overtake him. We know now what a vicious reptile we are dealing with. There'll be no replay of today. I can be a reptile too.'

In the shadows Michael smiled. What sort of reptile did Isobel imagine she was? But at least it meant that her spirits were reviving. Again he tightened his arm around her. 'This is my anaconda hug.'

She groaned in pleasure and took hold of his hand. She moved it back. 'Ever since I was young, I've loved having my back stroked. It's so soothing. I need soothing now.'

He pushed back the sheet, revealing the smooth sweep of her

back, all the way down to the top of her buttocks. He touched her skin. He moved the tips of his fingers up the line of her backbone, across her shoulders and down to her waist. He scored a fingernail back up her spine. Around the base of her neck, he softly massaged the tops of her shoulders. Then all the way down again.

'Mmmm.'

She manoeuvred on to her front so that he could stroke more of her back. He traced arabesques with his fingertips, lozenges, figures of eight, loops, parabolas, swans' necks.

'Mmmm. We can't stop now.'

'If you feel sure. I don't think Grainger will have done any more searching tonight. You can't dig in the dark but he'll be at the castle at first light tomorrow. *We* won't – there's no way we can be. We've no money, hardly any clothes, no car until I find a key that fits. All that will take two or three hours to fix at the very least. So the reptile might still win – but, yes, I agree that we can't stop now. It's a risk, not bringing in the police – but I suppose I'm glad you feel that way too.'

She twisted her head and looked at him, then reached over her shoulder and grasped his fingers as they brushed her neck. 'Michael,' she said, kissing the tips of his fingers. 'When I said we can't stop now, I wasn't, actually, thinking of Grainger.'

12

At breakfast Michael again raised the question of whether they should proceed. Isobel's lovemaking had been tentative at first but, in response to Michael's stroking, the shapes he continued to draw, deeper down her body, barely touching the skin, she had grown more and more demonstrative. So responsive he was distressed that her release, when it came, turned quickly into a sob – stifled, but unmistakably despairing. He had not said anything but had lain in the amber light with his arms around Isobel as she cried and cried. He felt the warm, sticky tears fall into the crook of his elbow until they both fell asleep.

Michael kissed her awake before phoning down for breakfast but she did not move until the tray was brought into the room.

'Coffee,' Michael said, putting the cup down on the table at the side of the bed. 'Eggs, tomatoes, sausage, bacon, mushrooms, toast . . . Eat it all – you need nourishing . . .' He spoke more softly. 'I'm sorry you were so upset last night . . . but it was natural.'

Now she turned to look at him and reached out for his hand. 'Have you got a chill in your arm? All those tears.'

He smiled. 'I'll do what schoolboys do. Never wash that part of my arm again.'

As Isobel drank her coffee, he went on, 'You were more upset than you thought last night. That's natural too.' He kissed her hand. 'Why don't we go to the police this morning? Let them do all the hard work. We could have a nice lazy day here, kissing and things.

I *like* this bed. As Clarissa would say, it's my second favourite spot. After the jetty in Southwold, where I first kissed you.'

Isobel smiled back at him and shifted lower down the pillows. 'I like this bed too. I like Michael Whiting, as well, even though he doesn't even begin to understand me.'

'Here we go . . . doing a Sylvie on me already?'

'You'll deserve it if you keep talking about other women while we're in bed. I wasn't crying about Grainger last night – well, that's not true . . . It was partly about him, or what he tried to do to us. But it was more about Tony, really.'

'Now you're talking about other men in bed.'

'I have to, just this once.' She looked hard at Michael and the angle in her eyebrows sharpened. 'Last night was the first time I've been to bed with anyone since I was in Beirut. You must have guessed that. It was the first time I *wanted* to. And it was lovely . . . warm, willowy, wonderbloodyful!' She squeezed his hand. 'I wouldn't have cried if it hadn't been so good, Michael. Don't you see that? I was crying goodbye to Tony. I was crying because I couldn't help the fact that at last, at long last, I wanted someone to do to me what you were doing. I was crying for what felt like a hundred reasons. But I was looking back for the last time. That was sad, inexpressibly sad. I loved Tony. Now he's behind me. It could probably only have happened in this way – I was crying about that, too.'

She drank some coffee. 'Grainger had something to do with it but only in the sense that I was so frightened yesterday, and so keyed up, that I saw everything more clearly.' She took Michael's hand again and kissed it. 'I'm happy to stop now and hand everything over to the police if you really want to. We *could* stay in bed all day but I rather think it would be more exciting to spend the day *thinking* about tonight, anticipating it, talking about it.' She laughed. 'And my farm is still losing money.'

Michael laughed as well and handed her a plate of breakfast. 'Now I see why the paper sent you to all those hotspots – bravery verging on the foolish, incredible powers of recovery, the ability to concentrate on the job in hand–'

'The ability to fall for the man I work with–'

'I rest my case. Let's stay here.' He clambered back into bed and slid his hand down Isobel's thigh.

She caught it by crossing her legs and holding it in a scissors grip. 'Slowly, Michael. Look at our day on the Broads. Sail, not steam.' She uncrossed her legs and he lifted his hand and stroked her cheek.

She swallowed a mushroom. 'Mmm.' Speaking with her mouth full, she went on, 'In any case, I don't know about you, but I can't get my mind off Grainger. You said yourself that his violence must mean we are very close. You talk of kissing but do you really want to kiss all that goodbye?' She took his hand in hers and placed it on her thigh. 'I want you just as much . . . I shall want you even more tonight.' She stared at his breakfast plate. 'If I give you another kiss, can I have your mushroom?'

After breakfast Michael tried first to phone his sister Robyn, who now didn't live too far away. She could perhaps lend him some money. When he got through, however, there was a message on her machine to the effect that she had taken an injured tiger to London Zoo for emergency treatment and wouldn't be back for forty-eight hours.

'Robyn has a lot in common with the big cats,' said Michael, turning back to Isobel and smiling. 'She used to be a man-eater too.'

Her absence in London, however, meant that he now had to explain their predicament to the hotel's Sunday manager. He was understanding and said that, if Michael would leave his watch and Isobel her gold necklace, he would advance them £200 in cash until the following day.

Their clothes were ready by ten o'clock. The police constable rang up from Woodsford and said that though it was Sunday he had persuaded the nearest Mercedes dealer, in Yeovil, to bring down to Dorchester the whole range of keys – for a fee, of course. Finally, Michael was lent a pair of wellingtons so he could collect his car. All this took time and it was 2.30 before Michael and Isobel could get into the car and retrieve their cases. Isobel did not have much money in her handbag but she was relieved to be reunited with her make-up. They drove back to the hotel, changed into fresh clothes, then went back to the boatyard, where Michael gave the youth his

238

address and assured him that he would pay for the lost boat. The youth did not appear at all concerned – the boat was insured. Finally, Michael stopped off at a garden centre on the outskirts of Dorchester where he bought a garden fork and a scythe. 'If we *do* meet up with Grainger again,' he said in response to Isobel's curious looks, 'he may still have his boat-hook. This is our reply.' He put them into the back of the car and then, just after three o'clock, they headed for Woodsford.

Mercifully, the road took them south of the river, opposite the bank on to which they had been forced the day before. For a while they followed a railway line, then ran parallel with the river at the edge of the valley. The river looked glassy, the silvery reflections of the clouds disguising the strength of the current which they both knew was there. They saw the spire of Woodsford church before they came to the village and Michael slowed. On the left a track led to the bridge where, the day before, they had first tried to put ashore. Michael stopped, then drove in.

Isobel stiffened as they drew near the river. 'What are you doing?'

'Looking for Grainger, for his boat. If he's here, we need to know. To be prepared.'

But there was no boat moored by the bridge. Michael got out of the car, walked halfway across and looked upstream and downstream. He could just make out White Mead and the leaning tree. There was no sign of any craft at all.

Michael returned to the car. 'No launches, though of course he may by now have changed to a car.'

He steered the Mercedes back to the road and turned towards Woodsford, again moving slowly. After a hundred yards a brown wooden sign announced, 'Woodsford Castle'. He pulled in through a gap in the hedge. With misgiving, he counted two parked cars and a van. Carefully, keeping a lookout for people, Michael turned the Mercedes so that it was pointing back to the road, just in case there was the need for a hurried exit. He looked at the other vehicles.

'Hold on here while I have a look inside the van. The picture could be there. That would explain why he's changed from a motor bike.'

'Be careful, Michael. I'm getting nervous again.'

239

'I'm not going far. You'll be able to see me. Keep the car locked while I'm away, just in case.'

He got out and walked leisurely towards the van, passing close by its bonnet and looking in casually as he went by. There was no one in the front but the back was screened off by something. He was alone in the parking area so he went quickly to the back of the van. The windows here were high and he would have to climb on the bumper to see in. Before doing so he looked around again. Still no one. Gingerly, he stepped on to the bumper. As he did so, the van moved under his weight and he also heard something move inside the vehicle.

His heart beating faster, he straightened his legs and lifted himself up. As his eyes came level with the window, he was startled to see another face staring out. As soon as the other face saw him, its mouth opened and a ferocious barking filled the van. The first Alsatian set off a second, which was also cooped up inside, and between them they made enough noise for a hundred dogs. Michael jumped down and ran back to the car.

'Come on,' he said. 'I've announced our arrival so we might as well walk straight on in.'

Two figures, both women, approached them as Michael and Isobel walked into the castle ruins. They crossed a grassy ridge from where they could see that the place was more ruin than it was castle, more a layout than a real structure any more. And it was immediately obvious that Grainger wasn't there. They could see a bald man with a child, and a young couple who looked Dutch or German. That made three groups of people, accounting for the three vehicles.

They relaxed and wandered around the site. The ruins were well kept; there wasn't much rubbish and the grass had been cropped recently and was otherwise well tended. They could find no signs of recent digging or excavations – nothing dislodged or broken which might have indicated where Grainger had searched. The ruins consisted essentially of three concentric walls, with the remains of most of the buildings within the inner wall. There was also the rubble of a couple of towers on the outer line. Isobel and Michael explored each of these. They were thorough, and, by the time they had finished, everyone else had left.

240

Isobel found a grassy place in the afternoon sun – it was nearly five by now – and got out her photograph of the painting which, thankfully, she had left interleaved in one of the reference books in the back of the Mercedes when they had hired the boat. Michael's photo had gone down with his jacket.

'The next clue,' she said, 'is a skeleton. See – the figure carrying the ivory crosier. That must refer to a cemetery, don't you think?'

Michael nodded. 'Or a tomb.'

'I didn't notice either around here, did you?'

Michael shook his head. 'Can a skeleton have another meaning, do you think?'

They went back to the car and looked at the books again. 'All I can find is the Last Judgement,' said Isobel after a while. 'And that doesn't help much.'

'I suppose it might imply it is the last figure, the last real clue. We already know that the ninth figure is facing the wrong way.' He looked at her. 'Do you get the feeling we've been in this situation before?'

'Something is being underlined for us, you mean?'

'Not exactly. I can't help thinking that we are missing something. Like the Jesse window at Godwin Magna.'

'But we must be close. Why else did Grainger stop at White Mead?'

'We never asked him exactly. Maybe it was simply a call of nature.'

'Michael! You don't believe that.'

'No, I don't. But I'm not so sure this castle is the site, either. It's too old. It may have been a ruin even by the sixteenth century. No one could have buried anything here – it would have been too risky. If we do find the final hiding place, it will make sense in relation to Monksilver, it will be a place they would have known and trusted. This castle doesn't fit the bill.' He paused, then said softly, 'Which perhaps means that White Mead is wrong.'

'It was *your* idea!'

'I know. I've been wrong before, remember. We were guessing that White Mead was named after the almond flowers. Maybe it was a wrong guess.'

'But we saw Grainger there!'

241

'Maybe he had the same thought process and maybe he thought it was wrong too. Don't forget, he saw us coming upstream. All he knew is that we had been further down the river – so he may have thought that we had the right solution all along. Perhaps that's why he went for us. He may have been in the process of concluding that White Mead didn't matter when he saw us coming from the general direction of where the treasure *is* actually hidden. That's why he was so vicious – he thought we were ahead of him at last, might even have found it already. That would explain a lot. It would explain his violence.'

'But that Nora woman seemed so certain the flower is almond.'

'Okay. It's just that we are misunderstanding the allusion.' Michael asked Isobel what the time was. It was half past five. 'We had a rough day yesterday. There's no sense in stretching ourselves today. We've got a lot of thinking to do. More work with the books. I don't know about you but I don't feel like The Yeoman again. Too many odd looks last evening.' He drummed his finger on the driving wheel. 'We're not too far from Burning Cliff, where I know there's a smashing hotel overlooking the sea. I could stroke your back again.'

'Yes, please,' she said. 'To both things.'

He called the hotel from a phone box in Woodsford. Yes, he was told, there was a room. Burning Cliff was no more than five or six miles away and so they arrived not long after six. They checked in, took a walk along the cliff to the old village of Ringstead, had a whisky in the pub, then strolled back to the hotel in time for dinner. All evening they tried out ideas on each other but reached no conclusion.

After dinner, up in their room, they sat for a while listening to the waves and watching the Channel traffic far out at sea. Then, while Isobel was in the bathroom, Michael took out the maps and a sheet of paper. He started scribbling.

'What are you doing?' she said as she came out. Tonight, reunited with her clothes, she was wearing a white lace nightdress.

'I'm making a list of every place marked on the map that could have been a burial site in the sixteenth century and is visible from the river. Then we can see what possible links the things on the list could have with skeletons and almonds.'

242

'Wouldn't you rather come to bed?'

'I thought you wanted to solve this puzzle.'

Isobel got into bed. 'I've been thinking about it all day.'

Michael smiled, put down the maps and started to undress.

When Isobel awoke next day, Michael was already sitting on the balcony in his dressing-gown. She put on hers and joined him. Below them the Channel was already alive with craft, busy in the early sunshine.

She stroked his hair. 'Come back to bed.'

'No.' He looked up. 'Not this time.' He smiled. 'There's no hurry. The list is nearly done. Order breakfast up here in the room. By the time it arrives, I'll have everything down on paper and we can talk it through over coffee and toast.' He kissed her, then gently pushed her away.

The breakfast took fifteen minutes to arrive and Michael was as good as his word. He buttered some toast and said, 'I've got seven names in a fourteen-mile stretch of river.'

'Okay, tell me.'

'Some of them are better candidates than others – but here goes.' He ate some toast. 'Fossil Farm. I thought fossil might relate to bones, as in skeleton. Not too convincing, I agree. Whitborne. That's a village that could, I suppose, be a corruption of White Bones – not very convincing either. Four churches – at Moreton, Pallington, Stokeford and Woodsford – which will all have cemeteries and which also border the river. And, the best candidate, Black Hill.'

'Black Hill – why is that so good?'

'Because it's the site of an ancient tumulus – a burial chamber that would definitely have been around in the sixteenth century.'

Isobel shook her head. 'Michael, you're getting carried away by your own cleverness again. The reason you ruled out Woodsford Castle is because it had no link with the monastery at Monksilver. How can Black Hill have any link? *We* may recognise it as an ancient burial site, but they didn't have archaeologists in the sixteenth century, so the site may not have been recognised for what it was. Like White Mead, Black Hill may be a neat solution, but it is wrong.'

243

Michael munched his toast. She was right. His silence told her she had scored a direct hit.

'I don't much care for Fossil Farm, either,' she continued. 'Whitborne is slightly better but – well, you know, Michael, I've been thinking, and I wouldn't rule out Woodsford Castle entirely. Not yet. Grainger may have had his problems and may not have been able to get there yesterday. Or he may be lying low. After all, he did attempt to murder us – me. He may think we have brought in the police.' She helped them to more coffee. 'I think we should go back to Woodsford this morning and look again, only harder.'

After they had dressed, they did as Isobel suggested. First, though, they had to go back to The Yeoman to settle their bill. Michael had called his bank manager in London from Burning Cliff and, by the time he reached the Dorchester branch of his bank, the money transfer had come through. At The Yeoman, they thanked the manager again, paid what was outstanding and retrieved the watch and the necklace. Then, having put the incident on the river behind them, they sped off for Woodsford. It was another glorious day and they drove with the sun-roof open. The wind was rising and the wheat swayed in the fields like crowds cheering at a rally.

When they reached the castle there were several visitors who had beaten them to it. Grainger was not among them. They searched again for signs of disturbance and for a cemetery or tomb. They could find neither. Even Isobel began to have doubts that the castle was the right place. After an hour they gave up and drove into Woodsford village where they found a pamphlet on the castle in the church. It was no help. The details were skimpy and there were no references to burial sites or practices.

'In any case,' said Michael, 'people were rarely buried in castles. Unless they had their own chapel, they would have been buried here, in the local church.'

Michael stood outside the church, looking across to the river, at the far side of the cemetery. Isobel stood in the sun watching a woman weeding the churchyard which was, for the most part, beautifully laid out. After a moment, the woman tidied up what she was doing and came towards them. As she drew close, they could see she was carrying a basket of apples which she must have picked earlier. She offered them both one.

244

'Isn't it unusual for apple trees to be growing in a churchyard?' said Michael.

'Very,' replied the woman. 'But this is the church of St Dorothea. The church was founded by pilgrims who had been to her shrine in Asia Minor. Her symbols are roses and apples, so rose bushes and apple trees have always grown side by side here in the churchyard.'

The apples were delicious and Michael and Isobel strolled back to the car munching them.

'Apples and roses . . . There are so many beautiful and poetical things about Christianity,' said Isobel. 'It's a pity more people don't believe.' She looked up at the sky. 'Shall we have a picnic today?' She looked across to Michael. 'If we found a quiet spot, you could stroke my back. You haven't done that in the fresh air.'

'What did that Nora woman say about almond?'

'Yes, you *are* English, Michael Whiting. I'm talking about making love and you mention another woman.'

'Seriously. What exactly did she say?'

'That the flowers were almond. Very common in the Mediterranean countries, not so common here. That she didn't know where to direct us – we were supposed to be on a treasure hunt, remember?'

They had reached the Mercedes and Michael immediately dipped inside and reached across the back seat. He snatched at a reference book, straightened up and riffled through it. 'Useless!' He bent again, threw it back into the car, grabbed at another book and riffled through the pages of that. Again: 'Pitibloodyful!' He tried a third.

'Yes!' He banged the palm of his hand on the open pages of the book. 'The almond is rare in Britain. That should have been our clue. Whoever painted the picture wasn't directing us to look for real almonds. He knew they were rare and would be hard, if not impossible, to find. That was a clue of sorts. We keep forgetting we're dealing with a religious mind. A poetic Christian mind, as you put it a moment ago. For him, almond was a symbol, just as roses and apples are symbols for Dorothea. White Mead *was* a red herring. Look, read this.'

He passed Isobel the reference book and pointed to a paragraph.

She read it out loud. ' "Almond: The allusion is to the Book of Numbers, chapter seventeen, verses one to eleven. Among all the tribes of Israel, only Aaron's rod flourished, with ripe almonds.

245

Fulfilling this poetic prophecy, the House of Levi became the fore-most, the royal house, and the white blossom of the almond became a symbol of the Virgin's purity." ' She looked at him, her eyebrows arched. 'The Virgin?'

'Easy, isn't it?' said Michael. 'When you know how.' He kissed Isobel's cheek. 'Like everything else in this damn trail, it's simple, if you can only work it out. Somewhere along this river, right next to it, is a medieval church dedicated to the Virgin.'

'Of course,' breathed Isobel. 'The ecclesiastical mind again.'

Michael snapped the book closed. This church here is St Dorothea, so that leaves the three others I mentioned this morning – at More-ton, Pallington and Stokeford.' He was already getting into the car. 'Let's go to Moreton first – that's closest. Then we can cross the river to Pallington. There's a straight road from Pallington to Stokeford – they are both on the north side of the river.'

Excited again, they moved off.

Woodsford to Moreton was just under four miles. It took Michael six minutes. As they drew up at the church, they immediately saw a big board saying 'St Nicholas, Moreton". Michael didn't even bother to stop but instead hauled the car around and headed north.

The lane twisted through Hurst, then crossed the river to Wad-dock, where they had to turn left. Pallington was a mile further on. The church was visible from the road but there was no sign this time. Instead there was a gate and a path made of local sandstone. It was chipped and had eroded in layers. Michael left the engine running and ran to the church. There was still no sign outside. He tried the door. It opened. He looked about, found a row of hymn-books. He opened one. Damn! It wasn't marked. He looked around again. Yes, there it was. A white satin standard hung down the front of the pulpit. On it, in gold, were the words 'St Mary the Virgin, Pallington'.

At last. Halleybloodylullah. He hurried back to the car. 'This is it! St Mary the Virgin.'

Isobel's eyes gleamed. 'Any sign of Grainger?'

'No – but I can't say I've looked hard. I think we should hide the car before we inspect the church. We can't be far away now.'

They drove back the way they had come for a couple of hundred yards, to where Isobel had noticed a leafy track. Michael eased the

246

car in there. About fifty yards along it, a gate opened on to a field, enabling Michael to turn the Mercedes. Before they got out they looked again at the last clue in the photograph. It was actually the eighth figure, but the seventh and the ninth were facing the wrong way.

'It's very grisly, isn't it?' said Isobel. 'I suppose, strictly speaking, a skeleton doesn't mean a cemetery, but death. So we could be looking for a grave outside the church, or a tomb inside it.'

'But which one?'

'What is it the skeleton is holding as well as the crosier – a glass container of some sort?'

'Yes, I'll look up glass.' A pause. 'Nothing.'

'Jar?'

Another pause. 'No. Nothing at all.'

'What other words are there? Bottle? Phial? Flask?'

'I'll try. Hold on.' Silence. 'Nothing under "bottle".' Another silence. 'Got it! "Phial, a small glass flask, is the attribute of Bishop Januarius." That must be right because he's holding a crosier – a crosier is the symbol of a bishop.'

'Funny name, though.'

'No. It's obvious. We're looking for someone who died in January. There must be another clue here as to the person's name.'

Isobel was inspecting the figure in the photograph. 'What about that? It looks like an arrow sticking through his hand.'

'Okay, okay. I'll try arrow.' More silence. But not for long. 'Perfect. Listen to this. "Arrow. The arrow is not merely a weapon but the carrier of disease, traditionally the plague . . ." Lower down: "The arrow is also the attribute of several saints. Arrows piercing the breast are the symbol of St Augustine; arrows held by a richly dressed maiden symbolise Ursula; several arrows piercing a nude body refer to St Sebastian" – I knew that, of course – and this: "an arrow piercing the hand depicts St Giles." '

'Aha! So, we are looking for –'

'A Giles who died in January.'

Isobel grinned, took the book from Michael and threw it into the back of the car. She kissed his cheek. 'Neat. Very neat. Let's move.'

Instead of walking on the road, they kept to the fields, always with a hedge between them and the church, just in case Grainger was about. As they approached the church, Michael said, 'He can't be far away. One of us should keep a lookout while the other searches in the church and the graveyard.'

'Let me look, please. I'll die of nerves if I have to act as lookout for Grainger.'

Michael hid behind the hedge opposite the church as Isobel ran swiftly across the lane. She began systematically going around the graves outside the church. It wasn't easy. Over the centuries, the writing had in many cases become so eroded it was virtually imposs-ible to read. Moss covered the stones, like brown liver spots on old skin. There were grey streaks from rain down the years.

'Car!'

She dived behind the church, heart pounding.

A moment later, the vehicle sped on and out of sight. 'All clear!' Michael shouted.

Isobel resumed her search. It took her about forty minutes to inspect the churchyard properly, by which time she was reasonably certain that there was no one in the graveyard who had been called Giles and died in the month of January. Where she couldn't read the names, the month didn't tally, and, where the date couldn't be read, the name was wrong. She went round to the front of the church, stood by the porch and waved at Michael.

He sprinted over. 'No luck?'

'It must be inside. It's not out here.'

'Do you think we still need a lookout?'

'I'd be happier.'

He nodded. 'You'd better go in, then. I'll wait here and only disturb you if a car stops.'

'Right.' She went inside.

Michael felt very exposed in the porch, and not a little ridiculous, so he ducked behind the door, which he kept open a little.

Inside the church, Isobel found that it was light but rather cold. The Norman walls were thick, cut into by only small windows. At the back of the church was a large semicircular arch containing a Crucifixion scene and carvings of people, birds and fish. She tried to imagine what this building must have been like, all those centuries ago, packed with people truly frightened of God, facing the small, bleak apse beyond the altar. This was a church built before the

248

Crusades, or before the early Crusaders had come back. God was not glorified in this church. There was little art, no magnificent soaring architecture to lift the spirits or to carry singing on high. Apart from the arch of carvings, this was a dour church, efficient, businesslike, built when people didn't need convincing of God's authority or majesty.

There were memorial plaques, in stone or plaster or brass, let into the walls and covering much of the floor. Isobel soon established that the dates of the plaster and brass ones were much too late. The stone slabs, on the other hand, were mostly on the floor, shiny and worn and far more difficult to read. She decided to work systematically down from the back of the nave towards the altar.

She hadn't gone very far, however, when Michael suddenly hissed, 'Someone's stopping!'

He rushed in. Isobel had already got to her feet. 'There!' she whispered. 'Behind the organ, by that curtain.'

The organ, a small, modern instrument, was kept in the north transept, and was mostly hidden by a red brocade curtain. They both scrambled to the far end of the nave. There was a space between the organ and the wall where they could wedge themselves.

They heard footsteps approach on the gravel. The door swung open, grudgingly. From where they were crouched they could not see who had come in, but they heard someone shuffling about in the nave, stopping every so often and then moving on again. Was it Grainger reading the tombstones on the floor? Just as Isobel had been doing only a moment ago? She felt weak just to be this close to him. The image of the boat-hook, glinting in the sun, danced before her.

The footsteps moved back and forth. Objects were picked up and put down. Isobel looked at Michael. She had begun to shake once more. Michael stroked her cheek and planted a gentle kiss on her forehead.

For over a quarter of an hour the footsteps moved around the nave. They went out but, just as Michael and Isobel were beginning to relax, they came back again. The footsteps retreated a second time, only to return once more. Isobel was growing weary and more terrified than ever. They were both aching from the need to remain in one position for so long. Was it Grainger, and did he know they were there? Was he teasing them, trying to flush them out?

After nearly half an hour the footsteps left the church a third time. They crunched away down the path. Still Michael made Isobel wait where she was. It could be a trap. They heard a car door slam and then the engine sprang to life. They relaxed, but still waited by the organ for a few minutes in case Grainger should drive off, stop the car and sneak back.

Eventually, they agreed that the threat was over. They stood up and rubbed their sore joints. Michael stretched. 'Now, was that, or was that not, Grainger?'

Isobel had moved out into the nave. 'No.'

'How come you're so certain?'

'Come here and look.'

He followed her into the nave and looked to where she indicated at the back of the church, where the semicircular arch of carved figures dominated the architecture. Michael smiled sheepishly. The flowers had been changed.

'I'll go back and be lookout again.' He made to move off but she caught his arm.

'There's no need.' And she led him back behind the organ. On the far side was a slab of stone, shiny with age. She had noticed it while she was hiding. It was slightly sunken in the middle and one corner was cracked, but the writing on it was clear enough: 'Giles George Beechey Bt: 15 April 1473 to 3 January 1531'. Below it was a motif, three straight vertical lines cut deep into the stone.

'I don't know whether to feel elated or frustrated,' said Isobel. 'If the treasure is under there, we'll never get it up'.

'It isn't,' said Michael firmly. 'Remember that man at the beginning? The one with the iron wand? The five steps to truth. Giles-who-died-in-January was only the fourth figure – you pointed that out, remember? There's one more step to go and it must have something to do with these lines on the tomb.'

'What are they, do you think?'

'They look like Roman numerals – yes? For three. There must be some symbolic meaning in the number.'

'The Trinity?'

'That's one.' Michael looked to the back of the church. 'That's

250

the Crucifixion back there, with the Virgin at the top. Two figures only. Besides the Trinity there are the Three Fates, the Three Graces . . .'

Instinctively they both moved to go out of the church. At the bottom of the nave they stopped and looked up at the tympanum.

'What are all those little carvings around the edge of the circle?' asked Isobel.

'Looks like the Labours of the Months to me.'

'Meaning?'

'You start at January, bottom left. A little carving of men felling trees, gathering wood for winter. Next to it, the zodiac sign for January, Aquarius. The medievals were quite superstitious, even in churches. Anyway it goes all the way round to December, bottom right.'

Michael led the way out, back to the Mercedes and the reference books. They were halfway down the drive when another car pulled up. They had forgotten to keep a lookout and they both tensed.

A tall, thin man got out of the car. When he turned, however, they were relieved to see the flash of white at his throat. It was the vicar. He saw them staring at him and smiled. 'Good morning. I hope you enjoyed the church?'

'Thank you,' said Isobel, recovering first. 'Yes. And such lovely fresh flowers.'

'Mrs Summers has been, has she? Then I've missed her again. Oh dear, now she'll be angry.' He gave them a rather resigned look. Mrs Summers was clearly a trial to him. He went on past them into the church.

Isobel grinned at Michael and they hurried back to the track where the Mercedes was hidden. Inside the car they fell on the reference books. Silence for a few moments, save for the rustling of pages. Then:

' "The Trinity . . . God is of one nature yet three persons, Father, Son and Holy Ghost . . . is often represented as three interlocking circles . . . The Father was shown as a hand, an eye on a crown . . . The Son is shown on the Cross . . . and the Holy Ghost as a dove . . ." ' Isobel read the rest in silence. 'No . . . I can't see anything relevant here.'

Michael sighed. 'The Trinity is the most obvious but it's vague

251

in my book as well.' He paused, then read aloud: ' "The Three Graces . . . were often the handmaidens of Venus, the Roman goddess of love and fertility . . . Their names were Aglaia, Euphrosyne and Dice. Typically the two outer Graces face the viewer while the middle one turns away. Seneca said they stood for the threefold aspects of generosity – the giving, receiving and returning of gifts . . . The humanists of Italy in the fifteenth century saw in them the three phases of love: beauty, arousing desire, leading to fulfilment." Sick joke maybe . . . we're no nearer to fulfilment.'

Isobel arched her eyebrows. 'The Three Fates aren't much better. "Old and ugly, their names are Clotho, Lachesis and Atropos and they are shown spinning the thread of life with Atropos about to snip the thread with her shears . . ." Hold on, the next paragraph I didn't know about. "The three Maries at the Sepulchre." It says: "See Holy Women at the Sepulchre." ' Quickly, Isobel riffled the pages back through the book. ' "Three Maries, or myrrhophores, bearers of myrrh, accompanied the body of Jesus to the tomb after the Crucifixion. They had come to anoint the body but discovered that the stone sealing the entrance had been rolled away and the body gone . . . In art the tomb usually takes the form of a conventional stone sarcophagus . . . There is a figure sitting on the tomb, either simply a young man, which is Mark, or with wings – Matthew – or a sceptre tipped with a fleur-de-lis, which identifies Gabriel." Maybe *that's* what we're looking for – a sarcophagus with one of those three names on it.'

Michael nodded and closed his book. 'It's the best bet yet. Come on, let's hope the vicar has gone.'

They retraced their steps.

The vicar *had* gone. Not only that, he had locked the church. 'Shhhanghaied again!' said Michael. 'That, presumably, was what he had come to do when we bumped into him.'

Isobel examined the church board in the porch. It said: 'Services: Sundays and other designated feast days: 7.30, 9.30, 11.30, 6.30. At other times the church is open from 10.00 am to 2.00 pm.'

'I don't believe it,' said Isobel. 'This means we'll lose another day.'

'Not if the sarcophagus is in the graveyard,' said Michael. 'Come on.'

This time they both inspected the stones and didn't bother with a lookout. They had no luck, however. So far as they could tell, there was no Mark, Matthew or Gabriel in the cemetery. They tried all the graves as well as the handful of sarcophagi.

They walked back to the car. 'Surely,' said Isobel, 'the tomb would have to be inside? Even in those days they must have known that the weather does awful things to gravestones.'

'You're right,' replied Michael. 'What's more, we are forgetting that our painter and his abbot were very religious men. They would never have countenanced hiding something in a sarcophagus. It was sacrilegious.'

'Maybe it was a fake tomb.'

'That would be a serious offence too, for a very religious person. They didn't toy with death in those days. There's something we are missing here. We're not thinking like medievalists again.'

They had reached the Mercedes. Michael looked at his watch. 'This is annoying. Only two-thirty and we're stymied for the day. I could weep.'

'We could ask the vicar to let us in.'

'And draw attention to ourselves? No. It hasn't come to that yet. Let's go back to Burning Cliff, have a sandwich and browse in the books for a while. You never know, we might come across what we're looking for, just as I did that night when I saw those dance figures which told us Peverell Place was a red herring.'

He held the door of the car open for Isobel. She was just about to get in when they both heard the rattle of an engine stopping outside the church. They looked at each other. Then they ran down the track to the road. Carefully, they peered out.

A red motor cycle was parked by the gate to the church. There was no one on it. 'Wait here,' said Michael. 'We can see perfectly well and whoever it is can't see us. It's not the vicar or the flower lady, that's certain.'

They didn't have long to wait. After a few moments, they both flinched as they watched the dreadfully familiar figure of a tall man wearing a helmet get back on to the motor cycle. Instinctively, they hid deeper in the hedge, but he wheeled his bike around, kick-started it and rode off in the direction he had come from.

'Should we follow him?' said Isobel.

'I doubt if we could catch him now. By the time we've got back to the car and crawled out of this track here, he'll be miles away.'

'Is this the first time he's been to the church, do you think?'

'Nnno – he wasn't there very long and he didn't bother with the graveyard. That must mean he already knows the answer is inside. He went off to do his research on the three Maries, or three some-things, just as we did. Except that when he came back the church was locked, just as happened to us.' Michael sighed. 'We were very lucky we didn't bump into him again.'

'Hmm. I'm not such an easy target on dry land, Michael.' Isobel's expression was fierce, though it wasn't really directed at him. 'What I *am* frightened about is that he's the scholar and already knows what to look for. He's ahead of us.'

'Correct.' Now Michael looked at Isobel. 'This is where it gets very messy, Inspector Sadler. We have to think this through hard, and accept the consequences.'

'Meaning what, exactly?'

He took her hand and kissed her little finger. 'Start with the fact that, if our reasoning is right, we are one move away from fabulous relics which are hidden somewhere near here. So too is Grainger. Although he arrived here after us, it looks as though he's actually half a step ahead.' Michael kissed Isobel's third finger. 'Add to that the fact that Grainger knows we're around, that although we can't read the clues as well or as quickly as he can we may be on his tail.' He kissed her middle finger. 'And, finally, consider the fact that we know Grainger can play rough, very rough. What do you deduce from all that?'

Isobel stared at Michael.

'I'll answer for you, in case you're afraid to say it. There are three important deductions to be made. One, he won't wait until the church is opened tomorrow. *He's going to break in*! My guess is that he won't do it in daylight. He'll do it tonight, while it's dark.'

'How can you be so sure?'

'I'm not sure. I'm not a detective or a psychiatrist or an astrologer. But we are nearly there, Isobel, and so is he. The pace always hots up near the end of a chase, the prize is so close.'

'And the second deduction?'

'We know he's violent, explosive as an oil rig. We don't want to

254

tangle with him if we can avoid it. The only way to beat him *and* avoid him is to get into the church ourselves, first.'

'You're not suggesting *we* break into the church, are you?'

'Normally I wouldn't dream of it. We could quite happily wait until tomorrow. But if Grainger is going to break in tonight we have to beat him to it. We could try to convince the vicar to open the church for us but, as of this moment, we don't know what to tell him. That's where my third deduction comes in. We now need to bring in Veronica Sheldon.'

Isobel stared at him.

'This is an emergency, agreed?'

Isobel didn't move.

'Veronica is an old girlfriend. She's on the staff of the V and A Medieval Department. We were only an "item" for a few months but we keep up, sort of. It might take you and me hours – days – to find out what those three lines stand for. But it's Vron's bread and butter. She could help us in minutes, if you'll okay it.'

Isobel hesitated. 'We've come so far without – '

'This may be as far as we get!'

'It can't be that easy to break into a church.'

'No, but I have some ideas – '

'Such as?'

'Isobel! We're wasting time . . . we can discuss that later. Please! Can I call Vron?'

She was silent.

'Isobel! Isobloodybel! If we know what we're looking for, we can stop Grainger taking it.'

Isobel thought again.

This time Michael was silent too.

After a moment, Isobel said, 'I'm sorry, Michael. You're right. Let's do it.'

He led the way back to the car at a dash, then hustled the Mercedes down the track as fast as the branches would allow. Reaching the road he turned left, away from the church and from Grainger. 'I'll make for Burning Cliff and stop at the first telephone box I see. Veronica will need a little time to check her books and it will do us no harm to have a little early sleep, if we can. It gets dark around nine-thirty. We'll have to hope that Grainger plans his escapade for later rather than earlier, when fewer people will be about. Well after the pubs close. Say from midnight on. That means we have to be ready about ten. Dangerous, but it can't be helped.'

He turned left at Tincleton, returned to Woodsford and stopped at the callbox in the village. It had been vandalised. Cursing, he drove on, to Crossways. Thankfully, the phone there was in order. He dialled Veronica's number in London.

She was surprised to hear from Michael, but pleasantly so. He knew that her speciality was medieval sculpture and that she was preparing a new catalogue for the museum. He asked her how it was progressing.

'Academics have three speeds, you know that. "Slow", "Dead slow" and "Stop". I'm in the middle lane.'

He laughed and then outlined his problem, promising to explain more fully at a later date. 'What I need, Vron, are all the meanings and associations in art for three, the number three. What it refers to symbolically. What we have is the Roman numeral for three. We – I – have thought of the Trinity, of course, the Three Graces, the Three Fates and the Three Maries. As a result, we – I – have one possibility that might work but at the moment I'm stymied, having to tread water for a little while, and I'm by no means convinced that what I have is enough. There have to be other symbolic meanings and I need to know what they are.'

'Is this another coup, Michael?'

'It might be, if you can help me. There's a rival in the fast lane.'

'The same old Whiting. A fish doing the fishing. Sounds more exciting than sculpture catalogues . . . Oh well, let's see . . . Off the top of my head there are the three theological virtues, faith, hope and charity, the three denials of St Peter, the three faces of Prudence, the three aspects of time . . . Jesus rose on the third day, of course . . . the three ages of man, the three ages of the world – gold, silver and iron . . . anything there of any use?'

'Nnnot sure,' said Michael. 'Tell me about the ages of the world, silver especially.'

'I can't, not just like that.'

'Aren't there any books you can check in?'

'Yes, but they're not here. I'd have to go to the library.'

Careful. 'Vron . . . that's what I'm asking.'

At the other end, silence.

'Vron, *please!*'

Veronica breathed out heavily. 'Some people don't change. Oh, all right. If you're sure it's that urgent.'

'Vron, some day soon I'll tell you just how urgent it is.'

'It will take me ten minutes to get to the library. Give me three-quarters of an hour there . . . Can you call me back in – oh, an hour and a half?'

'I'm in a phone box in Dorset, but I should be at a hotel by then. Sure. Vron, you're an angel.'

Michael jumped back into the car and drove south, towards Burning Cliff. When they arrived at the hotel the sun was beginning to turn the Channel a pale straw colour. It was close to four o'clock when they entered their room and flopped down on to the bed. Neither had done very much that day, but the nervousness brought on by the constant tensions was wearing.

Michael slipped his arm under Isobel's shoulders and hugged her to him. She kissed his neck. The contact was settling for both of them and their breathing became more regular.

Isobel put her arm around Michael's waist and drew him closer. 'I've been a burglar once, already. I'm nervous about doing it again, in a church.'

'Worried you'll get used to crime?' He kissed the top of her head.

'Like I'm getting used to vice?'

She kissed his neck again. 'You call this vice?'

'This is not all I had in mind.'

Around five, Michael got up, stepped out on to the balcony and lit a cigar. He looked out to sea. Sailing boats, white wedges no bigger than fingernails, zigzagged across the water. To the west there was a line of them: a race. Somewhere, nearby, Michael could hear a tennis match being played. *Qwoq*, as the ball was hit. Squeals of excitement, shouting when a point was disputed. Laughter. All of them, the whole world, unaware of the treasures so close in Pallington church. Unaware of Grainger's wild attempts to kill.

Michael pulled on his cigar. If they got it wrong tonight and they had to deal with Grainger . . . His skin itched at the thought. It

257

struck him how very brave Isobel was being. She must know they ran that risk yet she wasn't deterred. Or, if she was, she must have overcome the feeling. She must have learned to overcome such fears when she was working all those hotspots around the world. He smoked on. Could you ever learn to overcome something as basic as fear? He had never been truly frightened at any point of his life. There had been a time when an aeroplane he was on, flying from New York to Toronto, had caught fire and been forced to turn back. Other people on the plane had panicked. But you never knew, with planes, just how bad it was. They never told you. And there was nothing you could do, personally, to remove the danger. The danger wasn't *aimed* at you personally either, that was another difference. Maybe he should have been more scared on the flight than he had been. It had taken seventeen minutes to get back to New York. It was a long time to be kept in suspense, knowing that at any minute an explosion could kill you. It had happened not long after the space shuttle disaster, and mid-air explosions were more familiar horrors than usual.

Isobel's bravery warmed him. He looked back into the room to where he could just see her hair on the pillow. She looked so calm. Their lovemaking was getting slower and better. No tears now. Instead, Isobel murmured very soft, very erotic words. He had never known such a captivating surrender.

It was time to phone Veronica. He went back into the room, shook Isobel awake and lifted the receiver. He was put through. At the museum Veronica was located easily enough but when she answered the phone she sounded tetchy.

'Vron, what's wrong?'

'Someone else has got the book I want.'

'What? Oh no!'

'Yes, but all is not lost. I know who took it out. He's away this week but he's not allowed to take books home, so what I want must be in his office. If I can find a security man with the right key, I can get into his office and look at the book. But it's an odd request and it will take time.'

'How long?' Michael knew he sounded ungrateful but couldn't help it.

'Another twenty minutes, maybe. My problem is my mother.

She's picking me up from the museum in about an hour and we're going to the theatre. If I can't get at the book by then, I won't be able to help. I'm sorry.'

Michael's heart sank. But all he said was, 'Yes, Vron. I understand. Will you call me – or shall I call back?'

'No, give me your number. I'll call you if I have anything to tell you.'

'No, no . . . Call me either way.' He gave her the number and reluctantly hung up.

'Let's have some tea,' he said to Isobel after he had explained the problem with Veronica. 'Anything to be doing things. I shall go mad just waiting here.'

They ordered the tea and it came. They drank it. That took twenty-five minutes at the most. Vron would only just have got to the book, even if all had gone well in London.

Michael decided to have a bath. It was something else to do. He managed to drag it out for twenty minutes. He put on his dressing-gown and tried some more tea, but it was cold. Isobel was under the sheets and trying to catnap. Michael looked out again at the Channel. The sounds of the day were everywhere – children's voices, a horse whinnying, the throaty growl of a power boat. It felt odd to be in the room, in a dressing-gown, with Isobel almost asleep and a summer's day raging all around them.

He noticed a woman walking towards the hotel. She had been to the beach and was carrying some towels. But what attracted his attention was her hair. It was the same kind of red as old Julius had uncovered in the Victorian portrait and it reminded him that he would have to research those three families whose coat of arms featured emeralds. He'd start with the *Dictionary of National Biography*, then the library of the Genealogical Society. Genealogy was a passion these days. People compiled histories of families that were often so run-of-the-mill they stood no chance of being published. But the manuscripts were lodged in the Genealogical Society and could be very useful to someone like Michael. Then there was that weird chesspiece or turret she was holding in her hand. What could that mean?

The phone, when it rang, seemed to Michael unnaturally loud and he flinched. Isobel, who had risen from her catnap very quickly, lifted the receiver from its cradle and passed it to him as he sat on the bed.

'Are you ready with pen and paper?' said Veronica without any preamble. 'Let's get on. Entertaining my mother isn't my idea of heaven but at least she pays for the tickets.'

'Ready. I'm ready. Shoot.' He motioned to Isobel for a pencil and notepad.

'Which do you want first – all the meanings "three" can have, or the three ages of the world?'

'Give me a tour of all the meanings first. Then we can close in on some of them.'

'Okay. I won't say this too fast, so you can get it down. But I don't have all day.'

'I'm ready, I'm ready . . . Dictate away.'

'In no particular order . . . the three generations, three violent deaths – execution, murder, suicide – the three zones of the church, the three angels welcoming Abraham. Three feathers are the symbol of Lorenzo de' Medici and a couple of popes, three bells are the symbol of music, three nails are the instruments of the passion, a crown with three heads on it stands for philosophy, a three-pronged fork symbolises Neptune – are you keeping up?'

'Three yeses.'

'Three forms of love, Christ had a vision of three arrows, three crosses stand for Golgotha, Paris judged three naked beauties, there is a legend of the three living and the three dead, though that makes six, I suppose, the three "nodi d'amor" symbolise the problems of love – that is, two's company, three's a crowd – a tower with three windows is a symbol of chastity, a crosier with three transverses stands for the pope, and three children in a barrel stand for Nicholas of Myra. And I think I'm scraping the barrel here, Michael. That's about it.'

Michael was scribbling furiously. He grunted approval, finished writing and then said, 'Fine . . . okay . . . Here are my three queries . . . what more can you give me on the silver age, the three zones of the church and the tower with three windows?'

'Hold on while I look them up.'

Michael handed Isobel the list he had copied down and prepared to write more notes on a fresh sheet of paper.

260

'Ready? There are actually *four* ages of the world, it seems – the gold, silver, iron and bronze ages – but in art bronze is usually omitted. I'll read it out. "In the golden age man lived in a state of primal innocence . . . without tools he fed on berries, and Saturn, the ancient Roman god of agriculture, reigned . . . In the silver age the eternal springtime was over, man learned to sow and knew right from wrong. In art the female figure of Justice is seen holding a sword and scales . . . . Iron was discovered "to the hurt of man" and usually soldiers are shown slaying a figure crowned with laurel, to personify learning and the arts." Hold on . . .'

Veronica riffled the pages again. 'Three zones . . . three zones . . . Here we are. "As a result of Byzantine influence, in medieval times churches were divided into three zones. Crudely speaking these were heaven, the Holy Land and the terrestrial world. In the dome of the church, heaven was portrayed, with Christ, the Virgin and the Apostles peopling this zone. The second zone was the upper areas of the vaulting and the arches below the ceiling, where the events of the gospels in the Holy Land were depicted. In the third, the lowest zone, are shown saints, martyrs and more notable ecclesiastics." Enough?'

'Yes, yes. Next.'

' "There are several legends of a daughter shut in a tower by her father to ward off her suitors. In time, therefore, towers came to symbolise chastity and the attribute of Barbara, whose tower often had three windows, as well as the Virgin, and Danaë." '

'Tell me about Barbara – please.'

Another delay while Veronica turned the pages. ' "Barbara's father shut her in the tower to discourage lovers. The tower had two windows but Barbara persuaded the workmen to build a third window because, she said, they symbolised the Trinity which lighted her soul. Barbara was often invoked against sudden death by storms and lightning and thus sometimes held a chalice and wafer, implying the last sacraments. She may have a cannon at her feet." ' Veronica sighed and said, 'I hope that's enough, Michael. I'd like to go now, if that's all right with you. I hope it's been worth the wait.'

Michael wasn't sure. But what he said was, 'Terrific, Vron. Saved my day. I owe you one. Many, many thanks . . . See you soon.

Give my love to your Ma –' and he put the phone down as Veronica shouted her reply.

He explained everything to Isobel. Neither of them could see any immediate way forward.

'I didn't notice . . . but maybe the tower of the church has three windows. Or perhaps there's a Barbara in the church.'

Isobel shook her head. 'It can't be a tomb. We decided that.'

'I suppose you're right.' Michael paused. 'No "suppose" about it. You're right.' He was still sitting on the bed and she stroked his arm.

'Now what?'

Michael looked at his watch. 'The Three Maries pointed us to a sarcophagus – which must be wrong. The silver age points to scales, for Justice. The three zones of the church and the Barbara business suggest the top of the church somewhere. Conbloodyfusing.' He looked at Isobel and smiled. 'It's just coming up to half past six. It gets dark around nine-thirty tonight – '

'Michael, do we have to? Break into a church, I mean.'

'We've been through this before, Isobel. I don't like it any more than you do. But there's no other way. You burgled Grainger's office, after all. Is this so much worse? What I suggest is that we get some sleep now. It will take – what? – half an hour to drive back to Pallington and we should aim to arrive just before ten.' He pulled the curtains closed and shut out the raging day. Then he took off his dressing-gown and got into bed. For a moment he had a glimpse of Isobel's flesh but firmly told himself that, just now, he needed the sleep more.

13

Michael awoke around 8.30. The sun was going. He kissed Isobel awake, then called down for a bottle of whisky and some sandwiches. They ate as they dressed.

Isobel wore trousers and a brown woollen shirt and carried a dark sweater in case it should turn cold. Michael put on his navy blazer and a pair of brown corduroys, the darkest clothing he had.

To anyone watching them as they left, they looked as though they were going out for a casual dinner in a nearby pub. On the way to Pallington, Michael stopped for petrol. The 190 was running low and, all being well, they would be coming back in the small hours, when there would be no petrol stations open.

They arrived at Pallington just after 9.30 and installed themselves well down the track they had hidden in earlier. It wasn't yet fully dark, so Michael switched off the car lights and they waited. As their eyes adjusted they found they could still see quite well.

'How long are we going to sit here?' said Isobel.

'At least until it's fully dark. I also want to watch the traffic. It's only a lane that goes past the church but lanes can carry a surprising number of cars. I'd like some idea of how busy, or un-busy, this lane is at night. It will give us a feel of how safe, or unsafe, we are. Also, we might listen out just in case I was wrong about Grainger. Maybe he *will* try to get into the church earlier.'

'How are *we* going to get into the church? You said you knew what to do.'

'As a matter of fact I do. I was once burgled in London because I used to hide my key for the daily woman. Burglars know all

263

the hiding places and afterwards I received the briefing which the Metropolitan Police issue about places *not* to hide your key in. I'll bet the vicar doesn't know about all that. I'll bet he hides the key somewhere and I'll find it.'

'You sound very cocky.'

'I'm whistling in the dark, to keep my spirits up.'

'It's nearly ten. Why don't we listen to the news?'

Michael switched on the radio. It was the usual mix. Isobel tensed involuntarily as Beirut was mentioned. But it was a raid by the Israelis that was making news and there were no references to hostages. The programme also carried a short preview of the next day's papers, which consisted of a great deal of speculation on whether the Queen was about to announce her abdication. There had obviously been a high-level leak of some sort. But for Michael the gloomiest item was the news that there had been a multiple pile-up on the M25 and a twenty-nine-mile tailback had formed near Guildford. That could easily be a winning bet – but it wasn't his. Was it an omen?

The news slid smoothly into a late-night music-and-chat show. 'Don't switch off,' said Isobel. She moved in her seat and leaned her head against Michael's shoulder, then reached down and clasped his hand. 'I don't think I'll ever get used to cigar smoke, Michael Whiting, but I've come to like you rather a lot.'

Michael turned his head and kissed her hair. 'How much?'

'Well, if I was your goddaughter, I'd probably say you were my third favourite thing.'

'Third! After *what*?'

'Oh . . . rivers . . . boat-hooks . . .'

'Flattering.'

'Kiss me.'

She turned towards him. In the light from the car radio, he could just make out Isobel's face, her skin disappearing here and there into shadow. He kissed her mouth.

On the radio, a slow sentimental song was coming to an end.

Michael brushed Isobel's cheek with his lips and kissed her throat. As he did so, she tilted back her head so that the muscles in her neck flexed. Michael ran the tip of his tongue down to her collar bone.

264

The smooth voice of the presenter could be heard on the radio. He was introducing a regular guest, an astrologer. The astrologer was giving horoscopes and she began with the presenter's own sign, Leo.

Isobel began to undo the buttons on her shirt. The collar widened and Michael was able to kiss the skin on her shoulders.

'Leo cannot be coaxed or forced,' said the woman on the radio. '. . . But you need to come to terms with events and developments of the past few months . . . A major career change could be in the offing . . .'

Michael moved his lips across Isobel's skin. She finished unbuttoning her shirt and unfastened her bra. Michael gripped its edge with his teeth and pulled it upwards, revealing her breasts, the shadows curving around them.

'Virgo . . . Circumstances beyond your control will bring all major issues to a head . . . This month will mark a significant turning-point in your life . . . Putting others first may not come naturally . . .'

Michael kissed Isobel's nipples. She stroked the back of his neck. He held one of her nipples between his lips, and squeezed. She gave a soft moan. Gently, he touched the nipple with his teeth. Again he squeezed.

'Brute!' But it was a whisper. 'Do it again.'

'Libra . . . At some point this month you may feel trapped or at odds with partners and close friends . . . But there will be a catalyst and before long a balance, as befits a Libran, will be restored . . .'

Isobel's nipple glistened in the dim light, fleshy and swollen. Michael transferred his attention to its twin. He lowered his lips again.

He stopped. 'Balance!'

Isobel opened her eyes. 'Beast!' But the spell was broken. 'What?'

'I am a beast, you're right. Only a dinosaur would stop what I'm doing when he doesn't have to.' Michael manoeuvred Isobel so he could look at her as he spoke. 'Don't be angry, please, but three, the number three, among three hundred other things, stands for the ages of the world – remember? We're looking for silver and, as Vron said, in the silver age man learned right from wrong. So . . .

265

the symbol of the silver age was the figure of Justice holding a sword and scales. The sign for Libra is scales, or a balance.'

'Yes. So?'

'So . . . at the back of the church is that tympanum, that semi-circle of carvings, with the Labours of the Months . . . January, February —'

'Michael!'

'September . . . Libra, Isobel. The sign for which is scales! That has to be it. What's more, it's high up in the church, in the third zone. I've only just thought of that. It must be right. Come on, let's go!'

'Michael!'

Softly, he said, 'I'm not being unromantic. If we get this sorted out we can make love in all sorts of exotic places, not just Mercedes cars.'

'I was enjoying it. You said you wanted to wait for a while.'

'I was enjoying it too. Believe me. And I did want to wait. But now we know the final clue we stand a real chance of getting into the church and away before Grainger appears. Come *on!*'

He switched off the radio and got out of the car. From the back seat he took his blazer and from the boot he took a torch, a large screwdriver and a spanner. 'Elbow grease may not be enough,' he said. 'Ready?'

Isobel refastened her bra, buttoned her shirt and pulled on her sweater. She nodded.

They walked gingerly down the track to the lane. It was now nearly 10.30 and properly dark but, as they came to the lane the headlights of a car swept by.

'You don't think we're too early, do you?' said Isobel. 'I'm scared we'll be seen.'

Michael didn't answer but jogged down the road to get to the church gate before the next car arrived. Isobel followed.

They turned into the graveyard and just had time to duck behind some headstones when the next set of headlights flashed by.

After the car had gone, they stood up. 'Pity about that bend in the road,' said Michael. 'It means headlights shine right into the church. One of us will have to keep a lookout.' He moved off towards the porch.

'Now this is the really tricky bit,' he said when they got there. 'I'm going to have to use the torch to find the spot where the key is hidden. If you see or hear anything, give me a whistle or something, so I can put my light out.' He kissed her cheek and moved off.

From time to time he flashed the torch into a shadow. Isobel could hear him moving further and further away from her. Then he came walking back. 'Any luck?'

'No,' he whispered. 'It must be on the other side.' He went past her.

Moments later she hissed, 'Car!' He snapped off the light and they both ducked down behind the gravestones.

The car approached, but slowly. The light from its headlamps looked strangely wobbly, throwing large quivering shadows over the walls of the church. When it got close enough, however, they could see it wasn't a car, but a tractor, going home late. Its rumble filled the air as it reached the church and trundled by. Isobel's eyes were now quite accustomed to the gloom and from where she knelt she could see the silhouette of the driver quite clearly. The tractor rattled on without stopping and its clatter disappeared behind the pine copse next to the churchyard. Isobel breathed again. She heard Michael moving about too.

Moments later she heard voices. 'Michael!' she hissed, but he had heard them too, for his light snapped off.

Isobel's eyes raked the road, searching for the source of the voices. She heard a laugh, off to the right. Was it some people out for a walk? Was it the vicar, coming to the church? Please God, not that.

'Get back!' said Michael's voice, out to her left.

Deftly, she slipped behind the end of the church and turned to watch.

A moment later from behind the trees came two small lights, almost as wobbly as the tractor headlamps. It was two bicycles, two old men by the sound of it, riding home after an evening in the pub. Isobel's heart almost burst when, halfway along the graveyard, the men stopped. Were they coming in? What would they want with a church in darkness? Maybe one of them was a policeman and Michael or she had been seen. A moment later she had her answer. 'That's better,' said a voice. 'That's the trouble with beer. Goes right through you.' The other man laughed and the two lights wobbled off into the night.

Isobel moaned softly in relief and moved back to her vigil. A moment later, just as she was beginning to relax, she heard another voice.

'Allebloodyluia!'

It was Michael, coming towards her. As he approached she could see he was smiling and holding a key. 'In the gutter on the next gable. According to the Metropolitan Police, a gutter is the seventh favourite hiding place.'

'What are the first six? – no, don't tell me. Let's get a move on.'

They crowded into the shadow of the porch. The night was absolutely still, save for the cry of a bird on the river. Michael inserted the key and turned it. The lock rotated but with what seemed to Isobel a dangerously loud rattle. She was reminded of the lock that had rattled in her own house, the night of the burglary all those weeks ago. She looked out, back towards the road. Everything appeared calm.

Michael pushed the door and they went in.

Inside, the church was very dark. 'Should one of us keep a lookout?' said Michael.

'No. Please. Don't let's separate now. Please.'

Michael led the way to the main aisle, turned left and stopped in front of the west wall. He switched on his torch and found the curve of figures at the edge of the tympanum.

Isobel craned her neck.

'See the first figure, someone chopping trees. And the second, a figure carrying a bucket —'

'Aquarius.'

'Correct. Now we proceed round —'

'Car!'

Michael snapped off the beam and froze. The car came towards the church, its headlamps filling the interior with a silver light that rose up the walls, swept across the ceiling, and died rapidly as the car turned the bend and sped off. As it did so, the light brushed over the tympanum at the end of the nave. The beam threw the huge semicircle of stone carvings into a jigsaw of shadows shimmying around the high figure of the Crucifixion in the centre. Then the light was gone.

Michael gripped the torch but he didn't switch it on just yet. He waited for his eyes to readjust to the dark. After a moment he said, 'September is three-quarters of the way through the year, so it must be on the right, near the top.' He shone the light again. 'Threshing, that's right . . . and next to it . . . aha, the Balance.'

'Michael!'

'Fingers crossed. We've got to get up there somehow.' He looked around and flashed the light across the nave. 'There! That table with the hymn-books on it. Let's clear it and bring it over here.'

Together they moved across and started lifting off the books. The dust they disturbed made Isobel sneeze, and they both froze for a minute. In the silence they heard a bird squawk on the river but that was all. After a moment they continued clearing the table. It was heavy, but with a mixture of lifting, pushing and dragging they managed to manoeuvre the table back across the nave and slide it beneath the tympanum. Michael climbed on to the table but when he stood up he still couldn't reach the top of the semicircle.

'A chair!' he whispered. 'Quick, get me a chair from the choir.'

Isobel tiptoed down the aisle to where several chairs were laid out opposite the organ. She carried one back and handed it up to Michael. He placed it on the table and tested it to see if it was firm. It was.

He climbed on to it, and straightened himself up. His face was level with the feet of Christ on the Cross. In one hand he had the torch and with the other he reached up.

He could just grasp the scales. He pulled.

'Any luck?' whispered Isobel, peering up out of the gloom.

'No, it must be stuck. Look, why don't you climb on to the table and shine the torch for me. Then I can use both hands.'

Michael waited as Isobel hauled herself up. It wasn't easy with him and the chair already in the way. Then she had to shuffle herself into a position where he could hand her the torch and she could shine it so that he could see what he was doing. But eventually it was arranged. Michael reached up and grasped the scales with both hands. He pulled. The carving wouldn't budge.

269

'It's ossibloodyfied!' he hissed. 'It must have silted up over the years.'

'Try again.'

He reached up and pulled again. He pulled and almost hung his entire weight on the stone. 'Give, damn you,' he hissed. 'Give!'

'Try twisting,'

Michael twisted. The carving of the Crucifixion hung before him as he reached up. He was sweating and aching. 'It's no good,' he whispered. He lowered his arms and got down from the chair. 'I was *so* certain I was right.'

Isobel lowered herself from the table to the floor. 'Maybe it's to do with the tower after all. If there is one.'

Michael, disappointed and breathing heavily, followed her down off the table. 'Where would the stairs be, do you think? Behind the organ, by the vestry?'

They moved across the church but there was no doorway out of the vestry. It appeared there was no tower, at least not one that could be climbed from inside.

'I'm lost,' said Michael. 'My brain's gone on "freeze frame" again.'

'Could we have been wrong about Beechey?' said Isobel. 'Shine your light down, he's right here.'

They were indeed standing behind the organ curtain, where earlier in the day, they had hidden from the woman changing the flowers. Michael switched on the torch and shone it on the gravestone. 'No, we're right this far. Beechey . . . Giles . . . born in April. And the symbol for —'

'Car!'

Again Michael snapped off his light and they both stood still, waiting for the car to go by. The headlights flashed across the ceiling as before, down over the tympanum and died as the car disappeared into the night.

'Michael? What are you doing . . . ?'

Michael had fallen to his knees and switched on the light. Isobel also lowered herself so she could study his movements. He had taken the screwdriver from his pocket and was scraping the tomb.

'Michael, that's more than burglary, that's —'

'Watch!' He was scraping at the numerals, the three slashes on

270

the tomb. Dirt, crusts of grime and stone dust began to come away.
For thirty seconds, a minute, he kept at it.

'I don't see —'

'Look, this isn't a three –'

'Of course it is.'

'Yes, well it *is* three, but not *just* three. It's three *somethings*. See
– the slashes are slightly broader at one end, and they have narrow
points at the other. When that car flashed its lights in here, I suddenly
saw where we've been going wrong. This isn't a Roman three . . .
it's three *nails*.'

'You *are* going to explain this conundrum, I hope.'

'Not much explanation needed, inspector. Three nails, the instruments of the passion, that's what Vron said.'

'Maybe dear Veronica did say that. I don't see –'

'You didn't stand on that chair, Isobel. You didn't press your face
against the Crucifixion while you were straining at Libra. I did. And
I can tell you there's something very odd about that Crucifixion. At
least, I see that it's odd now. Jesus is on the cross but there are no
nails sticking through his flesh. No stigmata marks at all.'

Isobel stared at him.

'The nails are the clue.'

She still didn't speak.

'We have to hammer the nails, or this screwdriver here' – and he
took it out of his pocket – 'into the carving. Where the nails should
go.'

Isobel's eyebrows arched but even now she didn't speak.

Michael shone his torch on the tomb again. 'Look. I'm right.
Those are nails – they have flat heads and sharp points.' He rose and
walked down the aisle. Isobel followed.

He climbed on to the table but as he was about to stand on the
chair he felt Isobel tug at his trouser leg. 'You can't do it, Michael.
It's horrible, the worst thing I've ever heard. It's worse than sacrilegious, it's sick.'

He looked down at her. 'In normal circumstances, yes, I agree.
But we now know the mind we're dealing with here. And it fits
perfectly. No one would do what we . . . what I am about to do,
by accident. It's the perfect hiding place. You have to be in on the

271

secret to even attempt it. And, in being in on it, we know it's not really sacrilegious.'

Isobel shook her head firmly. 'I don't like it.'

'We'll beat Grainger, if I'm right.'

'And we'll be turned into a pillar of salt if you're wrong. And deserve it.'

'Stop peppering me with objections . . . and hold the light, so I can see what I'm doing.'

Reluctantly, Isobel climbed on to the table and took the light. She shone it up at the figure of Jesus.

Michael stood on the chair, steadied himself and then placed the tip of the screwdriver in the palm of the figure's right hand. He pulled the spanner from his blazer pocket.

'Do we have to?'

'Shhh!' He turned the spanner flat and banged it against the head of the screwdriver. The crack echoed around the church. The figure didn't budge. He tried again.

'The noise!'

Michael said nothing but transferred the screwdriver to the open palm of the figure's other hand. He hammered the screwdriver a third time. Again the crack ricocheted down the nave but still the figure didn't move.

He shifted the screwdriver to a point in the middle of the figure's feet, where they were crossed, one above the other. Isobel went to speak but Michael snapped, 'One more. One more.'

He drew back his hand and brought the spanner down on the screwdriver. This time the crack was muted as the lower half of the figure swung inwards and the top half, swivelling about an invisible axis in the wall, dipped outwards, revealing an oval cavity in the centre of the tympanum.

'No pillar of salt,' said Isobel quietly.

'The light! Quick!'

Isobel handed up the light to Michael, who shone the beam into the hole. 'A box! Hold the light again. Shine it up here.'

As Isobel did so, Michael reached into the cavity. It wasn't very big but he could just curl his hands around the box or casket, which felt as if it was made of metal but covered perhaps in leather which had dried and cracked. He couldn't see but it also felt as if it was covered in dust and crumbs – mice or rat droppings.

He took the box out. It measured perhaps a foot square and was about nine inches deep. It wasn't heavy, and Michael handed it down to Isobel. She placed the light on the table and took the box from him. He stood up straight again and felt into the cavity a second time. His hands explored the dusty , dirty edges. The hiding place was empty.

Michael got down from the chair and followed Isobel off the table on to the stone floor of the church. He held the box while Isobel pulled back what they could see was an old leather casing, now so dry it was solid like a biscuit. A lid was revealed which was fastened. Michael took the screwdriver and inserted it between the lid and the side of the box. With difficulty, he prised upwards. There was a rattle, another crack, and the metal began to buckle.

'Careful!' hissed Isobel. 'We're not vandals.'

Now Michael inserted the screwdriver between the metal flap over the lock and the lock itself. He prised outwards. Nothing happened.

'Hrrgh!'

Next he twisted the screwdriver and as he did so the top of the flap sheared away from the lid, which lifted open a fraction. Michael jerked it back and Isobel shone the torch inside.

Involuntarily, Michael grunted in horror.

'It's a joke,' gasped Isobel.

'Well, it certainly isn't silver.'

Isobel held the light as he reached into the box and took from it, one by one, three small, fragile objects, each of them roughly the size of an egg.

'They look like skulls,' said Isobel.

'Not human. Rats, cats, dogs, rabbits . . . foxes perhaps.'

'What's that other thing?'

Michael reached into the box again and took out what was still inside. 'A bracelet, a necklace?'

Isobel shook her head. 'The central opening is too small. And you couldn't wear it – it's like a plate or a record.' The object was a series of metal rings, one inside the other and fastened together so that they formed a flat disc. 'Three skulls, nine rings,' said Isobel, counting them. 'Twelve in all. Michael, I don't like this. It was all supposed to end here. Now we're landed with another, entirely unexpected . . . joke?'

'It's not a joke. It must stand for something very simple. The rings of Saturn? We've been following the Landscape of Lies, remember. The painter lied about the final number of clues. It's a last-minute failsafe.' He put the skulls back into the box. 'Vron will know what these mean.' He took the rings from Isobel. Or he thought he had, but in the gloom she had let go before he could take hold of them. The rings slid over the smooth edge of the wood to the stone floor.

The heavy iron of the rings pealed and clattered against the stones, a baritone clang that rolled down the nave.

'We're going to wake everyone here,' said Michael grimly, moving across to pick them up. 'Shine the torch over here, will you, so I can see what I'm doing.'

'Allow me,' said a voice, and a powerful torch beam immediately flooded the floor where Michael was kneeling.

He went cold. He had never heard Grainger speak but he had no doubt whose voice it was. As he looked up, he heard Isobel gasp and he saw why. Grainger was holding a shotgun – and behind him was a boat-hook.

In the dark behind the light of the beam, Grainger chuckled. It sounded to Michael like a death rattle. 'Lucky for me you were here after all. Moving the table all by myself was going to be a problem. That's why I gave myself all night. I came back here yesterday for a close look at the Crucifix but the damn building was closed. So I wasn't *absolutely* certain. But you have done the hard work for me. My congratulations to you both. Very dogged of you to stick with me for so long.' He waved the gun in his hand. 'But this, I think, makes me the winner.'

He moved a step further into the church.

'Now, this is what we are going to do. First, Miss Sadler, you will push back the part of the tympanum which is open. Then you will both lift back the table to where it came from and replace the hymn-books. Very enterprising, that was, if I may say so. You will also put back the chair in the choir and kick away the dirt that fell from the boxes, so that we leave no sign of what's been happening.'

Michael was shaking with anger and fear, mentally kicking himself for being so stupid as to leave the church unlocked and
unguarded. How could he have been so foolish? Grimly he did as
he was told.

Grainger watched as his instructions were obeyed. He took
Michael's torch and slipped it into his own pocket.

'Now, Miss Sadler, you will carry the box. You will go first, Mr
Whiting, followed by Miss Sadler. I shall bring up the rear, with
this gun and this boat-hook. I shall have to switch off the torch as
we leave the church but, if you act in any way unusually, Mr
Whiting, please remember that I can damage Miss Sadler with this
boat-hook in absolute silence. I shall only use the gun second, on
you. Is that clear?'

Michael didn't move.

'I said, "Is that clear?" '

Michael nodded.

'Good. Now please step out of the porch, turn right, then right
again, and follow the path across the cemetery.'

So that was it! Michael had been wondering why they had not
heard Grainger's car or motor bike arrive. *He had come by boat up
the river!* Michael now recalled that cry from a bird on the water. It
must have been disturbed by Grainger. What idiots they had been,
not to anticipate that and to abandon their lookout. On the other
hand, they could never have got the treasure down without both of
them helping . . . They had played straight into Grainger's hands.

Isobel clutched the box containing the skulls and the rings.
Michael wanted to reach out and stroke her hand, but just then
Grainger snapped off his torch and barked, 'Right, in single file
please. And no adventures along the way. I don't want to harm you
but if I have to I will.'

'Just a second,' Grainger added as they stepped out into the night.
'Mr Whiting, I see there's a key in the church door. I take it you
found where the thing was hidden. Please lock the church and put
the key back where you found it. We don't want to draw attention
to ourselves but if we do I want *your* fingerprints on the door.'

Michael obeyed Grainger but now saw a small chance to leave
word that something was wrong. Grainger couldn't possibly know
where the church key should be hidden. He hadn't been hiding,

275

watching them all of the time, surely? Michael tried to recall how many birds he had heard call out . . . and when. Had that been Grainger arriving?

His idea was worth a risk. He locked the church and then walked purposefully towards the gable where the key was normally hidden. Instead of lodging it in the guttering, however, he put it on a window-sill. In the dark, Grainger couldn't see exactly what he was up to, but anyone looking for the church key in daylight, and not finding it where it should be, might well stumble across it, in the new hiding place. They might think it suspicious and examine the church carefully. There was a slim chance they would conclude St Mary's had been burgled.

Michael returned to the porch.

A grassy path led from the church through the graveyard and into some bushes which, Michael guessed, bordered the Frome. By the time they reached the bushes their eyes had adjusted to the murk and he recognised, beyond the dark mass of rhododendron branches, the white bulk of Grainger's launch.

'Hold it there.' Grainger spoke in barely more than a whisper but his words carried and they all halted. 'We can't have you throwing things into the river, Miss Sadler. Leave what you are carrying here.'

Isobel put the box on the bank.

'Now, Whiting, board the boat and stand at the prow.'

Michael did as he was told. He was itching to act but he needed no reminding how terrified Isobel was of the boat-hook and that inhibited him. Grainger manoeuvred Isobel to the stern and, still keeping the boat-hook so that its point rested against her flesh, he reached over and with the twin barrels of the gun pressed a button. The launch's engine coughed and died. He pressed the button again. The engine stuttered into life.

He turned to Isobel. 'Untie that rope, will you?'

The rope was wound around two mooring poles some ten yards apart. Isobel was made to unwrap first one, then the other. Grainger wedged the boat-hook under the arm that held the gun. That left his other hand free to put the engine into gear. Moving with the current, the boat was soon in the middle of the river.

Now he put the engine into neutral. He spoke to Isobel. 'I want you to face forward and put your hands behind your back.' He waited for her to do so before saying, 'I am now going to put down the boat-hook and wedge the shotgun just here, by the wheel. Then I'm going to tie your hands. Any sudden movement by either of you, anything not in the script, and I shall use the gun.'

He waited a moment while he straightened the launch in the river, then laid the boat-hook near his feet and picked up a length of rope which was coiled there. He leaned the gun against the wheelhouse and expertly fastened Isobel's wrists together. He was very strong and the ropes were fastened tightly. Bending down again he took from the deck a roll of wide, heavy-duty plastic tape, unwound some inches and snapped it off with his teeth. Then he wrapped it over and around the knots he had just tied in the rope binding Isobel's wrists.

'That should make it a good deal harder for you to fiddle with,' he said. 'I have the gun in my hand again. Please move over by the cabin, Miss Sadler, and sit down.' This time he tied her feet. Again he wound tape around the knots. 'Stand up and turn again to face the bow.'

As she stood, Isobel could hear more tape being unwound. Before she realised what Grainger had in mind, his hands came over her head and a strip of tape was slapped across her mouth. Instinctively, she opened her mouth to scream but it was too late. Grainger's hands went round her head three times, pulling the tape harder so that her lips were firmly stuck together. While she was concentrating on breathing through her nose, Grainger opened the cabin door and pushed her inside. She fell heavily, bruising her thigh, her shoulder and the back of her head. Grainger banged the door shut immediately.

'Now we repeat the process, Mr Whiting. Come back here.'

Michael had watched, horrified, at Isobel's treatment from Grainger, his anger rising. But what could he do? The gaping barrels of the shotgun eyed him unblinking. He moved to the back of the launch as Grainger again adjusted the wheel. They had already drifted nearly fifty yards downstream from the church landing. Michael could now see that the launch was also towing a small boat, rather like the skiff Isobel and he had rented. The one Grainger had sunk.

'Turn, and put your hands behind your back.'

Michael decided this was his moment. While Grainger was trying to tie his hands, with the gun no longer actually in his hand, that was the best opportunity Michael would get. As he held his hands behind his back he kept his fingers spread wide, ready to grab Grainger's wrist.

He heard a swift movement behind him and realised late that Grainger was too cunning to expose himself in that way. The twin barrels of the shotgun came hammering down on his head and, before he hit the deck, he passed out.

14

A hard dome of glass, shiny with pain. Red blisters bubbling and boiling and exploding noiselessly. Michael's skull was filled with a heavy, molten, flammable sea. The pain poured out of his ears, beat in waves against the inside of his forehead, squeezed under the base of his cranium at the back. As he came to, as the hot red tide eased, he found it difficult to move. Only after some minutes did Michael grasp that he was tied up. His wrists were fastened behind his back. His ankles were wrapped together equally firmly. Only after what may have been another half an hour, or a week, did he realise that his lips were sealed with some sort of tape. And only then did he remember the blow on his head. In haphazard order he recalled the events – except that he didn't remember falling. Concussion, he supposed, was like that. It involved some memory loss.

His eyes had watered and the dried tears caked his cheeks. He grunted and groaned. Slowly he began to appreciate where he was. The bottom of Grainger's launch. Michael's right shoulder and arm were sodden with dirty, oily water, cold and smelly. His forehead itched where something sticky had dried – he couldn't see but guessed it must be congealed blood from the blow to his skull. His cheek lay against a coarse substance and he saw, inches in front of him, the rough interior of the fibreglass shell of the launch. It curved away above him, hard, stained, scuffed with the marks of riverboat life – plastic coloured buoys, cans of grease, wooden boxes, rusty anchors. The sound of water chasing along the hull conveyed two things: he was below the waterline, and the boat was moving at a

279

fair pace. But then he realised the tone of the throttle should have told him that. The whole boat vibrated with a power that only came from a strong engine, fully open.

The sound of movement, and a sob, very close, surprised him, until his memory, still affected by the blow to his head, reminded him that Isobel's plight was similar to his own. With difficulty, he manoeuvred on to his back, then on to his other side. It was still dark and although he could make out a couple of windows, high above him, he could see only vague outlines of the other shapes in the cabin. The shadows inside the boat were too deep for him to make out Isobel's face.

Michael had no idea how long he had been unconscious or where they were on the river. He wasn't fully conscious now and, for some time, drifted between sleep and full alertness. Now and then he was attacked by stabs of nausea.

What was Grainger's plan, he wondered in his more lucid moments? He dimly remembered that, when moored, the launch had been pointing downstream. Did that mean Grainger was heading for the coast? He supposed that made sense. In a launch the size of Grainger's, they couldn't go very much further upstream. But if they were going downstream were they going out to sea? And, if so, what then? With a head that felt it had grenades exploding inside it, he couldn't begin to guess.

He thought back to his trip on this same river with Isobel. Including stops at Quarr Abbey and that pub in Wool, it had taken them about five hours to get to Wareham. In Grainger's launch they could do the journey in – what, four hours? Three and a half? If his memory served him right, the Frome at Wareham issued into the same complex of waterways as Poole, and there was a long estuarine channel before they actually reached the open sea. Another hour or two. At least it should be daylight by then.

The fact that Michael was thinking meant he was, in some sense, recovering. He turned his attention to the rope that bound him. He was only now beginning to take in Grainger's cleverness in covering the knots in the rope with tape. Michael could just feel its slipperiness with the tips of his fingers. Grainger was a strong man – he seemed at times almost wholly made up of long bones and stringy sinews – and he had tied Michael's feet and hands very securely. Without the tape, however, it would probably have been possible, given time, for Michael to find one of the ends of rope binding his feet and then gradually dislodge the knots. Michael couldn't feel the end of the rope under the tape. For a long time, he couldn't even find the edge of the tape, so that he could start to unwind it.

It must have been a full twenty minutes before he found the join. He was groaning in frustration long before that. Then, for the next five or six minutes, he worried at the tape, trying to wedge his fingernail under the join, to dislodge it so that he could get enough free to pull on it. In the confined space of the boat it was difficult, even painful, to manoeuvre. Ridges of fibreglass ran like ribs around the hull and often cut into his arms when he moved, so that he occasionally had to stop. Nor could he wriggle too much. The launch wasn't large and if he moved too suddenly Grainger would be able to detect it.

Eventually, however, after what must have been three-quarters of an hour, he freed enough of the tape to pull with two fingers. Slowly it came away. He unwound it halfway around his ankles . . . three-quarters . . . the whole way. Suddenly the tape came away in his hands. Thank God! He reached with his fingers for the rope.

No! What he found almost made him weep. There was another layer of tape. Now he had to start all over again, searching for the join, prising it up with his nail, unwinding it.

While he was struggling, Michael suddenly detected that it was getting light. He could see bushes going by on the bank outside and he could now make out Isobel's features. He could see her frightened eyes above the tape around her mouth as she watched him struggle. The fact that they could not speak to each other made their situation more pathetic. If they could have talked they could have shared their misfortune. As it was, they were each locked away, alone, with their fear and their inability to hit back at Grainger.

Michael, though, had now found the join in the second piece of tape and was prising it apart with his thumbnail. Though it was summer, because it was early morning and they were on a river it was very cold. His fingers were by no means as supple as they might have been and it took him another half-hour to free enough of the join so that he could start pulling with his fingers.

As he was doing this, he noticed, through the window of the

281

launch, an oil tank slipping by. He recognised the tank, since it was more or less where Isobel and he had 'gone about' in their skiff, three days before. They were coming into Wareham.

It was now fully light, though still very early. From his experience of sleeping on the couch at Peverell Place, Michael judged it must be around 5.30. What were Grainger's plans now? Was he going to sail straight through Wareham and out into the estuary, making for the Channel, where no one could help them?

Michael redoubled his efforts. Aware that they were passing the buildings of Wareham, he unwound the rest of the tape. Yes, underneath was the naked rope. Immediately he found one end and pushed it, pulled it, poked at it, waggled it, trying to loosen the knot. He couldn't see what he was doing and had to feel his way. After a quarter of an hour of pushing and pulling he managed to slip the end of the rope through one of the loops that had contained it. His heart leapt and he experienced a new surge of energy.

No sooner had he gathered himself for another assault on the knots than he noticed something else. The launch was slowing down. The engine tone changed and the angle of the hull in the water grew more level. Michael also felt the boat begin to turn. It slowed even further. Outside was a white forest of yacht masts; there must be a marina in the open estuary. The launch stopped completely, though the engine still turned over. Now Michael could hear Grainger moving about on deck; he got off the boat and then back on – he was tying up. Then the engine was killed.

A moment later the cabin was flooded with silver daylight as Grainger threw open the door. Michael held his breath. Grainger stooped and looked in. Holding the shotgun, he looked down at the bodies, grinned and grunted with satisfaction. Michael prayed he wouldn't think to examine the ropes at his feet which, thankfully, were in the shadow caused by Grainger himself standing in the doorway. But neither of them had moved all night and presumably Grainger concluded that his handiwork was successful. Quickly he closed the cabin door. There were more sounds of his moving about on deck, then he stepped off the boat and on to what sounded like a wooden pontoon. His footsteps receded into the distance. Michael counted off 120 seconds to ensure that Grainger really had gone. Then he frantically resumed pulling and poking at the rope around his ankles. It was very firmly tied; Grainger was a depressingly strong man. It took Michael five minutes to finish dislodging the first knot and a further fifteen minutes to untie the other two. But then he quickly unwound the rest of the rope and rubbed his fingers over his ankles. Isobel was watching his every move.

Now that he could move his legs, he manoeuvred himself first so that he could stagger to his feet and peer out through the windows. Again, Grainger had been cunning. He had not moored the launch in Wareham at all but well out in the estuary on a pontoon where several other boats were tied up. They were about half a mile from the bank and the same distance from the nearest houses in Wareham. Even if they could shout, there would be no point; no one could hear them this far out. Sounds travelled over water, but not that far. Grainger must have taken a rowing boat ashore. Had he left them? Or was he coming back? How long had they got?

Michael didn't waste time thinking but set to work, though still unsteady on his feet. First he leaned over Isobel and brushed his face next to her fingers, to let her know he wanted her to pull the tape off his face. Once he could talk he could give instructions. As he did this, however, he felt Isobel's fingers clutching at the lapel of his blazer. They crawled down his jacket in a mystifying way. But Isobel's hands were really quite strong and she clearly had something in mind so he allowed himself to be manoeuvred.

Her fingers were now at Michael's pocket and he twisted his body so that she could delve inside. He heard keys rattle. Then Isobel grunted and the pressure on his blazer eased as she took her hands out of the pocket.

He straightened — and then grunted himself. She had found his matches. She was right, too. It had taken him for ever to undo his ankles but they might be able to burn through the ropes much more quickly.

Isobel twisted on to her side so she could see Michael round her shoulder. He held his wrists where she could both reach and see them.

She lit the first match. After a moment Michael smelled the acrid stench of the tape burning. Beneath it the rope smoked — but then the match went out. Grainger, he judged, had now been gone for an hour and a half at least. It must be 7.30 by now. Was he coming back at all?

With the second match the rope smoked a good deal more. But then the flame licked Michael's wrist, he grunted and jerked away, knocking the book of matches out of Isobel's hand. When he looked down, he saw that the book had fallen into the water at the bottom of the boat. No! Still, he bent and sat on the floor. The water was cold as his fingers scrabbled around, searching for the matches. He found them, clawed his fingers around them and stiffly regained his feet.

Isobel took back the matches. The first failed to strike – it was too wet. Under the tape Michael cursed. The second match failed to strike. How many did they have left? Michael couldn't remember. The third match didn't work either but the fourth flared. Again the flame licked his flesh but he was more prepared this time and only flinched. The smell of burning rope filled his nostrils. The match died and Isobel tried another. No luck. Michael cursed again, louder but equally incoherently. Another two dud matches but the next one worked.

As the smell of the singeing rope again filled the cabin Michael suddenly felt the pressure on his wrists relax. Two ends of rope fell away. He pressed his fingers together and prised apart the balls of his palms. Something shifted, though he couldn't tell what. When he relaxed his hands again, however, the ropes were definitely looser. He pulled, hoping to slide one wrist through the loops. It nearly came free but the ropes scorched his flesh.

He sank to the floor again. This time he dunked his wrists in the water at the bottom of the boat. It was more than cold, it was slimy.

He tried to ease his wrist out a second time. Nearly . . . nearly . . . suddenly the rope slipped over the oily water on his knuckles and he banged his elbow as his arm jerked free. He hardly grunted, though, as he immediately got to his feet.

Almost simultaneously he heard footsteps at the far end of the pontoon. Was it Grainger? Or someone else? If he pulled the tape from his mouth and called out and it was Grainger, that would give the game away. He decided to keep silent but tried the door that led out on deck. It was locked. He searched the cabin for a weapon.

All he could see was an oar, a few cushions and a plastic buoy. The oar would have to do.

The footsteps were getting closer. They stopped for a moment. Then the angle of the launch changed. It *was* Grainger and he had stepped back on board. Michael waited, holding the oar, ready to rush the door.

Suddenly the cabin door opened and daylight again splashed in. But Grainger stood back, his gun covering both of them. It happened so quickly that Michael had no chance to wield the oar.

'I thought I saw a little excitement through the window.' Grainger grinned. 'Mr Whiting, please lie down again in the bottom of the boat.'

Angrily, Michael did as he was told and lowered himself into the cold, oily water.

Grainger inspected Isobel's wrists. Satisfied that they remained firm, he shifted his attention to Michael. 'Face down, please.'

'Ah,' he added after a moment. 'Burning, that's how you did it . . . And here are the matches, what's left of them. I'll pocket these.'

Resting the gun so that its barrels lay next to Michael's down-turned face as a warning, Grainger secured his wrists again. Then he did the same with Michael's ankles. 'I can see that I need to modify my boy-scout knots. I think three strips of tape on each piece of rope.' Michael heard Grainger tearing off the strips. 'And the last one, to make sure you can't find the join, I'll tie in a knot itself.' This, Michael realised, was a deadly trick. Once the brown tape was crumpled up it became even stronger, almost impossible to break, and if it was tied in a knot there would be no join to prise apart. Grainger stood up and slammed the cabin door behind him.

Soon Michael heard the engine being started up and the launch was moved out into open water. The estuary was breezier than the river had been, the wind sweeping uninterrupted across sand and water, and the launch began to dip and rise on the small waves.

For half an hour the launch beat into the wind and it got even colder in the boat. Then Michael felt them slow again, and stop. He heard Grainger move forward to the prow, and felt the shudder and rattle as the anchor chain slithered overboard. For a moment the only sound was the breeze and the slapping of the water against the hull. Then the cabin door was opened again.

'Whiting?'

Michael grunted.

'Okay. In a moment I am going to take off the tape around your mouth – there are some answers I need from you. Before I do, however, you should know two things. One, the boat-hook is now resting against Miss Sadler's thigh.' There was a movement, then a muted gasp from Isobel as Grainger jabbed her with it. 'Two, we are anchored near Fitzwilliam Point in the middle of the estuary. We are about a mile and a half from the nature reserve on Brownsea Island and the nearest house is over a mile away. The nearest boat with anyone on it is, I should say, six hundred yards. Once I take the tape off your mouth, there is obviously no point in your yelling but if you do I can promise you that whatever you shout will be drowned by Miss Sadler's screams. Is all that understood?'

Michael grunted again.

He was rolled over on to his back. A pair of scissors was roughly wedged under the tape stuck to his cheek. The tape was sliced. Roughly, Grainger pulled it all free. Michael winced as a piece of skin on his lower lip was taken off. He felt blood seep into his mouth. He sucked in gulps of air.

It was the first chance Michael had had to study Grainger close to, in daylight. He was struck immediately by his intelligent – his wickedly intelligent – eyes. They were small for such a large face, but restless, aware. There was also something else in those eyes. Something that Michael couldn't quite put a name to.

'Now,' said Grainger. 'I have some questions. If you answer them honestly and fully, you can have some coffee and a sandwich I bought when I was ashore in Wareham.'

Till then, Michael hadn't given food a thought. Now he realised how hungry he was. Isobel must be feeling the same way.

'Have you been in touch with the police at all?' Grainger asked. His voice was harsh, higher pitched than Michael expected in such a tall man.

Should Michael tell the truth, he wondered? If he pretended the police were on Grainger's trail, maybe he would panic. Then again, if the police were really in on everything, why hadn't they been at the church in Pallington? He decided to add no embellishments. 'No. We thought about it but, in the end, decided against it.'

'Hmm. And how did you find out my identity – after I had taken the picture?'

'Helen Sparrow told us the design she uncovered looked like a coat of arms. We figured you had to visit the College of Arms and on which day you had to have been there. With a little trickery we managed to see the college register. We got your name there. You're an author, Dr Grainger, and we found one of your books. That led us to the Royal Institute of History where a little burglary produced the number of Peverell Place Hotel.' Michael couldn't resist a triumphal tone in his voice. They *had* been clever.

'Ahh. Burglary. I can't complain, I suppose. You were clever there. Allow me to congratulate you. Now, one last question. Who, if anyone, have you talked to about me? Anyone else here in Dorset? In London?'

This time Michael had to lie. 'Well, there's my partner, Gregory Wood, of course. He knows all about you. There's the man we bribed at the College of Arms: he knows who you are now. We asked the vicar of Pallington if a Dr Grainger had visited his church recently.'

Grainger played with the roll of tape. He smiled. At least, he smiled with his mouth. His eyes didn't smile. They bit into Michael like boat-hooks. 'You're over-egging it, Whiting. You seem to have told the whole world about me. You *have* been busy. Well, I think you're lying. I called your office the other day and spoke to Wood. I introduced myself as Grainger. I asked if you had left any messages for me. He said no, then added: "What is this in connection with?" You're lying, aren't you? Isn't he, Miss Sadler?'

Michael heard Isobel whimper in pain above him. 'Okay, okay, I'm lying. The only person who knows is Helen Sparrow.' There was a silence. Michael watched as more tape was unravelled. He played for time. 'What about the coffee?'

Grainger smiled his cold smile. 'I've changed my mind. Think about coffee, think about food. Now I've mentioned it, you won't be able to take your mind off it.'

Just then, Michael realised what it was in Grainger's eyes that he hadn't been able to put a name to. Now he could. It was vanity. A form of smugness. Grainger was not only very intelligent, he was very aware of that intelligence in himself. Pleased with it. Some very bright people were like that. He was one of those intelligent people who despised anyone less sharp than themselves. Suddenly, Michael realised how it must have destroyed Grainger to be publicly humbled at Oxford. At once, it explained his single-mindedness, his sadism and his violence.

It also gave Michael an idea.

'You must have felt pretty slow, last night, when you found we had beaten you.'

'I wasn't beaten! You're the one who's tied up.'

But Grainger had spoken too quickly. And the glint in his cold eyes told Michael he had scored a direct hit. He pressed his advantage.

'I'm a gambling man, Dr Grainger, and I'd wager a sandwich to a Sandby that you would have given anything to have been the one who found that box last night, not us. You started weeks ahead of us – and we still got there first.'

'You had the picture!'

'Only until you stole it. But you had two weeks' start on us – and still you lost. Like you lost at Oxford.'

'Shut up, Whiting!' Grainger glared at Michael. 'Shut up.' He took several large breaths, as though he was preparing to strike Michael. But then he calmed down. 'You're right, Whiting, damn you. Nothing would have given me greater satisfaction than to have discovered the cavity for myself . . . On the other hand, I listened to you and Miss Sadler talking before I . . . interrupted you. And you don't know what you've found, do you? You have no idea what the skulls and rings mean.'

Grainger paused, looking from Michael to Isobel and back to Michael. 'No. You're as much in the dark as you were in the church last night.' He grinned his grin. 'But *I* know. You two think you're pretty clever but I've been in this business all my life. As we have been motoring downstream, I've worked out the last move in this little game of ours. It wasn't immediately obvious what the skulls and rings added up to, but I've got there now. After all, I can read these signs and symbols as easily as I shall read your obituaries.'

At this, Michael's skin flushed in fear. But he knew he had to keep talking. 'We caught you, and overtook you. You're not as good as you think you are.'

Grainger's eyes narrowed and again Michael thought he was going to be hit.

But the other man fought back his anger a second time. He swallowed. 'You were lucky. And I was delayed for a day, finding this launch.' His eyes bit into Michael again. 'Intelligence, however, real intelligence, means being adaptable to any situation. During the night I have had to adapt to this new situation I find myself in – two cleverdick prisoners who can spoil my coup. I flatter myself that I have come up with a solution that is wonderfully neat, easy to execute and foolproof. It wasn't easy and I might have overlooked something. Only time will prove me right or wrong. Neither of you, however, will live to see it put to the test.'

Grainger stepped forward and wound more tape around Michael's mouth. 'Don't bother to try to squirm free. From now on I shall look in every so often to check your ropes.'

The cabin door banged shut. The engine rumbled to life. The rattle of the anchor chain was soon heard. In the next half-hour Michael felt the waves getting rougher as the launch approached the open sea. It may have been a nice day but it was certainly more than a little windy.

Michael's mind was in a whirl as, no doubt, Grainger intended it to be. Michael was hungry too. He was uncomfortable. He was cold. Worst of all, he was afraid. How must Isobel be feeling?

The day wore on. The wind did not abate, and for endless hours the launch beat steadily into the waves. Each of them was thrown about the cabin now and, true to his word, Grainger opened up the door every so often to check on their ropes. It was pointless to struggle or attempt to dislodge anything. In the shifting waves it would have been exhausting as well as fruitless.

At one point, Isobel began to heave with what Michael realised was sea sickness. With her mouth taped over, this was extremely dangerous. Michael beat on the sides of the cabin with his feet to attract Grainger's attention. The door opened – and then, a few moments later, closed again. It clearly mattered little to Grainger if either of them choked in their own vomit.

Michael tried to control his fury. Anger was wearing and he was tired enough from bracing himself against the waves all the time. He would need his strength later. Later . . . he didn't dare think. He didn't know what Grainger would do so he could have no plan. He couldn't talk to Isobel, so they could co-ordinate nothing. He didn't even know what state she would be in. She might be so weak as to be scarcely able to stand. He stared at the fibreglass roof of the launch. He couldn't help it. He was seething.

Just then the cabin door opened again. Grainger had the gun in one hand, a bucket in the other. He walked across to Isobel, put down the bucket and cut the tape from her face. He was rough in his actions and Isobel cried in pain. 'Here, be sick into this.'

The sound of Isobel's retching filled the cabin and a faint stench of vomit reached Michael's nostrils. God, he thought, don't let me be sick. Being sick, he knew, was exhausting in itself.

Resting the gun near the door, Grainger unravelled a fresh strip of tape. He was just about to apply it to Isobel's mouth when she suddenly said, 'Now I know what it was like, sleeping on that sofa.'

'Shut up! Close your mouth.' Grainger wound the tape around Isobel's face, stifling her sobs, and picked up the gun. Then he shuffled out and the door banged shut again.

Isobel lay groaning for a while. Then, to judge from the regularity of her breathing, she fell asleep.

The waves were dying down now, as the wind dropped, and the movement of the launch was more comfortable. Less uncomfortable.

Michael turned over in his mind what Isobel had said. Code? Not really. She was just being Isobel, good under fire. Cheering him up. Themselves up. More than that. She was telling him she was alert, that Grainger might have them physically beaten but that was all. She was watching, waiting.

Michael felt himself growing drowsy. He fought it. The dirty water in the bottom of the launch continually splashed against his face and that helped to keep him awake for a while. But then he too fell asleep.

15

When he jerked awake, Michael was immediately conscious that the light outside was different. It was yellower somehow. Evening was coming on. The sea was now much calmer and he could hear again the slap-slap of water against the hull as it raced past. He had a consuming desire for a cigar.

The only satisfaction Michael could salvage from the situation was that he was refreshed now and Grainger could not be. The other man had been up all night and had needed to handle the launch in fairly heavy seas all day. He was a tall and sinewy man but he *had* to be weaker now, Michael hoped.

The light began to fade. The sun must have just set. Funny how quite blustery days often settled down towards sunset. It was true the world over. Involuntarily, he thought back to the places he had been where he had watched wonderful sunsets – Jamaica, California, Chile, British Columbia, Australia. Michael was suddenly angry all over again. For a few moments since he woke up he had forgotten to be angry.

He heard the rattle of the door handle as Grainger opened it. 'Nine-twenty,' he shouted. 'We left Portland Lighthouse over an hour ago . . . there's no one else in sight and it's time to make a start.'

The tape was unwound from Isobel's face. Once more she cried out as it was pulled roughly from her flesh. Then the scissors were wedged under the tape which fastened Michael's mouth. He pressed his lips together as best he could so that no more tender tissue was torn away.

'There, you can both talk if you wish. Yell all you like. We're out of sight of land.'

Neither Isobel nor Michael spoke.

'Very wise. Now I'm going to let you in on my plan. I want you both to know that, despite what happened at Oxford, and despite the fact that you beat me – by a whisker, I might add – my solution to the problem of your disposal is possibly the most brilliant conception I have ever devised. Given the circumstances . . .

'I also want to get it off my chest. Think about all this from my point of view. I have worked out the most elegant solution to a problem. All the loose ends are tidied up, the problems smoothed away; the red herrings, the false clues I shall leave, are simple, clean and will work perfectly . . . the intellectual satisfaction is immense. But I can hardly tell anyone, can I? It's not like the solution to an academic controversy which I can publish.' He laughed. 'But I can tell *you.*' He looked at his watch. 'Since I am going to drown you shortly, there's no harm in your knowing. In fact,' he chuckled, 'it helps me to let you in on my plans. Now I shall know that someone, even at such a - well, embarrassing – time, has appreciated my guile. So I shall feel . . . content. I can do what I have to do, knowing that someone, someone I respect, knew – for however short a time – knew that George Grainger's mind was as sharp and creative as ever.' He stopped smiling. 'You are a safety valve. That is your value to me. In telling you, I shall never again be tempted to tell anyone else. If we were not having this chat, I might be tempted in years to come. But not now. The fact that you are listening makes it safe for me. I ought to thank you but that really would be silly.

'It's now getting dark. We've sailed west all day and are now about five miles offshore of Weymouth. According to the maps there are about four hundred feet of water at this point. I have just transferred the box with the skulls and rings in it to the skiff at the back of the launch. Also the two fishing rods I bought at Wareham this morning, my radio, coffee flask, bits of silver chocolate paper, the seven fish I caught today. When I motor into Weymouth in about – oh, two hours – I shall look like a perfectly ordinary but very keen fisherman who's been out all day. It will be dark, so no one will pay any attention to an old box. Everything will all look so natural.'

Michael went to speak, but Grainger raised his voice and hurried on.

'Before all that, however, there comes the bit I'm most proud of. Where I've been really clever.

'As soon as it's completely dark, I shall invite each of you out of the cabin and on deck. There I shall remove the tapes and the ropes – and all of your clothes. The cabin is too small for such sport. Then you will be . . . persuaded back into the cabin, and locked in again –'

'Why –'

'Then I shall scuttle the launch. It's quite easy – I just turn a tap by the engine. The boat will take about seven or eight minutes to sink. After about four minutes, I shall take to the skiff and watch the rest of the proceedings from there. As soon as the launch is safely out of sight I shall head for the shore. I should reach Weymouth about eleven-thirty. Late but not suspiciously so for a fishing fanatic on a summer's evening.'

'The launch will be missed before we are.' Michael could keep silent no more.

'No doubt. But it can't be traced to me – or to you, for that matter.' Grainger shifted, to make himself more comfortable. 'I must confess that, like you, I expected to find the silver in Pallington church. Unlike you, however, after I'd worked out that the church was the place, I always considered it risky, from my point of view, to use a car to take everything away in. There's traffic on a country lane even in the depths of night and I couldn't risk being seen. That's why I chose the river. Unfortunately, the launch I was in when we had our . . . encounter . . . on the river had been hired only for a day. That's why you caught up with me and even overtook me; I had to search for another.

'It wouldn't have been clever to hire one, of course. They don't let you keep these things out after dark. So I had to . . . help myself.'

'You stole it?'

Again the chuckle. 'The least of my sins, as you will shortly find out.'

Michael stared at Grainger, trying to control his hatred.

293

'It was remarkably easy. There's a large basin at Poole, a wide stretch of water just inside the drawbridge and on one of the banks is a rather nice pub. I had a drink there on Sunday afternoon and watched a couple moor their launch in the middle of the basin, on a pontoon. They covered the deck area with a tarpaulin and then rowed ashore. They joined a crowd they knew in the pub, had a couple of drinks, then got into their car, waving to everyone and telling the world, or anyone who cared to listen, that they would be back next weekend.' Grainger shook his head from side to side, mentally congratulating himself on his cunning. 'Yesterday morning, very early, I rowed out to the launch, fiddled with the ignition – it's just like a car or a motor bike – and, well . . . here we are.' He stared at Michael. 'This launch won't be missed until next Saturday morning at the earliest and even then it can't be linked with either you or me.'

He stroked the crease in his cheek. 'If your bodies *are* found, then it will look as though *you* stole the launch. Once your bodies have been identified, people will then remember that you have already had one "accident" with a boat, and ended up in the water. They will assume you were careless, fatally so, a second time. If they *don't* find you, as I suspect will be the case, they will assume you flew off –'

'– but if they find the bodies *and* the car, miles away, that will look suspicious.'

'No. If you were going to steal a boat, you wouldn't park your own car nearby, would you? If the launch were to be missed early, a nearby car without a local registration would be one of the first things the police would check – and it would lead straight to you. A sensible thief would leave his car some way away . . . like a long-term car-park where it wouldn't arouse suspicion. You can get from Bournemouth to Poole very easily, by train or bus.'

Michael forced all the hatred he could muster into his eyes. They were his only weapon.

But Grainger only chuckled icily again. 'Keep trying. Your objections just show, so far, how clever I've been in working things out.

'Now, let me get on with explaining my plan. This is the next clever bit . . . I left my motor cycle in a side road in Wareham. If I have missed the last train from Weymouth to Wareham, I shall

294

simply take a taxi. From Wareham I shall ride to Moreton station. It's about half a mile outside the village and, as you will see, is necessary to my plans. I see from the map that it also has two caravan sites – which means that, at this time of the year, there is a lot of strange traffic in the area. I shall not be noticed. Moreton is, of course, barely two miles from Pallington. I shall walk there keeping to the hedges so that no one sees me. It should take me no more than an hour. Between two and three o'clock tomorrow morning, I shall therefore locate your car, which must be hidden somewhere near the church in Pallington. And that reminds me: where are the keys?'

Michael was silent.

'Come along! Or I shall harm Miss Sadler here.' And he jabbed Isobel's thigh with the boat-hook.

'Here, in my jacket,' breathed Michael softly. He was feeling totally humiliated by Grainger's treatment.

Grainger reached forward, found the keys, but also noticed the cigar which was still in Michael's top pocket. He laughed, took it out, smelled the leaves. He put it in his own jacket pocket and then stood back again near the door. 'I shall search your car for any incriminating documents or other evidence and dispose of them. I shall then drive your car to Bournemouth airport. Somewhere along the way I shall "lose" the fishing rod and the rest of the junk. As soon as everyone else wakes up, so I don't draw attention to myself, I shall park the car in the long-stay car park and then take a bus to Bournemouth railway station. No one will pay any attention to me – I shall just be one of hundreds of bus passengers that day. I shall then take a train back to Moreton and pick up my motor bike. I shall drive *that* to Bournemouth airport and leave it in the same car park. Then I shall go back into Bournemouth, this time by taxi, and catch a coach or bus to Weymouth. It would be quicker to catch a train but if I used the railway station twice in the space of a few hours it might look suspicious. In Weymouth I shall take the ferry to Jersey. I can't fly out of the country because I would have to use my real name. And in any case it's as good a way to get to Jersey as any, which is where my first stop will be. The banking system there, being what it is, is perfect for my plan. As you may know, Jersey is stuffed with safety deposit centres which are open at all hours and are much more anonymous than banks proper. I shall deposit the Pallington box in one of them.

'Next, it is just a short hop from Jersey to France, where I should arrive by early tomorrow evening. They never stamp your passport these days. A train should get me into Paris some time late at night.'

Michael's mind involuntarily went back to the Bibliothèque Nationale and the coffee he had drunk in the square outside. He realised how much his body ached for coffee now. And a cigar.

'Next comes the third clever part. You cannot, of course, stay in a French hotel without registering and giving your name. If anything should go wrong with the rest of my plans, and people should want to know where I was at the time of this . . . incident . . . then I would need an alibi and the dates on hotel registration forms might not stand up. Therefore I shall enjoy myself and spend tomorrow night at Barbara's, a rather busy brothel just off the rue de Seine. One can spend a night there very pleasantly. Expensively, but pleasantly. No one, of course, expects anyone to use his real name, nothing is ever written down, all transactions are in cash. The next day I shall proceed to Amsterdam and repeat the same process at the Chequered Flag, a not dissimilar establishment. All the while I shall be sending postcards to friends and colleagues. They will, of course, be pre-dated. The postcards will turn up days later and people will never remember when they got them, still less work out when they were posted. That's the way with postcards – some take a day or two, some take a week. But if called upon to be witnesses, months later, these friends will confirm that I was certainly in Paris and Holland at this time. I shall also look up university colleagues in Paris and Amsterdam.

'Then I shall return to England and retrieve my motor cycle. That was another brilliant touch. I haven't ridden one of those things since I was a boy, so no one will associate a fifty-year-old don with motorbike leathers. The helmet came in very handy, of course, as a disguise. Most probably, your bodies will never be discovered and my elaborate plan will have been unnecessary. Pleasant, expensive, but unnecessary. If, however, for some reason your bodies and the boat *are* found, the situation will be clear. Being naked, you were engaged in having sex, you didn't notice the boat was sinking and, too late, were inadvertently locked in the cabin. You probably haven't noticed but there is a bracket attached to the wheelhouse outside the cabin which clips on to the door to keep it open. In a moment I shall pull it away from the wood it is screwed into and then fix it to the fitting on the door, so that it will appear as if the door slammed shut accidentally after the restraining bracket broke loose. But, as I say, I don't expect your bodies ever to be found, and most probably people will think, weeks from now when the airport authorities finally pay attention to your car, that you flew off somewhere. You will be listed missing and that will be that. Now, we'll start with you, Miss Sadler. Get up, please.'

Michael's brain was a jumble of questions and delaying tactics. 'What about Helen Sparrow? She can link you to us.'

Grainger smiled his cold smile. 'Can she? I wore my helmet all the time I was there. And at that point, Whiting, even you thought I was called Molyneux.'

Michael groaned. Grainger was right . . . No, he *wasn't* right. He was overestimating his own cleverness and underestimating the police. It was that intellectual vanity again – and it was what made him so dangerous. Helen would obviously alert the police if she didn't hear from Isobel and Michael, or if their bodies were discovered. She would tell them about Molyneux. That might not lead straight to Grainger but the police would know that the launch 'accident' was no such thing.

All these thoughts flashed through Michael's brain as fast as a guillotine but he didn't speak. Grainger's vanity was leading him on and no amount of argument would change his stubborn mind. Michael had to watch for his chance, then seize it. Rather than waste energy on arguing, it was better to nurse his strength.

The tapes and ropes around Isobel's ankles were cut. She was led out on deck. Her wrists were now fixed to the gunwhale.

'Don't think of jumping overboard,' said Grainger. 'You'll only be dragged along behind the launch and get caught up in the propeller. There . . . I think that's tied firmly enough. Let me just pull it hard, to see . . . Yes, that's fine. Struggle if you want to. You won't get free.' He turned back to the cabin. 'Now, Mr Whiting. You. I'm going to untie your feet. Please don't think of kicking out at me. The gun isn't in my hand but it isn't far away. If I need to I shall hit you over the head with it and undress you myself while you are unconscious. That may spoil my plan a little but I shall wait for you to come round before I drown you.'

Michael watched in silence as the tape was pulled back from his knots, then the knots themselves were loosened. His legs were free.

'Stand up and walk towards me.'

Out on deck it was a beautifully clear night. As Michael came out of the cabin and felt what was left of the breeze on his cheek, Grainger grabbed his arms from behind and pushed him quickly to the back of the launch. Michael started to turn to kick out at Grainger but was neatly tripped by the other man. He fell, crashed into Isobel's legs and banged his head against something hard. The pain made his eyes water. Before he could recover, Grainger was on him and tying another rope around his wrists. His arms were jerked up behind him, painfully, as Grainger hurried to tie Michael to the gunwhale.

Michael regained his feet. Steadying himself, he looked all around him. Grainger was right: there was no land in sight, no other boat or ship, not a light or a sail, not anything.

Grainger, who now had Michael's cigar wedged in his mouth, addressed him. 'No reason why you shouldn't enjoy the show, Whiting. I don't know whether you'll find it erotic or embarrassing. I don't really care. Now, Miss Sadler, I'm going to untie you. As I do so I shall stand about six feet from you. In one hand I shall have the gun. The boat-hook is also very close. At that range I can do you serious damage the minute you depart from the script. First I want you to shake free of the ropes on your wrists.'

Michael had to stop it. 'Helen Sparrow may never have seen your face, Grainger. But she saw – and cleaned – the picture. So, even if you do find the missing silver, you can never sell it or publish how you found it. It won't help your academic reputation.'

Again the cold smile. 'Oh, but you are wrong, Whiting. Very wrong. You surprise me and underestimate me. The Pallington box could not suit my purposes better. You are probably interested in – oh, the gospels perhaps, as the most valuable item, financially. Or the crosier, which is probably the most beautiful piece. I, however, am not. For the first part of my plan, the most useful items are the hand reliquary and the map of the True Cross. The reason? Very simple. They both contain jewels. The hand bears exquisite rubies, while the map shows the sites of the cross, each one designated by an emerald. Some of them are fairly small, but by no means all. There's an account of the Monksilver treasure in a sixteenth-century manuscript in the British Museum. You may not know about that.

'Assuming all goes well tonight, I shall allow a suitable interval to pass. Just to be on the safe side, I shall take a trip abroad, perhaps. But then I shall return and retrieve the Pallington box from Jersey. Unlike you, I already know where I shall find the silver hidden, don't forget that. Discreetly, I shall remove it. At my leisure I shall carefully detach the rubies and the emeralds from the hand and the map. Then, over the following weeks, in London, Amsterdam, Israel, New York and India, where I gather there is now a thriving jewellery market, I shall dispose of the jewels, one or two at a time. The emeralds must be worth a million and the rubies nearly as much. Not as much as if I sold everything, of course, not by a long chalk. But in selling the jewels I shall become comfortably off without drawing attention to myself.'

'Only a freak would vandalise the treasure!' Isobel put all the contempt she could muster into her words.

'Don't be so quick to judge me, Miss Sadler.' He stepped closer to Isobel. 'Now, my dear, let us begin.'

Michael watched as Grainger untied the rope from the gunwhale. With scissors he cut the tape which covered the rope around Isobel's wrists. He undid two of the knots and then stood back and picked up the boat-hook and the gun.

Slowly, Isobel worked her hands free. She rubbed her wrists.

'Now, begin with your shirt and trousers. And, Miss Sadler, as you take off your clothes throw them into the bucket over there.' He indicated with the boat-hook and then turned back to Michael.

'Once the sale of jewels has been completed and I am a . . . sufficiently well-off man, I shall allow more time to elapse. With you two dead there will be no hurry. Then, after a year, maybe two years, I shall return to Pallington, to St Mary's. Again, at my leisure, I shall observe where the key to the church is hidden – since I am sure you returned it to the wrong place last night, Mr Whiting, in a silly attempt to raise the alarm. Maybe they will have changed the lock and the hiding place. But security is a boring business, the most boring there is, which is why it always fails. I shall have no real difficulty, being in no hurry, in discovering how to enter St Mary's late at night unobserved. As you know only too well.'

He looked fiercely at Isobel and stabbed the boat-hook into the wooden deck inches from her feet. 'Do it!'

Isobel's fingers sought the buttons on her shirt. She undid them and took off her shirt.

'Throw it into the bucket.'

She threw the shirt where Grainger said.

'Now take off your bra. Let Mr Whiting and me see your breasts.' Grainger pulled the boat-hook from where it still quivered in the deck and stood ready to throw it again should Isobel not obey him immediately.

But she did. With one hand she unhooked her bra at the back, took it off and threw it on top of her shirt. Then she bent to undo her trousers, took them off and threw those on to the pile.

'Now the rest. I'm enjoying this.' Grainger stretched his arm holding the boat-hook so that its tip brushed Isobel's breasts. Then he stepped back further.

Isobel had stiffened as the boat-hook touched her but she now bent again, removed her pants and threw them on to her other clothes. She stood up straight. As she did so every inch of her body was displayed to both men. Embarrassment and defiance mingled in her eyes. Michael realised that Grainger, in forcing him to watch, was making the situation humiliating for them both. And it stopped them thinking of ways of escaping.

Isobel stood in front of Grainger, turned slightly away from Michael. Her hands were at her sides, not hiding anything. Either from fear, or cold, her nipples were erect. Her eyes bore into Grainger's. Was he aroused? Could she, with her body, with its promise, distract or delay him? She could bring herself to use no form of words but if –

Grainger smiled and blew cigar smoke at her. 'Into the cabin please.'

As she moved he held the boat-hook no more than six inches from her skin. Michael could see as well as Grainger that the boat-hook was still more terrifying for Isobel than the gun.

Grainger slammed the cabin door behind Isobel and turned to Michael. 'When I have discovered how to get back into St Mary's,

I shall return again, as last night, and force my way into the church. This time, however, I shall not take anything but put it back! That is the really beautiful part of my plan. I shall also return the silver to *its* original hiding place. I shall sprinkle it with dirt and dust and then leave it for several months to accumulate still more, genuinely so.

'Then comes my final, glorious coup. I shall approach the directors of the British Museum, and the Victoria and Albert Museum, the vicar of Pallington and somebody from one of the quality Sunday newspapers. I shall say that I think I have found the Monk-silver treasure, which has been missing for centuries, and will ask them, or their representatives, to accompany me to the church. They will, of course, be unable to resist. After suitable diversions and mistakes, we shall finally discover the cavity in the tympanum. The skulls and rings will lead us to the silver. Sensation!'

'What about the missing jewels?'

'Everyone will be so overwhelmed by the discoveries that they will automatically agree with my suggestion that the actual jewels were looted at the time the silver was hidden away. It's the kind of thing that happened. Neat, eh? The discoveries are what matter. They will make the front pages all over Europe and North America. I shall then be famous as well as quite rich – but that is not all. A court will no doubt adjudicate later on who the treasure belongs to. I shall announce in advance that my share, should there be any, will be donated to the V and A or the British Museum, whichever decides it is the more suitable home. I shall then settle down to write a book about the whole affair. This will reveal that I was set on the trail by the sale of documents at Sotheby's but that later I noticed a picture in a sale catalogue in Switzerland, called the Land-scape of Lies.'

'Then Helen Sparrow will go to the police –'

'Hear me *out*, Whiting. I shall have sent the picture for sale, in Switzerland as I say, but through a fiduciary. The Swiss have these convenient people, who make a good living acting as barriers for people who wish to do things anonymously. The picture will be entered for sale with a low reserve. It will be printed in the catalogue and – who knows? – someone will buy it. Or I shall buy it back through another fiduciary. It doesn't matter because I shall base my

301

coup not on the picture itself but on the photograph of it in the sale catalogue.'

'But Helen will report its theft.'

'Let's assume she does. Okay, the picture was stolen from her studio. Now it has turned up in Europe, battered. Miss Sparrow will say that you asked her to clean a particular part of the picture which you were interested in. She, and the police, if they are interested, will find that the area of the picture which you were interested in is now covered over again with grime – that tile with the coat of arms is hidden again. You see, Whiting, what you are overlooking is that the part of the picture which you went to so much trouble to have cleaned, and which I went to so much trouble to steal, *is not necessary to the solution of the mystery*. You found out the hard way, just as I did. But, knowing what I know now, in my book I shall make it plain that the figure is facing the wrong way and therefore is a non-clue. There is therefore no *need* for me to have gone anywhere near Helen Sparrow's studio. The puzzle actually *can* be solved using a photograph of the painting, even though part of it is grimy and hidden. I will be able to argue convincingly that I never needed to see the actual picture, to solve the problem. The police will conclude that the theft and my discovery are completely unrelated.'

'That's ridiculous. You're being stupid, Grainger. Helen is bound to alert the police when we disappear. She will tell them everything about the painting, and the silver. Lots of people will know and the police will simply not believe the coincidence.'

'I am not stupid, Whiting, you know that. Coincidences happen all the time, and that's very often all they are.'

With a jolt, Michael recalled himself using those very words to Isobel at their first meeting.

Grainger went on. 'Remember, a couple of years will have elapsed between a theft at Aldeby, which was regarded as so unimportant at the time that it was never reported to the police, and a small auction in Switzerland. There is no link between Miss Sadler and me, you and me, or Miss Sparrow and me. On top of that, the fact that I have discovered the treasure and donated my share to the nation will put me entirely above suspicion. Who would think to raise doubts about an academic who did such a thing?'

Michael's mind was racing again. Grainger's vanity awed him. His plan made intellectual sense. As a piece of reasoning, Michael had to admit that it was brilliant. But it made no *psychological* sense. Neither Helen nor, more important, the police would believe Grainger. After twenty years they might, but not after two. Once he came out with his discovery he would come under suspicion and, when that happened, the police would ferret out some error . . .

But for now that wasn't the point. The point was that *Grainger* believed Grainger and his intellectual pride was leading him forward.

He was behind Michael now, beginning to undo the ropes at his wrists. As with Isobel he left Michael to work free the last knot as he retrieved the gun and the boat-hook. Michael knew that he had to do something while he had his hands free. It was the only chance he would get. He also knew that Grainger knew. The other man would be expecting Michael to try something. Whatever that something was, it had to be a complete surprise. And to work it had to be simple.

'Isobel's farm manager will recognise the picture. He will put two and two together. He may even remember your visit.'

'Rubbish. He never saw me, and Miss Sadler brought the picture up to you herself. And he's a farmer. No one will query me, Whiting. So far as anyone knows, I shall have made no financial gain. I shall have had no motive to kill you, just as I shall have had no motive to burgle Helen Sparrow. That's where the beauty, the elegance, of my plan lies. My reputation will soar. When the donation of the treasures is made, I think I can be sure that, within the not too distant future, I shall be *Sir* George Grainger. It's not quite as good as a professorship at Oxford but it's not bad as a second best – eh?'

Michael shook the rope from his wrists and rubbed his flesh where it was sore. He turned to face Grainger. The other man looked at his watch.

'Nearly ten. We're running a bit late. No matter, I'll have less time to wait in Bournemouth. Now, come over here and start undressing. I prefer to watch you from over there!'

Warily, the two men changed places so that Michael was standing, still fully clothed, with his back to the locked cabin door, and Grainger was again by the tiller.

303

'Start with your shirt, as Miss Sadler did. But don't be too long about it.' Grainger stooped and turned something near the engine: it was the tap which scuttled the boat. Immediately a gurgling was heard and Isobel started shouting from within the cabin. Michael began to unbutton his shirt, thinking furiously. What could he do? They had less than seven minutes now to live.

He took off his shirt and unfastened his belt. He unzipped his trousers and slid them down his legs. He took off his socks and shoes so that only his underpants remained. There was an inch or so of water in the boat now. Isobel was still hammering on the cabin door.

He bent so that he could slide his pants down over his feet. Now he too was naked. His clothes were in a heap on top of Isobel's. Presumably Grainger would make Michael take all the clothes into the cabin with him, so the sex scenario would look more plausible. There were nearly four inches of water in the boat now. It covered his feet to his ankles.

He saw his chance.

Michael straightened his body facing Grainger. As he did so Grainger's eyes instinctively followed his own upwards. In one sudden movement Michael kicked out with his right leg. Water from the deck flew in a splash of spray towards Grainger and he flinched. In that moment Michael threw himself violently to one side, deliberately making the boat roll. Grainger, not expecting it, stumbled and fell on to one knee. He looked away, throwing out one arm to help keep his balance. Michael lunged for the cabin door, turned the handle and pulled the door open. He kicked more water at Grainger as the other man started to recover. Then Michael threw himself towards the stern of the boat but to one side so that the launch now rolled the other way. There were already six or seven inches of English Channel in the bottom of the boat.

Michael had bruised his shoulder when he threw himself towards the stern. He was kneeling in water as Grainger began to recover and raised the gun.

Michael saw the boat-hook lying between them, its hook pointing towards him. Grainger was levelling the gun. Michael scooped more water at him. This time the other man didn't flinch but he did close his eyes for a fraction as the water hit his face. That was when

Michael reached the boat-hook and grabbed it. It was heavy in the water and now Grainger was pointing the gun again.

Michael raised the hook, which suddenly jerked free of the water and slammed upwards. Grainger parried it with his free hand but the force of the blow unbalanced him again and he swayed. Michael jumped and before Grainger could take aim a third time he had reached the gun. The boat-hook had dropped back into the water swirling around the deck. Michael's hand closed around the barrels of the shotgun. The two men struggled. Grainger's teeth, amazingly, still gripped Michael's cigar. The water in the boat was above their shins. Grainger pulled one of the two triggers on the shotgun. The explosion was deafening – but the barrels were aimed harmlessly at the waves. Seeing a way out, Michael sank to his knees, dragging Grainger with him. He pulled at the gun. Grainger tried hard to stop him, but he *was* exhausted and, slowly, Michael pulled him down. The water was still rising, and therefore Michael's ally for a moment. He gave one last heave - and submerged the gun in sea water. Now it would surely not work.

Grainger must have thought the same, for he let go of the gun before Michael did and reached quickly for the boat-hook.

'Michael!'

Michael turned in time for Isobel to throw him a very wet pair of trousers. 'Jump!' he yelled to her. 'Get clear!' He turned back to face Grainger.

Grainger lunged at him and Michael did his best to parry the blow with his trousers. Grainger lunged again, harder this time, and the hook pierced the wet cloth and dug into Michael's arm. He screamed. Grainger was immediately on him, his long thick fingers at Michael's throat. Grainger couldn't know it but the hook had sliced into Michael's wrist at precisely the point where he had suffered his skiing accident. The agony was immense. A hot tide of pain rushed up his arm. It meant he now had only one hand to fight with.

He saw Grainger above him. He could smell the other man's breath – the coffee he had drunk mingled with tobacco smoke. It was stale and made Michael feel sick. He felt himself being pushed down. The water was rising to meet him: now it was Grainger's

305

ally. He felt the cold Channel water at the back of his head, lapping his ears. Grainger was forcing him down.

Behind Grainger he saw Isobel. She hadn't jumped, but what could she do? Though Grainger was weaker than Michael might be, he was still too strong for her.

Suddenly Grainger snatched the cigar from his mouth and in one swift movement jabbed the lighted end into Michael's injured arm. The hot ash and blood mingled and Michael's screams shot across the waves. The pain filled every pore in his body. As Michael convulsed, Grainger shifted his weight and forced his head below the water. Michael spluttered and coughed and heaved as his mouth and nose sank into the salty water. All he could think of was the pain in his arm and hand, his raw nerves scorched by the hot cigar.

Then, through a blur of tears and sea water, Michael saw that Grainger's face had suddenly darkened. It wasn't shadow, though. It was brown. A brown strip. Two brown strips. Three. Isobel had found the tape! She pulled it around Grainger's eyes, then his nose, then his mouth. He couldn't breathe.

Grainger's hands now sought to free the tape around his nose, but Isobel continued winding. She wound his hands to his face. That didn't work for long but by then she had wound the tape around his body twice, twisting it to give it added strength.

Michael squirmed out from under Grainger. The boat was now nearly waist-deep in water and would be going under soon. The pain in his arm was scalding.

Grainger was still caught up in the tape. Isobel had now wound it round his legs. She screamed at Michael. 'Look at your arm. Try to stop the blood! And jump! Free the skiff. I can manage.'

Michael saw what she meant. He grabbed his floating shirt and pressed it to his wound. The amount of blood he was losing was alarming. Then he jumped. The skiff was tied to the launch and would go down with it.

As he jumped, the whole episode seemed to move into slow motion. He had time to kick himself over to the skiff. Using his good arm, he untied the smaller craft from the launch. Then he hung on. The pain in his arm was too much for him to be able to haul himself out of the water unaided. Through his pain he watched Isobel as, twice more, she wound tape around Grainger's legs. He had pulled the tape away from his face but his arms and hands were still caught among the sticky strips. Then, very calmly, Isobel took three steps back from Grainger, unwinding more tape as she went. She stood for a moment, then wound the tape around the gunwhale now only a few feet above water.

She turned back to the struggling Grainger and brandished something at him, something Michael couldn't quite see.

'I can cut you free, Grainger!' she screamed.

Michael realised she had the scissors Grainger had used to cut the tape from their faces.

'What do the skulls and the rings mean? Where's the silver? Grainger!'

Grainger screamed back. 'You can't let me drown! Cut the tape!'

'The silver!'

'Cut the tape and I'll tell you.'

'Isobel!' yelled Michael. 'Forget it – we've got the box. Get clear!'

Isobel seemed not to hear him. She was shouting again. 'You tried to kill me twice, Grainger. The silver! Say and I'll cut the tape.'

Grainger didn't reply but instead redoubled his efforts to break free. As he did so, the boat gave a lurch.

The pain in Michael's arm throbbed on, made worse by the salt in the water. He just summoned the strength to shout again. 'Isobel, it's going. Get clear. *Jump!*'

Isobel had been unbalanced by the lurch of the boat and suddenly seemed to realise how close to sinking it was. She turned and began to climb over the gunwhale.

'No!' screamed Grainger. 'No! The tape –'

Isobel stopped climbing and turned. But she remained where she was.

Grainger stared at her for a moment. It was a battle of wills and no one spoke.

Then the boat lurched again. Michael opened his mouth to shout another warning to Isobel.

But Grainger got in first. 'Hell!' he cried. 'Hell. The place is Hell.'

For a split second Isobel didn't know what to say. Then she jerked to life. 'Hell isn't a place,' she shouted back. 'You're still playing riddles. Hell doesn't exist.'

'It does, it does. I told you! The tapes, cut them! I told you all I know. Hell –'

'Isobel! Isobel!' Michael watched in horror as the launch rolled over, taking Grainger down and Isobel upwards for a moment as the hull was lifted. The roll just gave her time to dive clear. She took the roll of tape with her.

Michael's last image of the launch, as he still clung to the skiff, was of the huge wiry figure of Grainger, writhing in the sticky brown web, his screams suddenly silenced as the launch sank from view.

They put into Portland Harbour three hours later. After an hour at sea in the skiff they had seen the sweep of the lighthouse beam and aimed for that. The unannounced arrival of two naked adults puttering into a naval base in the small hours set off a full alert. But it was worth it, for Michael could take advantage of the superb medical treatment available around the clock at Castletown Naval Hospital.

Even so, the general view of the hospital staff was that he might not have survived if the woman with him had not shown such presence of mind. No one had realised beforehand that plastic tape can serve equally well as a tourniquet.

Epilogue

Isobel fought her way down the steps of Sotheby's and through the crowds of people straggling on to the pavement outside in the sunshine. She looked about for the others. She had been left behind, when the sale finished, talking to reporters from Fleet Street, old colleagues whom she had once known.

It was nearly a year later, April, and the day of Sotheby's main sale of medieval and Renaissance antiquities. Suddenly she saw Michael, Helen Sparrow, Veronica Sheldon, Michael's sister Robyn and Anthony Weaver, the vicar of Pallington, standing on the other side of Bond Street. They were avoiding the crush and she went to join them.

Michael had his head bent down, scribbling on the back of his catalogue.

'What are you doing?' she asked as she reached them.

'Michael's calculating the grand total,' said Helen.

'According to one of the Fleet Street people who cover the sale-rooms,' said Isobel, 'two million pounds is a record for any reliquary sold at auction.'

'Yes, I heard that too,' said Weaver. 'And eight hundred and fifty thousand is also a record for an ivory object, I believe.' There had been fierce competition for the ivory crosier, as there had been for all of the items.

The four of them stood for a moment, watching the crowds from the auction spill out on to the road. It had been such an unusual, historic occasion that people were not ready to leave. Instead, they stood talking to one another, describing and redescribing what they had just seen. The censer had gone to the Metropolitan Museum in New York, the eagle vase to the Berlin Museum and the candlesticks to a private collector in Tokyo.

'It's a rich man's sport, art collecting,' sighed Weaver, surveying the crowd opposite. 'I wish people felt as strongly about God.'

'How rich are *we*, Michael?' said Isobel. 'You once told me you were good at maths.'

'Hold on. Nearly there.'

'Maybe you can now buy a new suit, Michael. Something more . . . becoming.' Michael's sister Robyn was in London being interviewed for a job, at London Zoo, and had been to her first auction.

'What are your plans?' said the vicar, turning to Isobel. 'Now that all the excitement has died down.'

For a while Isobel didn't reply. A tall thin man was standing outside Sotheby's and, for the briefest of intervals, she thought it was Grainger. He was standing just where Grainger had stood when he first invited himself down to the farm. Suddenly her eye was attracted by a sign on the window above where he was standing. It said 'Molyneux Rose Gallery' – so that's where he had stolen the name from.

Such a lot had happened since Grainger had drowned. There had been an inquest during which the entire story had come out and been reported in detail in all the newspapers – including the nudity. Fortunately the verdict had been death by misadventure. The treasure had been declared trove and, as a result, the British Museum had claimed the map of the True Cross and the Victoria and Albert Museum the jewelled gospels. But, as was now the custom if not the law, Isobel and Michael, as the finders of the objects, had been offered the market rate for them, since only if the museums paid up in that way could they expect people to declare trove. The rest Isobel and Michael had been free to sell.

In view of her part in the misadventure, Helen Sparrow had been offered a share in the proceeds and, because they had had to break into Pallington church, they had decided to offer the altar cross to the parish. Anthony Weaver had attended the sale out of interest. Veronica Sheldon was there because, in the end, it was Veronica who had solved the last riddle.

She had not been at all mystified when they told her about Grainger's final admission – that the box from Pallington church had pointed to 'Hell' as the final destination.

'These are three dog skulls,' she said, examining the contents of the box. 'A three-headed dog is Cerberus, guardian of the entrance to Hades, the underworld. And these are nine concentric rings. People used to believe that both Heaven and Hell were made up of nine zones, nine concentric zones, with God at the top of Heaven and Satan in the ninth zone at the bottom of Hell.'

At first, however, she hadn't been able to take them any further than that. Only when they had described their adventures to her a third time, in ever-increasing detail, did she suddenly say, 'Tell me about Quarr Abbey again. Tell me everything.'

They told her.

She picked up on the sign they had read there. 'Tell me again what it said.'

Isobel had the better memory. 'That the abbey had fallen into disuse after a local woman had given birth to a child fathered by a monk in the abbey. She had been distraught, had killed her child and then herself. The monk who was the father had secretly buried the woman and her child in the abbey grounds. Being a suicide the woman's body should not have been buried on consecrated ground and the act deconsecrated the abbey. When the scandal was discovered, no one could be found who would exhume the body. The abbey, therefore, had given the deconsecrated land to the village but the villagers, being superstitious, hadn't wanted it and had just left it. Eventually other suicides were buried there and trees and undergrowth took over. It became known as the Wood of Suicides. We fought our way through it – the trees are nearly choked by undergrowth these days. The silver's not buried there, is it? We had that idea at one time.'

'Nnno . . .' said Veronica.

'You don't sound very sure.'

'I'm still working this out, Michael. Look, have you got a good map of the area?'

'Of course. The one we used all the time. It's in the car.'

Veronica had pored over it for some time before muttering, 'Hmm.'

'I agree, Vron. Hmm. Is that a place, like Hell?'

'Very funny. If I'm right . . . *if* . . . it's a very macabre joke and a very medieval way of scaring unwanted intruders away.'

'Yes. Okay. Fine. It's medibloodyeval. Vron, *please!*'

'It was the Wood of Suicides that alerted me. That and the three skulls. They are both areas of Hell. In the first layer, Charon ferried the souls across the Styx and Cerberus guarded the entrance. Lower down, in the Wood of Suicides, there lived harpies and monsters. Then I noticed that there were nine pieces of silver and that some of the other places you passed through, or by, were similar to Hell also –'

'Like what?'

'Blood River. Another part of Hell was the Phlegethon, a river of boiling blood –'

'But Blood River is red because of the red soil –'

'Yes. But it's symbolic. Then there was Helstone. Hell stone. In the third zone of Hell misers and spendthrifts spend eternity rolling great stones, Hellstones. Then there was the Valley of the Stones. The seventh area of Hell was the desert or wilderness of blasphemers – and a valley of stones is a good approximation of a wilderness. You went by Woodsford Castle, which is enclosed, like Limbo, the first zone of Hell. It is also crenellated, you said, like the fourth zone. And, near Abbotsbury, you explored some caves – the eighth zone.'

'You mean . . .' Isobel had begun, her eyebrows arched as never before.

'As you got closer to Pallington, you were descending through Hell. Only symbolically, of course, and you didn't realise it. But a sixteenth-century person who was capable of deciphering the picture would certainly have understood the allusions. It was obviously devised by the same mind as required you to re-enact the Crucifixion to get to the cavity in Pallington church. Only if you were absolutely certain of yourself and that you were behaving righteously would you dare to proceed.'

'Spooky,' breathed Isobel.

'And where does it lead, Vron? Does all this help?'

'Oh yes, I think so. So far, according to my count, you have been through eight zones of Hell. That leaves only the ninth, the deepest layer, where – ironically and naturally – Satan himself is found. The ultimate deterrent in those days, the devil himself, is guardian of the silver.'

'And that is?'

'The ninth ring, the deepest zone, is the well.'

'The well? But there's no well at Pallington and there must be hundreds of wells in Dorset. That can't be right.'

'Not just any well, Michael.' Veronica was smiling, enjoying having the upper hand. 'Think . . . Look at the map . . . As well as being in Dorset, you were also, symbolically speaking, in Hell . . . What is the most notorious aspect of Hell, the thing that everyone knows?'

Isobel answered first. 'It's hot.'

'Right. Good. Now look up Pallington on the map. Then look at the villages and hamlets close to it. Go on, tell me what you see.'

Isobel and Michael had hunched over the map. 'East Burton . . . East Knighton . . . Owermoigne – strange name – Warmwell, Broadhurst – Oh, I see . . .'

'Warmwell,' breathed Isobel.

'Correct. A hot, or at least warm, well. The deepest division in Hell. The most terrifying place in the sixteenth century for a devout Christian.'

The well, on the village common, had been blocked up years ago as a danger to children. But Veronica's authority, as a curator at the V & A, had been sufficient to have it unblocked.

There were no Sunday newspapers when Michael and Tom, Isobel's farm manager, climbed down the well.

It had been Tom who had had the sense to tap the bricks lining the well and had found an area that rang hollow. They had chipped away at whatever crumbly material it was which held the bricks together and, after about an hour and a half, had freed enough of them to reveal a chamber containing three very damp, badly corroded boxes. They had taken out the pieces, black with age, and raised them to the surface one by one.

So Grainger *had* been right and he had, in a sense, beaten them. He had correctly spotted the reference to Hell. Had he lived, though, he would almost certainly have beaten Isobel and Michael to the well. He had given them the answer but, being the man he was, not the whole answer.

He had been wrong about the jewels, however. The rubies and emeralds were all missing. Someone had obviously helped themselves to the gems long ago.

'Isobel? Isobel? I *said*, what are your plans?'

Isobel blinked and dragged her thoughts back to the present. She looked across to Michael.

He had needed another operation on his arm and wrist. He looked like making a good physical recovery but, after Grainger's cruelty in burning his nerves with his own cigar, Michael now felt about tobacco the way Isobel felt about boat-hooks. This pleased Isobel after a fashion, though she wasn't certain about Michael's new habit – old-fashioned humbugs. He was putting on weight.

Half smiling to herself, Isobel turned back to Weaver. 'I've already spent a lot of the money – on land next to the farm. With luck it will now work commercially. And I'm employing more people so I can spend weekdays in London. I'm going to open a gallery, for photographers.'

'No holidays in exotic places?'

'No. We're going to Texas, but only because Michael has sold a picture to the museum in Dallas and he wants to deliver it personally.'

'Is that the one I read about? The lost portrait of Sarah Kinloss?'

Isobel nodded. Their adventures hadn't entirely ended with the discoveries at Warmwell. Once Michael's arm had recovered (though it would always be stiff) and he was back in the gallery, he had found that the jewels in the picture Julius Samuels had cleaned led nowhere. On the other hand, he had found that the figure was holding, not a chesspiece, but a miniature lighthouse.

Researching lighthouses, he had found that the Kinloss family of Strathspey, between Aberdeen and Inverness in Scotland, had built one of the oldest lighthouses in Britain, at Findhorn, and that successive generations had kept it in good repair until it was destroyed by a gale in the 1820s. One of the Kinloss women, Sarah, had been a mistress of the Prince of Wales at the beginning of the nineteenth century. In the National Portrait Gallery he found another likeness of her – which confirmed who she was. All that explained why she had been painted over – once she was dead no one wanted to be reminded of her infidelity, amounting theoretically to treason. The Kinlosses had emigrated to America in the late nineteenth century and their ancestral home, at Dallas near Elgin, had been broken up. So there was no one in Britain who was an obvious customer for the portrait. The museum in the other Dallas in Texas, *had* been interested, however, to the tune of $350,000. Michael had promised his share to Isobel, to help open her gallery. That adventure had been written up in the papers too, which is how Anthony Weaver knew about it.

Isobel realised he was speaking again. 'And the painting? The Landscape of Lies? What's happening to that?' It had been found at Grainger's home.

'Well, since you ask, Michael had rather a good idea, I think. He said that, if you agree to marry us in St Mary's, we would give you the picture, if you wanted it. Since the whole Monksilver business led to St Mary's, it seems the proper resting place for it.'

Weaver beamed. 'I should be delighted, on both counts.'

Isobel laughed.

'Okay, everybody, I've done it,' cried Michael. 'Listen! The grand total, for the six objects sold today, plus what we were paid by the British Museum and the V and A, comes to seventeen million, four hundred and fifty thousand pounds. Divided five ways, since I have to give Greg a share, that means three million, four hundred and ninety thousand pounds for each of us.'

'Dear Lord,' whispered Weaver.

'Jesus Christ!' said Helen.

'Shit!' said Robyn.

'Let me see,' said Michael, closing his eyes. 'If I'm as good at maths as I say I am, my share gives me approximately three hundred and fifty thousand Havana cigars.' He looked at Isobel and smiled. 'Or, since I no longer smoke, two hundred and thirty thousand litre bottles of whisky. Do you think I could get decently drunk on that?'

Isobel smiled. 'I wouldn't bet on it.'